C000099814

# The Tsar'

To Marco
Best wishes
Stephen Davis

# The Tsar's Banker

Stephen Davis

*The Tsar's Banker* © Stephen Davis

ISBN 978-0-9929486-4-1
eISBN 978-0-9929486-5-8

Published in 2015 by Crime Scene Books

The right of Stephen Davis to be identified as the author
of this work has been asserted by him in accordance with the
Copyright, Designs and Patents Act 1988.

A CIP record of this book is available from the British Library.

Printed in the UK by TJ International, Padstow

## Dedication

To Paul, for being such a wonderful friend.

To Caroline, for being an inspiration.

To James and Lib, for their encouragement.

And to Sarah, for turning the dream into reality.

# Prologue

Following the death of Tsar Nicholas II in 1917, rumours abounded throughout Europe that vast riches had been deposited by the Romanovs in various European central banks, including the Mendelssohn Bank in Berlin and the Bank of England.

In 1933 the Berlin Civil Court granted a 'certificate of inheritance' to seven heirs of Nicholas II for all the funds held at the Mendelssohn Bank.

The Bank of England, however, denied holding any assets for the Russian Imperial Family and, despite a number of attempts by distant members of the Romanov family to establish if any money or property exists, none has ever been found in Great Britain.

In 1960 Sir Edward Peacock, Director of the Bank of England, stated to the newspapers: 'I am pretty sure there was never any money of the Imperial Family of Russia in the Bank of England, nor in any other bank in England. Of course, it is difficult to say "never".'

Despite Sir Edward's denials, it's been whispered since 1917 that the Bank of England has, in fact, been the guardian of a number of boxes, each embossed with the double-headed eagle of the Imperial Russian House of Romanov, which contain vast riches and secret papers.

The boxes are said to be locked in a treble-keyed, six-foot-high safe located in a vault deep in the basement of the bank and are considered so valuable that, during the Second World War and the Blitz, they were moved to the same secret location outside London that hid England's crown jewels and, like the crown jewels, were guarded day and night until the end of hostilities.

Today there are officially only a handful of people who know the contents of the boxes. They include four senior members of the British Royal Family, a couple of senior executives at the Bank of England, some members of the Royal Family of Denmark and a handful of senior officials within the Russian and British governments.

All agree on the need for secrecy.

# Chapter One: The Grand Duke

## London, 1913

Philip Cummings hated change. He was content with the life he'd created for himself.

His work as a director for foreign accounts at the Bank of England provided all the excitement and variety he required from life. His passions for bridge, opera and regular evenings dining out in London's best restaurants were shared with a few good friends.

He was a bachelor and intended to remain so: not because he thought women unattractive – quite the opposite, but because he viewed marriage as something hostile.

A wife would want to change him. He'd observed that too many of his friends had been changed after marriage and, in his opinion, rarely for the better.

Little did he suspect that the next hour was going to change his life for ever.

This was the fifth day in succession that a thick smog had wrapped itself around London, and Philip shivered as the cold reached his bones. Every day this week he had arrived at work with his clothes and face covered in a film of greasy water. It was like a damp blanket that polluted the roads, pavements and buildings, and made them look dark and dirty. There was no escaping a burning throat after even the shortest walk. Philip covered his mouth with his scarf and bent forward into the mist.

Arriving at the Bank of England precisely at his usual time he acknowledged the cheery 'Morning, Mr Cummings' from the doorman at the entrance reserved for senior staff.

'Morning,' he muttered in reply. Passing the executive elevator he climbed the stairs to his office. He had never ridden in the elevator since the unfortunate time he'd been trapped between floors as maintenance men ran around trying to rescue him, and junior clerks and secretaries gawped at his helplessness. He could not have caused more interest had he been a caged beast at the zoo; an undignified experience he intended never to repeat.

Walking purposefully down the thickly carpeted corridor, he was irritated to see Mark Johnson outside his office door pacing up and down in what Philip considered an overly excited manner. Staff at the Bank of England should pride themselves on never being flustered, on remaining calm even in the worst financial crisis, and it irritated Philip when junior staff panicked or displayed excitement.

'Johnson, you look positively distracted. What's the matter?'

'Mr Cummings, good morning, sir,' Johnson rasped breathlessly. 'The Governor would like to see you, sir.'

'Now?' said Philip, hiding his irritation at what was going to be a deflection to his routine.

'Immediately you arrived, was what I was told, sir.'

'Oh, very well,' said Philip, wondering what crisis had erupted overnight that demanded his immediate attention. Doubtless it would be something trivial, would eat up too much time and would disrupt a day he had meticulously planned with his secretary the previous afternoon.

'Take my hat and coat and leave them in my office, please.'

Philip turned and walked back down the corridor to the Governor's office. On his arrival in the anteroom, a secretary indicated he should go straight through. Walking into the Governor's office he could see two other directors, Edward Lascelles, a pale-skinned, slim man seven years Philip's junior, and the best bridge partner Philip could hope for. The other director was Neville Porter. Philip felt Neville's fast promotion at the bank was due more to the fact that his father was the third son of a viscount than to his actual ability. However, being the third son of a viscount brought neither money nor title and so Neville had had to find his own way in the world, and this had made him resentful and greedy. Philip also disliked the rough manner he adopted when speaking to junior staff and the fact that he always blamed others for his own errors.

4

The Governor of the Bank stood at the far end of the room in a hushed conversation with a stranger. The Governor waved Philip into the room and the secretary closed the door, leaving the five men alone.

'Cummings,' said the Governor. 'Thank you for coming. Gentlemen, this meeting is highly confidential.'

Philip, Neville and Edward nodded in agreement, understanding the Governor's statement was more for the benefit of the visitor than for the three employees. Confidentiality was a by-word at the bank, and had been ever since it was established in 1694.

Philip looked hard at the stranger. A tall, good-looking man in his early fifties with brown hair parted down the middle, a soft, pale complexion, a well-groomed beard and moustache. His suit, starched white collar and shoes were all hand-made from Saville Row and his navy blue silk tie was fastened with a diamond and ruby pin that Philip assumed contained genuine stones.

'Sir,' said the Governor to the stranger, 'You've met my other two colleagues, but may I introduce to you Philip Cummings? Philip, may I present His Royal Highness, Grand Duke Konstantin Konstantinovich of Russia.'

Philip bowed his head. The royal guest smiled and without extending his hand said with a perfect English accent, 'Delighted, Mr Cummings. Thank you for giving up your valuable time to meet me; I know you are all busy.'

The Governor addressed the group.

'Time is pressing; we should begin. Please, gentlemen, let's be seated.'

The Grand Duke moved to the highly polished board table at the side of the room and sat in a leather seat with his back to the window. The Governor sat at the head of the table, while Philip, Edward and Neville took seats facing the Grand Duke.

Once they were all settled the Grand Duke pursed his lips as though he were thinking how to begin, then drummed his fingers on the polished table to indicate that he had made a decision. 'Sirs, I have been commanded by his Imperial Majesty

Tsar Nicholas to instruct the Bank of England on a matter of the greatest importance.'

The Grand Duke looked directly at Philip. 'His Imperial Majesty is conscious that his daughters are growing up and wishes to establish a base from which they can live and entertain in the style expected when visiting Europe. The Grand Duchesses Olga, Tatiana, Maria and Anastasia Nikolaevna, to give them their correct titles, will require funds to do this.'

He drummed his fingers on the table again.

'It's considered sensible to transfer substantial funds for the Grand Duchesses and their retinue for use when they visit Europe for extended periods. However, as these funds will be for the private use of the Imperial Family and will not belong to the Russian state, it's not appropriate that their existence should become public knowledge.' He smiled.

There was another pause as the Grand Duke took a cigarette case out of his pocket, extracted a long, slim cigarette, lit it and took a long pull. A stream of smoke floated towards the ceiling. He placed the cigarette case on the table and the four bankers were transfixed by the beauty of the item. Just three inches wide by five inches long, covered in deep royal blue enamel and at the centre a letter 'A' picked out in diamonds, surrounded by a laurel leaf of amethysts, Philip thought it one of the most beautiful pieces of jewellery he had ever seen.

The Grand Duke continued. 'In addition, the Tsar has proposed that two banks in Europe should contain substantial assets to allow for immediate payment for goods that the Tsar has in mind to purchase from England.'

Philip assumed that 'goods' was a euphemism for armaments.

'It's proposed that these deposits will be made in a series of shipments to be collected from St Petersburg. I have agreed with the Governor that the bank will take responsibility for the deposits at the time they are handed over to your representative. I am aware that this is an unusual method of transporting funds between banks, but we hope to avoid the many layers of civil servants that would compromise any hope of maintaining the confidentiality of the transactions. The private incomes, travel arrangements and marriage plans concerning any of the Tsar's daughters must remain a state secret in Russia.'

There was another pause as the cigarette was extinguished.

'Mr Cummings, the Governor has indicated that you would be able to travel to Russia to arrange for the collection and transfer of the items in question and that the entire project could be completed before the end of next year.'

The Governor spoke directly to the Grand Duke as if Philip were not present. 'I'll be instructing Mr Cummings directly, Your Royal Highness.'

The meeting concluded, everyone in the room stood.

'Mr Cummings, it's unlikely we will meet again, but I thank you for undertaking charge of this matter for His Majesty.' The Grand Duke picked up his cigarette case, pocketed it and left the room with the Governor. The three men bowed their heads as the visitor was ushered from the room.

'Well, it looks as if you're off to Russia. I'm pleased it's not me; I've got too much to do here,' said Neville Porter and limped from the room to return to his office.

'Beetroot stews, dumplings and freezing blizzards,' added Edward Lascelles unenthusiastically, 'and all to act as a glorified delivery boy.'

Philip smiled at Edward's teasing, knowing that his comment contained more than a little envy. 'So how about steak and kidney pudding and a bottle of Bordeaux in Covent Garden to see me off?' he asked.

Edward beamed. 'I'll make the reservation. Rules as usual?'

'Perfect,' said Philip.

Philip returned to his office lost in thought. There was more to this task than the Grand Duke had revealed. He stared out of the window at the smog-filled streets and the shadows of people rushing about their various tasks.

Philip knew he'd been chosen because Russian was his first language. His father, a British diplomat in Moscow, had fallen in love and married the daughter of a successful Russian merchant. During Philip's early years, his mother's English had not been good and she preferred to speak to him in her native Russian, and he had enjoyed nothing more at bedtime than to lay his head in her lap as she told stories of beautiful snow princesses, dashing Cossacks and their adventures in Siberia and on the Steppes.

On his sixth birthday his father was posted to the British Embassy in Paris and it was there that Philip began his education. Thus French became his language of learning while English was the language his father used and was thus the language of authority. By the age of twelve he was holding conversations with his parents in all three languages, and with a Parisian, Muscovite or English accent.

Philip thought about the meeting. Why did it take a senior member of the Royal Family to arrange a task that a junior secretary from the Russian Embassy could have achieved just as easily? The Tsar was the wealthiest man in the world. He could arrange credit provision for his daughters at a moment's notice, so why all the secrecy?

He pressed the bell on his desk to summon his secretary and asked her if she could bring him the Russian file.

The Bank of England isn't just a repository of the nation's wealth: it's also the primary adviser on financial matters to the British government. Information on every country is regularly updated to provide short-, medium- and long-term assessments for their economic, political and social future. The information it collects is used by the Home Office, Foreign Office and the War Office to plan for conflict.

Ten minutes later Philip was settling down to read the three thick folders. After studying the columns of figures detailing income from mining, manufacturing and all manner of other business, he then moved on to the written assessments.

*Strictly confidential: not to be removed from the Bank of England.*

*Sources:*
*a) Crédit Lyonnais: Financial assessment Russia 1912*
*b) Report by Count Sergei Witte: 'The fight for Russian industry', 1912*

*[...] the transformation of this financially backward empire into a modern agricultural and industrial superpower has been dramatic [...] by 1948 Russia's population is expected to have reached 343.9 million – three times that of Germany, six times that of Britain and eight times that of France [...] If expansion continues in the future as it has between 1900 and today it could be expected that by 1950 Russia will dominate Europe, politically, economically and financially [...]*

*The empire's geography, however, presents a daunting challenge to the movement of goods and people. Decent roads are few and far between [...] Fewer than one-tenth of one per cent of Russian villages have local telephones, and there is no public telephone line connecting the Russian Empire to the outside world. Russia's rail network, in which the French are keen to invest, in order to speed their ally's mobilisation against Germany in a time of war, is only a quarter as dense as that of the United States. A study of Russia's railway timetables shows that it would take a minimum of 75 hours and nine minutes for an express passenger to travel from Chelyabinsk, where Europe meets Asia, to the German border...*

Philip picked up the financial assessment.

*[...] Russia is lavishly endowed with natural resources, mainly located in Siberia, is self-sufficient in all major industrial raw materials, and has reserves of less essential, but nevertheless significant, natural resources, including diamonds and gold [...] The ease of access to these resources is hindered by Siberian inaccessibility [...] despite the Tsar being the wealthiest man in the world and Russia being one of the wealthiest nations, Russia's huge size means that the nation is almost ungovernable...*

Philip moved on to the final file, the political assessment.

*Twenty-one tsars of the House of Romanov have ruled Russia since 1613, and will celebrate three hundred years of rule in 1912. Japan's defeat of Russia in the Russo-Japanese War (1905) caused a financial crisis, resulting in social conflict and unrest that nearly dissolved into anarchy [...] The situation was further exacerbated when workers marched on the Winter Palace to present a petition to the Tsar, Nicholas II, for better working conditions, and were fired on by soldiers. The Russian press dubbed the massacre 'Bloody Sunday' and two weeks later, Grand Duke Sergei Alexandrovich, the Emperor's uncle, was assassinated by an anarchist's bomb…*

*To calm matters, Nicholas II agreed to elections and the establishment of the 'Duma', an equivalent to England's House of Commons, but without any of the same powers…*

As the office clock quietly chimed six in the evening, Philip stretched his stiffening muscles and closed the file. None of his questions had been completely answered.

Arriving home to his townhouse, he told Mr and Mrs Evans to prepare for his trip to Russia. Mr and Mrs Evans had come to work for him after a weekend's shooting at a country house some years before. Mr Evans had been allocated to act as his personal valet, but after the first evening had been replaced by another man.

The new valet informed Philip: 'Mr Evans has had a bad fall and broken his hip, sir. Such a tragedy, as the doctor expects he will, very likely, be left with a pronounced limp, and the butler says a valet with such a disability will be unable to perform the job to the standard required. The butler's never liked Mr Evans and says if he has a limp then he'll have to clean the shoes and bring in the coal in future. Mrs Evans doesn't know how they are to live on the reduced wages the butler's saying he will be paid.'

Having just bought a townhouse in High Holborn, Philip needed some servants and asked if he could meet with Mr and Mrs Evans. A manservant with a limp didn't matter to Philip and they agreed that when Mr Evans was fully recovered he and his wife would come to London to look after Philip. It was one of the best decisions Philip had ever made and, although the wages he paid were high, the house was kept immaculately. His shirts were perfectly starched and ironed, his suits were pressed, and the food that Mrs Evans cooked was absolutely delicious. The only other servant was Elisabeth, a part-time girl who helped Mrs Evans each morning with the dusting, preparing the fires and bringing in the coal.

At the end of her first week Mrs Evans confided to her husband: 'Mr Philip's far too thin. There's not enough fat on him to keep out the cold; he needs building up.'

She set about turning the kitchen into a horn of plenty, delivering huge breakfasts and even larger dinners, interspersed with delicious cakes, homemade biscuits, jams and glasses of hot milky chocolate before he retired to bed. After a few months, Philip complained to Mr Evans that his trousers were tight around the waist.

'I'll arrange for the tailor to let them out,' said Mr Evans.

'Not for the moment,' replied Philip. 'Tight trousers will remind me not to have that second helping of your wife's delicious puddings.'

They both laughed.

The battle between Mrs Evans's fine food and Philip's desire to keep his waistline unchanged resulted in him walking to work, avoiding lunch and regularly sacrificing Mrs Evans's food for a modest meal at the Criterion or the Ritz. Mrs Evans didn't understand why he ate out, an event that happened, in her opinion, far too regularly.

'He should find a nice girl, settle down and marry,' she told Mr Evans.

At the end of a hard day Philip would often visit Mrs Evans in her kitchen. He delighted to see her broad smile, listen to her stories and her continuous laugh. It swept all the day's troubles away. He loved to hear Mrs Evans, covered in flour, waving a pastry cutter and laughingly putting the government and the British Empire to rights.

That night before Philip was to travel to Russia Mr Evans laid out the suits, evening wear, jackets, trousers, shirts, cufflinks, collars and shirt studs, leisure wear, hats, toiletries, smoking jacket and dressing gown Philip would need for his trip – the bare essentials for a gentleman travelling abroad.

## Chapter Two: St Petersburg

### March 1913

Philip was delighted to arrive at St Petersburg. The ship voyage had meant endless hours looking out to sea, small talk over dinner, reading books and not being able to work, and it bored him. To be able to walk down the gangway and onto firm land and be greeted by an officer of the Konvoi guard, a Cossack regiment of the Tsar's household, was a delight. As he shook hands with the officer, Philip felt positively underdressed. The officer wore an olive-green jacket with a fur-trimmed dolman, a similar green coat to the rest of the uniform with fur trimming and slung over the left shoulder with the sleeves hanging loose, knee-high boots, and a conical fur hat topped with a plumed eagle feather that effectively made him stand over seven foot tall. The sabre hanging loosely from the officer's waist lent the man additional authority.

'Good morning, Mr Cummings,' the officer said in perfect English. 'I've instructed that your luggage will be sent on to your hotel.' He waved Philip towards an open landau. Philip settled into the plush velvet seats.

'Is this your first visit to St Petersburg?'

'I was here as a boy with my parents,' said Philip.

'Very good! Then may I welcome you back, and I hope your stay will be an enjoyable one. If there's anything that I can do to make it a more comfortable time, then you need only to contact me. My card, sir.'

Philip took the card, looked at it and placed it safely in his waistcoat pocket.

The officer tapped the door of the landau with the hilt of his sword. The driver snapped his whip, the horses took up the strain and the carriage jolted forward.

Known as 'The Venice of the North', St Petersburg is one of the most beautiful cities in the world. Cut in half by the three-quarter-mile width of the Neva River, its golden domes and massive pastel-coloured palaces projected imperial power and prestige. The horses trotted towards the Nevsky Prospect, the grandest boulevard in the city and equal to the Champs-Élysées in Paris or Berlin's Unter den Linden in size, length and grandeur.

Philip was captivated by the multitudes of people. Russians mingled with Ukrainians, Finns, Poles, Swedes, Latvians and Turks, reflecting the huge size of the Russian Empire. Diplomats, businessmen and academics from every European country raised their hats to each other. The women, dressed in the latest Paris fashions, were escorted by officers in smart uniforms resplendent with medals and gold epaulettes; a priest with a long flowing beard hurried past a prostitute. In the roadway hundreds of motor cars and open-topped landaus transported their passengers to lunch or business appointments. Philip took in the sights.

The landau passed a church with blue domes painted with golden stars, Gostiny Dvor, an arcaded bazaar that specialised in Russian goods; Druces, an emporium that imported English soaps and perfumes, bright woollens from Scotland as well as linens from Ireland; past Wolf and Beranger's, the confectioners where the nobility bought exquisite pastries; the jewellers Bulgari, Bolin, Cartier and, of course, the most famous jeweller in the world, Fabergé, eventually arriving at the far end of Nevsky Prospect and the most fashionable hotel in the city, the Hotel European.

After checking him into the hotel, Philip's escort saluted, informed him that he would call for him at exactly ten in the morning to take him to his appointment, and left. The hotel manager and three porters ushered Philip to his suite. On the way Philip glanced around the lobby. It resembled the art nouveau style and décor of the Savoy Hotel in London. He would be comfortable.

\*\*\*\*

That same afternoon, two men met in a house in London's Belgravia. The district takes its name from one of the Duke of Westminster's subsidiary titles, Viscount Belgrave, and is one of the most fashionable addresses in the city.

Relaxing after a long lunch, the two men helped themselves to the cognac and cigars left by the butler.

'Earlier this morning I had a meeting at the war office,' said Sir Charles Cunningham, a career civil servant in his mid-fifties with thick brown hair greying at the temples. Sir Charles was proud that he had served the British Empire for almost thirty years and that his influence had reached far beyond the Foreign Office and even as far as the King's private secretary.

He knew people described him as being proud and arrogant; a description he dismissed as belonging to those without his ability and intellectual capability, people who couldn't create a plan that would extend Britain's control over weaker, inferior nations and their peoples. The British Empire was the greatest institution in the world and it needed him.

After sipping his cognac, Sir Charles spoke. 'The War Office has confirmed the present strength of the armed forces as two hundred and fifty thousand men – it is considerably smaller than the French and German counterparts. Half of the regular army is stationed in garrisons throughout the British Empire and, unlike the French and German armies, is made up exclusively of volunteers. If there were a war in Europe, we'd have difficulty winning it.'

The second man put his drink down on a side table. 'I was speaking to the Prime Minister this morning. He's worried that France and Germany both have larger armies than we do, and that Germany's building up its navy. It presents a threat to peace.'

'That's why I'm not pleased with Britain's treaty with Russia. If Britain has to come to Russia's aid in the event of war, we'll end up unable to win a European war.' He took another sip of cognac before continuing. 'I also disagree with the Foreign Minister that peace will continue for the foreseeable future. Relying on treaties that deliver mutual destruction is no way to ensure peace, yet Russia guarantees to support

Serbia, Germany has promised to support Austria-Hungary, and Russia and Britain will come to the defence of France, Belgium or Japan if attacked. As a result of all of these treaties, he thinks war is inconceivable. Personally, I think the man's an idiot, a pygmy, who can't see clearly into the future. One bullet could make war irresistible. So I've persuaded the Minister for War to let me draw up a plan for the British army to be increased by half a million men within weeks – should it be required. With my plan we can only be the victors.'

'That's excellent; I think that calls for a toast.'

'To war!' said Sir Charles, raising his glass.

'To war!' repeated the other man.

****

After a comfortable night at the Hotel Europe Philip awoke refreshed and after a breakfast of pastries and strong black coffee dressed carefully in a dark suit and looked at himself in the mirror. He looked sober; just what would be expected from a representative of the Bank of England. Looking at his pocket watch, he was satisfied he was ten minutes early for his appointment. People who were dilatory were undisciplined, he reminded himself as he walked downstairs to the lobby.

The same officer of the Konvoi Guard arrived to escort him to the Winter Palace. Philip was looking forward to seeing inside the palace he'd only seen from the outside as a child.

'It has over one thousand rooms, one hundred and seventeen staircases, needs an army of servants and, despite that, it's probably cold and draughty,' his father had said to five-year-old Philip.

The car passed through the fifteen-foot-high gates adorned with gilded double-headed eagles and headed towards the yellow and white façade of the huge palace, and two Cossack guards saluted as they passed.

Arriving at the visitors' entrance, Philip entered the vast hall with its vaulted ceiling and smelled a strong odour of oranges hanging from the trees that framed huge mirrors, allowing for a final adjustment to ball gowns, uniforms and dark bankers' suits before entering the Palace. Philip gave his reflection a quick glance and made a small adjustment to his cravat.

Philip followed his escort through two enormous doors into another hall that rose two storeys high to a ceiling covered in military banners and trophies. Officers and liveried servants hurried in and out. From the corner of one eye Philip saw a man drop a bundle of papers that slid onto the highly polished floor and scattered everywhere. Philip sensed the man's panic. The servant fell to his knees in a hopeless effort to recover what he could, but his efforts were frustrated as other messengers, too busy to lend any aid, walked through the papers, scattering them further. Philip wanted to run over to help the man but his escort had no intention of stopping – even though he had observed the man's plight.

They marched through three huge halls of increasing opulence, arriving at a room over two hundred feet in length and lined with the portraits of Russian and Allied commanders who had fought against Napoleon Bonaparte. At the far end of the gallery hung an immense portrait of Tsar Alexander I astride a prancing grey horse displayed beneath a gilded canopy hung with crimson velvet and crowned with a golden double-headed eagle.

As they arrived at the top of the gallery Philip's escort stopped and pointed to a picture of the Duke of Wellington. 'You will, of course, recognise your General Wellington who helped in Tsar Alexander's defeat of Napoleon and the French.'

Tempted as he was to correct the description of Wellington's role in defeating Napoleon, Philip smiled at his guide as if grateful at being given this critical historical fact. Satisfied with the impact he had made, his escort marched towards the next room and in the distance Philip heard the unmistakable tune of the British national anthem. He began to mutter the words: 'God save our gracious King...'

'You know the tune?' asked his guide.

'Of course,' replied Philip. 'It—'

'Was once the national anthem of Russia. Known as "The Prayer of the Russians", it will be played at a concert tomorrow attended by the Tsar,' interrupted his escort.

'Fascinating,' said Philip as he once more trotted alongside his escort.

Eventually Philip was ushered into a library and his escort discreetly faded away. Inside the room the walls were covered by elaborately carved walnut bookcases filled with leather-bound volumes. At the centre two sofas stood on a brightly patterned Oriental carpet. Seated on one of the sofas was a man in a grey morning suit and a neat cravat. Behind the sofa stood another man in military uniform adorned with rows of medals and gold epaulettes on each shoulder.

The uniformed man smiled and approached Philip, extending his hand in greeting. 'Mr Cummings, my name is General Alexander Mossolov. I'm head of the Imperial Chancellery.'

Gesturing to the man on the sofa, he went on, 'May I introduce Piotr Bark?'

Philip knew of the man by reputation. A brilliant mind, totally dedicated to the Tsar. After studying law at St Petersburg University he had studied banking at the Mendelssohn Bank in Berlin and was now Assistant Minister of Commerce and Industry, the Russian day file had told him.

'I hope your journey was comfortable and that your hotel is acceptable?' enquired the General.

'Perfectly,' smiled Philip.

The General waved a hand at the bookshelves. 'This is His Majesty's private library. He's an avid reader and this library contains over thirty thousand works. His Majesty speaks five languages fluently.' The General pointed towards the shelves. 'The volumes covered in brown leather are works in Russian, blue in French, red English and green German.'

Philip remembered what his father had told him when he was a child. 'Remember, my boy, that Russians have an inferiority complex, brought on by the fact that they know many Europeans believe them to be backward and uncultured… which can't be true when you consider their many writers, composers, artists and the wonderful buildings their empire has produced.'

'His Majesty has asked us to conduct the arrangements on his behalf.'

Philip, the General and Piotr Bark all knew that a meeting between the Tsar and a banker from Britain was quite impossible.

'Mr Cummings,' said Piotr Bark, pointing to a wooden box on a side table. 'This is His Majesty's first deposit.'

Philip looked at a box of polished beech with brass corners and a gilded double-headed eagle affixed to the top.

'We'll check the contents so that you can agree and sign for them on behalf of the Bank of England.'

The lid was opened to reveal a silk-lined interior and a number of Moroccan leather-bound pouches, each embossed with a double-headed eagle.

'This pouch contains one hundred gold ten-rouble pieces,' said the General.

A second revealed a gold chain holding square-cut emeralds, each surrounded by a diamond border. A third held a diamond and ruby tiara with drop pearls suspended along the crown that would swing as the wearer moved. In all, there were eighteen pouches of diamond bracelets, necklaces, gold coins, jewellery, loose diamonds, emeralds and rubies as large as bird's eggs. Philip had never seen so many beautiful pieces of jewellery.

'The total value is nine hundred and fifty thousand roubles,' said the General, as he passed Philip two sheets of paper with the inventory to sign. The box was repacked and locked.

The General handed a key to Philip, who placed it carefully in his coat pocket. A hidden bell was pressed, informing two servants in the outer office that the meeting was at an end.

'You will receive an escort to your boat and I wish you a safe and pleasant journey back to England. We shall see you again in a few months for the second shipment.'

Philip bade both men goodbye as the two liveried servants picked up the box and escorted Philip out of the Winter Palace and to his waiting boat.

Passing through the gates he heard a distant military band strike up the national anthem and a group of bystanders began to sing:

*God save the Tsar!*
*Mighty and powerful!*
*May he reign for our glory,*
*Reign that our foes may quake!*
*O Orthodox Tsar!*
*God save the Tsar!*

# Chapter Three: Reflections and celebrations

Ten days later Philip was back in London. The concerns he had had over his trip to Russia quickly faded, as it turned out to be an interesting time to be in London. Life in all sorts of ways was changing. The price of gold rose to four pounds per troy ounce and Philip wrote a report for the British Treasury on inflation or, as the bank referred to it, 'advance in prices' and its effect on imports from the empire.

In April the newspapers reported that Emmeline Pankhurst, the suffragette who wanted to change the electoral voting system, had been sentenced to three years' penal servitude for smashing windows and assaulting police officers. In June Emily Davison, another suffragette, ran out in front of the King's horse, Anmer, at the Epsom Derby. Trampled by the horse, she died four days later.

When he read of the death of Emily Davison Philip reflected on his own mother's death who had also died after a horse riding accident. He had been inconsolable when she died on his twelfth birthday. The pain had been strange and terrible; like having an aching tooth, it was constant.

On that day his father had looked at him and could only see his dead wife in the child before him, and to hide that vision he sent Philip away. Philip ran to his room, crawled into bed, pulled the covers over his head and sobbed alone in the dark.

The darkness continued long after the funeral. Philip's presence reminded his father of the love he'd lost and generated in him an irritation that always ended in Philip being ordered from the room. Philip understood his father was in pain, but so was he. His greatest wish was to hug his father and ease his own suffering a little. Instead, his father would constantly admonish him for being lazy, feckless and irresponsible. Philip convinced himself that if he worked harder at school, played sport with even more determination, then his father might love him and show him some of the affection he desperately longed for. Every night he climbed the steep stairs to his room and cried himself to sleep, vowing to try even harder to be better so that his father would show him the love he so wanted.

On the morning of his father's funeral the family solicitor handed him a letter, written in his father's hand:

*My boy,*

*I know that things have been difficult between us since your mother's early departure and I'm truly sorry for that. I never knew how to replace the love she gave you, and so avoided doing so. I always hoped that by giving you a good education you would be able to cope with the struggles of this world, but in my old age I've come to know that this wasn't enough.*

*I wish now I'd given you the love and the affection you craved – and deserved. I realised, only when it was already too late, that I also needed your love. You should know it's always been with immense pride that I saw you excel at school and forge a career in banking that's taken you to the top of your profession, all with no help or support from me.*

*While it may have seemed that I abandoned you, it's with great appreciation that I know you never abandoned me. I can never thank you enough for the many, many kindnesses you showed me in these past years of my illness. I do hope, my boy, that one day you will find the happiness you so much deserve and that I was unable to give you.*

*Much love and many hugs, your father.*

It was the last time Philip had cried.

Even after his father's death he continued trying to please him, thinking nothing of spending fourteen hours at his desk and then working another hour or two when he was at home. When he was alone and nursing a whisky and soda he would wonder how things might have been had his mother lived.

\*\*\*\*

1913 was also a busy time for the Russian nation, as three hundred years of Romanov rule was celebrated around the empire. Champagne flowed and huge banquets were consumed in royal palaces and in restaurants, where the middle classes toasted the system that had made them wealthy and Russia the wealthiest country in the world.

The Tsar toured his empire waving to his subjects through the windows of his private train, saying to his family and government ministers, 'My people love me.'

Endless rows of soldiers were inspected; cheering naval ratings were saluted from his yacht *Standart*; at the opera he acknowledged the cheers of the audience. All of Russia was in a fever of patriotic devotion and eagerly anticipated another three hundred years of autocratic rule.

****

In the mind of the aristocrat there are two things that create a gulf between himself and ordinary people. The first is wealth and the second is their hereditary title. Not all titled families have money but, given the choice between wealth and a title, the aristocrat will always elect to retain the title. The ancient House of Tagleva might well have been one of the impoverished aristocratic families to be found all over Europe when the then Count gambled most of the family's estates on the turn of a card – which turned out to be a deuce rather than an ace. Luckily the Count's son, Michael Tagleva, who had a natural aptitude for business, took what was left of the family's fortune and worked hard to double it. Fifty years later much of their wealth, though not their lands, had been restored. With a title and money, the Taglevas were welcome in the grandest houses throughout Moscow.

Sergei Michaelovich Tagleva was dressing for the third ball in ten days.

Sergei was considered by the matrons of Moscow as an 'excellent marriage prospect' for their daughters whilst their daughters would look over the tops of their fans at the tall man of twenty four with the athletic, muscular body, curly blond hair, large blue eyes and permanent smile and would often describe him to friends as 'probably the best-looking man in Moscow, if not the empire', and, as a result, his dance card was always full. Sergei genuinely didn't understand why women were attracted to him. He thought he was no better looking than many of his friends, no better a dancer or a horseman, and he thus had none of the arrogance or cockiness that so many young men adopt when they believe themselves to be irresistible to women.

His friends knew the effect he had on women and after every ball took the opportunity to provide comfort and sympathy to the disappointed females he left in his wake.

On more than one occasion Sergei had accepted an invitation to dine with the family of a pretty young girl only to discover, too late, that the girl's mother was the only person in residence and both husband and daughter were 'away in the country'. How he had managed to avoid being challenged to a duel by an outraged husband, brother or fiancé he didn't know.

As he dressed, Sergei thought of his father, Count Michael, and how much he respected him for having managed the family business so successfully after his grandfather had nearly lost everything at that game of cards. It was with pride that Sergei knew his father was considered a model administrator and employer as well as a man with a social conscience by the most important merchants in Moscow.

His father often told his children of the time their grandfather had forced him to watch the flogging of three peasants found guilty of theft. Their crime? Stealing a bag of rotting parsnips destined to be served to pigs and stolen to feed their starving children during a famine. The men were brought into the village square and tied to a triangular wooden frame; their shirts were ripped off their backs and a burly man unravelled a 'knout' to administer the punishment of twenty lashes. The men's wives and children were brought to the front of the crowd by local police to watch the punishment, which was administered with enthusiastic brutality by the executioner, himself a criminal, let off his punishment in return for his services. The knout consists of a handle about the length of a man's arm to which is fastened a flat leather thong twice the length of the handle. At the end of the thong is a large copper ring which is bound with a strip of hide, soaked in milk and then dried in the sun to make it as hard as rock. After twenty lashes, their backs were broken and they were crippled for life. The young Michael cried with the men's wives and children, no older than himself, forced to watch as the family was reduced to a lifetime of poverty and empty bellies.

That night Michael had promised himself that, when he became Count, none of his servants or tenants would ever be flogged. When his father lost most of the family's money at that game of cards, Michael used the little that was left to set up a clothing manufacturing business. The family title helped to gain contracts to supply the army. The factories thrived. Over the years that followed, workers' housing was built; the working week reduced to five and a half days; a doctor engaged to provide basic healthcare to all tenants; and a school established for the children. On hearing that a tenant was ill, Count Michael would arrive at their door with gifts of meat, cake and salt. At Easter, baskets of painted eggs, Easter bread and sweet cheese spread would be delivered to every household. The whip had never been used in the Tagleva factories and whenever Count Michael, now an old man, travelled around his estate he would hand out candies to the throngs of children who rushed to greet him.

Sergei adjusted his collar in the mirror and thought about his younger sister, a beautiful young woman with an infectious laugh. He smiled when he thought back to when they were young and she had delighted in running through the regiments of toy soldiers lined up to be inspected, scattering them in every direction. Now that they were adults, he had forgiven her the decimation of his armies and instead took pleasure in their trips to the theatre and picnics, where they would talk about their hopes for the future.

His elder brother Sacha, on the other hand, had been the rebellious one. When a student he'd been warned by the *Okhrana*, the secret police, to moderate what he said in public when speaking against the government. His father hoped that

Sacha's political leanings would mellow as he grew older, but it was not to be. In fact, as Sacha got older his anger at the injustices he saw all around him made his language more violent. He was arrested for distributing pamphlets criticising the war against Japan. His father managed to free him from prison by promising the magistrate that he would not do it again, an undertaking achieved by sending Sacha into exile. Now Sacha was in London and acting as a secretary, or some such thing, for a socialist group. Sergei missed his elder brother.

Much to his father's delight, Sergei had always been interested in the family business. After leaving Moscow University he helped his father manage the clothing factories. Two of the factories made clothes for the fashionable shops in Moscow and St Petersburg and the third specialised in military clothing and officers' uniforms. Sergei began by learning every aspect of the work of the factory. He ordered the gold and silver thread that would be sewn into collars, epaulettes and cuffs, the fur that covered the military caps, the feathers for the plumes of the officers' caps and the ladies' hats. He spent time sewing the materials himself so that he knew how it was done, which materials complemented each other, how to dye cloth and shape feathers.

To keep up with modern production techniques Sergei's father had sent him to the cotton mills in Lancashire in the North of England. There he studied how the bales of raw cotton were broken open, combed and processed. He liked the North of England and particularly the humour of the women who worked in the mills. On seeing him they would nudge each other and ask, 'Are all Russian boys as fine as thee?'

'Wi' so much snow, wha' do folk do te stay warm on winter nights?'

Often he would find himself blushing at their questions, which only encouraged even more teasing and laughter. No matter how carefully he answered, his words were frequently turned into meanings he had not intended which always caused immense hilarity. Often one of the older women would shout out the pleasures that could await him on a dark and cold night, and the whole factory would laugh out loud at his reddened face.

In London he enjoyed the dance halls, fine restaurants and the gracious living that the city afforded. The main difference between London and cities in Russia was the absence of large palaces. The largest, the Palace of Westminster, which housed not a monarch or some wealthy prince but the British parliament, was modest by Russian standards. One day Sergei managed to get a seat in the strangers' gallery to listen to a debate and was shocked to hear people argue with the King's ministers without fear of arrest. He thought it was a system that would serve Russia well, but he knew how slow Russia's rulers were at adopting change that would reduce their own powers and resigned himself that it would be many years before the Tsar would allow Russia to be democratic, if ever.

One evening he had managed to meet his elder brother. Typically, Sacha took him to a political meeting in Pimlico, where the topic of debate was 'The downfall of the Romanovs in Russia'. Sergei was amazed that the meeting wasn't broken up by the secret police and that the lone policeman guarding the door greeted him with, 'Evening, sir' as he entered the hall. Sergei thought the debate a waste of time, as did most of the British public, judging by the size of the audience, a bare dozen people, half of whom seemed to have come in from the street to keep warm.

There was, however, one man that stuck in his mind: the leader of the Russian Social Democratic Party, the organiser of the debate, one Vladimir Illich Ulyanov, whom Sacha called Lenin. Sacha was helping Lenin to write a pamphlet titled 'What is to be done?' that argued for a party of professional revolutionaries dedicated to the overthrow of Tsarism. At the end of the evening Sergei politely wished him luck, convinced that Sacha was wasting his time.

After the meeting he was taken to a workers' café and presented with a plate of jellied eels and potatoes. He looked down at the grey glutinous mass on his plate and, despite not having eaten since breakfast, Sergei didn't feel at all hungry.

It was obvious that Sacha was living on very little, so one afternoon Sergei gave Sacha a hundred pounds. It would allow him to pay off some debts and buy a new overcoat for the winter. Sacha stuffed the notes into his pocket and slapped his brother on the back, saying, 'When the revolution comes, my brother, I'll be sure to repay you by making sure you're not shot.'

'Thank you,' replied Sergei.

Three months after Sergei returned to Russia the cotton machines were delivered from Britain and both productivity and profits increased. Within a year the Tagleva family was managing the largest cloth and clothing factory in Moscow. The following Easter the factory workers, now some of the best-paid factory workers in the city, presented Sergei's father with a silver egg. In return, each worker received a loaf of bread, some salt and a five-rouble piece. The workers knew that, while the work was hard and the hours long, they were some of the luckiest workers in the whole of Moscow. Sergei took a final look in the mirror, adjusted his cuff and content with his reflection, walked down the stairs to wait for his father and sister.

# Chapter Four: A puff of wind

## London, November 1913

Sir Charles Cunningham was having another meeting at his Belgravia home.

'Since our last meeting the Belgian war ministry has authorised the use of the .303 British round for their Lewis gun,' said Sir Charles.

Cunningham believed that the Lewis machine gun was essential for the British army and had met with its inventor, Colonel Isaac Newton Lewis, when he heard that the US army had initially refused to buy the weapon. With Cunningham's help and finance, the Armes Automatiques Lewis Company was established in Liège in Belgium to manufacture the new Lewis gun for the British army.

'Will the Americans be a problem?'

'No; one advantage to these arrangements is that the Lewis gun can only be manufactured in Belgium for the British army. The Americans have their own version of the gun, made by Savage Arms in America. Although the two guns are largely similar, there are enough differences to stop them being completely interchangeable, and they will even fire different-sized bullets,' replied Cunningham.

'That's better than we had hoped for. In fact, it's perfect. The army won't be beholden to the Americans for supplies, and the manufacturer will be completely independent.'

'I thought you'd be pleased.'

'Pleased? I'm ecstatic.'

Cunningham watched a cloud of blue cigar smoke rise to the ceiling before continuing. 'The order was smaller than we'd hoped, but I suspect that more will be needed fairly soon. The idiot Foreign Secretary told me last week that war in Europe will never happen and, even if it does, Britain hopes to be able to stay out of it, so he sees no reason for the army to have lots of machine guns. He's wrong, of course. His expectation of peace is just a house of cards and the problem with a house of cards is that there's always a puff of wind to blow it down.'

## Moscow, June 1914

The puff of wind predicted by Charles Cunningham arrived seven months later and more quickly than anyone could have expected. In Moscow, Count Michael Tagleva was eating his breakfast and reading aloud the latest news of the assassination of the heir to the Austro-Hungarian throne. What had seemed a minor incident at first had over the past few days developed into a crisis.

'The first two terrorists were unable to throw their grenades because the streets were too crowded and the Archduke's car was travelling too fast. A third terrorist did manage to throw his grenade, which exploded under the car and severely injured attendants, who had to be taken to hospital. After attending the official reception at the City Hall, Archduke Franz Ferdinand asked about the members of his party who had been wounded. Told they were badly injured, he insisted on being taken to see them.

'On the way to the hospital, the car took a wrong turn. It was here that Gavrilo Princip happened to be standing on the corner. The nineteen-year-old, burning with the fire of Slavic nationalism, envisioned that the death of the Archduke would be the key that would unlock the shackles binding his people to the Austro-Hungarian Empire.

'Princip took the opportunity presented to him, stepped forward, drew his gun and, at a distance of about five feet, fired twice into the car. Archduke Franz Ferdinand was hit in the neck and his wife in the abdomen, a shot that killed their unborn child.'

Count Michael took a sip of his tea and continued to read the account. 'As the car quickly reversed, a thin stream of blood spurted from the Archduke's mouth and Count Franz von

Harrach, who was riding on the running board and serving as a bodyguard, pulled out a handkerchief to wipe away the blood.

'The Duchess cried out to her husband, "In Heaven's name, what has happened to you?"

'At that she slid off the seat and lay on the floor of the car. Princip's bullet had pierced the Archduke's jugular vein but despite the pain, he pleaded, "Sophie dear! Sophie dear! Don't die! Stay alive for our children!" The bodyguard seized the Archduke by the collar of his uniform, to stop his head dropping forward, and asked him if he was in great pain. The Archduke replied quite distinctly, "It's nothing." The car sped the royal couple to the Governor's residence, but they were both dead.'

The footman slid a plate of ham and eggs in front of Count Michael, who folded the newspaper and placed it down beside him.

'I was talking to Prince Igor at the reception last night,' he said to Sergei. 'He told me that Austria's sent Serbia an ultimatum which Serbia can't possibly accept, thereby giving Austria a pretext for launching a war.'

'But the Tsar won't allow Austria to attack Serbia, will he?' asked Sergei, as a servant poured more tea into his glass.

'It seems that the Austrians, afraid of an attack from Russia, have made a treaty with Germany to come to her aid should Russia declare war. Despite this, the Tsar's ordered the army to be mobilised. We should prepare for the worst.'

'But we can't have war. The Tsar and the Kaiser are cousins,' said Sophie.

'Family feuds are often the bitterest,' said Sergei, and the old Count inwardly smiled. He'd always been delighted at the way his two youngest children loved each other. He found it fascinating they had never argued and were so devoted to each other.

As a baby Sophie would follow her brother with hesitant steps, arms outstretched as if looking for a hug. If she fell she would land on the marble floor, push herself up again and with a smile take another few wobbly paces towards her brother.

Her antics could keep the family amused for hours. Even today, whenever one left the house they would seek the other on their return to excitedly recount what they had been doing and to share any gossip or news. As children, if ever Count Michael scolded one he could anticipate that, within the hour, the other would approach him and plead for clemency. Inevitably he forgave the misdemeanour. Such laxity on his part could have made them unruly and wild, like their eldest brother, but for as long as he could remember his two youngest children had been polite, caring, obedient and respectful, and he continued to spoil them far too much.

'What will the Tsar do?' asked Sophie.

'I'm not sure, but I was speaking to Count Zubov, who told me that he thinks Russia is on the verge of events such as the world has not seen before. He's convinced that we're about to enter a time of barbarism that will last for decades. I fear he may be right.'

Turning to Sergei, he asked, 'What do you think?'

'If there's war, it'll mean a huge demand for military uniforms. I think we should make an order for more cloth.'

'Good idea; you do that,' said the Count and returned to reading the newspaper, noticing out of the corner of his eye his daughter give her brother a wink to say, 'Well done.'

### London, 29 July 1914

Philip Cummings was having a very busy day. The talk in company boardrooms throughout the City of London was of war. The government, the bankers and the public alike had been frightened by the assassination of the Archduke. The stock market fell. Everyone wanted to protect whatever investments they had – and, in a crisis, that meant buying gold. At the start of the day the Bank of England held fifty million pounds worth of gold; by the end of the day twelve million had been withdrawn by France, Belgium, Egypt and Gibraltar.

The man in the street also wanted gold and demanded that the Chief Cashier kept the promise he writes on every British pound note to 'pay the bearer on demand the sum of…' in gold.

The first requests for gold arrived at Philip's office before the banks opened. Throughout the morning telegram followed telegram until the bank was swamped. Confidence was falling and Philip knew the situation was turning into a serious crisis with panic on the streets. Local banks fuelled demand, as some banks paid out gold to its customers as it was demanded, while others refused. This caused anger and near riots in parts of the capital. Police were summoned to maintain order.

Hasty meetings were held to discuss the crisis.

'If we don't honour the promise of gold for each pound presented to the bank then we debase the entire banking system and more chaos will be the result,' said one manager.

'But if we pay out every demand we could end up with no gold at all,' argued another.

'We should close the banks until the crisis passes,' said a third.

'The problem is the threat of war. Everyone's panicking.'

'The country can't afford a war. We'll be bankrupt within a month.'

'We should raise interest rates.'

Shocked at the way his colleagues were panicking, Philip tried to calm the meeting. 'Gentlemen, I would expect any rise in interest rates would increase the sense of panic, not reduce it. If Britain increases interest rates it'll force other nations to follow suit.'

Philip's was a lone voice urging caution.

That evening the government raised the interest rate from three to ten per cent.

On hearing the news, Germany, Austria and Denmark raised their own interest rates. There was no stopping the panic.

A messenger entered the room and delivered an envelope from the Governor. He opened it and read the paper inside: 'Austria has declared war on Serbia.'

All day the telephone rang constantly, as senior staff moved from one crisis meeting to another. Decisions made at one meeting had to be unravelled immediately as the next piece of news arrived on people's desks.

Acknowledging that Philip's advice over interest rates had been correct, he was asked for his solution to halting the financial crisis.

'Everyone needs to be given time to draw breath. Suspending trading might do that,' suggested Philip.

That afternoon the government closed the stock exchange and ordered all commercial banks to shut their doors for a week. Closing the banks calmed some people but increased others' anxiety. The streets outside many banks were filled with people hoping to gain access to their money. Jewellers in Hatton Garden and goldsmiths around Holborn were also told to close their doors to prevent their shops being overrun with people demanding to buy loose diamonds and gold.

At six in the evening Philip looked at his watch. He felt drained and suspected that this was only the start; that things were about to get much worse. The crisis had a momentum of its own: there was no stopping it. Every country in Europe was intent on a fight and the first one to strike a blow would cause the others to lash out at the rest.

The Governor of the Bank of England pleaded with government ministers. 'We have to remain neutral. It's the only sensible course of action to maintain Britain's economy.'

Lloyd George gave the government's position: 'Austria declaring war on Serbia is of little consequence, but if Germany declares war on Russia or France we must go to war.'

In St Petersburg the Tsar's generals informed him that within six weeks Russia could mobilise the largest army in the world: six million men. Neither Germany nor Austria could compete, and would have to back down.

Stepping from his swimming pool, he gave the order to mobilise.

In Berlin the Kaiser told his generals that 'Russia's mobilisation of six million men was an aggressive act' that Germany could not ignore. Twelve hours later, at ten minutes past seven, Germany declared war on Russia.

Bound by its treaty with Russia, France declared war on Germany and Austria.

Two days later, Germany invaded neutral Belgium. Britain,

34

bound by the terms of a seventy-five-year-old treaty, felt obliged to come to Belgium's aid and declared war on Germany.

The house of cards had collapsed.

****

Troops all over Europe paraded in front of their tsars, kaisers and kings. Generals drank champagne and young men intoxicated by the thought of honour and glory donned uniforms and marched off to war, promising their loved ones that they would be home in time for Christmas.

Philip thought the events of the previous four weeks utter madness. Nevertheless, he felt a sense of patriotism and made an appointment with the Governor.

'I'm tendering my resignation to join the army to fight. I feel it's my duty,' said Philip.

'Damn foolish,' said the Governor. 'Your duty's here helping manage the nation's finances – besides, you'd be a useless soldier. You'll be far more effective here than running around Belgium with a pop gun.'

Philip could see the sense in what the Governor was saying. All the same, he felt he wasn't doing his duty by staying at home, in comfort. Then the Governor looked at him and smiled. 'Philip, my dear chap, by the time you've learned to march and to get to France it'll be Christmas and it'll all be over, and such a waste of time. Resignation is refused.'

Philip returned to his office feeling as if he were letting someone down.

****

At the start of the war there was a general outpouring of patriotism in England, Germany, Austria and Russia – and the Tsar, the Kaiser and George V found themselves more popular than at any other time during their reigns. They spent their days reviewing troops. No one had time to meet with a banker from Britain and organise the transfer of the final box from Russia to the Bank of England.

Like most of his countrymen, Philip was anxious for any news of the war. Mr Evans brought him *The Times* each morning with his breakfast. The start of the war had gone well for Russia. Germany had expected that Russia would be slow to mobilise, allowing Germany time to thrash France and then turn and transfer its victorious, battle-hardened troops along Germany's superior rail network to fight the Russians on the Eastern Front. However, quite unexpectedly, Russia invaded East Prussia on the seventh of August. The Germans were forced to retreat. The Kaiser appointed Hindenburg Chief of the German General Staff and he sent eight divisions against the Russians in the Battle of Tannenberg. The battle was brilliantly executed and resulted in over thirty thousand Russians captured and eighteen thousand killed. The Russian General Samsonov, blamed for the defeat, shot himself.

After Tannenberg the Russian army went from defeat to defeat. The infantry was poorly equipped; the cavalry was cut down in thousands as they charged German machine guns; and, to make matters worse, the communications, equipment, food, munitions, horses and trucks had to travel eight hundred miles to the front. When reinforcements arrived they were forced to walk the last fifty miles to the battle front, exhausted even before the fight. They were thrown into battle before they had time to recover, and the terrified peasants who'd never seen an aeroplane decided that 'God must be on the side of the enemy that had flying machines' and deserted.

As casualties rose and battles were lost the Tsar appointed himself as Commander in Chief and in homes and palaces all over Russia people began to blame the Tsar for every defeat and setback. As the war dragged on, millions more men were dead, equipment was in short supply and the morale of the army so low and so many had forgotten why they were fighting that whole units would desert and walk the hundreds of miles home to their farms and loved ones.

# Chapter Five: Death in Petrograd

## London, October 1916

The Governor walked into Philip's office. Unusual, thought Philip. Perhaps the Governor had acquiesced to his most recent request to join the army in France.

'I've had a telegram from the Foreign Office. You're to go to Russia to pick up the final box. You sail tomorrow.'

So much for my application to fight, thought Philip.

The following day Philip arrived in Southampton and boarded a merchant ship sailing to Petrograd, the new name of St Petersburg changed to associate it with the glories of Peter the Great. The ship brought essential supplies for the Russian war effort. If the first three trips had been tedious – and they had been on cruise liners – then this final trip was likely to be long, uncomfortable and dangerous. German U-boats were sinking Allied merchant ships whenever they found them. To protect itself, the ship sailed without lights at night, and during the day lookouts at port and starboard trained binoculars on the sea. On a couple of occasions the ship's captain was forced to alter course to avoid known minefields, but no submarines were spotted. The ship arrived unscathed in Petrograd and began to offload its cargo. As Philip disembarked the captain told him that his orders were to sail only when Philip was ready to depart.

## Petrograd

Compared to Philip's first visit the city was drab and depressing. Gone were the brightly coloured uniforms hung with glistening gold braid, the Paris fashions, the colourful shops filled with goods. In their place were the old, the very young, soldiers with missing limbs, and beggars.

For the first few days Philip waited to be summoned to

collect the final box and passed his time walking through the city. He couldn't help but notice the many people waiting in queues, a few kopecks in their pocket, for a cup of hot soup and a slice of grey bread. Too often those at the back of the queue would wait for hours only to find that the food had run out before it was their turn. Life was so difficult that many of those who had previously confined themselves to the city's slums, dark and hostile places even the police avoided, were now forced to beg in more prosperous areas and to prostitute their children, girls and boys as young as ten to find the money to buy food to survive.

In the evenings, however, those from the slums noticed that the city took on a more vibrant feel as many of the palaces lining the Neva River continued to resound to music, champagne flowed, and carriages arrived at the opera and the ballet so that the wealthy could escape the privations felt by most. Even the Hotel Europe had fresh flowers delivered daily and its restaurant and bar were filled each night with diners who ate the choicest food and drank the finest wines.

If Philip left the hotel for a walk in the fresh air after dinner he noticed groups of people looking into the large windows of the grand houses at the wealthy enjoying themselves, dancing the night away, seemingly without a care for those dying in the mud to preserve their carefree lifestyle. Philip was amazed at their insensitivity.

After three weeks Philip was still waiting to be summoned to the Winter Palace, and boredom was beginning to frustrate him. Whenever he sent a telegram to the Bank of England he was never sure that it was delivered and he never received a reply. He was beginning to feel imprisoned in a gilded cage.

Needing to escape the confines of the hotel, and despite the dangers of walking the streets, he was walking by the river when a woman approached him. She was not the usual beggar he saw on the streets. Dressed in a long overcoat, the collar turned up to protect her from the chill, she asked him for 'some kopecks to feed the poor'.

Philip delved into his pocket and brought out two fifty-rouble notes and gave them to the woman.

'That's very generous,' said the woman.

'And what will my money pay for?' It was a stupid question, he thought; typical of a banker, but he hadn't had a conversation of any significance with anyone for so long and was desperate for someone to talk to.

'There are so many men from the war who need help: the homeless, those without a job, wounded soldiers. I feel it's my responsibility to try to help them, even though I can do so little.'

'I'm sure that what you are doing is much appreciated,' replied Philip.

'Would you like to see what your generous contribution will pay for?' She looked up at him without any expectation that he would accept.

Philip had nothing else to do other than to return to the Hotel Europe and another tedious evening. 'Yes, why not?' he said, 'and what should I call you?'

'My name's Marie.'

'Then lead on Marie.'

They walked a few blocks to a cellar from which a dim light glowed. As Philip approached he was overcome by the stench of damp and excrement. He coughed and, as he got closer, his throat objected to the stench. He bent over and retched. He retched again at the top of the stairs leading down to the cellar. He didn't want to enter but the woman had already begun to descend the stairs and motioned him to follow. Holding a gloved hand over his mouth and pinching his nose, he hoped he could stem the awful smell. At the bottom of the stairs his eyes adjusted to the light of a dozen candles. Sitting at a table made of planks were some thirty men. At least, he thought they were men – at first he wasn't sure. Yes, they were faces, but they were like the agonised and tortured faces painted by Michelangelo above the entrance to the Sistine Chapel to remind corpulent cardinals in Rome of the terrors that awaited those descending into Hades. Philip looked into the sunken black eyes, which stared back at him with the indifference of the starving waiting for death. Every man was dressed in a threadbare overcoat; some had woollen mittens; all had unkempt beards growing almost to their waist; and matted hair to their shoulders. As Philip's eyes grew more accustomed to the flickering candlelight, he saw lice and maggots crawling in their hair and open wounds making their homes in the still-living flesh.

'My God,' whispered Philip to himself, hardly believing what he saw.

A rat the size of a small cat scurried along the wall of the cellar and Philip shuddered. None of the men moved. It was as if a favourite pet had scampered through the room. On the table there were plates but no food.

'These people haven't eaten in three days,' said the woman.

'How can I help?' asked Philip.

'You've helped already by giving me money to buy food, sir.'

'It's not money you want. Come outside,' said Philip.

They returned to the street. 'Come with me.'

They walked two blocks to a restaurant. At the door the woman grasped his arm roughly. 'I haven't come to eat,' she said angrily.

'Neither have I,' said Philip.

The head waiter approached them.

'What is your soup of the day?' asked Philip.

The head waiter smiled at the thought of two more customers. It had been a quiet evening.

'We have a choice of *solyanka*, made from fish, vegetables and pickles, and *okroshka*, a cold soup of meats and vegetables, served with boiled eggs and sour cream.'

'Fine. I'll take thirty portions of each with bread.'

'I'm sorry,' spluttered the waiter, thinking he had misheard.

'Thirty portions of each, with bread – and some waiters to carry the pots two blocks down the road.'

'I'm sorry, sir,' protested the waiter. 'I regret, we only serve food in the restaurant.'

'And if the food was for a party at the Novo-Mikhailovsky Palace?'

'That would be entirely different, sir,' smiled the waiter, recognising the name that had once been the official residence of Grand Duke Mikhail Nikolaevich.

Philip placed a small pile of gold coins on the table in front of the head waiter. 'I'm sure this will cover the cost, as well as give you a substantial tip, and you'll do the same each evening for the next week.'

Twenty minutes later Philip was supervising the transport of the soup, not to the Novo-Mikhailovsky Palace, but to the cellar, where it was dished out to the amazed diners.

When everyone had eaten their fill, and most were sleeping, exhausted, Philip told the woman he would return each evening to make sure that the waiter fulfilled his task.

'Who are you? What's your name?"

'It doesn't matter. I'll see you tomorrow.'

As Marie watched the man melt into the darkness, she crossed herself. She couldn't have expected more if Saint Spyridon or Saint Nicholas had visited the cellar that night.

After visiting the cellar for a week, word had spread and the numbers needing to be fed had swelled. Nonetheless, Philip insisted that no one should be turned away, and he spent hours in the cellar serving soup to those that came for a meal. He would wait at the door, sometimes with a cloth over his arm, and Marie gently teased him, saying that he looked like a head waiter.

He would return to the Hotel Europe, undress, have a bath and hand his clothes to the floor butler to be cleaned and washed. The floor butler would depart to the laundry holding the clothes at arm's length and wondering if the gentleman worked as a sewage engineer.

One evening, Philip was sitting in the lobby wondering how he could continue the soup kitchen even after he had left Petrograd. His payment to the restaurant had increased and their kitchens were now exclusively cooking soup for him. He knew he could never feed all those in need, but was determined to do as much as he could and for as long as he could. He picked up a newspaper that had been discarded on the sofa and settled down to read when his attention was drawn to a disturbance towards the main entrance. A man dressed in the uniform of an infantry regiment had managed to slip past the doorman. His beard was matted and his face covered in grime, and a purple scar, probably a sabre cut, ran from his ear to his mouth.

He was obviously a deserter – and drunk. The man swayed, squinted in the bright electric lights in the lobby and, through his alcoholic fog, surveyed the twenty people in the lobby dressed in their fine clothes. Everyone froze.

Philip feared that one of the men from the cellar had followed him to the Hotel Europe, and he watched as the man swayed and threw pamphlets into the air. They drifted down to the floor and across the lobby, and he shouted, 'God fuck bloody Nicholas, the murdering Tsar!' He raised his right arm and fired a revolver at the ceiling.

One woman screamed, another ran away from the scene and got no further than two paces before colliding with another woman. They fell to the floor. Many of the onlookers thought that the women had been shot by the gunman, and there were more screams as people panicked and ran away. From one side of the lobby a heavily built man pulled a revolver from his jacket and fired. He hit the vagrant in the chest and blue smoke drifted across the lobby.

Philip was transfixed. He'd never seen a man shot before and watched as the man slowly crumpled to the floor. As he fell, the man's left arm seemed to wave as if he were saying goodbye, and his mouth opened as if he were trying to cry out, but Philip heard no sound. In fact, he was to recall later, the whole event happened in complete silence: he just had a vision of the man waving to him as he fell to the floor, landing with his legs bent unnaturally underneath his body. His left arm was the last part of him to reach the floor, with one finger pointing towards Philip, and it twitched before lying still.

It was only once the man stopped moving that Philip became aware of the screams and shouts, the smell of cordite and the panic in the room. One of the leaflets thrown into the air drifted into his lap. He picked it up. On it was a crudely printed cartoon of Rasputin and the Empress of Russia. The monk, a favourite of the Empress of Russia, was believed throughout Russia to be a charlatan and hypnotist who had wormed himself into the Tsar's palace and acquired a limitless power over the hysterical German born Empress. Many blamed his influence for the war's disasters. The picture showed Rasputin fondling the

Empress's exposed left breast. The message of the pamphlet was clear.

Philip instinctively folded the paper in half, hiding the offending picture, then heard a soft voice behind him. 'Oh my God, no!'

How Philip heard the whispered exclamation above the commotion and panic he didn't know: perhaps it was because it was in English. He turned to see a woman in her early twenties, dressed in an ivory dress with lace collar and a hat with an ostrich feather curled around the brim. One hand covered her mouth, and her complexion was as pale as her dress.

Forgetting his own shock, Philip stood up, held out a hand and said, 'Let me take you to another room.' Without another word she took his arm and together they walked to the back of the lobby, where they found a sofa behind a pillar that would hide them from the sight of the man crumpled on the floor. On the way Philip could smell the water of roses she used for perfume.

Settling her down, he asked, 'Would you like a brandy?'

'No thank you; I'm so sorry to impose on you.'

'Please don't apologise,' said Philip, mesmerised by the large violet eyes looking back at him. 'I should introduce myself: Philip Cummings at your service.'

She smiled. 'Sophie Tagleva,' and held out a hand.

Philip took her hand in his, noticing her long fingers, delicately manicured nails, the softness of her skin and the absence of any rings. He feigned a kiss, as appropriate when meeting a strange woman.

'How did you know I was English?' he asked.

She looked at him quizzically, not sure what he meant.

'When you cried out you spoke in English,' explained Philip.

She smiled. 'Oh, I hadn't realised I had. My mother was English and as a child I always spoke to her in English. So tell me, what's an Englishman doing in St Petersburg... I mean Petrograd... changing a name so that it didn't sound so German and to link it to a Great Tsar is so confusing, don't you think?'

Philip smiled. 'The change of name is confusing when it's

the only one we've used and to answer your question I work for the Bank of England and I'm here on business. So what brings you to Petrograd?'

'I'm here to meet my brother. He's been wounded at the front. He's in a hospital somewhere in the city and I've come to take him home to Moscow, but I haven't found which hospital he's in yet. It's become a nightmare and I'm worried for my brother and also for my father, who's alone and unwell in Moscow.'

'What about your mother?'

'She died when I was a child.'

'Oh... I'm so sorry,' commiserated Philip, who wished he hadn't asked. 'Can I get you anything?'

'You've done more than enough, thank you.'

He didn't know why but he didn't want to walk away. He felt drawn to her, perhaps because he too had lost his mother as a child; perhaps because she looked so vulnerable; perhaps because she was so beautiful.

'Then allow me the privilege of staying with you until things are calmer and afterwards will you allow me to buy you dinner?'

She smiled. 'That's very kind, but I can't impose on your time further.'

'I'm alone in the city and you are too. It would be silly for us both to dine alone – that is, unless you have other plans.' He hoped she didn't.

She smiled again. She was used to men pressing their attention onto her, but somehow she thought he seemed different. Besides, she was tired of eating alone in her room and having no one to talk to.

'That would be very kind and I would be delighted,' she said, hoping she wouldn't regret it.

They walked to the lounge on the first floor, Sophie averting her gaze from the front door where the man had been shot. Philip noticed the body had been removed and a rug hid the bloodstain on the carpet.

That night Philip and Sophie enjoyed a long dinner. They talked of business and politics and Philip was fascinated by her knowledge and understanding of both. Over three hours they shared stories about their childhood, families, the arts, the music they enjoyed and the places they had visited. He was captivated by her hair and complexion, which glowed gold in the candlelight, and by the dimples that appeared on her cheeks whenever she smiled.

Sophie told Philip of her excitement whenever her father took her for a ride in their troika as a child. Covered in blankets of ermine and sable, she described the sound of the horses' hooves, the bells on their harness the swish of the runners as they glided over the snow as her father told her stories of Russian princes, fairies and goblins.

'My elder brother and I would sneak down the kitchen steps to watch and listen to the servants as they cooked the family's meals, knowing that if Cook spotted us peering around the door a couple of biscuits would magically appear on her table. Then as Cook pretended to attend to the oven they would dash to the table holding their fingers to their lips so that the other servants would say nothing, grab the biscuits and rush out of the door before we were seen by Cook. On returning to her table, Cook would discover the biscuits were missing and would demand from all the other servants to be told the names of those responsible. When all said they had seen nothing, Cook would declare it must have been "Ivan the fool". It was such a wonderful game,' said Sophie.

During a main course of duck breast cooked in red wine and cherries Sophie asked Philip about his family. She listened attentively to Philip's stories and laughed out loud at his description of his father's mother.

'She was a tall and imposing woman to a five-year-old, and I never saw her without a large hat covered in feathers. Around her shoulders she would invariably have draped a mink stole with the stuffed heads of the unfortunate animals hanging down her back. My mother, never a favourite daughter-in-law, told me that my grandmother would leave her house early each morning, catch the poor animals for her breakfast and those creatures she hadn't eaten would be wrapped around her neck in case she felt hungry before her lunch. I spent much of my childhood believing that women with such furs were to be avoided in case, as my mother said, their appetites turned to little boys.'

Sophie laughed. 'My mother had the same type of fur! Oh, that's so funny.'

They talked about the authors they loved: Jane Austen, Dickens, Voltaire, Rousseau and Helena Blavatsky, the Russian author of *Isis Unveiled*. They discovered their musical tastes included Bach, Handel, Tchaikovsky, Shaporin and Napravnik.

Despite her initial fears, Sophie was fascinated by Philip. He wasn't arrogant in the way that so many Russian men could be. Too many Russians dismissed female opinion as being of little consequence. He was genuinely interested in her opinions, even when they contradicted his own. For her part she was particularly attracted to his hands: the signet ring on the little finger of his left hand, the way he would rub and twist the ring as if the action increased his concentration. She liked the wrinkles at the edges of his eyes, the way he smiled and how his eyes lit up whenever he smiled.

Over coffee a flower seller entered the dining room and Philip bought a white rose and presented it to her. Sophie blushed as he handed it to her.

'I'm sorry, I've embarrassed you. I apologise.'

'Please don't apologise. I'm touched, truly I am. It's been a very special evening, and I will treasure this time always.' She reached out and touched his arm. He was disappointed she quickly withdrew her hand.

Philip watched Sophie close her eyes and smell the bloom, smile and place it gently in front of her. At the end of the meal Sophie carefully carried the rose to her room and placed in a glass of water on the table beside her bed.

As Philip walked into his own suite, intoxicated by the pleasure of the evening, he saw that a note had been pushed under the door. Opening it, he read that his appointment had been confirmed for the following morning at eleven o'clock at the Alexander Palace, Tsarskoye Selo. A car would arrive at the hotel at ten.

# Chapter Six: The final box

## October 1916

The following morning Philip travelled the fifteen miles to Tsarskoye Selo, the luxurious private retreat of the Emperor's family. As grandiose as the Palace of Versailles, it boasted immense lawns, boating lakes and formal gardens.

Philip was escorted to an antechamber and met by General Alexander Mossolov. 'Mr Cummings, I have the last deposit for the Bank of England.' The General pointed to two leather-bound boxes each about ten inches square. Smaller than the other boxes, they also had no gold cypher embossed into them. The General opened them to reveal three rubies the size of hen's eggs, and a number of smaller stones. 'A gift to the Imperial Family from the Shah of Persia,' he said.

The second box had six small compartments. The first was filled with ten huge cut diamonds, the second three ingots of platinum, the third gold ingots, the fourth diamond and ruby bracelets, one with a huge ruby set in the front, the fifth four diamond and sapphire necklaces, and the final compartment a huge emerald, the size of a hen's egg, on a platinum-studded chain with diamonds and rubies that had once belonged to Catherine the Great.

This being his last visit, Philip had decided that he'd try to discover the reason for the transfers being made in such a strange manner.

'General, can I ask why I've been entrusted with such riches when you could have transferred these items more easily through your embassies or sent them direct by your own couriers to the Bank of England?'

'I suppose that you deserve an explanation.' The General took a seat and motioned to Philip to sit. 'You were chosen for this task because you speak Russian fluently and, more importantly, the Governor of the Bank said that you were utterly honest. In fact, he described you as incorruptible, which is an interesting notion to many Russians.'

The General continued. 'Just after the 1905 attempted revolution, His Majesty concluded an agreement with your government to provide refuge to some members of the Royal Family, namely his daughters and the Empress, should they need to leave Russia for a short period. These items are intended for their care and welfare. However, people in Russia might misinterpret such preparations if they were to become known.'

Looking at Philip he paused as if thinking how to continue, 'There's one more thing. Some time ago our secret police arrested a man close to the Tsar – a traitor. During interrogation the man revealed a conspiracy that caused Russia untold damage during the war, things that have resulted in the collapse of our armies. Unfortunately, we didn't get all the details he knew, as he was shot trying to escape, but it's a conspiracy that also involves people in your own country.'

The General picked up a long brown manila envelope and held it as if it were more precious than any of the jewels he'd shown Philip earlier.

'Inside this envelope is all the information we know about the conspiracy, how it has affected your own country and the people involved. You must deliver this information to your Prime Minister or the Foreign Secretary, Sir Charles Grey – but be careful: trust no one else with this information.'

'I will do what I can,' said Philip, taking the envelope and placing it inside the box.

'Now I have some bad news for you. Unfortunately you'll be unable to return to England by boat because the captain received orders from your Admiralty to set sail for Portsmouth. The ship left yesterday and unfortunately the Russian navy can't spare a vessel for you.'

Philip knew that there was no chance that a Russian ship could give him passage. The Russian Baltic Fleet had mutinied and wouldn't sail out of their own ports.

'I suggest that you go to the Crimea by train and take a boat from there.'

Another brown leather wallet was handed to Philip. 'I realise that these new arrangements will cause you some expense, and this wallet holds a thousand roubles in notes and fifty gold five-rouble pieces. There's also a letter signed by the Tsar himself that'll guarantee you safe passage anywhere in the empire. That should be more than enough to get you to England.'

Philip placed the wallet inside his jacket. They shook hands.

'Mr Cummings,' said the General. 'We'll not meet again, and I urge you to leave Russia in all haste and may God be with you.'

Philip travelled back to his hotel deep in thought. He had to leave Russia as soon as possible but, instead of travelling by boat, a journey that would take only a few days, he now had to travel a thousand miles across Russia from the Baltic to the Black Sea.

When he arrived back at the Hotel Europe his head was spinning. He had a valuable package to transport across Russia; some important papers to deliver to the government in England; he wanted to ensure that the soup kitchen would be able to continue its work, even for a few days, and then there was Sophie. He'd only known her for twenty-four hours but desperately wanted to see her one last time. He didn't want to leave without saying goodbye. He would delay his departure, just for a few hours, so that they could have a final meal together, laugh as they had last night... he wanted to touch her soft hand again and look into those violet eyes.

As he entered the lobby of the hotel he saw Sophie by the stairs. Her face was radiant and her eyes sparkled as she rushed over to meet him.

'It's Sergei,' she said slightly breathlessly. 'He's in Petrograd. He arrived last night, he's wounded and at a hospital on the other side of the city. I'm off to see him. Please, Philip, would you come with me?' she begged.

'Of course,' he said. There was no power on earth that would have made him refuse. 'Let me put these parcels in my room and I'll come down in a few minutes.'

'Thank you,' she said excitedly and smiled broadly so that her dimples showed.

Philip rushed upstairs. What was he doing? He should be preparing to leave the country, not agreeing to go on a hospital visit with a woman he'd met a few hours before. What was he thinking of? As he hurried to his suite he heard his father's voice: 'You're not being logical, young man; remember your duty. Duty first, no matter what the personal sacrifice.' He knew it was the first time he would defy his father.

Philip looked around his suite. He needed to find a place to hide the contents of the boxes and the letters. A place where the chambermaid would not look. Under the bed would be the worst place, and the wardrobe would not be secure enough. Walking into the bathroom, he pulled back the panelling that surrounded the bath and pushed the packages into the gap designed to provide easy access to the water pipes. Replacing the bath panel, he checked to see if someone could see that it had been moved. Not the most original hiding place, he thought, but unless a plumber looked for a leaking pipe it would be out of sight of a cursory inspection. Satisfied he'd done what he could to conceal the treasure, he walked down to the lobby.

Sophie was so excited she could hardly sit still as she waited for Philip. She felt like a dizzy little girl waiting to go to her first grown-up party. As the taxi moved off to go to the hospital she grasped Philip's hand in a grip that was not altogether comfortable – but Philip didn't complain, in case she stopped holding him. They travelled for fifteen minutes through the early afternoon traffic. Sophie seemed not to notice the beggars on the street, the small groups of people stamping their feet and blowing into their hands to keep themselves warm, the priest in his black cassock rushing to take confession from a dying woman. She could only think of her brother.

Arriving at the hospital, Philip paid the taxi and together they walked into the building. They smelled the terrible stench of boiled cabbage and disinfectant. Nurses in white habits, looking more like nuns, bustled about. Philip and Sophie approached a table where a nurse in starched uniform and tall helmet-like hat with a bright red cross on the front sat writing.

'Please could you tell me where I could find Captain Sergei Tagleva?' Sophie asked nervously.

'When did he come in?' replied the nurse without looking up from her papers.

'Last night, I think.'

'Then he'll be in ward nineteen on the first floor.'

'Thank you.'

Sophie's excitement seemed to disappear, to be replaced by anxious anticipation of what she might find. Her fears increased as they negotiated their way past groaning soldiers lying in the corridor, covered in thin blankets. The walls reverberated to moans from those in pain and doctors shouting for medicines or fresh bandages. Sophie and Philip passed men with horrific wounds. She tried not to look at the man with a hole in his face where his nose was meant to be and who stared at them as they passed, nor at the crutches and walking sticks leaning against walls and lying alongside their new owners. Sophie tried not to look, not because she felt no compassion, but because she feared what she might find in ward nineteen. Her stomach cramped, the palms of her hands were wet with perspiration; she prayed to God.

They located ward nineteen, a smallish room with twelve iron beds. A volunteer nurse approached.

'Can I help you?'

'I'm looking for Captain Sergei Tagleva,' said Sophie, looking from bed to bed anxiously.

'Are you his wife?'

'No, I'm his sister.'

'He's over there,' said the nurse, pointing to the far wall.

They walked to the bed to find a man lying still, as if asleep. Sergei's complexion was grey, and Sophie said to herself that he looked tired and weary, but was as handsome as ever with his blond curly hair.

Sophie breathed a sigh of relief. Her wonderful brother was fine. She approached the bed slowly, as if afraid of waking him, but as she did so he opened his eyes and, seeing his sister, his face lit up and a broad smile greeted her. He looked like a little boy receiving a birthday gift, and some of the greyness in his complexion left him.

'I was worried about you,' Sophie said softly and couldn't help the tear that fell onto his cheek as she bent forward to kiss her brother on his forehead.

'Shh, don't cry,' said Sergei as he moved his left arm to embrace her.

It was then that Philip saw that his right arm was missing and, as he looked down the bedclothes, he saw that they covered one leg.

'I've been so worried about you, my brother.'

'I promised you I'd come back,' said Sergei.

'I know. I remember the day you told me you'd joined up because it was your patriotic duty. I was so angry at you. You told me then you would come home safely but I couldn't help but worry. The news was always so awful,' and another tear ran down her cheek.

'Don't cry.'

'I can't help it,' she said. 'I'm so relieved to see that you are safe.'

'How's Father?' asked Sergei, changing the subject.

'He's not so well, but that's more to do with old age than illness. He sends you his love.'

Just then Sophie looked down at him, the bedclothes could no longer hide his missing arm and only one leg.

'Oh, my darling brother, what—' Sophie wiped her tears from her cheeks. 'It's all so awful.'

'Let's talk about this later,' said Sergei. 'Tell me,' he whispered, looking at Philip, 'who's your escort?'

Philip was stunned at the composure of the man. He'd lost an arm and a leg and was behaving as if they had just been introduced at a dinner.

'Oh, I'm sorry. May I present Mr Philip Cummings? We met after a… a problem at the hotel and he's been so very kind to me over the past day.'

'Thank you for looking after my sister.'

'Think nothing of it,' said Philip.

The formalities over, Sophie once more looked at her brother and her hand began to shake in shock.

'So when can you leave hospital?' she asked as she sat in the chair next to the bed.

'They would like to throw me out now if they could but I'm classed as a Grade Three case. It means I'm waiting for a wheelchair, as I can't walk with crutches.'

Sophie stifled a sob.

'Oh, don't cry,' said Sergei. 'Your arrival here is the best thing to have happened in two years at the front.'

'Sorry,' said Sophie. 'But it's so hard seeing you like this.'

'It could have been worse,' said Sergei comfortingly.

'How?' gulped Sophie as she held back her tears.

Philip looked down at Sophie. All he wanted to do was sweep her into his arms and comfort her.

'I will ask the doctors if we can move you to the Hotel Europe and we'll look after you until you are well enough to travel,' said Sophie, looking at Philip.

'Of course, and anything I can do to help, I will,' replied Philip before he could stop himself.

'We'll bring a wheelchair tomorrow,' said Sophie.

A doctor in a white coat approached. Looking at the patient, he smiled and said, 'So, Count, I see that you have found your family.'

'Doctor, may I present my sister, Countess Sophia Tagleva, and Mr Philip Cummings, a friend.'

The doctor bowed. 'Countess, I'm delighted to meet you.'

'I'm going to arrange to take my brother to the Hotel Europe to recover, tomorrow if that's convenient,' said Sophie.

'The earlier the better,' said the doctor. 'Since he arrived all my nurses have fallen in love with your brother; it's making the other patients jealous.' He laughed. 'But he'll need a wheelchair, and I don't have one to spare so you will have to see if you can find one in the city. He'll also need constant nursing to allow for his injuries to fully heal. That could take a couple of months. You'll both be able to manage that?'

'Of course,' said Sophie.

Half an hour later Sophie said her farewells to Sergei, and promised to return the following day. As they walked out of the ward the doctor approached them.

'Countess,' he said looking directly at Sophie and then at Philip. 'Despite appearances, your brother is heavily troubled and has very bad nightmares. Last night he screamed so much that it took three nurses to hold him down. During these dreams he becomes delirious. I suggest that you have someone strong who's able to help during these attacks. The dressings on his wounds will need to be changed regularly, and he may develop sores from lying down, which will need careful attention. Do you think you'll be able to manage that?'

'We'll do whatever's necessary, doctor,' said Sophie.

'Then I will see you both tomorrow.'

In the taxi travelling to the Hotel Europe Philip looked at her. 'You didn't tell me that you were a countess.'

Sophie looked at him and smiled. 'It didn't seem important – and, anyway, I forget half the time. It's just something you grow up with. Walking around saying, "Hello, I'm Countess Tagleva, good afternoon, my name is Countess Tagleva" isn't something one does. What's more,' she continued, 'there are too many people in Russia who would reply, "Good to meet you, I'm Prince or Princess so and so".'

They both laughed and the tension of the previous hour was broken.

He looked at her saying to himself, 'Title or no title, you're wonderful.'

Philip knew it would be some time before he left Russia.

# Chapter Seven: The baker's house

## The same afternoon

Walking down any of the miles of corridor at the Foreign Office in London past the hundreds of identical oak doors, one is able to guess the work undertaken on the other side of any door simply by reading the gold leaf letters that face the corridor.

The casual visitor isn't invited to know the work being done on the other side of the oak door of Room 380. Its work is intelligence, clandestine operations. Its work is secret.

It is an office where Sir Charles Cunningham feels distinctly comfortable. The employment of espionage, blackmail – in fact, any tool that furthers British aims and ambitions – is acceptable and to be relished.

'So what's the latest news from Russia?' asked Sir Charles of the thin man with the hooked nose and protruding eyes, who was sitting behind the desk.

'The news from Russia isn't good.'

Sir Charles admired the man opposite. He was probably one of the most loathsome men in England, able to be utterly indifferent to people's suffering. A skeleton of a man, dressed in the formal dark frock coat which was the uniform of the British civil service, and a starched winged collar, two sizes too large, leaving a one-inch gap between it and his neck. The large collar was necessary so as not to impede the movement of his Adam's apple as it leaped up and down his throat whenever he spoke. The vision reminded Sir Charles of a farmyard hen.

The hen continued. 'In fact, to quote an undersecretary, "It's a bloody disaster." The Russian army's all but collapsed. Most units have deserted, usually not before shooting their officers in the back. Reinforcements can't get to the front because the railways don't run, and even when reinforcements do arrive there isn't enough ammunition for more than three bullets per man.'

The Adam's apple came to rest for a second before leaping up again. 'I'm reliably informed that the Russians are now attacking the Germans with kitchen knives and farm implements and the Germans are mowing them down with machine guns and without a single loss of life.'

'So what's your assessment?' asked Sir Charles.

The man coughed and his Adam's apple leaped up his throat once more.

'Our informants tell us that there's a chronic food shortage in most cities, and strikes in Petrograd and Moscow. Most of the population believe the Empress is a German spy, and I have it on good authority that even members of the Romanov family are questioning her loyalty. We anticipate that a group of officers will attempt a coup, possibly from inside the Royal Family, and it's likely to happen within a few weeks, if not days.'

'Will that keep Russia in the war?'

The Adam's apple moved up and down his neck again. 'Unlikely. Most Russians want to make peace with Germany. If that were to happen, Germany will move her troops from the Russian front and reinforce their western front against England and France. In such circumstances the war could last for another two or even three years.'

'Thank you.'

'To change the subject, is there any news of that banker?' said Sir Charles.

'I'm informed that he's stuck in Petrograd. As you requested, the ship that was to bring him back to England sailed without him.' Sir Charles opened a cigarette case, took a cigarette, lit it, took a deep drag and said, 'As planned, we can expect him to remain stuck.' Sir Charles smiled and left the room.

\*\*\*\*

In Petrograd that night sleep didn't come to Philip. His mind was flooded with thoughts and arguments that had him tossing and turning in bed and then pacing his room. His mind worked through the various situations, the possibilities, the known facts.

At the bank he could have accessed a card index for each country he managed. One side of the card recorded a known fact with all important information detailed. The reverse held all the links and references to all the other cards that could influence or affect any decision. It made it much easier to arrive at a decision after analysis. Such was the success of his system that it had been adopted by various other departments at the bank.

Alone in his bedroom Philip visualised cards and added to them all the relevant information. The first card was titled 'the Tsar's package'. It recorded the packages and letters he'd been given; the cumbersome jewels and money that would attract unwelcome attention. If discovered, it would be an irresistible prize to steal.

Card two was the sailing of the ship that had left him stranded. The captain had clear orders that the ship was to transport him back to Britain, so who'd given the order to sail?

The soup kitchen was card three. He couldn't fund the soup kitchen for ever, and he'd done more than anyone. Yet if he just disappeared it would only be a few days before those desperate creatures were starving again, and he knew that thought would haunt him.

The final imaginary card was titled 'Sophie and Sergei'. How could he abandon Sophie now that she had found her brother and needed his help? Alone in Petrograd with a political system collapsing around them, hers would be an impossible task. If he were to abandon her now he would have a lifetime of recriminations.

He would often remind his juniors at the bank that emotions clouded an issue and could hide a pathway to solving a problem. All the cards he was looking at were clouded by emotions. At four in the morning he had decided on a course of action and crawled into bed.

Two hours of disturbed sleep later he woke, shaved, dressed and met Sophie in the lobby. Finding a wheelchair wasn't easy in a city where demand for wheelchairs and crutches outstripped supply. Time and time again they were told that it would take many weeks or even months for one to become available. After eight hours of walking the streets from one furniture shop to another, they found, by chance, a furniture maker who had a completed chair on order for a client who had died before final payment had been made. Philip didn't haggle with the shop owner, but paid him what he demanded (which was equivalent to three times the cost of a fine dining table that would seat ten).

At nine in the evening Philip and Sophie arrived at ward nineteen to collect Sergei. They were greeted by the same doctor they'd spoken to the day before, and who was delighted at the thought of having an empty bed for a new patient. Sophie went to speak with Sergei. As she did so the doctor indicated to Philip that he wanted a quiet word.

'I have to tell you,' said the doctor. 'The Count's wounds are healing well. When he arrived his wounds had been properly cauterised, probably using a red-hot poker. He was lucky that someone at the front knew what to do. However, his mind's badly affected. He has night sweats and only sleeps a few hours before he wakes screaming. It's not unusual – we see many soldiers in the same condition – but during these nightmares he's unable to control his bodily functions. My problem, as a doctor, is that I don't have the time or the ability to treat an illness of the brain. In fact, we don't even try; we repair broken bones, treat some of the burns and try to put back together the shattered bodies as best we can. When we've done that, we discharge the patient as soon as possible. There's no after-care and there are no medicines that will help. It's barbaric, but it's all I can do. You need to know that the Count will need months to recover before he'll be fit enough to travel to Moscow. By rights I shouldn't be discharging him, but I need the bed.' The doctor looked over to where Sergei was lying. 'Count Sergei will need a great deal of care, and I don't think his sister understands how exhausting that will be.'

'Thank you for the information, doctor,' said Philip.

Philip knew that any plans he'd made to leave Russia would be delayed.


They put Sergei in Sophie's bed at the Hotel Europe. It had been a long time since he'd slept in cotton sheets. His head sank into the duck down pillows and he was soon asleep. Philip and Sophie walked to the window and whispered to each other.

'The doctor told me that Sergei will need a few months to recuperate before he'll be fit enough to travel to Moscow,' said Philip.

'The nurse told me the same thing.'

Philip looked at Sophie. She looked tired.

'I don't have the funds to stay in the hotel for that long, and I don't know what to do,' she said quietly.

'Don't worry about that, I have some money,' said Philip.

'I couldn't take your money,' she replied.

'Yes you can, and you will,' replied Philip, and bent down and kissed her forehead. It was an instinctive action; he hadn't meant to, but it was done and Philip feared that Sophie might misinterpret his advance and be angry at him.

'You're such a kind man. I don't know what I'd have done without you,' she whispered and stroked his cheek with her forefinger and smiled.


The following morning Philip left the hotel early and returned to find Sophie in her room watching over Sergei, who was fast asleep. 'I've bought some leather and horsehair to make the wheelchair comfortable for Sergei. I'll take it to my room so the hammering doesn't disturb him.'

Back in his room Philip locked the door. He measured the wheelchair and cut the leather into shapes to make a padded seat, backrest and armrests. He retrieved the packages he'd hidden in the bathroom, unpacked the contents and laid them neatly on the bed.

He began work on the backrest, fixing the leather with small tacks at the base of the seat. Inside the seat he carefully fixed the gold and platinum ingots with tacks so that they wouldn't move. At the edge of the backrest he fixed the diamond bracelets and necklaces. When these were all in place he filled the cavity with horsehair stuffing. As he filled the cavity he tacked up the sides, adding more jewels as he went. Every so often he'd check that the jewels couldn't be felt through the leather and on a couple of occasions had to undo his work to make adjustments.

At the top of the headrest he inserted the papers so that they could be recovered without having to remove too much stuffing or tearing the leather. He finally added some more horsehair to pad out the leather into a cushion. Next he turned to the arms. He placed half the gold roubles onto each armrest, covered them with horsehair padding and neatly tacked down leather on top. He placed the larger gems at the back of the seat where Sergei would be unlikely to feel them. He then covered the jewels with stuffing.

After a couple of hours he was satisfied that the chair hid the contents of the boxes. He completed the effect by tacking a crimson velvet ribbon around the edges to hide the brass tacks. Philip finally sat in the chair to see if he could feel any of the precious stones through the padding. He was satisfied that Sergei would be unaware of the treasure he was sitting on.

Philip placed the remains of the horsehair in the empty jewellery boxes, stuffed them into a valise and went for a short walk. Finding a pile of rubbish in a side street, he buried the valise at the bottom and returned to the hotel.

When Sophie saw the chair she was delighted and clapped her hands silently so not to wake Sergei. 'Oh, you're so clever,' she said, and sat in the chair. She stroked the soft leather and wiggled her bottom on the seat. 'It's so comfortable.'

The following day Philip asked some of the shopkeepers he had befriended if they knew of any rooms for a couple to rent, to nurse a wounded soldier. Most said that they knew of nothing available, but one told him that he thought the baker on Dzerzinsky Street had some rooms.

On arriving at the baker's shop he found a group of disappointed women slowly walking away after the last loaf of bread had been sold. The baker, covered in flour, greeted him with a smile and said that he did have some rooms to let.

There were only two bedrooms, a living room, a small kitchen and a bathroom. The rooms were warm and, while the furnishings had seen better days, they consisted of two beds, some chairs, a sofa and a couple of tables. Shutters on the inside of the windows would keep out the chill of the nights.

Philip paid the baker three months' rent in advance.

Before returning to the hotel Philip decided to visit the soup kitchen. He intended to discuss with Marie how the soup kitchen could be financed for a few more months.

As he walked towards the cellar he wondered if similar miserable places existed in London. He suspected that there might be, hidden unless you went looking for them. It would be awful if in the twentieth century there were such crippling poverty in his homeland. As soon as he returned to London he would find out and, if he found any, would see what he could do to help. He recalled Edward Lascelles saying to him after he had dropped a half-crown into a beggar's hat, 'You're the only banker I know with a social conscience.'

As he neared the soup kitchen he could see a small group of people. It was a bit early in the day, he thought. As he grew closer, he saw that the group wasn't of beggars waiting for food, but of policemen and curious onlookers.

'What's going on?' enquired Philip of one of the policeman.

'We've orders to close this soup kitchen. Some merchant's funded it so well that the number of homeless has grown so much that it causes a nuisance. Local residents are complaining.'

'So where's it moving to?'

'Nowhere. It's closed.'

Philip looked to see if he could see Marie among the faces, but they were all strangers. She wasn't there. The homeless and the hungry had been moved on, had been scattered to the winds, the 'nuisance' hidden from the sight of those who were lucky enough not to need a soup kitchen. Angrily he walked away. He wanted to scream at the injustice. Had he a red flag he would have waved it and shouted for a revolution against those who could turn the hungry away from their door. This nation deserved the whirlwind that was surely coming – and when it came, he couldn't care less if it swept away all the palaces, all the estates, the wealthy who crossed themselves three times as they presented money to a priest to buy incense, and yet could avert their eyes from the sight of the poor and hungry so as not to be offended.

****

It's easy to imagine nursing a loved one back to health. Most people have childhood memories of being confined to bed with a cold, mumps or measles as their mother sat beside their bed reading to them from their favourite book and occasionally having their pillows plumped to make them more comfortable. The reality of nursing a grown man with one arm and one leg is very different. The simple act of moving such a patient so that they can comfortably sit, lie, eat or drink needs more than a couple of hands.

Then there are practical difficulties, such as washing and going to the toilet. It was apparent to Sophie that she would need to find a way for Sergei to relieve himself without moving him to the bathroom. He was too heavy for her to move on her own, and she didn't want to ask Philip for help. When she tried to move him, it caused Sergei great pain and distress.

Together they came up with a solution, like the process that had been used in the hospital. To collect his urine Sophie propped him up with pillows and a wine carafe, borrowed for the purpose from the restaurant, conveniently positioned so that Sergei could control the process with his remaining arm. For a bowel movement, Sophie pushed a towel underneath Sergei, and he relieved himself on the towel. It was messy, but with care Sophie could remove the towel and clean Sergei without the need to replace soiled sheets. Sergei found the whole process embarrassing, and became angry and upset at Sophie's attempts to help clean him.

When he had been cleaned up, Sergei would feel contrite for being so difficult and snapping at his sister. She was trying to do her best and he felt no less embarrassed with her than he had with the nurses in the hospital when they performed the same messy process.

'Sorry for being so moody. I am so grateful for what you are doing.'

Sophie smiled lovingly back at her brother, kissed him on the forehead and went to add the towel to the pile that would need washing. She was upset by his distress and felt so sorry for him.

When he slept, it wasn't always peacefully. He mumbled and his eyelids moved as visions of trenches, charging infantry, mud and destruction played out in front of him. When he cried out and woke with a start Sophie could see the fear in his eyes. He saw her watching him, and the death and destruction faded as he settled his head back into the pillows, relieved that he was safe.

Having eaten some soup, Sergei was sleeping when Philip quietly entered the room and whispered into Sophie's ear. 'I've found some rooms on Dzerzinsky Street above a baker's shop, close to the Semerovsky bridge.'

Sophie rose from her chair, walked over to the window and Philip spoke quietly so as not to wake Sergei. 'It's not much, a room for Sergei, one for you and a small living room where I can sleep, kitchen and bathroom, but we'll be able to look after Sergei and it'll be cheaper than the hotel. I've paid for three months in advance and we can move in tomorrow.'

'How clever of you! And above a baker – at least we won't starve,' she said and smiled. Philip went downstairs to inform the hotel that he and the countess would be leaving in two days, and paid both their bills.

The following day Philip decided on the essential things he needed to take with him to the baker's apartment. He left his evening dress, smoking jacket, carpet slippers, toilet case and some of the other 'Essentials for a gentlemen' packed by Mr Evans in the wardrobe – he wouldn't need them where he was going and he needed the room in his suitcases for the five sets of sheets, towels, blankets, pillows and soap supplied by a hotel maid, given a week's salary in roubles to leave them in his room.

Two days later a pony and trap took them and their luggage to Dzerzinsky Street.

On arrival they discovered a loaf of black bread and a small container of salt on the kitchen table as a traditional welcome from the baker to his new tenants. The bread was still warm from the oven. The three of them felt it was a good start.

Both bedrooms held a metal sprung bed, a small wardrobe, a chest of drawers with a wash bowl, and a small fireplace. They decided Sergei would have the small bed; it would make it easier to nurse him. Sophie would take the larger bed and Philip would sleep on the living room sofa.

Philip was delighted. The sofa had a number of cushions and was long enough for him to stretch out on.

The living room was large, with a bay window looking out onto the street but which didn't let in much light. The window was covered in a mixture of dust and flour, and Sophie resolved to clean it as soon as she could. There were two small chairs, a table, and a rug that had seen better days. Above the fireplace was a wooden icon of St Catherine.

'Stealing the sheets was a good idea,' said Sophie.

'I didn't steal them,' objected Philip. 'I paid the chambermaid for them.'

'Well, it was a good idea.' Sophie giggled at the thought that her banker had turned into a thief.

'I must go and find some food, cutlery and plates.'

'I assume the head waiter at the Hotel Europe couldn't be bribed?'

'Quite incorruptible,' said Philip, and she laughed.

Sophie went to change the dressings on Sergei's wounds. The doctors had told her to treat the stumps with a mixture of vinegar and salt to harden the skin and had given Sophie tiny salt bags to bandage tightly next to the wound. They would aid the healing process, she had been told, but the bags of salt, small as they were, inflicted such excruciating pain that Sergei kicked and yelled as the salt burned into his lacerated flesh.

After two applications Sophie couldn't bear to see her brother in such pain and decided to wash the stumps with a small amount of vinegar and salt dissolved into water. Before bandaging the wounds, she wiped them with vodka, the only disinfectant readily available. After replacing the dressings she talked softly to Sergei as she stroked his forehead and hair until he fell asleep.

Two hours later Philip returned with pots, pans, cutlery, three cups, a couple of tea glasses and a small mixing bowl. Sophie had managed to light the fires, with wood and some coal she'd found in a store cupboard on the landing.

'Where did you find these pots and pans?' asked Sophie.

'A small restaurant was closing, and the owner was pleased to get some money for them.' Philip revealed, in one of the larger pots, a salami, a small cabbage, four eggs, two apples, a small bag of tea and a bottle of vodka.

'How wonderful! Where on earth did you find such riches when the city's so short of food?' she cried and wrapped her arms around his neck.

'I have my connections,' said Philip, without revealing he had parted with the equivalent of a month's wages for the meagre rations. The money he'd brought to Russia was fast running out.

That night they moved Sergei into the wheelchair so that he could sit at the kitchen table and eat with them. Despite his pain, Sergei felt almost normal as they ate cabbage soup, a couple of slices of salami and black bread, and toasted each other with a glass of vodka. Afterwards, Sergei felt slightly drunk, not having drunk alcohol for some months, and thanked Philip for helping him and his sister again and again – much to Philip's embarrassment and Sophie's amusement.

After the meal they helped Sergei back into bed and Sophie cleared the table.

Once they had washed and stored the plates, Philip took Sophie's hand. 'I bought you a present today.'

'Oh, you've done so much for us already.'

Philip handed her a leather-bound book.

Sophie looked at it. *'The Brothers Karamazov*... it's my favourite Dostoyevsky story! You're so kind,' and she wrapped her arms around his neck and kissed him on the lips.

He held her in a tight embrace, feeling the warmth of her body next to his as their lips met. Her eyes were closed and she didn't open them even after the kiss finished.

'Take me to bed,' she whispered.

Philip gently picked her up and carried her to her room.

****

Philip had always been anxious around girls. In his late teens he'd listened to friends describe in graphic detail how to flirt with girls and catch sight of an exposed ankle. Philip tried all the recommended techniques but got nowhere. He suspected that girls just laughed at him.

One day near his twentieth birthday he decided that the time had come for him to lose his virginity. He told his father he had been invited to a party and would be staying overnight with a friend. Instead he travelled to Covent Garden in London, took a room in a small hotel and during the evening nervously enquired from the porter if he knew of 'a girl'. The porter said he would do what he could and Philip paid him a shilling.

Five minutes later a large, full-bosomed woman in her late fifties walked towards him. Thick make-up unsuccessfully hid her pock-marked face and her cheeks and lips were covered in rouge which didn't disguise the fact that she was much older than she wished her clients to know.

'I hear you are lookin' for a twist 'n' twirl?' she said as she squeezed her ample body up next to his on the sofa.

Philip didn't know what to do. The woman was quite repulsive; not at all what he had imagined in his bedroom at home. An embarrassing five minutes followed as he extracted himself from the situation. As the woman rose from the seat to leave, she said loudly, so that the porter could hear, 'You won't get a better one than Maisie.'

Philip was mortified, he could see the porter laughing and rushed upstairs to the safety of his room.

Lying alone on the bed, he concluded he'd probably die a virgin.

Despite the events in Covent Garden, he did eventually lose his virginity, and there followed a few occasions when a woman had encouraged him into her bed, but they had always been hurried affairs that had left him feeling awkward and unsatisfied.

Sophie didn't make him nervous. In fact, it seemed like the most natural thing in the world. He kissed her neck, cheeks, eyelids and forehead, breathed in the smell of the rose water she used as a perfume, stroked her soft golden hair and gently bit the lobe of her ear, thinking how perfectly formed it was. Looking into her face, he thought her the most beautiful creature, and never wanted the moment to end.

Sophie felt Philip's arms hold her tightly and gently pull her to him. She could feel his strong, broad chest and powerful arms, and was surprised by how muscular he was.

Their gentle kisses became more passionate. His head swam and Sophie moaned with pleasure. Then she stepped back from him and Philip wondered if he had gone too far. But Sophie just looked at him. She was not running away and he watched as, without taking her eyes off him, she undid the buttons of her dress and allowed it to fall in a heap at her ankles, followed by her two silk slips. She now stood naked before him, her hair falling down her back and over her shoulders towards her small breasts. As the fire crackled and the flames leaped her skin was bathed in a shimmering gold.

Sophie had never made love to a man. In fact, apart from her brother she'd only ever seen a naked man once before. That was when she and her best friend happened upon some youths bathing naked in the river one summer's afternoon. On seeing them, the four boys stood up out of the water, exposing their manliness, and invited the two girls to choose their lover. Secretly fascinated and wanting to look more, nonetheless they had hurried away, giggling.

Now she was naked, being carried to bed by a man who was not her husband, and it was everything her parents and the church would condemn. None of this she cared about; she knew that she wanted Philip and knew it was the most natural feeling in the world.

They made love slowly.

Having climaxed, they lay looking at each other, without a word. After only a few minutes Sophie could feel that Philip was aroused again. The second time, there was more urgency to their lovemaking.

Sophie loved exploring Philip's body. His tight chest and stomach, the few hairs in the centre of his chest, the mole on his back, his face, ears and the way his back tapered to his waist – she loved it all. Twice more that night they made love. It was as if neither could stop, and each time was more passionate and more confident.

'Oh God, I hope it's always this good,' she whispered finally.

'Complain if it's not,' replied Philip, amazed he should say such a thing with such limited experience himself.

'You can be sure of it.' She giggled and pressed herself into the warmth of his body.

Wrapped in each other's arms, they fell into a deep sleep as the embers of the fire slowly died.

****

The following morning they were woken by Sergei scream-ing. They donned dressing gowns and rushed to his room. He was thrashing about in bed, bathed in sweat, his eyes wide in terror. Sophie took her brother into her arms and rocked him as if comforting a baby. In turn he held her tightly with his one good arm as his body shook with fear from his nightmare.

Philip watched a tear slowly run down Sophie's cheek and make a small dark mark on Sergei's nightshirt. He clenched his fists in frustration and felt his fingernails press into the palms of his hands. Their lovemaking a distant memory.

After a small breakfast Philip helped Sophie make up the fires, wash Sergei and change his bandages. He then left their rooms and walked to the restaurant where he'd bought the

68

salami, to find it closed and the owner gone. Snow was beginning to fall, so he took shelter in one of the hotels at the top of the Prospect. It took twenty minutes – and another of the precious gold roubles – to persuade the head waiter to give him two small tins of butter, some tea, six potatoes, a very small cut of cooked ham, some candles, two salamis and a small bar of chocolate. The two small tins of butter he put into the large pockets of his overcoat, together with the packet of tea. The salamis and ham he placed inside the legs of his trousers with their strings wrapped around his belt and he tied the potatoes to his waist by a cloth wound round his waist. The chocolate he hid in his inside breast pocket. Walking with the food was awkward and he felt as if everyone was looking at him with his valuable hoard. As he turned a corner, one of the potatoes came loose. It rolled in front of him and under the wheels of a passing truck. Two boys, presuming the potato had fallen off the truck, both claimed it as theirs and began to fight over it. Philip hurried past, hoping the other potatoes were safe.

On his arrival at their rooms, Sophie laughed as he recounted the episode of the escaped potato. Sophie brewed tea and was surprised when, having finished the warming brew, Philip announced that he was going out again.

Having temporarily solved the problem of food, he now sought to prevent boredom. While he could have easily passed every night making love to Sophie, he didn't want to presume she would feel the same. Finding a book store, he paid the owner for a dozen books and a pack of playing cards that were carefully tied with twine so he could carry them easily. In another shop he bought a small chess set and board.

As he left the shop, an old woman stood there with a bundle of bedcoverings, some tablecloths and some fur-lined boots for sale. She told him that the bed coverings were filled with the best duck down.

'Why are you selling your best linen?' asked Philip.

'My husband and my three sons have all been killed in the war. I have more need for food than fine bedcoverings,' she replied, sadness in her expression.

'Here, Mother, have this,' said Philip and handed over some money for the bundles.

She looked at the precious money and as tears welled up in her eyes she kissed his hand. 'God bless you, sir.'

Before he was halfway home Philip was stopped by a small band of army deserters, demanding to inspect the bundle he was carrying. The deserters searched through his pockets, but found no food and nothing of value they could steal. One of them picked up the bundle of books and accused him of being an intellectual.

'There's no wood for fuel, so I'm taking them home to burn in the fire,' declared Philip. Laughing and satisfied with his answer they said, 'Don't let us see you again, comrade,' and let him go. Philip was grateful he'd not been stopped earlier with the food.

After a week the days took on a familiar pattern. Philip would go downstairs to meet the baker, find out the gossip from the street and collect a loaf of bread, if one was available. Together he and Sophie would bathe Sergei, change his dressings, comfort him through his nightmares and depression, wash whatever linen was soiled from the night before, cook some soup and cut a chunk of bread to have with a slice of ham or salami. They entertained themselves by reading to each other, playing chess or cards. At times their isolation was interrupted by the sounds of gunfire in the streets and, on occasion, the rattle of a machine gun. Each night Sophie and Philip would close the shutters so that their lights would not be seen from the street, to prevent a mob of soldiers breaking into their rooms looking for things to steal.

Philip tried to make each evening entertaining, especially for Sergei, but both he and Sophie longed for the time they could go to bed and make love.

Sergei was not oblivious to how close his sister had become to Philip. How one would gently brush their hand against the other's finger or exchanged a secret look. On more than one occasion he heard them making love. He should have been angry, furious at how his sister was behaving, but his childhood attitudes changed after he watched thousands of men ordered to march towards a trench and be mown down by machine guns; when he'd seen starving soldiers tear the flesh off a dead horse and eat it raw; when his sympathies were with the hundreds of men that had deserted his regiment; when he'd lost an arm and a leg in a hopeless war and was being nursed by the very sister he should be angry with.

Sergei was grateful to Philip for the care he took when he carefully washed his stumps when Sophie was too tired to do it herself, and how Philip took care not to rub the sore, inflamed skin of his leg and apologised each time Sergei winced with pain. Whenever he asked, Philip was always ready to adjust his pillows, read to him, play draughts or chess and would tease him by asking 'Are you sure?', when the proposed move would place an important piece in danger. Their score at chess was about even, and Philip played chess well even if, as Sergei suspected, Philip let him win on occasion.

****

As the days turned into weeks, Sergei gradually grew stronger. After a month he was able to move himself from his bed to his wheelchair without assistance. Philip had modified the chair by hinging the left armrest so it could be dropped down to allow easy access to the seat from the bed. Sergei would prop himself up in a seated position and with his hand pull his leg round so that he was seated on the edge of the bed. Then, leaning over to grab the far handle of the wheelchair, he stood and twisted his body so that he fell into the wheelchair. Then he lifted the hinged armrest and locked it in place. When Philip and Sophie saw Sergei achieve this for the first time, Philip was afraid the wheelchair might fall over, Sophie clapped madly for a full minute, and everyone celebrated with an extra slice of salami and a glass of vodka that night. Even Sergei's nightmares had begun to be less frequent; his face had lost the greyness it had had in hospital; and he was smiling more. Sergei insisted that being able to get out of bed on his own gave him a little independence and he was determined to be able to dress himself. He would practise for hours, putting on trousers and shirts, until, bathed in sweat and exhausted, he slumped back on the bed.

Each afternoon he would sit in the bay window looking out onto the street as Sophie read to him. On a few occasions Philip asked if he would like to talk about his experiences at the front. Sometimes Sergei would say no, but on other occasions he would talk for hours about how, at the start of the war, each soldier had been given five bullets a day and, as supplies were affected by corruption and incompetence, the number of bullets issued to each soldier fell from five to three and finally to one a day. He spoke over and over about how rifles had become scarce and soldiers were marched to the front and ordered to charge the Germans. If they didn't have a rifle, they had to pick one up from a dead comrade. He explained how men had rushed towards the German machine guns armed only with kitchen knives and farm implements.

'Another officer told me of a platoon starved, cold, without ammunition, being ordered to attack the enemy. The men remained motionless, ignoring the order, and the officer pulled his pistol from his holster and aimed it at the men, ordering them to move against the Germans. Instead they pulled the officer from his horse, trampled him to death and began the long walk home to their farms and families.'

Philip was appalled at the incompetence of the Russian military and wondered if similar things were happening in the trenches in France and Belgium. Surely not, he thought, but feared that many of his own countrymen could also be dying due to incompetence and corruption.

The following day Philip left the house to look for more food, knowing it would probably take him much of the day. After only an hour outside he learned there was a general strike in the city. As many as a hundred thousand people were said to be demonstrating on the streets. Women from the textile factories from the Vyborg district were marching around the city, demanding that the war finish, the Tsar abdicate and the people be fed. He watched as wave after wave of people passed, shouting to anyone who would listen to join the strike.

In response, police battalions and mounted Cossacks were preparing to restore order. He would not be able to find fresh food supplies that day but there was enough in the cupboard, so they would not go hungry.

On his way home he watched a crowd of youths stop a couple of men. They had picked on them because they were Jews. Within seconds they were being beaten by the gang, only being released when the youths tired of their sport and joined another group of workers marching towards the centre of the city.

'Russians have always blamed Jews for all their ills,' said Sergei when Philip recounted what he'd seen over dinner. 'Tsar Nicholas and his father believed, like so many throughout Europe, in the "worldwide Jewish conspiracy". They said that Jews became wealthy at the expense of the rest of the population. It's so untrue! They work harder than many other people, and help each other in their community, but Russians have always resented it. The pogroms against Jews during Nicholas's reign were more vicious than those under his father,' Sergei said to Philip before adding, 'The worst episode was in Odessa, when nearly a thousand Jews were hacked to pieces with sabres and axes, watched by their wives and children, who were held back by the police.'

Sergei paused before whispering into his plate, 'I hate that man for what he's done to Russia.'

After their meal Philip suggested that they play chess, but Sergei wasn't in the mood. Instead he sat in his chair and watched the embers of the fire die in the grate.

# Chapter Eight: Sophie's confession

## December 1916

During their time at the baker's apartment, the three were hungry – not just for food, but also for news of the outside world: Russia's progress in the war, the strikes, the demonstrations in the city and what was happening in other parts of the country. The situation moved so quickly that newspapers couldn't keep up with events, and people came to rely on pamphlets printed in their thousands and thrown from trucks to the waiting crowds.

It was through a pamphlet that they learned of the assassination of Rasputin, the demonstrations that had taken place for International Women's Day, with a crowd of a hundred thousand people, how the Tsar had ordered the use of military force to break the strikes. They read how Cossack troops had fought with the police to protect protestors, that half of the city's soldiers had sided with the demonstrators, that the city's police headquarters had been ransacked and the files of the secret police, the *Okhrana*, burned. Sergei and Sophie were shocked when Philip told them how the red flag had been raised over the Winter Palace as people shouted 'Long live the revolution', how the Imperial government had collapsed, had been replaced by a Provisional Government, that Tsar Nicholas had abdicated and that three hundred years of the Romanov dynasty had come to an end.

Sophie and Sergei were stunned to read the news of the Tsar's abdication. Sophie remained silent for a long time as she thought about how a system she had known her entire life had just collapsed in such a short time. It seemed only a few months since they had been dressing in their finest clothes to attend balls celebrating three hundred years of Romanov rule. All that had suddenly been swept away.

'So who will be Tsar?' she asked.

'There won't be one. Russia will be a republic like France,' replied Sergei.

'I hope there won't be the same reign of terror the French had after their revolution,' Sophie remarked.

Philip and Sergei remained silent.

That evening, Sophie told Philip that she intended to tell her brother they were lovers.

'I can't deceive my brother. In fact, I want him to be pleased for me, but he can't be pleased if he doesn't know,' she had explained to Philip. 'And even if he disapproves I think he deserves to know.' In fact, she was bursting to tell her brother that she was in love: she wanted to throw open the shutters on the windows and announce her news to every person who passed in the street below.

Philip understood her desire to tell Sergei. He wanted to shout his love for her from the balcony of the Winter Palace.

The following morning she plucked up her courage as she was washing him.

'My Bliznets, I have something to tell you.'

Sergei knew that when Sophie used the Russian word for 'twin brother' she was about to say something serious. Although they were not twins, he being the elder by three years, the family had always referred to them as such because, as children, they were inseparable.

'Do you like Philip?' she asked.

'I do,' replied Sergei.

'I think he's so kind and thoughtful. He found this house for us, you know.'

'I know.'

'He does all the shopping and pays for it all.'

'I know. I know.'

'We are lovers,' she blurted out. There, it was done. Now she would remain silent and wait to be scolded by her brother for the first time in her life

Sergei's expression became stern and Sophie feared there was going be harsh words said. How she dreaded the thought of upsetting him! She bowed her head, waiting for the admonishment she knew was coming.

Instead he roared with laughter, feeling more than a little sorry for teasing her.

'My little Sestra, you don't think that I have been stupid enough not to guess what was going on, with all the noise coming from the next room every night?'

She looked at him, embarrassed at the realisation he'd heard them making love.

She blushed, bit her lip and couldn't look him in the eye – but had to supress a little giggle at the same time.

Sergei reached out to hold her hand. 'I'm happy for you.'

They hugged. 'I was afraid you'd be annoyed,' she said.

'By rights I should be,' he said, mimicking a stern voice again. 'In fact, I should be challenging Philip to a duel to preserve the family honour… but, luckily for him I left my pistol at the front.' He laughed out loud.

She went out to tell Philip, determined that their lovemaking would be quieter in future.

****

When Philip left the house to look for food the only outward indication the government had changed was the absence of the Imperial double-headed eagle from shops and government offices. In their place, he could see the shadow of the outline against the brick or wood where the Tsar's coat of arms had once proudly hung. It was not just double-headed eagles that had been torn down: anything that reminded people of the past had been removed. The squares, monuments and building names had been removed, even some streets were now nameless.

There was one thing that had not changed, though, and that was the crowds on the streets. Sometimes Philip would stop to listen to people delivering speeches to crowds on street corners. Speakers demanded support for the new Provisional Government continuing the war against Germany, while others wanted to make peace no matter what the cost, confiscate the riches of the aristocracy and give it to the people, abolish the church, put the Tsar on trial, or execute the Tsar without a trial. There was only one topic he never heard debated: the restoration of the monarchy. The reign of the Romanovs was over.

On a number of occasions he was detained by groups of soldiers looking for money, jewels or food to steal. He never told Sophie of these encounters so as not to worry her, but knew that each time could be dangerous. Soldiers used soft hands and clean fingernails to identify enemies of the revolution. Good clothes would be stripped from their owners, sometimes leaving them almost naked. To avoid such incidents, Philip had begun to take the precaution of rubbing coal dust into his fingers, and purposely allowed his fingernails to become ragged and ingrained with dirt. If he was stopped his dirty hands, unshaven face, threadbare clothes and worn boots meant he was never detained for long. Even so, he marvelled that in some respects life went on as before in the city. The opera still performed, theatres were sold out every evening, the aristocracy continued to entertain, and many openly supported the new government in the hope that it would restore a little of the order they had known before the revolution. Philip was content to remain as invisible as possible. The streets outside the safety of the baker's were becoming more dangerous

****

Philip woke to find Sophie sitting in the chair next to their bed, her head bowed, her knees pulled up towards her chest, tears flowing down her cheeks.

'What's the matter?' he asked as he knelt on the floor in front of her.

'I can't take any more. I've been stuck in this house for months looking after Sergei and I need to get out.' She looked around her. 'It feels like a prison.'

Philip stroked a tear away from her cheek. 'I'm sorry,' he said. 'I thought that you and Sergei would be safe if you stayed indoors; it was insensitive of me.'

Sophie placed her arms around his shoulders and her

bottom lip quivered. 'I know you're doing your best, but Sergei is much stronger and could be left for a few hours or we could even take him with us…' Another tear fell.

Philip was concerned. The streets were dangerous but he knew that she must feel so frustrated.

'We'll go out for a walk along the Neva River.'

'Yes, please,' she said and smiled through the tears.

'This afternoon,' he said, knowing that daylight hours would be safer than the evening.

They hugged and from the room next door they heard Sergei: 'An excellent idea; I've been wanting some peace and quiet. You two are always around and fussing,' he laughed '… and while you're out you can bring me a cake.'

Sophie went into Sergei's room and kissed him on the cheek. There were no secrets in their small home.

At two in the afternoon Sergei and Philip were sitting in the front room when Sophie appeared from the bedroom dressed in a long coat of fawn woven wool, a lamb's wool collar and a matching stole to keep her hands warm. She wore a hat with feathers that swept around the rim. Her face was fresh and eyes sparkled with anticipation.

Sergei raised his hand to greet her and said, 'You look like a Grand Duchess.'

Philip smiled and went over to her. 'Too much like a Grand Duchess, I fear,' he said and gently removed the stole and the feather from the hat.

'Woollen gloves would be better and less noticeable,' he said as he removed her fine coat and replaced it with the threadbare one he'd purchased for the purpose.

Sophie no longer felt dressed up; the outing wasn't going to be special. She quietly chastised herself for being so childish, for wanting to look her best, for not thinking the streets would be dangerous. She loved the care that Philip was showing. If he walked me through the streets naked I would still feel very special, she thought, and giggled.

'What's so funny?' asked Philip.

'Nothing,' she whispered and blushed ever so slightly.

Having settled Sergei near the window with some tea within

easy reach and promised that they would only be an hour, they left the apartment. At the bottom of the stairs they met the baker.

'Good afternoon, landlord,' said Philip.

'And a good afternoon to you and your good wife,' replied the baker.

'I see you had a delivery of flour yesterday,' said Philip.

'The Provisional Government has improved the ration, but much of what I make is taken by the military. I'll have a loaf for you tomorrow, however. Have you heard the news?' the baker asked.

'What news?' Sophie's voice was anxious.

'A friend of mine supplies food to the troops at the Alexander Palace. He told me that he was making his usual delivery yesterday but the guards stopped him. He saw a large number of cars and trucks leave the palace. There must have been forty or fifty, he said, and in one of the cars he saw the Tsarevich Alexi and one of the Grand Duchesses looking out of the window. My friend was shoved back to let the convoy pass, and when he went to unload his delivery of food he was sent away and told that he wouldn't be needed again. Poor souls! I was told they're being sent to Siberia. It's the young children I feel sorry for – they've done no one any harm.'

'Poor souls indeed,' said Sophie.

Philip and Sophie walked along the street in silence.

'I know the Tsar wasn't good for Russia, but it's all I've ever known and I can't help hoping they will be safe. None of this is the children's fault, so why do they have to suffer for their parents' sins?'

The sun broke out from behind some clouds and bathed the street in a golden glow and their spirits rose. Sophie clasped Philip's arm and neither heard the noise of the city as they began their walk towards the river.

Sophie saw that nothing was as before. Uncollected rubbish was piled up everywhere, and on many corners old women offered their treasures of pots, linen and blankets for sale so they could buy some food. Groups of soldiers, dressed in blue or grey uniforms, wandered the streets, rifles slung over their shoulders, and everywhere there had once been double-headed eagles, red flags and banners now hung.

They walked towards the Stranger's Court, a labyrinth of narrow alleys where more than ten thousand merchants had once worked. Here Sophie could almost feel herself back in the past, as a number of the church-ornament shops were open and some were still selling incense and perfumed candles. Sophie breathed in the aromas of sandalwood, cherry and camphor, remembering her childhood Easters. It was strange, she thought, that such things were available yet bread was so scarce.

After leaving the labyrinth of alleyways they paused at the 'handsome square' that contained a large, defaced, statue of Catherine the Great. Sophie took hold of Philip's hand and squeezed it tightly. 'I have something to tell you.'

He looked into her eyes. 'What is it?'

Suddenly she was afraid. She couldn't explain the feeling she had for him and simply said, 'Have I told you today?'

'Told me what?' asked Philip.

'That I love you.'

Philip looked at her. 'And I love you too, so perhaps we should marry,' he said matter-of-factly.

'Is that a proposal?' asked Sophie.

Philip looked into her eyes. 'I suppose it is.'

'I'm serious. I love you and nothing would make me happier than to be your husband and a good father to our children.'

'Do you want many?' asked Sophie.

Philip smiled. 'A whole cricket team of boys.'

'A cricket team?' Sophie asked, wondering how many that meant.

'Eleven boys,' Philip said helpfully.

'So few,' she said and giggled.

'I think we should have some daughters as well.'

'So you intend to keep me confined to bed?'

'All day and night.' Philip paused as he thought about his reply.

'But I don't mean to... Well, that's not to say... I hope you're not offended... I didn't mean...'

Sophie roared with laughter at his embarrassment. The thought of being in bed with him all day wasn't at all an objectionable one. She stroked his cheek with her gloved hand and blew him a kiss.

'What will Sergei say?' he asked.

She smiled. 'You'll have to ask his permission, of course.'

'Oh, will I?' he said in confusion.

'In the absence of my father, he represents the family,' she said.

'But what if he says no?'

'Then we will have to elope.'

He kissed her and hugged her close to him until she complained that he was hurting her.

Two older women passed on the other side of the road and, seeing Sophie and Philip embrace, looked at each other and smiled.

'Love, that's one thing the revolution can't stop,' said one to the other.

'Let's celebrate with that cup of tea,' Philip said.

They found a small café full of people all trying to pretend that times weren't as bad as they believed by having some hot tea and a small plateful of biscuits.

The owner came over and wiped the table with a cloth that left tram-lines of grease. He replaced the cloth in the pocket of his equally stained apron.

'Tea?' he asked in a deep voice.

'Have you anything else?' asked Sophie.

'Yes, your ladyship, hot water,' roared the waiter so that everyone in the room could hear, and everyone laughed. Sophie saw the irony and, sharing the joke, laughed too. The room returned to the friendly murmur of hushed conversation.

The tea arrived and they sipped it slowly as they looked around at the rest of the customers. Many were couples, trying to catch up on the latest gossip. In the corner near the window there was a group of four men wearing red armbands. Bolsheviks, noted Philip. Bolsheviks had a reputation for unruly behaviour and Philip didn't allow his gaze to linger on their table, pleased that Sophie had her back to them.

Sophie was enjoying being out, seeing some of the city, doing something as normal as having a cup of tea in a café with the man she loved and who'd just proposed marriage to her.

Once they had drunk their tea they paid the owner the few kopecks he demanded for the hot liquid, and got ready to leave. As they did so, a man rose from a table near the entrance and pushed past them. He squeezed himself between them and without an apology disappeared into the crowds.

Once they were on the street Sophie turned to Philip. 'How rude that man was, just barging into us.'

He agreed and felt her weave an arm into his. He slid his free hand into his coat pocket and felt a piece of paper. When they were out of sight of the people in the café he pulled the paper out and read:

*You and your friends are in great danger. You must leave Russia as soon as possible with the papers you were given and deliver them. Don't trust anyone with a message from London.*

Philip felt his stomach tighten. It meant that since leaving the Hotel Europe people had been watching him. The time had come to tell Sophie about his mission to Russia.

That night Philip recounted his meeting with Grand Duke Konstantin Konstantinovich at the Bank of England so many years before, and the several trips he'd made to Russia, and how he had come to be trapped in Russia 'before I could collect the final box. Then I met you and I fell in love.'

He had lied to her about the box and its contents: telling a woman about fabulous jewels could only mean that she'd want to look at them and that would mean tearing apart Sergei's chair – and he wasn't sure he could repair any damage so that it was invisible.

'And because of helping me and Sergei you're in danger,' said Sophie.

He took her hand. 'I've loved every minute of being with you and I can't leave you, particularly now, but the note slipped into my coat this afternoon shows that people know where I am and you could be in some danger because of me.'

Once in bed Philip couldn't sleep. He had much to think about.

Russia had collapsed into anarchy. The Provisional Government had survived one attempted coup by the Bolsheviks but another could happen any day. Many aristocrats flew red flags from their palaces: not just as acts of self-preservation but as real supporters of the revolution. However, to Philip, it was clear that demonstrations of support for the revolution wouldn't give aristocrats a passport to live as they had in the past. If they thought that, they were going to be mistaken. Philip had seen the mob that roamed the streets. They wanted the riches that their masters had enjoyed and would invade their fine homes, smash their pictures, remove their silver and gold plates and drink their wine cellars dry. The country would inevitably descend into civil war. A country fighting a civil war was a cruel and sadistic place. He had to get Sophie and Sergei out of Russia.

He thought through the possibilities. It would be dangerous to flee to Finland. The White Russians were reported to be shooting anyone they believed was a revolutionary, and coming from an area run by the Reds was seen as proof of being a revolutionary.

They could travel south to the Crimea. Many aristocrats were fleeing the revolution to their country estates in the Crimea. From there they could get a neutral ship to Cyprus or Malta, but travelling to the Crimea would place them firmly as supporters of the old order. Philip weighed up the two choices – Finland or the Crimea?

There was, of course, only one destination Sophie and Sergei would consider. Because there was one other person that Philip hadn't planned for, someone Philip had yet to meet, the old Count Tagleva, Sophie's father. Philip knew Sophie would never agree to leave Russia without seeing her father, and it was possible that her father could join them to escape. Their next destination would be neither Finland nor the Crimea; it would be Moscow.

****

Having sold his last loaf of bread, the baker was tidying up the shop and wiping the last remains of flour and crumbs of rye bread off the counter and onto the floor where it could be easily swept up. He was not a tall man, and his girth was proof of the thirty-two years he had spent working in the family business.

Ever since he helped his father as a young boy he'd loved the look of his hands, slick with water, as they plunged into the flour, water and yeast mixture. Working, pulling, stroking, pressing the sloppy mixture over the marble slab until it was like silk to the touch.

'It should remind you of your mother's soft cheeks,' his father had said, smiling down at him as his hands worked the dough. Now it was ready to be laid down to snooze in the warm proving cupboard. But there would be no rest for the bread; it needed to grow, and only once it had doubled in size could the air be knocked from it. The living dough could then be shaped into loaves and buns and become a thing of beauty, like his lovely daughter Moika. He never tired of the smell of the freshly baked yeast; it always put him in a jolly mood. He never tired of the queue of customers who came to buy his magic.

During the good times, he'd displayed eight or more breads. There was *Rossisky*, a rye sourdough; *Borodinsky*, which was very popular with his customers, using barley-meal that the baker recommended for its earthy flavour and best eaten with pickled herring; *Balubusky*, the little rolls speckled with caraway seeds and with a special texture and pleasant acidic flavour he created by adding sour cream. But his favourite were the sweet breads such as *kulich*, which was similar to a brioche, but rich with raisins, candied peel, angelica, chopped almonds and then iced and decorated with candied cherries.

He sighed. He hadn't made *kulich* for over a year. Finding the molasses for the black bread was difficult these days. He threw down the cloth on the counter in frustration as he remembered days when he hadn't had enough flour to make the bread demanded by his customers. To hear the abuse when the last loaf was sold and there was still a queue of people waiting, you'd think that all of Russia's troubles were his fault.

'If we have bread and *kvas* (beer), what more do we need?' was a Russian saying repeated by mothers to their children when there was no other food and they were hungry. Without bread, there was no life – and there had been too many days when there'd been no bread.

His other pleasure was gossip. He loved to hear his customers report the goings-on in the district. The woman having an affair with a worker from the neighbouring street; the priest seen coming from the sanctuary with the young choirboy long after the rest of the choir had gone home; the ballerina from the Ballets Russes who'd got pregnant; and the servant upset by his master's rough tongue, who'd pissed in the soup to get his revenge. He remembered every detail for his wife, who waited eagerly for the evening and the latest instalment.

The baker saw Philip leave the upstairs rooms and waved to his tenant as he passed the shop window. Philip waved back. The baker liked the tenants upstairs; they were always happy to spend a few minutes talking and the rent was always paid on time. It had been his only source of income when there was no flour to make bread, and he was grateful for it. He shook his head as he thought of the young man with such terrible wounds from the war – and such a good-looking boy too.

He'd almost finished tidying up. He looked through the window and noticed the man he'd seen earlier in the day, and the day before, standing at the same corner. Being a shopkeeper, he was used to recognising a face in the queue. It helped when working out who was next, a skill that saved arguments by serving people in the right order. It was also useful to recognise a face that appeared more than once as – one can never tell – they might turn into a regular customer. This man seemed to be waiting on the street corner and taking a little more interest in the shop than the baker liked. Someone just looking at the shop without buying bread wasn't welcome. He decided he'd keep his eye out, and he busied himself preparing for tomorrow's bake.

Twenty minutes later Philip arrived home and the baker waved a hearty greeting to his tenant.

'I hope all's well upstairs?' asked the baker.

'It is, thank you.'

'I'll have a loaf for you tomorrow,' said the baker.

Philip was used to the baker passing the time of day, but on this occasion he seemed to want a longer conversation.

'I was wondering if you'd noticed the man hanging around on the opposite side of the street, watching the shop?'

Philip looked towards the far side of the street but saw nothing.

'What does he look like?'

'A tall man in a blue coat with a lamb's wool collar with matching hat, and a scarf he pulls over his face, so it's difficult to see his face… It's probably nothing. I might be imagining it,' continued the baker unconvincingly. 'Just thought I'd ask in case you'd seen him too.'

Philip promised to watch out for the man.

Upstairs, he made a point of glancing out of the window every now and again.

'Why do you keep looking out of the window?' asked Sophie.

'The baker told me that someone is watching the shop, and I was wondering if I might catch a glimpse of him.'

'How strange! Sergei said that he'd seen a man hanging about on the street corner yesterday.'

'What did he look like?' enquired Philip.

'A tall man, he thought, with a long coat and lamb's wool hat. Sergei thought it strange, because yesterday was very cold and not a time to be hanging around.'

'Let me help you prepare dinner,' said Philip, changing the subject.

The following morning Philip glanced out of the window as he passed, but the street was empty.

The baker too glanced towards the opposite side of the street as he kneaded his bread, proved the loaves and stacked them on the shelves behind the counter ready for his customers.

It was around eleven, when Philip was reading a book, that he saw a figure in a long coat and lamb's wool hat, stamping his feet to keep warm. Philip studied him for a few minutes and noticed that he regularly glanced up at their windows. He wasn't looking at the baker's shop.

As Sophie was bathing Sergei, Philip collected his hat and coat from the back door and slipped out. Arriving at the street, he turned left and carried on walking. Would the man follow? thought Philip. Sure enough, Philip could hear boots matching his own stride. At the next street he crossed the road and turned right at the next alleyway and waited. A few seconds later the man turned the corner and came face to face with Philip.

'Sorry,' said the man instinctively, in English.

'Keep your hands where I can see them,' Philip said gruffly, 'and tell me why you're following me.'

'You're Cummings,' said the man.

Philip was shocked at the use of his name after such a long time.

'So?' he said, trying to stay calm.

'I've been asked by the bank to get a message to you. The boat that should've taken you home was ordered by the Admiralty to leave on a special mission. It's taken a great deal of time, but new arrangements have been made for you to leave Russia.'

'Who are you?' said Philip, relaxing a little as the man smiled.

'My name's Sidney Reilly. I'm also British and in Russia working for British interests. I've been asked to contact you and help you to escape.'

'Who told you to contact me?'

'I can't go into details now; we don't have time. Just to say that your employer is anxious to see you home.'

'Go on,' said Philip.

'Arrangements have been made for you to leave Petrograd and go to Finland. Once in Finland you will be taken to Kotka, a town near Helsinki, and from there to Sweden, then to England.'

'When's this to happen?' enquired Philip.

'In three days. You're to go to the port and find the steamer *Novordsk*. The captain is expecting you. Within two weeks you'll be back in London.'

'I have friends that I must look after,' said Philip.

'Don't worry about them; they'll be perfectly safe. I'll make sure they're looked after. It's important that you leave Russia as soon as you can. Things are becoming more dangerous by the day. By the way, were you given some papers to take to England?'

Philip realised that this man knew a great deal more than he was saying.

'Yes, they are in a safe place,' said Philip.

'It's important that you collect them and take them with you. They're needed in London. Be sure to be at the *Novordsk* in three days. Ask for the captain, his name's Albrekt.'

'Yes, I'll remember,' said Philip and the stranger walked away in the opposite direction.

Arriving home, Philip saw his landlord.

'I saw you speak to the stranger,' said the baker. 'Is everything OK?'

'Yes,' said Philip. 'He was looking for his wife and thinks she's having an affair with someone in this street. I don't think we'll see him again.'

'How did you convince him?' asked the baker, anxious for all the details he could get.

'I told him she'd met a Bolshevik leader and had gone to fight for the revolution in Siberia.'

'Did he believe you?' asked the baker, amused at the lie.

'He said he'd be off tonight to find her.'

The baker roared with laughter. 'That's good, I must tell my wife tonight, she'll love that one.'

Philip didn't go upstairs to Sophie and Sergei. He needed time to think about his meeting with Reilly and walked on towards the river. The demon that was his duty had reappeared. He knew he should go to the *Novordsk* and then to England. He knew that the papers were important. He knew he had been in Russia for too long.

'Damn everything,' he muttered to himself. What did it matter if the papers general Mossolov had given him were, or were not, delivered to England? What possible difference could a few scraps of paper make to the war? Yet he knew that they might.

'But Sophie and Sergei need me! I have a duty to them too,' he said into the wind and plunged his gloved hands into his coat pockets. He felt the piece of paper, pulled it out and unfolded it.

*You and your friends are in great danger. You must leave Russia as soon as possible with the papers you were given and deliver them. Don't trust anyone with a message from London.*

He read it a few more times before crunching the paper into a ball and throwing it into the river. He watched it float away towards the Baltic.

On returning to the baker's shop Philip told Sophie of his meeting with Reilly. 'I don't know why we are of such interest to these people, but it can only put us all in danger. I don't trust this Reilly man. What do you think we should do?'

Sophie stifled a sob. 'If it's your duty to go to Finland and then on to London, then you should go. I'll stay here and look after Sergei. We'll be all right and when we're able to make arrangements we can travel to Moscow.' She looked at him, knowing she was being brave and not wanting to be. She could feel her anger growing; she had no right to be angry at him, but she was.

Philip looked at her. 'I'm not going to Finland,' he said, reaching out to hold her hand. 'I think we should all leave for Moscow as soon as we can. The situation here is becoming too dangerous. My darling, I love you and I've promised to marry you: that's my duty now. London can wait.'

Sophie was relieved. She threw her arms around his neck and kissed him three times on the cheek. As they embraced Philip whispered in her ear, 'I'm sorry if I upset you, but I wanted your thoughts on the arrangements for travelling to Moscow with Sergei. I never intend to leave you, ever.'

'Then why didn't you say that?' Sophie whispered back.

'I thought I had,' he said, thinking that he still didn't understand women.

For the rest of the day and far into the night, the three of them discussed what they needed to take on the journey to Moscow. Sergei didn't need his stumps treated any more but he would need disinfectant and cream to treat the sores caused by sitting for too long in the wheelchair. They would need some changes of clothing, but fancy clothes and shoes were unnecessary.

Philip saw the baker and told him that they would be leaving in two days.

'I'll be sorry to see you go,' the baker said, but was grateful for the two months' rent that he would retain. He was also grateful for the things that Philip said they intended to leave behind, such as the bedclothes, some dresses and some coats that the baker's wife might like to have. I will be popular, thought the baker.

Two days later, all the essential possessions had been packed into three small valises.

Suddenly they heard a banging on the door. Philip wondered what the urgency was. Opening it, he saw the baker, out of breath. He didn't wait to be invited in, but rushed into the living room. The three of them looked at the baker as he gasped like a fish out of water.

'You can't leave,' said the baker between breaths.

'Why ever not?' asked Sergei.

'No one's paid the soldiers for over a month, and some idiot's decided that instead of money they would pay them with wine from the Tsar's wine cellar. Every soldier in the city's been given bottles of champagne, fine wines and vodka. They're all drunk! No one's safe, they've all become murdering mobs.'

Once the baker had left, Philip said that he would venture out to see if the situation was as bad as the baker had said.

'Do be careful,' said Sophie to him as he left.

Philip didn't have to go far before he came across a group of soldiers drinking the contents of some bottles of Château Lafite and Latour. In the gutters were the smashed and empty bottles of vintage champagne, whisky from Scotland, French brandy and wines from the Caucasus. More used to the burning sensation of homemade vodka, soldiers staggered all over the streets, promised women a night of passion they were incapable of fulfilling, and slapped each other on the back as they laughed at nothing much. Philip predicted that the soldiers would eventually turn into an armed mob. He didn't have to wait long. Near the baker's shop he saw a group of very drunk soldiers with six bottles of Château Margaux at their feet. Seeing a couple of well-dressed men, the group of soldiers stopped them. After they had stolen the men's coats, the soldiers told them to run for their lives. The two men ran from their tormentors as fast as they could, but four of the soldiers took aim and fired. The first man, the artery in his neck severed, fell to the ground with blood gushing like a fountain into the air, staining the street cobbles dark crimson. The second man, two bullets in his back, sank to his knees before falling forward, dead. The soldiers congratulated themselves on their marksmanship and toasted themselves with more wine. The orgy of drinking lasted three days. There was nothing Philip, Sophie and Sergei could do but stay in their rooms.

The time allowed them to discuss their plans to travel to Moscow. Philip was comforted by the thought that, as a group, they probably wouldn't be too conspicuous. Wounded soldiers were everywhere, and so many families were moving from one part of Russia to another to escape one political faction or another that another three people wouldn't be noticed.

Sophie filled the extra time by stitching her two strings of pearls into the hem of her coat. A gift from her mother, they were very precious and she had been upset at the thought that she might have to leave them behind. She remembered the first time she had worn them, to an aunt's birthday party. Each evening she would take them off, rub the pearls with a silk handkerchief and return them carefully to their velvet pouch.

Sophie also had a couple of rings: a diamond and sapphire given to her by her father, and another from a favourite aunt, a ruby held in a platinum snow leopard's claw, and she was looking for places to hide these. Then she saw Sergei's chair and wondered if she could pull apart some of the leather and slip the rings into the seat. As she bent down to inspect the chair, Philip asked, 'What are you doing?'

'I thought I might hide these rings in Sergei's chair. If I pull back some of this piece of leather then perhaps I can slip them underneath.'

'You might tear the leather and then it'll look as if something's hidden. It would be better to find another place,' he said quickly.

Sophie was surprised. He'd never spoken to her so gruffly.

'So where do you suggest?' asked Sophie, slightly irritated.

'How about the collar of your coat?'

A little taken aback, she put his mood down to the stress of the situation and being cooped up in their rooms for so long. Feeling a little chastised, she went off to look for her needle and thread.

On her return, he was smiling but she chose not to acknowledge the smile, pouted and looked away.

'Sorry I snapped; I didn't mean to,' said Philip anxious to know that she wasn't upset at him.

She tilted her head backward and looked down at him with feigned disdain.

'Apology accepted,' she whispered, and bent down and kissed him on the forehead.

'Thank you,' he whispered with the same feeling that he had as a boy when he had been told off for some misdemeanour.

# Chapter Nine: Escape from Petrograd

After four days the baker knocked on their door.

'I thought I'd come and tell you that the soldiers are now nursing huge hangovers and most are sleeping it off. The streets are quiet and I guess the Tsar's wine cellar is now empty.'

They thanked the baker for the news and Philip left to find transport to the train station. They would leave the following morning.

Ever since the railway had been built in the 1880s, the idea of connecting the two capitals, St Petersburg and Moscow, had led to controversy, with some officials predicting social upheaval if the masses were allowed to travel. It was finally decided that only the affluent would be allowed to use the railway line. Every passenger had been subjected to strict passport and police control and, despite the revolution, the need for travel papers had not changed. After a long wait, their travel papers had been granted by a minor official. No one had had time to reprint the travel permits, so there were three stamps. The double-headed eagle of the Tsar's regime had been partly blacked out, the stamp of the Provisional Government was also blacked out, and the final authorisation was from the Petrograd Soviet of Workers and Soldiers Deputies. When Philip showed the precious document to Sophie and Sergei they all agreed that with all three authorities allowing them the right to travel there should be no problems, and they laughed at the absurdity of it all.

The following morning they waited downstairs in the bakery for a sled to arrive.

'I wish you all a safe journey, and may the saints protect you,' the baker said. They each hugged him and Philip reminded him of the things they were leaving behind.

'Thank you, thank you, you're so kind,' he replied fervently.

The sled arrived. The baker and the sled driver bundled their possessions under the blanket at the back, Sergei was carried to the middle seat, and Sophie and Philip sat on either side of him. The whole procedure took over twenty minutes because Sergei found it difficult to get comfortable. Eventually the sled moved off in the direction of the rail station and the baker waved his final goodbyes. Sophie was sad to leave the baker's. Despite everything, she had been happy there. She had fallen in love with Philip, nursed Sergei back to some sort of health, and she had enjoyed the baker's warm smile each time they met. She felt she was leaving a friend. A few hundred yards down the road Philip took one last look back to the apartment where he had been so happy with Sophie.

Two cars had drawn up in front of the building and a group of militiamen surrounded the baker. They were pointing their rifles at the baker, who was kneeling in front of them. Before the sled turned the corner and drove out of sight he saw the soldiers rush, bayonets fixed, into the building. Philip turned his head to face forward and gritted his teeth. They had to leave Petrograd on the first possible train!

The sled arrived in front of the railway station, a white stone building held up with nine huge arches at the front. A stone pillar in the middle of each arch gave the effect that the station had eighteen entrances. Above the building was a clock tower, its hands permanently stuck at eighteen minutes past three. Everyone knew the time would make no difference to the running of the trains. There was no timetable, and the fourteen committees discussing the situation had yet to agree on a new one.

Philip and Sophie pulled their cases from the sled, helped Sergei into his chair and wheeled him and their belongings onto the main concourse, which was packed with people all waiting to travel. People stood, sat and lay in every space, and it was a struggle to negotiate their way to the platform.

Philip stopped a man in a blue rail uniform. 'Is that the train to Moscow?' he shouted above the noise, pointing to the steaming train.

'Yes,' came the reply.

'When does it depart?'

'The Workers' Committee will tell us when,' came the shrugged reply.

'How long will that take?'

'They've been arguing for two days, so your guess is as good as mine: this week, next week, perhaps never.'

Philip was dismayed at the news. He was certain that the baker would be pressured into telling the soldiers where they had gone. He estimated it would be ten minutes before the soldiers arrived. Finding two people with a wounded person in a wheelchair would be too easy.

Philip needed to disappear.

Turning to Sophie and Sergei, he spoke to them in a whisper. 'Don't ask any questions, just do as I say. In a short time some militia will come looking for us. When they question you, say we argued and I've left to go to the docks to try to find a ship to Finland, and you and Sergei are travelling to your home in Moscow.'

Sophie looked frightened. 'What's happening?'

'No time to explain now. Just do as I say. Take Sergei and the luggage and go and sit near the third carriage of the train, if you can. Cover yourself in a blanket and look as if you've settled down for a long wait. Now go.'

Sophie bundled their possessions up and slowly negotiated Sergei through the crowd. Her stomach was churning and she felt weak with anxiety, but followed Philip's instructions and eventually found a space in the third carriage. She placed her small suitcase on end so that she could sit on it and protect their possessions from being stolen, and so she could also speak to Sergei and tell him quietly what Philip had whispered to her.

Philip walked to the engine and looked up at the engine driver.

'Comrade,' he shouted in greeting. The driver looked down at the platform. This wasn't the usual man from the Workers' Committee, he thought irritably.

Philip looked up at him and smiled. 'I've always wanted to meet a train driver and shake his hand. You've an important

97

job here. So many people rely on your expertise, it must command great respect.'

The driver leaned down to look at Philip. He was beginning to like this stranger, despite the fact that he must be slightly mad to think that his job commanded respect. Since the revolution, he had been told when he could go, when he must stop, what speed he could travel, what cargo he could take. Everyone on the Workers' Committee was an expert, despite the fact that none of them did any work other than to argue.

'You would think so,' said the driver.

'Comrade,' said Philip. 'Since I was a young boy I've dreamed of being a fireman in one of these engines. Could you show me how it works?'

The train driver wasn't going anywhere soon, and any distraction was welcome.

'Step up,' he said, delighted to be able to share his work with an enthusiast.

Philip climbed into the cab and listened to the driver as he explained the workings of the beast; how it needed to be 'nurtured, loved like a woman if it were to make the journey to Moscow and back without complaining'.

Philip enquired, 'How long does the journey to Moscow take?'

The driver indicated that Philip should draw closer, as if he was about to impart some juicy bit of gossip. 'Before the revolution the journey used to take ten hours. Now it takes days' and he raised his hands to the heavens.

'I'll tell you something else,' he continued, and indicated that Philip should come closer still so that no one should overhear them. 'When we get permission to leave the station, we travel ten miles before we'll have to stop. Then we'll wait to get permission from another Workers' Committee that says they are in charge. We stop and start all the way to Moscow.'

'They should put *you* in charge,' declared Philip.

'And be arguing with idiots all day? No thank you. Let me tell you how stupid they are. The line from here to Novgorod is completely straight apart from an eleven-mile bend near the city. I was told last week by someone on the Committee that the reason for the bend was that when the Tsar selected the route he took a ruler and drew a straight line between the two cities on a map and accidentally drew around his own finger on the ruler. It was said that the planners were too afraid to point out the error and constructed the line with the bend.' He roared with laughter and continued.

'The Workers' Committee has said that they intend to change the tracks so that the line will be straight as intended and repair the Tsar's mistake. They are idiots! The line was originally built without the curve and up and down a steep hill. It caused all sorts of problems because trains heading to Petrograd or St Petersburg as it used to be would pick up so much speed they couldn't stop at the next station and those heading for Moscow couldn't get up the hill without the assistance of four locomotives. The Workers' Committee has argued about making the line straight for a whole week and none of them knows the reason for the bend. Fucking idiots, all of them!'

They both laughed – and then Philip spotted the militia walk through the arches at the entrance to the station.

'Comrade, I've always wanted to wear a fireman's cap and shovel some coal on the fire.'

'Be my guest,' said the driver. 'The fireman's cap's on that hook.' He indicated to the latch on the furnace.

Philip picked up the cap and scraped his fingers along the metal to pick up some coal dust, then rubbed his forehead as if removing an itch before placing the cap on his head.

'Now your face is all dirty and you'll look the part,' said the driver, laughing.

Just as Philip picked up the shovel and threw a small amount of coal into the furnace, three members of the militia and an officer walked past the cab. Ignoring the driver and fireman, they moved further down the platform to search for a man and a woman with a wounded soldier in a wheelchair.

They were easy to find.

'Your papers,' demanded the officer.

Sophie passed the tickets to the soldier and looked into his face. He wore the hat of an infantry regiment and there was a tiny hole in the cap where the regimental insignia had once been proudly displayed.

'There are three of you mentioned on this travel pass. Where's the other man?'

'He's gone to the port to find a boat.'

'Why?' asked the officer.

'I don't know. We argued. We want to go home to Moscow; he wanted to go to Finland. We quarrelled and he became angry with us and said he would get a boat.'

'Then you must come with us to answer some questions,' said the officer.

'Are we under arrest?' demanded Sergei.

'Yes,' came the reply.

'On what charge?' asked Sophie as she stood up. In doing so, she pulled the blanket they shared from Sergei's knees. The officer was startled to see Sergei's missing arm and leg. The crowd had also noticed and began to listen more attentively to what was happening.

They were being arrested. There was a murmur of disapproval. The soldiers were arresting a war hero, a fighter who'd bravely fought and suffered for Mother Russia!

'It's a shame,' said someone in the crowd loudly.

'What harm could a cripple and a woman do to the revolution?' said another.

'Pick on someone your own size,' shouted someone from the safety of the rear of the crowd.

'Disgrace,' cried another.

'Only brave enough to pick on cripples and defenceless women,' cried a woman.

The crowd roared its approval.

One large woman, her head covered in a patterned shawl, walked over to the officer.

'I suppose you feel brave arresting someone who's defenceless? Be brave and arrest a real counter-revolutionary, an aristocrat or black marketer. What harm is this war hero to the revolution?' she shouted and the crowd roared its approval once more.

The officer wanted to avoid trouble at all costs, and he could feel that the soldiers in his platoon were quickly losing their enthusiasm to arrest the pair.

'They are wanted for questioning,' the officer told the woman.

'What for?' shouted the woman in the crowd.

'I don't know, but those are my orders,' said the soldier.

'They are arresting a defender of the motherland – and a hero at that,' one man shouted, explaining it to the others.

'Comrade, don't you have more important things to do than to harass cripples?' shouted someone from the middle of the crowd.

The officer looked at his men. They were becoming increasingly nervous. He didn't want any trouble. He'd been ordered to arrest an English counter-revolutionary, but these people were Russian. He would go back and ask for clearer orders.

He returned the papers to Sophie. 'The port, you said?'

'Yes,' she replied.

The officer nodded, turned to his soldiers and said, 'We'll try the port.'

As they marched up the platform the small crowd cheered and clapped at its small victory. Sophie closed her eyes and breathed a sigh of relief.

She turned to the woman who had challenged the officer and thanked her. She looked like every peasant's mother, with her scarf pulled tight around her round chubby face, deeply lined from working outside in cold weather, and with red veins covering her cheeks like a map. Her smile and sparkling eyes gave her a friendly expression, but her huge frame, exaggerated by many layers of warm clothing, created a dumpling of a woman of formidable proportions.

'No need to thank me,' said the woman, with a wave of her fat arm. 'We get rid of one tsar and up jump all sorts of little tsars who think they can boss everyone around. My name's Anna – Anna Vyrubova.'

'Nice to meet you, Anna. I'm Sophie and this is my brother Sergei.'

'So, you are off to Moscow?'

'I'm taking my brother home.'

'Well then, we shall travel together,' said Anna maternally. 'The journey's long and I'm sure we'll be good company for each other. My own husband was killed in the war against the Japanese so I'm all alone now, and the company would be most welcome.'

Sophie saw Philip out of the corner of her eye. Anna talked to Sergei as she patted his one good arm with her calloused hand.

Philip had seen what had happened. He looked Sophie straight in the eye and shook his head ever so slightly as he passed her. Sophie understood the message and was relieved as she watched Philip pass them and sit three feet away with another group of waiting passengers.

Three hours later a shrill whistle sounded from the railway engine, signalling that the train was about to depart. The cattle truck doors were thrown open and the crowd surged forward to board the train and claim their spaces.

The fitter people in a group climbed on board to reserve spaces for their families as the older and infirm helped each other climb on board. Pots, pans, suitcases and bundles of clothes were all thrown onto the train.

Philip slung the knapsack that held his clothes and some food onto his back and pushed past a few people to Sophie. He shouted, 'Here, let me help you with the chair,' and pointed towards Sergei.

Sophie climbed in ahead of them with most of the luggage and to reserve space for the four of them to sit. Philip and Anna lifted Sergei's chair into the carriage. Sergei extended his leg to kick an over-eager passenger out of the way and to prevent him from being tipped out of the chair and onto the tracks below. They settled into the space reserved by Sophie and found that they were all panting heartily with the effort and, despite the cold, sweat covered their brows.

'That was very kind of you, comrade,' said Anna to Philip.

The doors of each carriage slammed shut and a whistle blew.

They were all jolted as the train began to move. A couple of the passengers still standing were thrown to the floor and against others, who made their annoyance felt with curses. A thermos crashed to the floor and spilled dark tea over the carriage. A woman looked down at the tea stain and slapped a small girl for her carelessness. The girl sat down on the floor, her knees drawn up to her face, and sobbed into her skirt.

The rest of the travellers ignored the little girl and settled down to a long rail journey. As the familiar, hypnotic *tchh, tchh, tchh, tchh* rhythm of the wheels crossing the tracks drowned out the noises of the other passengers, Sophie succumbed to tiredness and fell asleep.

# Chapter Ten: The train to Moscow

## Spring 1918

In London Sir Charles Cunningham was almost at the end of his meeting with the King's Private Secretary. Lord Stamfordham had been the Personal Private Secretary to Queen Victoria in the last years of her reign and now held the same post to her grandson George V. A meticulous man, he knew most of the Royal Family's secrets and prided himself on protecting them from those who would use those secrets and the Royal Family for their own greedy ends.

Stamfordham knew his master, George V, was considered neither well-educated nor well-read by government ministers and senior civil servants, nor was he considered a wit or a raconteur. In fact, most people described him as being stiff and distant. However, Stamfordham believed that the King embodied diligence and duty. Unlike his grandmother and his father, George V accepted constitutional monarchy. Stamfordham told himself that it was the Private Secretary's duty to ensure that the Monarchy thrived, prevent anyone who hoped to gain unwelcome access or influence with the King and to ensure that the King was well advised. Stamfordham was adept at doing all of that.

The King was anxious to be kept abreast of what was happening in the war against Germany, and Stamfordham's meeting with Charles Cunningham was intended to give him valuable information that he could then tell his royal master.

Lord Stamfordham made notes as Sir Charles Cunningham spoke.

'At the start of the war the cry from government had been, "Damn the cost, we must win this war" – currently we are spending nearly four million pounds a day on ammunition. The cost of tobacco and cigarettes for the army runs at over two million pounds a year. The problem is that prices have doubled since the start of the war.'

Stamfordham asked, 'Does tax not cover the costs any longer?'

Sir Charles paused before answering. 'Tax only covers around forty per cent of the war costs. War bonds bought by ordinary people around the country cover another twenty per cent. There is currently a huge deficit. Up until 1916 Britain financed the Allies, then we ran out of money and had to borrow from the United States. Since 1917 the US has taken over financing the Allies but, as with all loans from the United States, it insists on being repaid after the war. The country currently owes almost as much in interest as it produces.'

Sir Charles waited until Stamfordham had finished writing in his notebook before continuing. 'The loans from the Americans are being spent on vast munitions industries to provide shells, guns, warships, uniforms, aeroplanes and a hundred other items.'

Lord Stamfordham asked, 'And are we sure that we are getting value for money? After all, we don't want to be indebted to the Americans any more than we have to be.'

'Currently they have us over a barrel. The Americans have the money and we need it.'

'But we are ensuring that there's no profiteering or overcharging by suppliers?' said Stamfordham gravely.

Sir Charles considered the question. 'There's very little profiteering; almost nothing at all. I check all contracts for supplies to the army and the navy. Any contract is given to the best supplier and I look very carefully at the price charged.'

'Very good,' said Lord Stanfordham, closing his notebook.

Sir Charles sat in the red leather studded chair and studied the glass of Madeira that had been poured for him and which he had carefully placed on the side table to his right.

'On another matter, I understand that an invitation has been sent by the King to the Tsar and his family to come and live in exile in England.'

'Yes,' came the reply from Stamfordham. 'The King feels that his cousin would be welcome here. In fact, I'm looking for suitable residences for them in Kensington this afternoon.'

'I see,' said Sir Charles.

'You don't approve?'

Sir Charles picked up the Madeira and took a short sip before replying. 'It's not my business to approve nor to disapprove but, under the circumstances, I wonder if the invitation is a bit rash.'

'What do you mean, rash?'

'Well, as we've discussed, the nation is essentially bankrupt and I wonder if that might cause some significant civil unrest if people learn that the Tsar, an autocrat, is living in the country at the taxpayer's expense. I don't think it would be popular. In fact, who knows, in these troubled times, with thrones in danger of being lost, what might happen if the people became angry? I just hope the King doesn't come to regret his decision.'

Stamfordham could see the sense in Sir Charles's assessment. It was the same sentiment that had encouraged him to advise the King to change the family's name from the Germanic Saxe-Coburg Gotha to the 'House of Windsor' at the start of the war.

Stamfordham left the meeting deep in thought.

The following day a telephone call was made to the Prime Minister instructing him that the King wished the government to withdraw the invitation to the Tsar and his family. The Prime Minister, David Lloyd George, was baffled by the decision but too busy to pay much attention to why the King had changed his mind. He did, however, share the news with a cabinet colleague, remarking that the King's just condemned his cousin to death.

# The train journey

The train was starting again. There had been no reason for the unscheduled stop, which was just one among many. Philip looked at some of his fellow passengers. Most were resigned to the long journey, and tried to make it as comfortable as possible. Children slept in their mothers' laps, wives leaned against husbands, who placed a coat behind their head for a pillow. A baby cried for want of food or a change of nappy, and the smell of a goat in the corner of the cattle truck filled their nostrils, but the passengers had stopped complaining about it as they were now used to it and instead complained of the cold. The noise in the carriage was deafening: the wheels clattered on the tracks, some cooking pans somewhere rattled against each other and a man snored. Within a couple of hours many wished they had stayed in Petrograd and wondered if the deprivations of the city hadn't been so bad after all. Most passengers were awake, having used the stop to empty the latrine, which had been carefully transported to the door so as not to spill any of its contents, and emptied onto the side of the tracks. Then the door had been quickly closed to prevent the stench flooding back into the carriage.

Throughout the journey Anna tried to keep the group entertained. To pass the time she recounted stories from her life as cook to a fat and often drunk owner of a factory in a village outside Petrograd.

'The bastard paid his workers very badly, gave them little time off and when drunk would often beat them for no reason at all. When the revolution came and a Workers' Committee was set up, the fat pig was moved out of his house and was put to live in his barn,' she said.

Everyone in the carriage felt that was a just and good result, and it sparked off lengthy conversations on the 'deserts' the wealthy landowners were yet due.

Their arrival in Moscow fifteen hours after leaving Petrograd was a source of relief to everyone on the train, especially to Sophie, who was worried that the journey had exhausted Sergei. After saying goodbye to Anna, they found a taxi to take them the short journey to their house. On arrival everything looked normal. The door of their house was opened by the housekeeper, who took one look at Sergei and placed a hand over her mouth as tears welled up in her eyes and tumbled down her cheeks onto her black dress.

'Oh, your ladyship,' she cried as she pulled the door wide open. 'I feared you might be dead.'

Philip and Sophie wheeled Sergei into the hallway as the housekeeper curtsied.

'Now, now,' said Sophie as she took the servant's hand. 'All that bowing has been swept away with. You don't need to curtsy any more. Where are the other servants?'

'All gone,' said Helena. 'I'm the only one left.'

'Where's my father?'

'He's not been well for some weeks. He's in bed in his room. The doctor's just left, but has promised to return before nightfall.'

Sophie turned to Sergei and Philip. 'I'll go up to see him while you organise a downstairs room for Sergei. I suggest my father's study. There's a large fireplace that we can light a fire to keep the room warm. I'm sure Papa won't mind.'

Sophie left the housekeeper, climbed the stairs and quietly entered her father's bedroom. He was propped up against his pillows, asleep, looking pale and old. Next to the bed was a small cabinet containing several icons of saints, and the silver surrounds that protected the old paintings flickered in the light given off by the candle in a glass cup. On the other side of the bed were the pills and medication left by the doctor with a carafe of water.

Sophie sat in the chair placed to one side of the bed, and as she did so her father opened his eyes.

He smiled and whispered hoarsely, 'My child, you're back. I've missed you. Thank the Saints you're safe.'

'Yes, Papa.'

'And Sergei?' He coughed.

'He's downstairs, but wounded, so we are going to set up a bed for him in your study.'

'Is he badly hurt?'

Sophie decided not to distress her father with the details of Sergei's wounds. 'He's well. You would be so very proud of him, and once he's slept we can bring him up to see you.'

Her father smiled. 'I'm sorry he's wounded, poor boy, but at least he's alive. It'll be good to see him... I've missed you both and I'm so pleased you're home and safe.' He patted her hand. 'I'm tired and would like to sleep. Go and see to your brother and promise to come back,' and he patted her hand gently again.

Sophie leaned over and kissed him on the forehead. Her father smiled and blew a kiss into the air without opening his eyes.

Sophie walked down the stairs and into the study. The bed had already been made up and Sergei was holding a cup of tea.

'How's Father?' he asked.

Sophie smiled. 'He looks tired and much older. He is sleeping. I said we would go up and see him later.'

Sophie went to see Helena in the kitchen. 'What food have we in the house?'

Helena took her to the pantry and showed her the empty shelves.

'Food is so scarce that I moved what we had into the cupboard behind the bookcase in the study. I was pleased I did, because a few days later some soldiers came into the house looking for food. I showed them the empty pantry and that we had only one can of soup, and do you know what? They even took that.'

They went to the store and Sophie viewed the meagre but valuable treasure.

Helena said proudly, 'I saved what I could. Some flour and some packets of tea, a few tins of fruit and some preserves left over from last year.' She pointed to six jars of jam. 'There are some cans of preserved meats I managed to exchange a couple of days ago for some spare salt. Salt is impossible to find – it's more valuable than gold but we have plenty of that,' she added helpfully. 'There are a few cans of stew, but these are four years

110

old and were part of a consignment of goods your father was testing out for the army the year the war started.'

Sophie reached up and pulled one from the shelf and read the English label on the can with the brand name of *Maconochie*: '*Contents may be eaten hot or cold. The unopened can should be heated in boiling water for 30 minutes.*'

'What's this?' asked Sophie.

'I don't know, I gave the Count some a few days ago, heated up. It was awful and I kept half for the following day and we ate it cold, hoping that it would taste better. But the fat had accumulated in a lump, and what I thought were chunks of meat and grey-coloured vegetables was only congealed gravy. It smelled awful too.' And as if to emphasise the point, Helena screwed up her face in disgust.

'What about the chickens we had at the back of the house?' asked Sophie.

'Stolen, soon after you left for St Petersburg.' The housekeeper looked at Sophie, hoping that she had an answer, but knowing she had none. It was only a few days ago that she'd seen the neighbours in the gardens opposite scavenging for acorns and even collecting grass to make soup. Helena was worried for the future, but perhaps things would be better now that the countess was back home.

Sophie picked up a can and read the label: *Cherry blossom boot polish*. Sergei had brought some back from England all those years ago.

When everything else has run out perhaps we could make a stew with the polish, she joked to herself

'The wine cellar still has a lot of bottles,' said Helena, wanting to sound enthusiastic. 'Though I've given some to some people, like the doctor, who's been looking after your father, and because I had no other money. I hope you don't mind. It's the only thing of value other than the furniture and paintings.'

'You've done very well, and thank you, Helena,' said Sophie softly, estimating that their meagre rations would last no longer than a few weeks at most.

That evening a meal was taken upstairs for the Count to eat in his bedroom and afterwards he settled down to sleep. The four remaining members of the household sat at the dining table. The meal was meagre, consisting of some sausage they had brought with them from Petrograd, the last of the bread and some jam. Sophie had decided that she, Sergei and Philip couldn't expect Helena to eat on her own in the kitchen and invited her to join them.

The housekeeper had never sat with the family before and was quite nervous. It was not her place, she thought, but Sophie insisted, saying it was only right. In celebration of their homecoming Sophie opened a bottle of champagne and a bottle of Crimean wine. By the time they retired to bed the entire household was satisfyingly drunk.

The following morning Sophie took a glass of hot tea to her father. She then asked Philip if he would look after Sergei while she went to see her best friend Yelena, who lived a few houses away. Ever since she had left Moscow she had worried about her best friend and her family.

She found Yelena at home and was greeted warmly and taken to the front room. Sophie wasn't offered anything to eat or to drink and assumed that they had nothing to give her, so was delighted that she was able to hand over a packet of tea. The gift was enthusiastically accepted, shown to the others in the household and it quickly disappeared into the kitchen.

'How are you all?' asked Sophie to Yelena.

'We're fine, but our estates in Tulsa have been confiscated by some committee and given to peasants. We heard that some of the servants resisted and were shot, and the manor house has been ransacked and all the furniture stolen – it's horrible. Two of my brothers have gone to see if there is anything to rescue and Mother's quite worried because we haven't heard from them for weeks. It just seems that anything people can steal, they just take. We've even heard they are digging up the bodies in graveyards and family vaults to steal the gold crosses and rings buried with the dead. It's awful,' Yelena spoke excitedly. 'There are rumours of people being thrown off their estates with only twenty-four hours to clear the house. I'm terrified it will happen to us. Father says we'll go and stay with Uncle Vasily until things calm down. Uncle Grigory says it'll be all right, that the Bolsheviks will soon be swept away by some Socialist Revolutionaries, and the quicker the better he says. Though it's never going to bring things back the way things were, is it? It's all so awful.'

After half an hour Yelena had run out of things to say. 'But what news of you and Sergei?'

Sophie told her friend of Sergei's wounds and Yelena was sincerely sad for him. She'd always had a schoolgirl crush on her best friend's brother and had even secretly hoped to marry him but, much to her annoyance, he had never seemed to notice her. If he was so badly wounded it was probably for the best; there was little point in having a husband, even in good times, who couldn't look after his wife.

They talked for another hour and as Sophie departed the two friends hugged and promised to call on each other again.

As Sophie returned to the house she found Sergei and Philip in the study. Sergei was propped up in bed reading some papers. His brow was creased and Philip looked grave. She could tell that something was wrong.

'What's the matter?' she asked.

'Sit down,' Sergei said and Sophie pulled a chair from a group surrounding a card table and sat in front of Sergei and Philip. She felt her stomach ache with anxiety about what was to follow. She knew it was going to be bad news; she had only to look at Sergei's face to see it.

Sergei began. 'While you were out a member of the local Soviet Committee called. They told us that all the houses in this street have more rooms than are necessary for a household of a few people. This house has only five people in residence, and we've been ordered to make room for some of those in need. The house was inspected last week and twenty rooms for five people is considered inappropriate.'

'My God,' shouted Sophie. 'It's our house – they have no right. Our father worked for it, gave employment to hundreds of people. Paid them well, provided a doctor when they were ill and now they want to take it away from us. I won't let them!'

'The new government has passed a law that says all property now belongs to the state,' said Sergei.

Sophie stood up. She was angry and wanted to shout at someone. 'This house has been in our family for years! How can the state just decide that it's theirs? It's theft – they are stealing it from us!'

Sergei looked at her. 'I know it's hard, but we have no option. The doctor's told them that father's old and will probably die soon. The chairman of the local Soviet Committee once worked for us and they acknowledge that he was always a good employer, paid good wages, looked after sick workers and even paid for education for the children. And as a mark of respect they've agreed to delay the confiscation until after Father's died. They asked the doctor how long that might be, and he said two weeks – and so the occupation is delayed for two weeks.'

'Two weeks!' Sophie sank her face in her hands and began to weep. 'They may as well come now for all the good that is. Our father gave them so much and they just want it all. Well, they can't have it all,' she shouted and picked up a vase off the side table next to her chair and threw it into the fireplace. It smashed into pieces in the empty grate and splinters flew out from the fireplace, covering the Persian rug with broken china.

Philip looked at Sophie, feeling utterly helpless. Sergei put down the paper and reached out for her hand, and Sophie knelt, rested her head on Sergei's chest and sobbed.

Philip looked at the pair and then at the maid who'd rushed in when she heard the crash. She guessed what had happened and bit her hand to hold back the tears. It was like a scene from a tragic play, thought Philip, and the curtain wasn't coming down any time soon. This was only the beginning – worse was to come.

Over the next few days Philip began making plans for their escape from Moscow. He pored over the maps of Russia he found in the library. He was looking for a route to safety and had seen three possibilities. The one thing Philip didn't know was the political situation in each of the areas they would need to travel through, and so he made alternative plans providing different options. All these he consigned to memory after Helena told them that three people had been shot as spies when the secret police had found street maps of Moscow and an old train timetable on them. Philip committed to memory all the towns and villages, the railway stations, roads and terrain between Moscow and the Black Sea. It had been no more difficult than memorising a page of financial accounts.

Sophie walked into the room. She wanted some private time with him. She had missed her period. It was two weeks late; she was pregnant. She would be an unmarried mother. There could be nothing more shameful. What would her father say of the disgrace of being an unmarried mother? What would Sergei say? And at the same time she was pleased that she was expecting Philip's baby; that she had proof of their love growing inside her. Philip smiled at her.

'How's your father?'

'Sleeping.' She paused. 'I have something to tell you.'

He looked up at her.

'Do you love me?'

Philip laughed. 'What do you think?' and he smiled broadly at her, wondering the purpose of the question.

'That's not an answer,' she said without looking at him, nervously biting her lip.

Philip had learned that when Sophie bit her lip she had something important to say, so he gave her his full attention.

'What's on your mind?'

Sophie knew she had to tell him she was pregnant. Her belly would soon start to grow; he would be sure to notice. She couldn't understand why she hadn't told him before now, but with all their troubles this was only going to add another problem.

'I'm pregnant,' she blurted out. *There, it was done.*

Philip smiled and stood up, wrapped his arms around her waist and pulled her close to him. She didn't resist.

'I know,' he said.

'How do you know?' she asked, shocked.

'You're sick most mornings, you keep holding your tummy and look distracted at times and then you just smile for no reason. But I thought I would wait until you told me.'

'Are you upset?'

Philip smiled. 'Why should I be? The woman I love and want to spend the rest of my life with is expecting my baby – my opening batsman. I'm the happiest man alive.'

Sophie wrapped her arms around him and hugged him tight. 'I was afraid you might abandon me as a fallen woman and not want to marry me.'

'I love the thought of you being a fallen woman. So very daring, so very revolutionary.'

'I will have to tell my father and Sergei,' she said.

Philip sat her in a chair. 'I think that we should do things in the right order. I'll ask his permission to marry you and then we'll do that as soon as we can.'

That afternoon Philip carried the wheelchair upstairs and to the Count's bedroom. Then Philip carried Sergei upstairs so that the three of them could see the old Count. Sergei in his wheelchair on one side and Sophie on the other and Philip stood at the end of the bed. The old man's breath rasped and his face was grey, but he smiled as he recognised his children and held out a hand. Sophie took it and patted it gently.

Philip coughed and the man looked at him.

'Count, I'm sorry to disturb you but I've come to ask for your daughter's hand in marriage. I'm very much in love with her, and wish to protect her all my life.'

The old man looked at his daughter, who smiled at him and nodded.

Looking back at Philip, he said, 'My daughter's told me much about you.' He paused to catch his breath. 'How you helped her... the care you've shown my son. These are difficult times... I've told my daughter that... it will be difficult to wait for a suitable Russian husband. She could die of old age.'

Looking at Sophie, he asked between gulps of air, 'You love him?'

She nodded.

'Then you have my blessing... on two conditions. My daughter remains... Orthodox... and... my grandchildren... the same... do you agree?'

'I do,' promised Philip.

The man raised his hand and placed it on his daughter's head. She kissed him on the forehead.

'Leave us,' he said to Philip. 'I want time with my children.'

Philip bowed his head, turned and left. He returned to the study, elated and all he wanted to do was to dance for joy. Nevertheless he composed himself and took out a map book from one of the shelves and settled down to study it. It was late when Philip looked up from the map, rubbed his tired eyes and caught a glimpse of his reflection in the mirror at the far end of the room. The man that stared back at him was almost unrecognisable. His usually neat hair had grown over his ears and his collar; his eyes had dark rings underneath; and his beard was showing some grey. What could Sophie possibly see in this old man? he wondered. He rose to go to his room and shave.

Sophie and Sergei looked at their father, propped up on soft pillows. He looked tired and old, his eyes were cloudy and they had lost the brilliance Sophie remembered when she had been a child. Sergei held his father's hand and thought how large and strong it was. He carefully studied the thick fingers and milky moons at the base of his nails, the liver spots and the signet ring on his little finger that glistened in the candlelight.

'I'm so very proud of you both... your mother... and you have made my life so joyful... so very happy.'

'Don't speak, you'll tire yourself,' said Sophie.

The old Count smiled. 'Russia's changed... things will... will never be the same again.' He sighed. 'I'm tired now, so very tired,' and closed his eyes.

His two children smiled at each other and a tear ran down Sophie's cheek.

Twenty minutes passed. The Count's breathing started to become more laboured, the pauses between breaths longer. Sophie raised a hand to her mouth to stifle a sob and Sergei continued to hold his father's hand.

There was a sharp intake of breath, the old Count exhaled slowly and was still.

Neither child moved as they looked at their father, waiting and hoping for another breath, but none came. Sophie began to weep and after a few minutes Sergei noticed that his father's hand was becoming cooler.

Philip, now shaved, was looking at his transformation in the study mirror as Sophie entered the room. Her face was tear-stained and Philip knew that her father was dead. With her arms around him and her face pressed tightly against his chest, she wept. They stayed like that for many minutes until finally she unwrapped herself and silently placed her hand in his and together they walked upstairs to join Sergei and Helena. The pillows and bedclothes had been straightened and a couple of candles in large candlesticks placed on either side of the bed. The lights flickered on the silver covering the icons. The old Count looked peaceful, and he held a gold cross to his chest. Helena curtsied as Sophie and Philip entered, before leaving the house to fetch the priest.

# Chapter Eleven: A funeral

As Head of Colonial Finances, Neville was working at his desk at the Bank of England when the tea tray was brought in and placed on the mahogany side table. The tea was his special blend, from the three best tea-growing regions of India: Assam, Darjeeling and Nilgiri. Having Fortnum & Mason recreate the blend was expensive, but a luxury he afforded himself. It produced a medium-bodied black tea. The Assam gave it a strong body, lightened by the Darjeeling, and the Nilgiri provided a unique taste and aroma. It was the same blend his parents had drunk when his father worked under the Chief Commissioner in Baluchistan when the Earl of Dufferin was Viceroy in India.

Twice a day the Indian servants would collect him from the nursery to have tea with his parents. His father would tell him of his important work at the colonial office and his mother would complain about the heat, the flies, the hornets and the servants – generally in that order.

Rising from his desk, he limped over to the sideboard and poured the golden liquid from the solid silver teapot, through the strainer and into the porcelain cup and saucer. It was a ritual he enjoyed. His childhood memories of India were vivid. As part of the white aristocracy he'd become accustomed to servants and luxuries, the idyllic atmosphere of protection and privilege.

In India none of the servants would have dared to mention the congenital *talipes equinovarus*, the deformation that made his foot turn inward; the club foot the doctors had tried and failed to 'cure' with a metal brace. The foot that made him look as if he were walking on his ankle. At nine years old he'd been sent home to England and to school to be educated. No longer the white aristocracy, he had had to suffer jibes and name calling from his fellow pupils.

How many nights had he spent in bed in his dormitory praying to God to release him from his burden? After all, didn't Matthew 7:8 say, 'For every one that asketh receiveth, and he that seeketh findeth, and to him that knocks it shall be opened'? But each morning he awoke to find his prayers remained unanswered. Unable to excel on the playing field, he hid himself in his books, particularly the Bible. He took comfort in the judgements that Moses visited on the Egyptians, the destruction of the tribe of Korah and the sons of Izhar, as recounted in the Book of Numbers: 'And the earth opened her mouth, and swallowed them up, and their houses, and all their men that appertained unto Korah, and all their goods.' Neville knew that the war had been God's revenge for man's arrogance and at its end many more men would understand, as he did, the meaning of suffering.

He took a sip of tea as Edward entered his office.

'I've come to deliver these files to you. They were brought to my office instead of yours,' he said and walked over to Neville's desk. As Edward placed the files on the blotter he noticed a note atop a pile of papers. He picked it up.

IN PETROGRAD STOP SITUATION COMPLICATED STOP WHAT INSTRUCTIONS STOP CUMMINGS

'This is a telegraph from Russia, from Philip. When did it arrive?'

'Months ago. It's in that pile of papers to be thrown away,' replied Neville matter-of-factly.

'But why didn't you mention it?'

'There didn't seem much point until we heard more. The telegraph was posted before the revolution – when it arrived the situation had become worse. We haven't heard anything since. Besides, what instructions or even help could we have given him? I think it's best we don't say anything about it to anyone else. We don't want to raise people's hopes, only to have them dashed later. He's fit, healthy and, if God wills it, he'll be back soon enough. If not, then things will go on as they are.'

120

'I suppose you're right,' said Edward hesitantly.

To ensure Edward's silence Neville added, 'We don't want any nastiness in the bank… we wouldn't want any risk of your dirty little secret becoming known…'

Edward blanched and left the office. Neville limped over to the desk, picked up the telegram, screwed it into a ball and dropped it into the waste bin.

## Moscow

Sophie, Sergei and Philip followed the coffin to the church a few hundred yards from the house. As was the tradition, the casket was open and the Count had been dressed in a plain grey morning suit. There were no flowers but Sophie had cut three white roses from the bush that grew over the arch that led into the garden and had given one each to her brother and Philip.

The three of them, the priest and the four pallbearers were the only mourners. That was, except for the small crowd of people watching the proceedings from the edge of the cemetery.

The priest chanted the prayers for the dead: 'Remember, O Lord, our parents and brethren who have fallen asleep and all those who have ended their lives in piety and faith…'

Sophie and Sergei heard little of the prayers, as their thoughts were of their father. They were numb. Sophie looked over at the group of people at the edge of the cemetery. She presumed they were her father's employees and, though she didn't recognise any of them, she thought how kind it was that they should come to say farewell.

'… the repose of thy servants who have fallen asleep, O Christ our God, and we render glory to Thee, with Thine eternal father, and with Thine all-holy, gracious and life-giving spirit, now and forever and unto ages of ages. Amen.' The priest sprinkled holy water over the body. Sophie remembered Helena's words about people stealing from graves. She let go of Sergei's hand and walked over to the crowd. The priest stopped chanting.

Sophie stopped in front of the group and addressed the onlookers. 'Thank you for coming,' she said. 'I know it's usual that a small icon of Christ and a gold cross are left in the casket, but I can tell you now that my father's coffin has no such treasures.'

The group just looked at her. Nobody moved.

'Come, have a look inside the coffin if you don't believe me.'

Still no one moved.

'Does no one want to look?' she challenged them again.

They stared back. Sophie wasn't sure they had even heard her.

'Then you can leave my father buried; there's nothing to be had.' She returned to the coffin and clasped Sergei's hand again.

The priest concluded the short service, the mourners placed the three white roses inside the coffin, the lid was hammered in place and the coffin lowered into place by the grave-diggers.

They waited as the grave was filled with earth and finally Sergei said, 'Let's go back to the house,' and they left in silence.

At the far end of the cemetery, watching the service from under a tree, was a lone figure in a greatcoat and cloth cap. He'd watched the small group, heard the short service for the dead, heard Sophie challenge the crowd and seen the priest hurry away. Once the cemetery was empty he walked over to the grave and looked down at the mound of fresh earth. He didn't stay long, just long enough to promise his father he would ensure that his brother and sister left Russia before the terror began.

****

When Sophie and Sergei arrived at the short driveway to their home and saw people carrying chairs from the house. Sophie ran to the front door. 'What's going on?'

A man with a thick scar down one cheek and the leather apron of a cobbler replied, 'Comrade, your father's dead, he's been buried and this house has been reallocated.'

Another man told her, 'It's all legal. In accordance with the instructions from the People's Soviet, this house has been given to the people.'

Sophie rushed into the house, followed by Sergei, Philip pushing his chair as fast as he could, to see strangers carrying their furniture, plates and fine linen in the hallway and to places in the house where the items didn't belong.

'What's happening to our things?' Sophie demanded of a large, pale-faced bear of a man standing in the hallway wearing a grey overcoat, a thick brown belt with a pistol tucked into it and a red armband on his left arm.

'Comrades,' he addressed the three of them. 'The Moscow Soviet has declared that this house is too large for one family. You have twenty rooms and the house has been reassigned to needy families, families that your class oppressed.'

'We didn't oppress anyone,' shouted Sophie angrily.

The man ignored her remark. 'However, you're lucky because the comrade here,' he pointed to Sergei, 'is wounded from the war and that entitles you to an extra room. You have four rooms allocated for you on the ground floor. As for your possessions, they are being redistributed.'

The four rooms they had been allocated were the drawing room, the study, the library and the family dining room. As they entered the study they saw Helena surrounded by possessions she had rescued from bedrooms and other parts of the house.

'Oh, my lady, I'm so sorry. I couldn't stop them.'

'Don't worry,' said Sophie. 'I know.' And she hugged her.

'I did manage to save some things from your dressing chest as well as the master's dress studs and the picture of your father that was beside your bed table…' She dissolved into tears.

Sophie comforted her and looked around at the jumble on the floor.

Just then, two men in knee-length boots and green uniforms entered and dropped Sophie's dresses on the floor. They then walked over to a pile of books and started to carry them from the room.

'Where are you taking our books?' cried Sergei.

Without looking at them, the first man replied, 'These books are being confiscated. They are bad for the mind.'

'But that's our family Bible,' said Sergei, indicating the large leather-bound book at the bottom of the pile.

'It's degenerate and confiscated,' said the man as he walked away.

'Philip, take me to the library please,' said Sergei angrily.

The library floor was littered with papers and books, and tables were overturned. On the floor in front of the large desk lay two pictures torn from their – now absent – silver frames. One was of their father by himself and the other was a picture of their father with Prince Felix Youssoupov, the former Governor of Moscow and the father of the man who had killed Rasputin.

Sophie walked into the room, gasped and then walked into the mess and picked up a photograph. 'My father treasured this picture of Felix Youssoupov. They worked very closely together when the Prince was Governor of Moscow. The Youssoupovs are such a nice family.'

Just then a small group of people appeared at the door. A man walked in and they watched in silence as he approached the mantelpiece, removed the marble cased clock and walked towards the door.

'Stop!' Sophie shouted. 'That's a valuable clock.'

'You have one, you don't need two,' sneered the man gruffly, motioning to a small carriage clock on the side table.

Sophie smiled at him. 'It'll only be valuable if it keeps working. You don't want it to stop and be worthless, do you?'

The man paused to think, and watched Sophie as she went to a small bowl on a bookshelf, extracted a brass key and returned with it to the man.

'Use this key once every three days to wind the clock like so' – inserting the key into the aperture in the face and pretending to turn it. 'Give the key three turns and it will keep perfect time. You have a good eye for something valuable; it's an excellent choice and I'm delighted it's going to someone who appreciates fine things.'

The man beamed a smile. 'Thank you, comrade,' he said and proudly marched from the room to show this valuable possession to his wife and children.

Once alone, Sophie and Sergei began to laugh helplessly. Philip was confused by their mirth. He couldn't see what was so funny.

Sophie explained. 'The clock was a gift to Father from a cloth supplier. Its chime is meant to remind one of the Kremlin's cathedral bells. It's so loud that Father banished it in here because he said it could wake the dead saints. It'll chime every hour; they'll not sleep at all.'

'Father is having his revenge on our new neighbours,' said Sergei and they all laughed.

Over the next two days the three of them tidied the rooms as best they could. Sophie pleaded for some of her father's personal possessions to be returned to them, and this was eventually done. Sophie and Sergei recognised that many of the people now living in the house were old retainers. They had fared much better working for the family than those who worked for other employers in the city. Now without the work that the factory brought they were poorer than before. They may be liberated, all comrades together, but nevertheless they were poorer.

With so many people living there, the house was now very noisy and cold. People shouted, children ran around the corridors, babies cried and the front door was opened and closed all through the day and night. A committee of residents was set up to manage the house, a committee which didn't include any of the original residents. The committee allocated times to use the kitchen and bathroom to every family. Sophie learned that leaving a pot with food cooking on the stove meant that pot and food alike were unlikely to still be there upon her return. The house began to take on the odour of boiled cabbage, sweat and urine. Many of the new residents relieved themselves against any corner of the room or landing. Soiled clothing hung everywhere, and the marble floor in the hallway soon became covered in a thick layer of mud.

One morning the house committee posted a cleaning rota on the front door. Sophie was required to clean the hall floor two days a week. It was evident that she had more tasks allocated to her than anyone else, and Philip was angry at the injustice. 'I'll go and tell the committee that it's not right,' he said.

'There's no point; they're getting their revenge on us. They want to see us work and show them that we can't cope with it. If we complain, we just prove that we are lazy and good for nothing. If that happens, we could end up cleaning the streets like the others I've seen, and that looks much worse as people shout abuse at you. No, I'll do the work and I'll do it perfectly,' she said.

On the day Sophie was to clean the hallway floor, a bucket of water and a hard brush appeared in the hall. Sophie donned a thick skirt and apron borrowed from Helena. As she arrived at the bottom of the stairs she looked up and saw residents leaning over the banisters and watching from open doors, and a group of eight children sat at the bottom of the stairs resting their heads on their hands.

*They don't think I know what to do. I'll show them.* Looking at her audience she rolled her sleeves up to the elbow then began by sweeping the dirt into a corner near the front door, where she would dispose of it later. Then she knelt, took a knife from her apron pocket and started to scrape away the stubborn bits of grease and wax that had stuck to the marble floor and which would never be removed by a brush alone. Seeing her do this, a number of women nodded to each other and left the throng to go about their business.

Despite the fact that people continued to walk all over the hallway, Sophie removed all the grease spots and then, without pausing to rest, washed and scrubbed the tiles and finally mopped up the water up with a cloth. Her face was running with sweat at the exertion but she refused to wipe away the droplets in case anyone in the audience thought the work too hard for her.

More people began to get bored of watching a floor being cleaned – there was nothing to entertain them, and they drifted away to go about their own chores. After an hour Sophie had managed to clean the whole floor. Then she produced a cloth covered in polish from her apron to buff the floor. When she had finished, the marble shone. The only people watching her were the children at the bottom of the stairs.

When she returned to the study, Philip was waiting with a hot cup of tea. 'I'm so proud of you, but when did you learn how to clean a marble floor?'

She slumped into one of the chairs. 'When I was little I used to watch the maid do it first thing in the morning, and I just copied what she had done. I showed them, didn't I?'

The next time she cleaned the floor there were barely a dozen onlookers, and within an hour no one was interested – even the children had disappeared to find something more entertaining to look at.

On the third day of her allocated work she took the rubbish to the communal rubbish tip. There was the clock from the mantelpiece, smashed, lying on the top of the pile. She looked at it dispassionately. So many wanted a better life; so many thought they would have a better life if they had more possessions; and yet when they had what they desired, it often turned out to be so much less than they had hoped. She turned away from the pile of rubbish and went back to the house.

Having discussed their situation, Sergei and Philip always greeted their neighbours kindly and with a smile. At first no one smiled back but, after a few weeks, a few of the older women smiled back in return, feeling sorry for the wounded soldier and the sister who looked after him. Then younger members of the house passed a few words with them, and soon everyone smiled at them. Then one morning a woman gave Sophie a small sausage. 'For your sick brother,' she whispered and hurried away before any of the others saw what she had done.

Philip would take Sergei for walks and for fresh air for about an hour or two each day. They always ensured that there was someone in their rooms to protect what possessions they had left, particularly as everyone in the house was told that locking their doors could lead to being charged with plotting counter-revolutionary activities. This meant that at any time people would open their doors and look into their rooms to see what they were doing; children, particularly, would spend a minute or two at the door just watching them. Then one day Philip became annoyed at one teenager who just stared at them from the doorway.

'Why don't you come in and we can talk?'

The boy fled, terrified.

After that, whenever anyone looked into the room they were warmly invited in. It had the desired effect: they all fled as if afraid of being caught fraternising with the enemies of the revolution. Among the four of them, it became a game to see how long a 'guest' dared stay, and they would wager matchsticks on the outcome.

This routine of communal work, exercise for Sergei and walks continued day after day, week after week. It was on these walks that they all noticed how smartly dressed merchants and former Tsarist officers were being forced into selling their possessions to survive – fur coats, small pieces of silver and jewellery. People who had never needed to work now had to learn how to, so that they were eligible for a small ration of food. They learned how to cook, wash dishes, sweep the streets and some even learned how to steal, all for food. The number of prostitutes had also increased and, simply from what they wore it was obvious that many were from privileged families.

So far we have been lucky, but the longer we stay, the more likely it is we'll have to do the same, thought Philip.

# Chapter Twelve: The arrival of Anatoily Snetkov

## October 1918

In a large room in the Kremlin the man now known as Fadeyka, meaning 'brave', was looking through a carefully compiled list of people. The seven hundred and twenty-two names on twenty pages were all enemies of the revolution. Included were grand dukes, princes, counts, their servants, priests, civil servants, writers, authors and intellectuals – in fact, anyone Fadeyka and the Central Committee considered a class enemy. The papers only included the class enemies known to be in Moscow, but soon every city would have their own list.

Fadeyka had been a revolutionary ever since he'd escaped the attentions of the *Okhrana*, the Tsarist secret police. Like many of his fellow citizens, he wanted to sweep away the privileged classes. It might have surprised some that he wasn't a peasant. In fact, his family were privileged by being wealthy, but he justified the contradiction by saying that, as a patriot, he had to fight for the people.

There were many people of his class who had joined the revolution – some out of ambition, others out of ideology, a few wanting to be part of history, some out of a kind of snobbery. Even Lenin himself was entitled to be called 'Your Excellency' but no one dared point this out to him. Fadeyka had joined the struggle when the revolution was a hopeless cause, when no one thought that they would succeed, and when hunger had gnawed at his insides.

He had realised why the revolution was so important when he had heard Lenin's speech. It was at that moment he understood the struggle that had been raging in his mind since he was a child.

Lenin's words were branded into his consciousness: 'Capitalism is just a stage of society... it has led to the concentration of social classes into two major groups. The proletariat, those who must work to survive and who make up a majority of society... then there is the bourgeoisie, a minority who gain their profit from the private ownership of the proletariat's production... the conflict between both groups will ultimately lead to the capture of political power by the proletariat. Public ownership and management of production will be established. All goods and services will be made freely available to the people. The result must be the disappearance of social classes and money and replaced with communism: a stateless, class-less and moneyless society, structured upon the common ownership.'

In any event, thought Fadeyka of the class struggle, as Trotsky had said to him, 'What's the point in belonging to a class that's destined for the dustbin of history?'

After years of hardship, the time had finally arrived: he'd travelled with Lenin to Petrograd and stood next to him as he had spoken to the crowds. He knew then that the revolution would bring them power. He worked tirelessly with the Central Committee to maintain that hold on power. Unlike many of his comrades, he never feared that they would be swept away. He knew only too well that the Bolsheviks needed two things to stay in power. The first was money and the second was the destruction of the old regime, to destroy the privileged classes so that they could never be a threat to the revolution.

Fadeyka worked unstintingly with Lenin and the others on the Central Committee to draft over thirty decrees national-ising private industry, manufacturing, the banks and credit institutions. Bank vaults and the safety deposit boxes of the wealthy classes were opened and the contents confiscated; private houses were inspected and anything that might be of value to the state and the common good was confiscated.

Since he'd helped to establish the 'State Treasury for the storage of valuables' (*Gokhran*), it had confiscated nearly fifty million roubles' worth of art, precious metals and gemstones, nearly half a ton of gold bullion, platinum and gold coins into the state's custody. Having collected the money to support the revolution, he now turned his attention towards those that might seek to destroy it: the bourgeoisie.

He walked down the corridor to Lenin's office at the exact time for his appointment. He had learned from many years in exile that Lenin had little patience for distractions, and a raging temper if disturbed. Even his telephone had been modified so that it had a light bulb on top rather than a bell.

Fadeyka was shown into Lenin's office by a secretary. He stood in front of the desk and watched as Lenin finished making notes in his notebook. He looked around the room and smiled when he saw the *No smoking* sign on the wall. Lenin would not tolerate smoking, an aversion that Stalin complained of whenever they had a long meeting. The bookshelves were filled with works such as *Women in Modern Industry*, *The New Japanese Peril* and *Cooperation in Danish Agriculture*. Fedeyka loved this man almost as much as he loved his own father. The difference was that Lenin was alive and leading the revolution while he had said goodbye to his father, part of the old regime, at his graveside a few weeks before.

Lenin took the list from him and gave it a cursory glance. The front page contained all the people one would expect: the grand dukes, grand duchesses, princes, counts and barons. He looked briefly at the other pages and then turned to the final page. 'I see that Count Sergei Tagleva and his sister are at the bottom of the last page.'

'You'll remember that the Count donated one hundred pounds to the revolution when we were in London, comrade. That money paid for a reprint of your pamphlet, "What is to be done?"'

'I hadn't forgotten his contribution. As far as I recall, he was an intelligent man who thought us all mad – far too good-looking to be a good revolutionary. Your list is approved.'

Lenin handed back the list and returned to writing in his notebook.

As he walked down the corridor, Fadeyka said to himself, 'There, my brother, I've kept my promise to save you from being shot – for the time being.'

\*\*\*\*

During the relative quiet of the evenings in their rooms Philip, Sophie and Sergei would spend the time planning how they might escape Moscow without being noticed by the people living in the house, who, they suspected, had been told to watch everything they did and report it to the house supervisor.

'We can't go back to Petrograd and then to Finland,' Philip explained. 'The White Army's ravaging the countryside. The rumours are that people who flee to Finland are being arrested by the Whites, who assume that all refugees are Red spies and shoot them on sight. Staying in Moscow is not an option; food is becoming scarcer and arrests are increasing. My feeling is we should go south to the Ukraine and try to get a ship to Greece.'

'Father used to take us there for holidays, to a place near Yalta called Koreiz. We have some friends there who I'm sure would help us,' said Sophie.

Sergei spoke. 'I know it's time to find another home. England or France would be my choice, but I've been thinking that you would travel faster and more safely without me. I think you two should leave me and flee as fast as you can. I'm afraid I'll be a burden to you and, besides, no one will suspect for a long time that you've gone if they see me about the house.'

Sophie hit the table with her fist and whispered through gritted teeth so that she wouldn't be heard outside the room. 'Stop being brave. I need both of you! We all travel together or not at all.'

'I agree,' said Philip. 'No one's going to be left behind; we'll be safer together than apart. So let's agree on our plan. I found that small gardener's shed near the back entrance. Except for some sacking it's empty; no one seems to visit it. When Sergei and I go for our afternoon walks we could take some clothes and other small items and hide them in the shed. It means when we do leave we won't have to carry bags out of the house. Anything like that would immediately cause suspicion. We would only be able to take one bag each and a little food for the journey, but we could get to the train station without being seen.'

Sergei smiled. 'It's a good idea. When we get to England we'll need money. I think it's time to show Philip Father's special place.'

Sophie rose and walked to one of the two marble pillars at the end of the room and, bending down, pushed a panel of marble around the base of the Corinthian column. It sprang open and she turned the panel upwards and slid it to the right to reveal a large secret compartment.

Philip's jaw dropped open. He would never have guessed that the column could contain a false compartment. The panel was cleverly disguised by the pattern of the pink marble.

Without removing anything Sophie quickly shut the panel in case anyone came into the room.

Sergei whispered an explanation to Philip. 'After the Moscow riots in 1905 my father built some safes in the house. There's one in his dressing room, but that's almost empty. We couldn't get to it anyway because that's the room with those three kids. The one in this room holds some gold five-rouble coins and some loose diamonds as well as some of Mother's best jewellery. They should be able to finance us for a short time in England.'

'I can turn the diamonds into buttons by sewing cloth over them and replacing all the buttons on our clothes, and the rouble pieces can be put into the soles of our shoes and into the bottom seams of jackets and coats,' said Sophie.

Sergei looked down at his chair. 'The seat of my wheelchair and the arms would hold a lot, and it would be unlikely that anyone would check if I was sitting in the thing.'

Quickly Philip cautioned, 'If we cut into the leather it would be difficult to match the colour, and that could make someone suspect that something was hidden under it. Let's leave the chair as it is and use it as a last resort.'

Much to Philip's relief, the other two could see the sense of that.

Over the next few days Sophie spent every waking moment unpicking her mother's jewels from their settings, covering the larger stones in cloth and sewing them as buttons onto their clothes. She unpicked the hems of underclothes and sewed small diamonds or gold coins into them. She even unpicked a corset and replaced the whalebone with gemstones, and sewed gold coins into belts and the cuffs of coats. Even an old hat was given a decoration of a cloth flower, the centre of which was a ruby covered in two layers of black cotton.

When Sophie completed one garment Philip and Sergei would go for a walk and deposit the finished clothes in the gardener's hut. No one in the hallway noticed that Sergei sat on a small cushion of clothing and that his height changed with each trip.

One afternoon they returned to the house to find a commotion in the hallway. A large group of people surrounded two women who were arguing. Two soldiers with bayonets fixed to their rifles held back the residents. In the centre was a man in a long greatcoat with a red armband. One of the women was accusing the other of stealing flour from her ration. They both denounced the other as a counter-revolutionary. The man with the armband lost patience and shouted for quiet.

'I don't have time for this stupidity. If you can't look after your provisions properly, I'll confiscate them and give them to more needy people and clear this house and send you all to a work camp.'

At the mention of the work camp the crowd quickly dispersed. Within seconds the hallway was empty.

Philip wheeled Sergei into their rooms, and the man followed.

The three of them looked at him framed in the doorway. He approached Sergei and stood in front of him. He pulled off the blanket covering Sergei's leg. Sophie gave a gasp and Philip took a pace forward to help Sergei. He stopped when he saw a pistol was pointed squarely at his chest.

Without taking his eyes off Philip the man spoke. 'Count Sergei Michaelovich Tagleva! I thought you must be dead!'

Hearing the man use her brother's full name, Sophie stared. No one spoke. He was a thick-set man with a handsome face that made him look younger than he probably was. His high cheekbones, olive skin and dark hair were in contrast to his blue eyes. The dark red scar running from his left temple to his jawbone, caused by a German bayonet, gave him a sinister look.

'You are English,' said the man to Philip. It was a statement of fact, not a question, and Philip thought it best not to lie.

'Yes. My name is Philip Cummings,' said Philip.

'What are you doing in Moscow?'

'I was sent here by my government to help the Russian government in their struggle with the Germans,' Philip exaggerated.

'The Imperial government fell months ago. I assume that the fact you're still in Russia means that you're a spy?'

'Not at all,' replied Philip. 'I work for the Bank of England and was trapped in Russia by the war and subsequently by the revolution.'

'What business did the Bank of England have with the government?'

'We were arranging letters of credit for food, medicines and other goods to be sent by my government to help with the Russian war effort,' Philip lied.

'Bullets, more like, to shoot more peasants with,' came the reply.

'No, it was for medicines and food.' Philip decided further discussion would only result in an argument, and resolved to remain silent.

Without lowering the pistol, the man looked down at Sergei. 'So what say you, Sergei Michaelovich?'

Sergei looked up. 'He's a kind, generous man. It's as he explained – he's here because of the help he's given to me and my family.'

The pistol was lowered and placed in the brown leather holster on the man's belt. 'Then, Count, as I've always known you to be an honest man, I accept your word. How are you, my friend?' The man bent down to kiss Sergei on both cheeks in the Russian manner.

Philip and Sophie exchanged glances. This sudden and unexpected change in atmosphere had surprised them, and they watched as the soldier retrieved the rug from the floor and placed it carefully over Sergei's leg.

'I should introduce myself,' said the soldier, looking at Sophie. 'I'm Anatoily Snetkov.' He looked at Sergei but spoke to Sophie. 'I heard you had returned from Petrograd and as your brother saved me from a mortar shell in the trenches and as a consequence finds himself like this, I wanted to pay my respects.'

'It was *you* that he saved!' said Sophie.

'It was,' said the man, looking at Sophie and smiling. 'I was temporarily blinded in no-man's land when your brother crawled through the mud to rescue me and pulled me into a shell hole. Just as we reached safety a shell exploded next to us and Sergei had his leg blown off. It was then my turn to save my commanding officer, and together we crawled the last few hundred yards to safety with your brother using his eyes to guide me. Even though he was in great pain, he saved us both, and I live today because of your brother.'

At the end of the account Anatoily looked at Philip. 'I've had a report of a foreigner in this house, and I wanted to investigate it myself.' He walked towards the door. 'Englishman, because of your help to this wounded soldier I won't arrest you today, but I suggest you make plans to leave Russia – and very soon. Situations have a habit of changing, and not always for the better.'

He opened the door and left.

Philip sat down and let out a long breath to relieve the tension he felt.

That night, over a dinner of thin soup and black bread, they discussed the visit.

'His message was unambiguous,' said Philip. 'I'm a danger to you and you would be safer if I left.'

'We've had this discussion already. If you leave, then we all leave,' said Sophie. 'In any event, our father's dead, our house has been confiscated, our possessions stolen, we have no business as it's run by a Workers' Committee and we have no means of supporting ourselves. There's no reason for us to stay and if we remain we will be in increasing danger. It's all or nothing,' she said and Sergei knew that once her mind was made up there was no changing her.

That same afternoon Anatoily Snetkov returned to the house.

Sophie and Philip were shocked to see him and initially feared that he'd come to arrest Philip. Instead he handed them travel documents to the Ukraine on health grounds for Sergei. Both Philip and Sophie were included in the documents as family carers.

'Leave within the next twelve hours,' said Anatoily and, turning to Sergei, went on, 'My friend, this now repays any debt I owe you for saving my life, but if you fail to travel within the next twelve hours you should know that I've orders to arrest you all for associating with and aiding the state's enemies.'

He looked hard at Philip. The message was clear to the three of them.

Walking to the door he came to attention, gave Sergei a final salute and left the room.

Anatoily walked over the road and spoke to the man who had been waiting for him in the street. 'It's done. They'll leave tomorrow.'

'Thank you, comrade,' said Sacha Tagleva, also known as Fadeyka.

# Chapter Thirteen: Feeling homesick

## October 1918

Edward Lascelles, Neville Porter and the Deputy Governor were in the boardroom at the Bank of England. There was only one piece of business to be considered: the death of the Tsar and the deposits held in the triple-locked safe deep in the basement.

Since Philip had been reported missing, his work at the Bank of England had been shared between Neville Porter, who was looking after any Russian affairs, and Edward Lascelles, who was undertaking the rest of Philip's work.

Neville had very little extra work to do, and would say, to anyone who would listen, that 'Cummings had carved out for himself a larger job than was merited by the amount of work involved. I manage to do in a couple of hours what he would take a week to do. Rather typical of the man, I'm finding. As it says in the good book, "Thou wilt say then, the branches were broken off, that I, Neville, might be grafted in".'

The female clerks recruited to replace the men fighting at the front didn't know Philip well and so assumed that Neville's assessment must be correct.

Edward, on the other hand, missed his friend. He often looked at the photograph of Philip – the official photograph the bank had commissioned to be given to the newspapers if needed, the one Edward had rescued from the waste paper basket and kept in a silver frame in the top right-hand drawer of his desk at home. If ever people asked about Philip, Edward said, 'A brilliant mind; able to assess a situation better than anyone I know.'

However, as time passed and Philip's absence grew longer, Edward recognised that looking after Philip's portfolio meant a promotion, of sorts. If Philip never returned, he would be in a perfect position to advance his career. The result would mean a better salary, greater status and, in time, could even lead to a seat on the executive board. Despite this, he missed his evenings out with Philip, the meals at Rules in Covent Garden, the evenings playing bridge, the intellectual conversations and the visits to the opera.

Neville opened the meeting. 'The information coming out of Russia is extremely confused, with the exception of one thing: that Tsar Nicholas has been executed. The Russian government says that the Empress and her children have been sent to a place of safety. Unofficial reports, however, say that the whole family's been killed. We do know that the White Army's captured Yekaterinburg where the family was imprisoned and found a lot of their personal belongings as well as a room covered in blood and bullet holes. The Whites have set up a team of people to investigate the facts.'

'So can we assume that the Tsar is dead?' said the Governor.

'I think we can,' replied Neville.

'Assuming, then, that the Tsar is dead, what should be our position as far as the deposits we hold?'

Before Neville had time to give an opinion Edward interrupted. 'If we believe that the Tsar's dead then the usual procedure applies. The account is frozen until proper ownership can be established. Once the Tsar's death has been confirmed, the assets belong to his wife or children and all they have to do is to present themselves at the bank, in person or via a legal representative.'

Neville, more than slightly irritated at the interruption, continued. 'In this case I feel the situation is more complex. The question is, are these assets the personal property of the Romanov family, or do they belong to the Russian state? If they belong to the state then we must wait until the new government of Russia is recognised by the British government. If, on the other hand, they belong to the Romanov family then they are the property of his wife and children – but if the entire family has been killed then ownership becomes much more complicated.'

Before anyone had time to interrupt again, Neville continued. 'If details of the deposits became public knowledge and the entire family is dead, then we can expect claims from all sorts of people, including distant relatives and even people who will claim to be relatives. There is even the possibility that claims would be made by the Empress's family in Hesse-Darmstadt or by the British Royal Family. I feel we should deny any knowledge of the Tsar's account until the situation becomes clearer.'

The Governor rubbed his chin in thought. 'An excellent suggestion, Neville. The bank will deny it holds any deposits for the Tsar until we can be sure of the survival of a member of the family or the rights of ownership. That'll be our policy until things become clear.'

Neville was pleased with the result of the meeting. As planned, the Tsar's account would remain a secret. He was tempted to pick up a telephone and have an immediate conversation with his contact, but there was always a danger that a switchboard operator might listen in. Frustrated by the necessary delay, he said to himself, 'The telephone's only thirty years old; a great invention but as a communication tool it's not confidential enough. Better when one could seal an envelope and have a post boy deliver it in the sure knowledge that the contents would only be read by the recipient.'

Once the meeting broke up Edward returned to Philip's office, the one he'd moved into the day after he had been given the responsibility for all of Philip's work outside Russia. He wondered where Philip was and if he had been killed in the revolution. He did miss his friend, and thought of him often in quiet moments. He worked hard to ensure that his superiors were pleased with his work, but opportunities had to be grasped. Unlike Neville, he couldn't use an accident of birth to gain position or power.

In the past, other opportunities had presented themselves. Like the time he became aware that a colleague was arranging for a takeover of a company and he purchased a great number of shares the day before the announcement. When they rose the following day, he sold them at a handsome profit.

Then there was the time, at the very start of his career, when he agreed a loan to a wine merchant so that he could expand the business. The business was well run, the wine merchant's business plan was a good one and the loan seemed prudent. A few months later he was approached by a competing business-man who persuaded Edward that they could both benefit if the loan was recalled and further credit was denied. Unable to fund the planned expansion, the business collapsed and the wine merchant went bankrupt. The business was bought by the competing wine merchant for a fraction of its real value, and Edward received almost three years' salary for his trou-bles. It was not a time he was proud of, and sometimes he had a sleepless hour or two when he remembered it, but they had all been opportunities.

Philip's absence was another opportunity. His prospects at the bank had vastly improved, though he did miss Philip. He hadn't eaten at Rules for months; Philip had always picked up the bill.

## The Tagleva House, Moscow

Philip and Sergei greeted a couple of the people they knew in the hallway and left the house at their usual time. Twenty minutes later Sophie also left the house, saying to Helena that she was going out to look for food. Many weeks had passed since Philip, Sergei and Sophie had begun to make their escape plans and anyone looking at them on this particular morning might think that they had all put on a little weight, as each was wearing two layers of underclothes, two shirts and a jacket as well as a heavy coat.

Leaving the steadfast housekeeper without so much as a goodbye made Sophie feel disloyal, but they'd agreed it was for the best. The less she knew, the less she could be blamed for. Sophie insisted on leaving a few gold roubles in the small wooden trunk that Helena used to keep her clothes and added to them the gold and pearl brooch in the shape of a bow that Helena so admired.

They met up at the gardener's shed and picked up the three small valises they had packed the previous night. Philip had arranged for a delivery truck to take them to the railway station. The truck was owned by a man who had once worked for a merchant. When the revolution came he'd confiscated it from his employer. Now he had his own business ferrying people and goods around and charging money for the service.

The truck had been arranged to arrive at eleven and already it was half past. Philip was beside himself with anxiety. As they all waited, each felt the tension and none of them spoke.

Philip feared having to go back to the house. They would have to replace their bags in the gardener's hut and the cases could easily be discovered. Once the gold coins and jewels were found, it would obviously implicate them.

Waiting in a group near the road, they would soon be noticed. Philip was almost ready to say they had to return to the house when the truck turned the corner. They walked to the edge of the pavement to be ready to climb into the back, and as they did so Philip's stomach knotted. On the back of the truck were four armed militia men. The three of them froze to the spot as the truck drew close.

'Sorry I'm late. I had some things to do, as you can see,' said the driver, gesturing towards four militiamen standing on the back. Under the Bolshevik code, running a business was disapproved of: it was expected everyone would work for the 'good of the state'. So the driver worked hard for the good of the state, always giving free rides to soldiers, running errands for workers' committees and generally being useful to those with power. He made his money off those with no power, who could afford to pay.

'Come on, you lot,' he shouted to the soldiers. 'Can't you see this comrade's a war hero and needs help to get on board?'

They put down their rifles, jumped down and lifted Sergei, still in his chair, into the back. Then the youngest, a youth of about twenty, smiled at Sophie.

'Here, let me help you,' he said and placed his hands around her waist and lifted her onto the back of the truck. He picked up her valise and handed it to her and, without waiting for the others, climbed onto the back so he could be sure to sit next to her.

Sophie smiled and thanked him. The young soldier smiled back.

'I hope you haven't been waiting long,' he said.

Seeing their young comrade flirting with the pretty woman, the other three militiamen nudged each and laughed.

'A pretty piece of skirt will be the death of young Ivan,' said one of the soldiers to Philip.

'Where're you going?' the young soldier asked Sophie, ignoring his comrade's comment.

Sophie repeated the explanation they had all rehearsed. 'My brother's been badly wounded in the war, as you can see, and the doctor says he needs to have some warm weather to help him recover. We're off to stay with my sister who works for a farmer in the south.'

The others engaged Sergei in discussion: where had he fought during the war? Which regiment had he been with? One of the soldiers, a man called Dmitri, had a brother in a regiment at the same part of the front.

'That was before he deserted and returned to Moscow.' He looked down at Sergei and felt sorry for him. There were too many wounded, but he thought he would prefer to be dead rather than suffer like the poor wretch in front of him.

On their arrival at the train station they helped Sergei out of the back of the trailer as another group of soldiers approached them.

'What's going on here?'

'These comrades are travelling to their sister's so that this hero of the revolution can have better health,' was the exaggerated response from the militiaman, who took it upon himself to defend his comrade in arms.

'Travel documents,' demanded the leader of the new group of soldiers gruffly as he held out a gloved hand.

'And who are you to demand them?' asked Dmitri.

'I'm doing my job, comrade, as part of the militia unit at the station searching for counter-revolutionaries and supporters of the old order.'

144

'Then go and find supporters of the old order in another part of the station,' said Dmitri sarcastically.

'Don't speak to me that way,' the soldier said aggressively as he moved his hand to his pistol.

'Gentlemen,' said Sergei. 'Don't argue over me – these comrades are just helping me. I can't even get out of my chair to have a piss, far less be a danger to the revolution,' and he removed his blanket to show his missing leg and arm.

The man looked down at him and his hand moved away from his pistol.

'Move on then.' The soldiers marched off to accost a group of Armenians.

As they moved away Dmitri said, 'Trumped-up nobody!' and straightened his jacket.

'I'll take you to your train,' the youngest said to Sophie, so the three were marched through the crowds to their train, protected by the soldiers. The train was made up of an engine, five carriages with compartments and two cattle trucks at the rear. A young man who had settled into his seat in the first-class compartment was roughly ejected to make room for the important travellers and, despite the torn velvet cushions and the absence of curtains, the three were settled and would have an easier journey to the south than the one they had had to Moscow. The soldiers departed with kisses from all on both cheeks and many good luck wishes.

Three hours later the train drew out of Moscow station and began its journey south. Philip looked out of the murky window and tried to plan ahead.

They hoped to leave Russia by boat from near Yalta, but from the scant information in the newspapers the area was being fought over by remnants of the German army – the Bolsheviks as well as supporters of the old regime. Travelling to that part of Russia might be dangerous. His thoughts turned to Sergei. Their stay in their family house in Moscow hadn't been relaxing, nor had it been healthy. Sergei had been showing signs of exhaustion and had developed a nasty sore on his buttocks and lower back as a result of sitting in the leather wheelchair and lying in bed for too long. The sores had begun to go septic

145

and needed cleaning three or four times a day. Philip admired the way Sergei bore the pain and never complained.

The other thing that puzzled him was the lack of news from the Bank of England. People in Moscow seemed to know that he was in Russia and had not returned to England. He thought of the soldiers who had arrived at the baker's in Petrograd just as they were leaving for the train station, and the Bolshevik policeman who had visited the house in Moscow to say that he would soon be arrested. In all the confusion of the revolution there were still people who knew who he was, were watching him and, despite all of that, he was being allowed to escape. Philip could make no sense of it.

Sophie and Sergei were sleeping and Philip continued to think as the countryside sped past. How long have I been in Russia? he thought desperately. There were the three weeks he had waited to go to the Alexandra Palace, then the few months at the baker's house, and a few weeks in Moscow. Then he looked down at a discarded copy of *Izvestia* and saw the date at the top of the page. He stared at the date. Was he mistaken? Surely he was mistaken? He squinted in an effort to see the print more clearly, but the date didn't change: 15th October 1918. There was no mistake. There it was, in black and white, the only fact in the crumpled newspaper that could be relied on to be accurate. He'd been in Russia for two years.

Suddenly he felt very homesick. He imagined having dinner at Rules and pictured a large steak and kidney pie, served by waiters in starched white aprons down to their ankles, the sommelier with a bottle of claret in his hands just waiting to pour the dark red liquid into the cut crystal wine glasses, supervised by the head waiter. The only dessert that could follow such a dish and do it justice: a huge treacle sponge covered in bright yellow custard. Suddenly, he felt hungry.

He wondered if *Joy-Land* was still running at the Hippodrome Theatre and if the programme still included Charles Berkeley and Irene Richards singing 'The swing song' and 'Our own dear flag'. It would be wonderful to escort Sophie to the opera at Covent Garden and to concerts at the Albert Hall and pictured her in the cream dress she had worn the night they had met. His thoughts moved to how Mr and Mrs Evans were coping and he was thankful that he'd taken the precaution of paying them a year's salary in advance and that they had access to emergency funds should they need them. Part of his salary was paid into the housekeeping account, to which Mr Evans had access, so he should be able to keep the house running almost indefinitely.

His thoughts were disturbed by Sophie moaning slightly in her sleep as she turned in her seat to make herself more comfortable. Her hair had fallen over her face and he smiled as, without opening her eyes, she brushed it away from her face. The train braked hard and the wheels screeched, everyone jolted out of their seats as the carriages shunted into each other. Pieces of luggage in the next compartment crashed down from the luggage rack and onto the passengers below, and a woman screamed as pots and pans fell to the floor further down the train. The passengers looked out of the window as five soldiers climbed on board. They were better dressed than the usual militias, with shiny boots, and the leader had an air of authority and importance. They passed the compartment, giving the occupants only a cursory glance, and, seeing Sergei's wheelchair, moved on. Philip noticed that most of the passengers continued to look out of the windows to avoid the soldiers' attention.

A few minutes later the group returned, pushing two men in front of them. They had long beards and felt hats and, judging by how they were dressed, most of the passengers assumed they were Jews. Philip wasn't surprised. The revolution hadn't changed centuries of prejudice against Jews and the Red Army arrested and harassed Jews on sight.

Philip watched through the window as the men were pulled off the train, their papers checked and the contents of their luggage emptied on the ground. One of the soldiers found some jewellery, held it up accusingly and struck the men in the face with the back of his hand. Blood spurting from his mouth, the man wailed and fell to the ground and used his hands to protect his head as another soldier kicked him in the ribs, making him cry out more loudly as a rib broke. The soldiers turned away from their captives. They re-boarded the train, which started to move off. The two men furiously collected their scattered possessions and stuffed them into their valises as the train moved faster and faster, leaving the men behind. All they could do was look on with resignation as the train disappeared into the distance.

Philip folded his jacket and, using it for a pillow, pressed his cheek into it. How would they escape from Russia? How could he explain such a long absence to the Governor at the bank? What would Mrs Evans make of Sophie and Sergei?

He closed his eyes, just for a moment, and fell asleep.

The train rumbled on through the night and into the following day, stopping regularly to take on water and fuel, when the passengers were allowed to stretch their legs and buy some fresh fruit offered for sale at inflated prices by the local peasants. It was on one of these stops that the guard came through the train to announce that, 'Due to White Army activity in the Yalta area, when the train arrives at Kharkov it will be diverted to Kuban.'

Many in the carriage were visibly upset. They had expected to meet up with friends and relatives, and now those plans had been frustrated. Philip pictured the maps he had seen and memorised in the study in Moscow. The Kuban area was on the opposite side of the Dardanelles to Yalta.

He looked at Sophie.

'You don't seem upset by the news,' he whispered.

'I'm not,' she whispered back. 'We often holidayed there as children, and we know the area very well. Some friends might be in the area and perhaps they will be able to help us.'

Philip was relieved. Perhaps things might not be so bad.

At Kharkov the train stopped for three hours to allow passengers off.

The train left Kharkov and continued on its journey south. Sophie settled down to more boredom and more discomfort. She shifted position to relieve her sore back, and wished there was a pillow she could put behind her. She was relieved when she slipped her feet out of her shoes. Were all pregnancies this uncomfortable, or was God punishing her for being pregnant and not married? She shifted her position again and remembered that Philip had teased her by saying that he wanted a cricket team of boys; at that moment she hoped a team of one would suffice. In one respect she felt fortunate: her stomach wasn't as huge as she'd imagined it would be but, even so, some of her clothes were becoming tight. She rubbed her hands in an effort to relieve the pins and needles. It had to be a boy to be causing so many problems, she thought.

When the train came to a final stop, it was at the end of the line. The three of them found themselves, with about eighty others, at a station with no transport. Some decided to walk into the small town nearby and others settled down to wait for another train to take them somewhere else, or in the hope that the train they had arrived on might go further. Philip thought it best to walk away from the crowd.

'What should we do now?' he asked.

Sergei looked up at them from his chair. 'We should be careful because the Kuban Cossacks used to provide the Tsar's bodyguard and many will still support the old regime. However, if this is the end of Bolshevik influence the city must be run by the Reds. Either way, the situation is prone to change at a moment's notice.'

Philip could see the sense in what Sergei was saying and out of the corner of his eye saw the guards who had ejected the two Jewish men earlier walking towards them. This time they were accompanied by a couple of soldiers wearing Cossack hats and with long daggers in their belts.

'Your papers,' asked the leader.

Their papers were handed over and given a cursory look.

'You will come with us.'

'Are we under arrest?' asked Sophie.

'Is there a reason why we should arrest you?' came the reply.

'No,' she answered.

'Then you're helping us with our enquiries.'

Sophie wheeled Sergei in the direction of the station house and Philip carried their bags as the group of soldiers escorted them to the station waiting room. A few of the train's passengers had begun to move in the same direction, saw the soldiers, thought better of their decision and walked away from any trouble.

The waiting room, once reserved for first-class passengers, was stark, with benches fixed to the wall on three sides. There was no decoration on the walls except the shadow of a picture that would have once held a portrait of the Tsar.

The three of them sat on the bench. No one spoke. Sophie smiled at the guard on the door but not a flicker of emotion was returned. Sergei's infected sore was paining him and he looked pale and tired. Sophie reached out to hold his hand.

After what seemed an age the door opened and a table and chair were brought into the room. A minute later the leader marched in and sat down.

He looked at them one by one and then spoke. 'By the orders of the Revolutionary Military Council for the revolution, I am instructed to question anyone for anti-revolutionary activity or aiding the state's enemies.' He paused. 'Why are you travelling towards an area that supports the White Army?'

He was a small man, but thickly set. His round face was emphasised by thinning hair and his face scarred by acne. Cold eyes, magnified by thick spectacle lenses held together by wire frames, contributed to his menacing appearance.

Philip had never been afraid of any man, but this man made the room seem cold. He knew by looking into the inquisitor's eyes he had the power of life and death and had used it time and again. The man looked straight back at him. Philip was afraid.

Sophie answered the question put to them. 'My brother's ill and needs warmth, and we think that salt water bathing will help his wounds to heal.'

The inquisitor ignored her and continued to look directly at Philip. 'And you?'

'I'm engaged to this woman, and helping her with her brother.'

'You're not Russian.'

'No, I'm English.'

'Why is an Englishman in Russia?'

'I was trapped here during the war.'

'That's not what I asked. Why were you in Russia in the first place?'

I was working for the government to help Russia with the war effort.'

'Which government, the British or the Tsar's?'

Philip saw the trap that had been expertly set.

'I was here to help Russia as an ally against the Germans.'

The inquisitor had fenced as a student and described an interrogation as reflecting the lunge and parry of a fencing match: the more intelligent the suspect, the more challenging the match. This looked as if it could be an excellent duel.

'As a spy?'

'No, I was here to help Russia in its war against Germany,' repeated Philip. 'I was trying to help with financing the war and to set up field hospitals and aid.'

'So why are you still here?'

Philip replied, 'As I've said, I found it difficult to return to England after the revolution and now I'm engaged to this woman.'

'So you now spy for England.'

'No, I'm not a spy, I'm a banker,' said Philip, feeling exasperated at having to answer the same question again, but not wanting to show it.

The interrogator slammed his hand down on the table, creating a cloud of dust as he did so, startling all three of them.

'Liar!' the man shouted. 'I don't care that you are using this woman and this man to help you hide. They are also enemies of the revolution. We will deal with them later. But you're an interfering foreigner. Russia is crawling with foreigners, all trying to take what they can from the people. Do you know how many foreigners we have in Russia, all trying to help us?'

'No,' said Philip.

'There are fifty thousand Czechs helping us by pillaging and raping Russian women all along the Trans-Siberian Railway, twenty thousand Greeks are helping us by doing the same in the Crimea, ten thousand French troops are helping themselves to our land in Odessa, and thousands of Italians, Serbs and Romanians in Arkhangelsk are helping us by stealing our corn. There are even two thousand Chinese troops helping us in Vladivostok and forty thousand English and Canadian troops supported by Americans also in Archangelsk. What their governments really want is to help themselves to the wealth that is Russia's, so why would you, Englishman, be different to any of these other invaders? Pardon me if I laugh at that, because you're a spy and a fucking liar.'

'I don't know what you're talking about,' replied Philip.

'He's telling the truth,' said Sergei. 'He helped me and my sister when I was ill at the time of the revolution and as a result was unable to get back to England.'

The inquisitor looked at Sergei for a full five seconds.

'Count Tagleva, I will come to you next, but until then please remain quiet.'

The use of Sergei's title shocked them all.

The inquisitor looked at the three of them. He hated the Tsar, the aristocracy and all it stood for. He'd joined the Vinnitsa Teachers' Institute as a student in 1912. At the end of his first year his best friend was arrested by the *Okhrana* for speaking at a student meeting discussing the need for socialism in modern Russia. The Tsar's secret police had beaten his friend so badly that his kidneys had ruptured. Ignoring his pleas for medical attention, they allowed him to die in great pain on the prison floor. The inquisitor had been forced to leave the institute when conscripted into the army to join the war against Germany. Stationed in a provisions unit a hundred miles from the front, he witnessed the corruption and the incompetence of the officers that resulted in hundreds of thousands of men being sent to their deaths sharing a rifle between two and with a single bullet each.

After six months he had begun to speak to his comrades about the incompetence, urging the end of the war and the destruction of the monarchy. The group was discovered discussing their plans to desert when a senior officer overheard them plotting. Two of his comrades were shot in the head, but before the officer could shoot them all the other group members overpowered him. Driven by revenge, the survivors dragged the officer to a deserted farm building that had once

152

served as an abattoir and hung the naked officer by his wrists from a meat hook.

He had enjoyed listening to the man's screams as he castrated him, cut out his tongue, sliced off his nipples and then skinned him alive. It took the officer five days to die. On more than one occasion, after tormenting the officer, he had found he'd ejaculated with pleasure. Since then he'd mastered the art of interrogation and could now keep his victims alive for as long as he wished. The longest had been three weeks until the man had, disappointingly, died of a heart attack. His superiors, unconcerned by his brutality, were pleased with his results and the information he got. He knew, however, that information gathered by pain was useless. People would say anything to save themselves from excruciating pain, they would admit to any crime, no matter how improbable. The only way to get to the truth was by fear, and careful and intelligent questioning. It was only once the truth had been extracted that he could reward himself by inflicting pain.

Turning to Philip the soldier said, 'Take your coat off.'

Philip did so and handed it to one of the soldiers, who began to empty his pockets. He removed some money, a half-eaten salami sausage, the train tickets and travel passes. Each item was placed on the table in front of the interrogator, who sorted through the pile with the tip of a pencil as if it were excrement.

'What are you looking for?'

'Anything and nothing,' came the reply.

The inquisitor looked at Philip.

Sophie's and Sergei's coats were searched in the same manner and then returned to them.

Finding nothing of interest for now but knowing he would most likely find things of interest sewn in the hems, collars and cuffs of their clothes once they started the serious and more pleasurable part of the interrogation, the inquisitor looked at them. 'So I have here two aristocrats and an English spy travelling to join our enemies and counter-revolutionaries... It doesn't look good, does it?'

'You know who we are. You used my name, so you must know we aren't counter-revolutionaries,' said Sergei. 'So why are you detaining us?'

The inquisitor looked back at him and rose from the table. 'You will all stay here until I decide what to do with you.' With that, he left the room.

The three sat in silence with the guard at the door looking at them dispassionately but with a slight grin on his face. It was menacing. Eventually Sophie rose and began packing their belongings back into the bags. It was something to do.

Three hours passed. Each hour the soldier on the door guarding them was changed by another. Eventually the inquisitor returned and took his place at the table. 'I am arresting you and am taking you to a place of interrogation.'

'On what charges?' said Sergei.

The inquisitor sighed. 'Does it matter? You're guilty of spying, attempting to take state secrets out of the country, being counter-revolutionaries, supporters of the White Army, spies for Germany, spies for England, assassins. Take your choice. Each comes with the death sentence and it's a shame we can only shoot you once.'

Philip stood. 'But these people have done nothing. This man,' pointing to Sergei, 'fought for Russia bravely and was badly wounded. What danger is he to you? His sister is only here because she is acting as his nurse. If any of us is guilty, then it's me for trying to help Russia in its war against Germany. But these people have done nothing.'

The soldier looked at them. 'English, I've noted your confession but you should know that we've known about you for some months. You were in Russia to transfer important documents and property to England. We want those documents and that property, and you will tell us where they are. Then and only then, perhaps, we will send you back to Moscow for trial and a firing squad.'

He knew there would be no trial. He would get what information he needed and then he'd keep his promise to his colleagues. The torture of the two men and particularly the girl would be an entertaining one for them to watch.

An hour later the three of them picked up their bags and were escorted towards a waiting train. Two of the guards walked on either side of them, bayonets fixed. Waiting at the train with his hands on his hips was the inquisitor. There weren't many other passengers and the train looked quiet. A truck from which vegetables were being unloaded by some farm hands was parked at the far end of the train.

Two cows and a young bull were being loaded into one of the cattle trucks just in front of them. One of the guards moved to one side to avoid the bull and Sophie took her chance to cause a distraction. She pulled the long hatpin from her hat and jabbed it into the rump of the bull, which complained violently. Upset at being stabbed, the bull kicked out and caught the unwary farm hand on the shin. Screaming with pain, his pipe fell from his mouth and into the dry straw covering the floor of the cattle truck. Writhing in agony, the man forgot his pipe and within seconds flames began to lick at the roof of the truck. The cows, already loaded, were frightened by the fire, jumped out of the cattle truck and charged towards the inquisitor. Cries from various bystanders alerted those around to the danger and the guards turned to see what the commotion was all about as the cattle charged into them. The inquisitor was tossed into the air and landed on his back, winding him. Another of the cows trampled over him and a hoof caught him on the head. His skull fractured, he cried out in pain. Everyone scattered to save themselves and the bull and cows stopped, turned and charged the soldiers once more. Sophie, Philip and Sergei watched as their guards ran to help their injured commander.

By now the fire in the cattle truck was consuming the wooden slats. Flames leaped into the sky and a second cattle truck caught fire. The farmer tried to recover his cattle, passengers rushed to avoid being trampled, and everywhere there was confusion.

Philip saw their chance as the train driver and fireman ran towards the end of the train to uncouple the flaming trucks.

Philip shouted to Sophie to wheel Sergei's chair towards the truck and together they pushed Sergei into the back and told him to lie down. Philip lifted Sophie up by the waist and threw her in after Sergei, then lifted the wheelchair after her. One of the soldiers noticed that the prisoners were escaping and ran towards the truck, but tripped over some luggage and fell heavily to the ground.

Philip climbed into the truck, slammed it into gear and pressed his foot hard on the accelerator. The truck jerked forward. Another soldier fired at the escaping prisoners but the shot went wide.

Looking behind them Sophie was able to see the train's engineer desperately trying to unhitch the two flaming cattle trucks, and soldiers hopelessly running after them, eventually giving up.

Within a few minutes they had put the train far behind them and, once Philip felt that they were safe and out of sight, he stopped the truck to check on Sophie and Sergei. He found Sophie sitting up, cradling Sergei's head in her lap. They both were laughing uncontrollably.

'What are you laughing at?' asked Philip.

'This truck must've been used to transport flour. Our clothes are now covered in it, so I suppose the soldiers were right when they thought we were off to join the Whites.'

As the truck moved ever closer to the coast the three of them began to feel free for the first time. The slow progress of the truck allowed them to look around and appreciate the natural beauty of the Crimea. Its mountains and dark green pine trees made an imposing background for the profusion of fruit trees, shrubs and vines which would fill the air with scent in summer. Almost every kind of fruit flourished in the valleys: apples, cherries, peaches and almonds. Roses would spread over every building and scatter their petals over lawns and pathways with a perfume that was almost overpowering.

It was no wonder that the Crimean coast had become a favourite place for winter holidays for the Royal Family. The presence of the Tsar's palace had attracted other wealthy aristocrats and merchants. The result was that the coast was filled with grand houses, high walls and sculptured gardens. Since the revolution, however, many of these grand houses had been abandoned and were uncared for. After several stops to allow the engine to cool down, they arrived at the coast, at a place signposted as Koreiz, which Philip easily translated from Greek as 'villages'.

# Chapter Fourteen: Koreiz

Sophie looked at the few people on the pavements. Most were Tartars, the men very tall and strong and the women almost invariably handsome. The men wore round black fur caps and short embroidered coats over tight white trousers. The women dyed their hair a bright red, over which they wore small coloured caps. Sophie remembered childhood bedtime stories of the Tartars. Honest folk, wonderful horsemen who compared favourably with the best Cossacks. Her father had said the best way to describe a cavalcade of Tartars sweeping by was to imagine centaurs, so perfect was the harmony between horse and man. She was dreaming when the truck slowed down and came to a stop.

'What's the matter?' she called out to Philip.

'We've run out of fuel,' came the reply from the cab.

The three of them unpacked their possessions, and Sergei's chair, from the truck and found themselves on the pavement, wondering what they could do. A few passers-by informed them that there was no petrol to be had in the area.

Picking up their bags and making Sergei comfortable in the wheelchair they began to walk down the wide street. Philip didn't like to abandon the truck but didn't know what else to do.

After half an hour they were exhausted. Seeing a modest house set back from the road, Philip told the other two to wait as he walked down the short gravel path to the front door. He hoped it might be empty and they could just break in and stay for a night or two. He lifted the heavy knocker and banged twice and, after a couple of minutes, a woman appeared.

'What do you want?' she asked without opening the door fully.

'I'm looking for accommodation for myself and two friends.'

'Who are you?'

Avoiding giving a direct answer, he said, 'We come from Moscow and I'm bringing a wounded soldier and his sister to recuperate from his wounds after fighting the Germans. But we can't travel further because we are all too tired.'

'Can you pay?'

'We have some money and wouldn't expect you to be inconvenienced.'

'I can give you two comfortable bedrooms for thirty roubles for a week – no paper money, mind. Paper's no good to me any more.'

'That would be fine,' said Philip, knowing that it was an extortionate rate for two rooms. The woman expected him to haggle and, when he didn't, scolded herself for under-pricing the accommodation.

The woman waited and watched as Philip returned to the street and the three walked down the pathway towards her. Looking at Sergei, she said, 'You'll never make the stairs in that chair, so we can bring down a bed from upstairs and I'll make one of the salons into a bedroom.'

'Thank you for allowing us to stay in your house,' said Sophie.

'Oh, it's not mine. I'm just the housekeeper. The owner is a wine merchant; it's he who owns it. I rarely saw him before the revolution, but since, not at all. Even the pay doesn't come as it used to, so now and again I'm forced to take in travellers such as yourselves. I keep the place ready for him as I've got nowhere else to go.'

'Is there anyone else in the house?' asked Sophie.

'No. At one time there were four servants and a gardener but I'm the only one now. The others left when they didn't get paid. Who can blame them? We all have to survive.'

After a small bed had been made up for Sergei, Philip and Sophie followed the woman upstairs to look at the room that they would share. It was large, bright and airy with a chaise longue standing at the foot of a large four-poster bed. After making up the bed with fresh cotton sheets supplied by the woman and an eiderdown quilt they lay, fully clothed, on the duck down quilt and fell into an exhausted sleep.

Four hours later they woke and went downstairs. At the bottom they found the housekeeper.

'I will have a small meal for you in a couple of hours,' she said to Philip.

Walking into Sergei's room they found him propped up against some pillows and reading a book.

'Did you sleep well?' he asked them.

'Very,' replied Sophie.

'So what are our plans?'

Philip took a deep breath. 'First, a long hot bath, if we can arrange it, and some food and then, I think, we need to find out what ships are in the area. We need to see if there are any boats available to take us to a friendly port. I don't know whether the Bolsheviks are in power here or even if this part of Russia is controlled by the Germans or another power. So we'll have to be careful, but the housekeeper should be able to tell us the latest situation.'

Sergei said, 'Well, the housekeeper – her name's Olga, by the way – has been very chatty and she tells me that the area's been invaded by the Germans, then by the Reds and the Kuban and is currently controlled by the Reds again, but they don't have many soldiers so don't trouble people much. Though it could change tomorrow, she says, as the Whites have small bands of supporters all over the region.'

'So, much the same as the rest of Russia,' whispered Sophie to herself.

'However, I do have some good news.'

'Oh, do tell,' said Sophie, wanting to hear something nice.

'We have some special neighbours. Olga told me that only a few miles away is Ai-Todor, Grand Duchess Xenia's estate. The Tsar's sister,' he added for Philip's benefit. 'The Dowager Duchess is staying there, as well as most of the Youssoupov family.'

'The Youssoupovs – I'm so pleased they are safe,' said Sophie with obvious joy.

Sergei explained for Philip. 'Our father was on the same committee for education when Felix Youssoupov's father was the administrator of Moscow and we used to play with his son, also called Felix.'

'The man who killed Rasputin?'

'That's him,' said Sergei.

'Oh, but he's such a nice, gentle man and wouldn't hurt a fly,' said Sophie, defending her friend, and then added, 'He was just doing his best to protect Russia from that monster.'

Sergei suppressed a giggle at his sister's contradiction but knew that it was one shared by almost every Russian, no matter what their political leanings.

'How does she know the Youssoupovs are here?' enquired Sophie.

'Apparently he's the only member of the Royal Family allowed to leave their estates. It seems that the local Soviet Committee consider Felix as a hero for killing Rasputin and he takes messages between the Dowager Empress and various relatives who live in other parts of the town.'

'I guess they're all trying to leave Russia. Tomorrow we should take a walk to the harbour and see what's going on,' said Philip.

'Let me go and see Olga and ask if we can have a bath,' said Sophie.

Sergei looked at Philip. 'Sit down, please. I have some things to ask.'

Ever since being interrogated by the soldiers at the railway station, Philip had been expecting this conversation.

'Philip, you seem to be a dangerous man to know. Those soldiers knew who you were and who I am. I can't think why we should be of such interest to people.'

'I'm sorry,' replied Philip. 'Association with me has brought you into direct danger and you have a right to know.'

Philip recounted the visit to the Bank of England by Grand Duke Konstantin Konstantinovich, the visits to the Winter Palace and the treasures he had taken back to England. He then told of the papers that he had been given and their importance.

Having met Sophie and fallen in love with her he had failed to return to England – and had placed them both in danger.

'I'm sorry and I can only apologise to you. My selfishness has placed you both in danger,' he said finally.

'No need to apologise. Had you not helped me and Sophie we would never have been able to see our father before he died and to bury him properly – we would still be in Moscow trapped in a house that's no longer our own and in a few months we probably wouldn't be alive. You have nothing to reproach yourself for as far as I'm concerned. And as for Sophie, she's so much in love that she won't reproach you either.'

'And I love her more than anything else,' added Philip.

Sergei looked at Philip and felt the same warmth he'd felt for his brother Sacha all those years ago in London.

'Perhaps I should be thanking you. I've not had such an exciting adventure since I was a schoolboy. So, where are these papers and jewels?'

'You're sitting on them,' replied Philip.

Sergei roared with laughter. He felt the leather and couldn't feel anything underneath. 'So that's the reason I get such bad sores' and held out his hand. Philip shook it and they smiled at each other with mutual respect.

Sophie returned. 'And what have you two men been talking about?'

'Nothing much, just man talk,' said Sergei.

'Oh, important man stuff then!' laughed Sophie, who'd heard the entire conversation from the next room.

*****

That evening they were ushered into the main dining room. Four places had been laid at one end of the long table and lit by two candles in the candelabra. Sophie looked down at the silver cutlery, the plates from the Kuznetsov factory in Moscow and the Venetian wine goblets.

She watched as Olga dished up a small portion of chicken stew and potatoes onto her master's plates and passed them down the table. A bottle of wine was produced and Philip asked if he would pour it. It was obvious to the three of them that, as Olga took her place at the head of the table, she was the mistress of the house and they were her guests. The stew was followed by some oranges and grapes. At the end of the meal Sophie looked down at the empty plates. It was the best, the grandest, meal she had eaten since leaving the Hotel Europe. Such a shame that she'd left her fine gowns in Moscow.

Back in Sergei's room Sophie looked at her brother. 'I wonder if Olga's employer knows that she's eating off his best plates and drinking his wine?'

'Probably not,' replied Philip.

Sergei said, '"For each new class that puts itself in the place of the one ruling before it, it's compelled to represent its interests as the common interest of all members and to represent those changes as only rational."'

'Who said that?' asked Sophie.

'Karl Marx,' replied her brother.

'And since when have you quoted Karl Marx?'

'I read some when I was in London with Sacha. He quoted Marx to me all the time and I would say that when you're in the company of revolutionaries it makes a lot of sense. In fact, there were times that I even thought of joining his revolution.'

'Why didn't you?' asked Philip.

'I couldn't live on the pay they offered, so decided to stay a bourgeois.'

'Father would have been shocked at you!'

'I'm not so sure. Father was quite revolutionary in his way. Look how well he treated our workers and stood up against the other employers who were against paying better wages. They were against him paying doctors when workers were ill and against Father when he shared some of the profits with them.'

'Your father was quite enlightened,' said Philip.

'He was, and he would have agreed with Marx when he wrote, "The mistake that all businessmen make is the error of examining surplus value, not in its purest and most beneficial form, but in the specific form of only profit."'

'If ever I return to the bank I'll have that quote put above my office door,' said Philip.

For the next few days Sophie bathed Sergei's bed sores with water and vinegar. They began to heal and he was soon able to sit in his chair comfortably. The walks the three of them took in the sun became a pleasure and to be looked forward to.

Olga was providing nourishing meals and a comfortable place to stay; the area seemed peaceful; the sun was warm on their faces; the flowers gave off a divine perfume; people bustled in colourful dress along the streets; donkeys brayed as they pulled heavily laden carts; and they could imagine that they were living at a normal time rather than in a country in the grip of civil war. They were happy to relax and recover their energy.

Most days they would stroll down to the seashore and Philip was cheered to see a number of large boats landing in the main ports and even in local inlets. Many were Russian fishing boats, but occasionally they sighted a large transport ship and even a few naval boats. Perhaps, thought Philip, when the time came, they could find one to take them away from Russia.

On this morning coming towards them was a couple dressed in walking coats. The woman wore a knitted cap and the man a hat that reminded Philip of a worker's cloth cap in England. As they approached Philip was struck by the girl's beauty. She had a lovely pale complexion with large eyes and brown curls peeping out from behind her cap.

As they approached, the man looked hard at Sergei and then at Sophie.

'Oh, how wonderful to see you,' said the man.

'Felix, is it really you?' asked Sophie.

'In the flesh.'

'We heard you were in the area.'

There followed an exchange of kisses and hugs between them.

'May I introduce my wife Irina?'

They all nodded as Irina continued to hold on to her husband's arm and smile.

Sophie replied, 'This is my fiancé, Philip Cummings. Philip, this is Prince Felix Youssoupov. As you know, as children we used to play together when our fathers were having meetings.'

'Congratulations to you both,' said Felix.

'Thank you, and it's a pleasure to meet you, Your Highness,' acknowledged Philip.

'What brings you here?' said Felix, in a perfect English accent which surprised Philip.

'We are hoping to find passage to England,' said Philip.

Looking at Sophie, Felix asked, 'Where are you staying?'

'We've taken rooms in the wine merchant's house just up the street.'

'Then, as you are so close will you please come to visit us for dinner at Ai-Todor tomorrow? Do say yes – the house is full of family and there's nothing more boring than a house full of Romanovs. Some lively company would be such a joy.'

'We'd love to, but we don't have anything to wear,' said Sophie.

'No matter; we don't wear ball gowns any more. Besides it'll be very informal, so come as you are. Shall we say eight o'clock? I'll send a car for you but I should warn you, the food may be a little thin compared to our usual standards.'

He bent down and whispered in Sophie's ear, 'Finding caviar any more is almost impossible.'

'Until tomorrow then,' said the Prince and Philip watched as the couple continued up the road arm in arm.

Once out of earshot Philip spoke to Sophie. 'He has a beautiful-looking wife.'

'Surprised?' Sophie enquired.

'A little. I imagined Felix Youssoupov was…'

'Homosexual?' Sophie said, smiling. 'Most of Russian society thought him so, but it was his mother's fault. She was so desperate for a daughter that when Felix was born she insisted on dressing him in girls' clothes and that continued even when he was well into his twenties. The poor boy grew up utterly confused. When Sergei and I used to visit his father's house, Felix could often be found dressed in girls' clothes. It was just one of those things, and everyone came to see it as quite normal.'

'I can imagine him passing for a very pretty girl,' said Philip.

Sergei chipped in. 'He was so pretty when dressed as a girl that when your King Edward VII visited Russia and attended a ball at the Winter Palace, the King asked Felix's brother, "Who was the pretty young woman?"'

Philip laughed. 'I wonder if King Edward was disappointed?'

# Chapter Fifteen: The Marlborough

## April 1919

At exactly quarter to eight, the Rolls-Royce arrived outside the wine merchant's house.

Fifteen minutes later they entered the gates of Ai-Todor Palace, the large white structure that imprisoned the surviving members of the Imperial Royal Family, the Dowager Empress, Grand Duchess Xenia, the Dowager's daughter, her daughter's husband Grand Duke Alexander and their six sons, together with the Youssoupov family. They were greeted by Felix and his wife at the front door and ushered into a private reception room. Irina left them and Philip assumed that the food wouldn't stretch to all the occupants of the house and so none of the other members of the Royal Family would be joining them. Their party would be just the four of them.

One of the things that had always struck Philip about Russian aristocracy was their exquisite good manners. Drinks were served by a servant as Felix enquired politely about all three of them and their adventures in Petrograd and Moscow. He listened politely and seemed particularly upset by the news of the death of Count Tagleva.

Philip was captivated by the man. He had grace, intelligence, a genuine interest in others and a quick mind, and Philip was amazed that this genteel man could have been responsible for the murder of Rasputin.

The meal comprised a *shchi* soup made from cabbages followed by some *pelmeni* dumplings cooked in garlic and a dessert of an apple with a few spiced grapes. Once they had finished, Philip complimented Felix on the meal and particularly on the excellent wine from Prince Golitsyn's vineyards.

'Wine is the one thing we have plenty of,' he replied, adding that the wine they were drinking came from the same vineyard that had supplied the wines at Tsar Nicholas's coronation banquet.

'Everyone in the house is drinking wine as fast as they can in case some soldiers requisition it for the state. Sometimes a meal consists of three courses of wine, wine and a dessert wine,' he laughed.

After the meal Felix enquired of Philip, 'How did you manage to be trapped in Russia during the war?'

Philip gave a short explanation, and, on learning that he worked for the Bank of England, the two men talked about investments and the relative advantages over shares and property. Philip found Felix's detailed knowledge of investments surprising.

At the end of the meal Irina joined them and engaged Sergei and Sophie in conversation. Felix motioned to Philip that he wanted to talk privately, and walked to the far end of the salon on the pretext of finding some vodka.

Felix poured two beakers of vodka. 'Were you aware there's a British battle cruiser anchored offshore with orders to evacuate members of the Imperial Family to exile?'

'I was not, sir.'

'It arrived this morning. Its captain sent a Lieutenant Pridham to negotiate with the Dowager Empress and the rest of the Royal Family to use it to leave Russia and go into exile. So far Her Majesty has resisted every plea to leave but I suspect that within a few days we'll have no option or we'll all suffer the same fate as the Tsar. In any event, it's my intention to leave with my wife on the boat.'

He paused to swallow the clear liquid and to pour himself and Philip another beaker.

'I suggest that, as a British subject, your best opportunity would be to escape on the same vessel. The ship's orders are to evacuate only members of the Imperial Family and their retinue, but I may be able to help you. Lieutenant Pridham will return tomorrow at midday to meet with me and I suggest that you're here to meet him.'

'Your Highness, I'm very grateful, but I could never consider leaving without the Count and Countess.'

Felix smiled. 'I never thought you would. I've known Sophie and Sergei ever since we were children. Unlike so many of my relatives, they never teased me and I felt that they liked me for who I am rather than for being a Youssoupov. It meant a great deal and still does.'

His insecurity surprised Philip, and he assumed the Prince's reference to being teased was possibly because he was so often dressed like a girl.

'Sophie won't remember this, but when we were small she gave me this,' and from his tunic he pulled a silver Orthodox crucifix with blue enamel on the edges. 'She told me it would always keep me safe. It was a childhood gift that can be bought on any peasant's market stall, but it was given with such genuine kindness and love that I've worn it every day since and consider it one of my most valuable treasures.'

He replaced the crucifix in his tunic. 'Be here at twelve and I'll introduce you to the ship's lieutenant. After that, it's up to you to persuade him to take you all on board, but I will do everything I can to help.'

That night Philip unpinned some of the brass pins holding the leather on Sergei's wheelchair and carefully pulled out the letter that had been given to him by General Alexander Mossolov.

The following morning Philip walked back to the palace, arriving a few minutes before midday, and was shown into the same room where they had had dinner the night before. Ten minutes later Felix entered with a British navy lieutenant.

'Philip, may I introduce First Lieutenant Pridham of His Majesty's ship, the *Marlborough*.'

They shook hands. The lieutenant had a thin mouth and a receding hairline, and the tops of his ears were bent away from his head, giving him a strange impish look.

'Lieutenant, this is the Englishman I was telling you about. Together with his fiancée and brother-in-law, he needs your help to secure passage out of Russia.'

'Your Highness,' said the naval officer. 'As you know, my captain's orders are to rescue Her Imperial Majesty and as many of the Royal Family and their retinue as can be accommodated. The Admiralty had thought a dozen people, but the retinue so far amounts to around seventy souls. My captain has no orders to include anyone else, even British citizens.'

Turning to Philip, he said, 'I'm very sorry, sir, but our orders are quite specific. I'm sure your party will be able to find some accommodation aboard some other vessel.'

Philip looked at the lieutenant and nodded. 'Yes, you are quite right, Lieutenant, and it's wrong of me to expect you to disobey any orders from the Admiralty. Even if my return to England is urgent and vital.'

'My orders are quite specific, I'm sorry,' Pridham said testily.

Philip removed the letter from his coat and handed it to Felix who immediately recognised the seal of the Tsar's private office. He took the package and reverently opened it and read the contents and then handed the note to the lieutenant, who read the English translation carefully.

Lieutenant Pridham was confused. 'Sir, I still can't see how this letter makes any difference to the ship's orders, which are quite specific.'

Felix smiled. 'Lieutenant, the contents of this letter are clear. They are to give him all assistance. It's a direct order from the Tsar and must be obeyed by even the Tsar's mother. Under the circumstances I don't think any of us have any choice.'

'But, sir, my instructions come from the Admiralty,' said Pridham.

'And that puts you and your captain in a quandary, Lieutenant. Should you fail to give this man the assistance this letter requires, then what explanation would you and your captain give the Admiralty if the information this man carries is proved to be vital to your government? Then there is the other problem that if the Dowager Empress or members of the family were to hear of your refusal to follow the Tsar's request and complained to the Admiralty or even to their family, the British King and Queen, what would be your excuse to a court of enquiry?'

Pridham knew he was between a rock and a hard place. Handing back the letter to Felix, he said, 'I'll speak to my captain.'

When the lieutenant had left the room Felix turned to Philip and passed the letter back to him. 'Clearly you are on some personal mission for the Tsar. May I enquire what your task is?'

Philip felt a sense of gratitude to Felix for his help in trying to save Sophie and Sergei and thought that Felix deserved some sort of explanation.

'I was asked by your government to transfer some documents to England during the war, documents which were designed to help both our countries,' replied Philip.

'I see.' Felix lit a cigarette and the thick blue smoke of his favourite Turkish blend sent clouds into the air. Felix watched the smoke as it drifted towards the ceiling.

After a few seconds Felix looked at Philip and said, 'I suggest that you tell no one else of this matter. The Romanov family is split by internal feuding over the possible succession to the throne. All sides would try to use you for their own ends.'

'Thank you for the advice,' said Philip.

'I'll send word to you as soon as I've heard back from Lieutenant Pridham, but I'm sure that he will arrange for you to travel with us. Keep your bags packed and be ready to leave at a moment's notice as soon as you hear from me. A moment's notice, mind you.'

On his return to the *Marlborough* Pridham saw the captain and that evening wrote in his personal diary, 'There will be four generations of the Romanovs on board and I'm sure that no British ship has ever before or will ever have four generations of Royalty, a great-grandmother, daughter, grand-daughter and great grand-daughter on board.' He thought of adding, 'As well as a British banker, under orders from the murdered Tsar', but decided against it.

****

173

Two days later at exactly three o'clock a car arrived outside the merchant's house. Half an hour later Sophie, Sergei and Philip loaded their luggage in the rear, said their farewells to Olga, and were driven to the estate, past the palace and down a winding road towards the seashore.

The road was busy with Royal cars, horse-drawn carriages laden with trunks and suitcases, and people walking down the hill. At the jetty Philip was amazed to see a mass of people and huge piles of packing cases, suitcases, boxes and even a set of golf clubs. Servants and English sailors shouted orders to each other as the group that Philip assumed was the Royal Family huddled together and watched the activity going on around them.

Philip saw an ornate statue of Minerva, the Roman goddess of wisdom, trade and strategy, atop a huge plinth at the end of the jetty. The goddess was pointing into the distance and at His Majesty's ship *Marlborough* as if blessing the enterprise they were all embarking upon. It was the first time Philip felt he could hope that they were safe, though that would only be certain when they were all on board.

Presiding over the throng was a very tall man dressed in full Cossack uniform, covered in medals, knee-high boots and with a long dagger tucked in his belt. A lambskin Astrakhan hat made his six feet seven inches extend to over seven feet, and he had a large nose, beard, moustache and hooded eyes that commanded unquestioned authority.

'Who is that magnificent-looking man?' asked Philip, indicating towards him.

'That's Grand Duke Nicholas,' said Sergei, 'the Tsar's uncle. He was commander of the Imperial army at the start of the war.'

'And the man next to him sitting on a suitcase in the dark suit and trilby and looking as if he's off to the office?'

'That'll be his brother, Grand Duke Peter. During the war he became a Lieutenant General. He was probably the most competent officer in the General Staff. My commander thought highly of him and said that had he been in charge we might have won the war, but his health was never good and he was forced to retire before he was able to make a great difference.'

The car door was opened by Felix Youssoupov. 'I'm so pleased you made it!' Philip shook his hand and Sophie kissed him on both cheeks.

'I've spoken to Lieutenant Pridham and you are all to be taken on board the *Marlborough* as part of my retinue.'

As two servants helped Sergei into his wheelchair Felix turned to look at Grand Duke Nicholas. 'There's a bit of a panic on,' he said softly so that no one else would hear.

'What's the problem?' enquired Sophie.

'The Grand Duke, never the most tactful of men, ordered the Dowager Empress to be here at a quarter to five. Apparently she's taken exception to being ordered about by her husband's brother and is complaining that it's given her only two hours to pack. The Grand Duke's afraid she might not turn up. He's frantic with worry and says if she doesn't hurry the Bolsheviks will discover she's planning to escape and prevent it. There's a rumour that a detachment of soldiers has been sent to arrest her.'

'We've twenty minutes before the deadline so perhaps she'll arrive,' said Sophie, trying to be helpful.

'What happens if she doesn't?' enquired Philip.

'God knows,' came the reply. 'We might all be stuck here and the *Marlborough* will sail without us.'

Philip looked out towards HMS *Marlborough*. The Iron Duke class battleship was an imposing sight and dominated the skyline. An armada of boats was transferring passengers, luggage, children and even pet dogs to the ship. Felix looked at his watch. It was twenty minutes past five. Grand Duke Nicholas paced even more furiously around the statue of Minerva.

Just then a landau appeared carrying two women. There was visible relief all around the quayside. The Grand Duke stood to the side and gave a smart salute at the arrival of the Dowager Empress, who ignored him, looking in the opposite direction. Descending from the landau, she shook hands with the coachman, walked round to the front of the carriage, kissed one of the leading ponies and walked towards the boat waiting to transfer her and her daughter to safety. Grand Duke Nicholas continued to salute until she was a good fifty yards from the shore. Half an hour later the jetty was deserted except for a few retainers and a discarded umbrella.

On board the *Marlborough* all was confusion as Lieutenant Pridham and other officers tried desperately to allocate the thirty-five officers' cabins to members of the Imperial Family. Having only ever seen royalty dressed in full military uniform with medals on their chest, the junior officers allocated the available space based upon who they thought looked important.

Sword-bearing bodyguards found themselves with large cabins, grand dukes were shown broom cupboards and princes hammocks. Those without uniforms were shown to mattresses in a corridor. Complaints were lodged, some were moved to better accommodation and the original occupants asked to vacate to more modest berths. The result was that the corridors were jammed with people moving large pieces of luggage from one cabin to another and finding they couldn't pass down the narrow corridors. Demands to allow people and baggage to pass were greeted with shouts and curses and counter-demands, depending on the seniority of the baggage being transported in one direction or another.

As the naval ratings spoke no Russian and the Russian servants spoke no English, both sides managed the situation with a great deal of gesticulation and raised voices, anticipating that increased volume would also increase understanding. The result was a noise that drowned out the roar of the ship's engines and the only people to find any enjoyment from it were Grand Duchess Xenia's young children, who thought their aunts and uncles arguing among themselves was the start of a great adventure.

Philip, Sergei and Sophie were allocated a small store cupboard that had once contained blankets, now distributed to the passengers. A cot, moved from the sick bay, had been placed in the small room. There was enough room for Sophie to sleep comfortably on a mattress on the floor next to Sergei's cot, though the door would have to be left open for ventilation. Sophie thought it very convenient because it adjoined a wash-room. The only disadvantage was that the Dowager Empress's dogs, Chi Foo and Soon, as well as those belonging to Grand Duchess Xenia and Duchess Dolgorouky, had been kennelled in the cupboard next door. The dogs viewed each other with the same sense of rank and importance that their human counterparts reserved for their own relatives. Barks and yaps could be heard as one dog or another transgressed their position in royal dog society and was firmly put back into their place.

Philip was allocated a hammock with the rest of the servants.

Lieutenant Pridham reported to the captain that all members of the Royal Family were on board, together with over seven tons of luggage. It was with some relief that the captain gave orders to set sail after dinner had been served.

Once Sophie had settled Sergei, two naval ratings arrived to say that they had been instructed to move Sergei, when the weather allowed, up on deck so that he could enjoy the scenery and have contact with the other passengers. While Sergei found it humiliating to be carried by two burly soldiers, he was grateful for the kindness and became instant friends with the two ratings. The members of the Royal Family failed to pay any attention to Sergei being carried on deck, being so used to seeing the sailor, Nagorny, carry the Tsarevich Alexei when his haemophilia was at its most painful.

Sergei discovered both sailors were from the North of England and all three exchanged stories. The sailors told him about their homes and their loved ones while Sergei recounted his experiences in the mills.

The first occasion he was placed in his chair on deck he found himself only a few yards away from the Dowager Empress and her sister, who sat in deckchairs, holding parasols to protect themselves from the sun. Sergei had never seen the Dowager Empress or her daughter and was struck at how small the two women were. Dressed in long dark overcoats, they seemed a lonely and sad couple. None of the other passengers approached them and they talked together quietly and watched the bustle on the deck. At one time the Empress caught Sergei's eye and, noticing his wheelchair, gave him a broad smile. Sergei bowed his head respectfully.

Sophie arrived and asked if he was comfortable and Philip glanced over to the two women in the deckchairs and was struck at the likeness of the Empress to Britain's Queen Alexandra. The resemblance was, of course, because they were sisters.

The *Marlborough* steamed towards Yalta, a few miles down the coast, to pick up the remaining members of the royal party, including Grand Duke Peter's daughter Nadezah and her baby. A further hundred tons of baggage and possessions sat on the quay ready to be loaded onto the *Marlborough*. The exiles intended to take with them items that would keep them in the style they took to be their birthright. One Grand Duke, it was rumoured, had managed to pack his entire silver and gold dinner service; another a writing desk inlaid with jewels. Even Prince Youssoupov was rumoured to have two Rembrandt pictures he had cut from their frames in his St Petersburg Palace, in the metal container he always carried with him in order to prevent them from getting lost.

The additional luggage took some time to load and some members of the Royal Family asked permission to go ashore. Philip decided to accompany them, if only to undertake a task he had promised himself. At the quayside Philip saw crowds of people all desperate to gain whatever passage they could and escape the Red army that was even now threatening the town. Children wandered the streets trying to find their parents, wives desperately held on to their husbands, the old and sick lay on stretchers next to piles of luggage, horses and carts were abandoned. Philip thanked their lucky stars they had not travelled to Yalta, as originally planned.

Sitting on a small wall overlooking the harbour was a small girl dressed in a cream dress trimmed with lace, a red sash around the waist, swinging her legs. In her tiny hands she held a wide-brimmed straw hat.

Philip walked over to her. 'Hello, what are you doing here?'

'Hello, sir,' she politely replied. 'I'm waiting for my daddy; he said he would come back for me.'

'How long have you been waiting?' enquired Philip.

'Since yesterday.'

'Would you like us to look for him together?' asked Philip.

'No, thank you sir, my father will come... he promised and he always keeps his promises.' She smiled sweetly and continued to scan the faces of those that passed.

Philip looked down at the girl. Her scuffed leather shoes were tied with red laces and she wrung her small hands anxiously as she desperately looked for her father. Philip turned away as a tear rolled down his cheek.

Philip returned to the *Marlborough* in a bleak mood. The atmosphere among the passengers was not helped by stories of friends and the thousands of ordinary people he had seen jostling for a place on board a ship – any ship, offering thousands of roubles to sailors for a place that would take them to safety. There were even a couple of men dressed in bowler hats, carrying rolled umbrellas, trying to persuade sailors from the *Marlborough* that they had family in England.

Yalta was descending into chaos, with bands of Tsarist supporters and Bolsheviks roaming the streets arresting those that supported the opposing side. Philip even heard of a band of White officers who had apparently hung a teenage boy, whose only crime was that he shared the same family name as the revolutionary Trotsky.

Four days later over one thousand people had managed to find passage on one of the ships in the harbour. Many more thousands had not, and the evidence was all around the quay, including a wide-brimmed child's straw hat left on a quayside wall.

\*\*\*\*

Philip was on deck when Lieutenant Pridham approached him.

'I hope your patient and his sister are comfortable?'

Philip smiled. 'Yes. Thank you for being so generous. Having the bathroom next to our cabin is very convenient.'

Pridham looked at Philip. 'I've received this from the Admiralty.' He handed him a telegram. Philip took the paper and read:

*From Admiralty Gibraltar: Response to passenger list. Repeat: only Russian members of the Imperial court and their household to be taken on board. Do not provide passage to any others, even if British citizens.*

Philip pursed his lips, crunched the paper in his fist and threw it into the sea, where it floated towards the shore. As he watched the paper drift towards the shore, a sloop passed, holding nearly two hundred members of the Dowager's bodyguard waiting to land at Yalta to fight the Reds. Noticing Her Imperial Majesty on the deck standing next to Grand Duke Nicholas, they came to attention, saluted and started to sing the national anthem.

*God save the Tsar!*
*Mighty and Powerful!*
*May he Reign for Our glory,*
*Reign that Our Foes may quake!*
*O Orthodox Tsar!*
*God save the Tsar!*

The sloop circled around the *Marlborough* as the soldiers cheered and waved their caps. The Grand Duke saluted and the Dowager crossed herself. Both had tears in their eyes at seeing the cheering soldiers and knew that many were distant relatives who would be going to certain death.

## Chapter Sixteen:
## *A marriage on a Greek island*

The following morning the English and Russian flags were hoisted. Philip was struck by the sadness of the situation. The Dowager's two sons and five of her grandchildren had been murdered. The other passengers were filled with apprehension about their future. He listened to their hushed conversations. How the war had been mishandled, how the Tsar had lost control, and how the Tsar's wife had caused the dynasty to fall, through her association with Rasputin. Even Grand Duke Peter, oblivious to his rescuers, complained that the British had landed munitions destined for the Russian army in an area captured the previous week by the Germans. Apparently, he said, British sailors hadn't known the difference between Russian and German uniforms when unloading the provisions.

Philip too was apprehensive. The note that Pridham had handed him ordering the captain not to take on board any person not related to the Imperial Family and their immediate servants confirmed that someone in England was intent on hindering his mission, but why? For their part, Pridham and the captain were complying with the Admiralty's order, and Philip, Sergei and Sophie were listed among Prince Felix Youssoupov's household.

On the seventh day the *Marlborough* anchored at Halki Island and Philip told Sophie, 'A number of the passengers are going ashore to visit the Greek Orthodox monastery on the island. We could marry there.'

'But it won't be Russian Orthodox,' said Sophie.

'Some Russian priests have fled to the island and taken refuge in the monastery and we could ask one of them to marry us.'

'That would be lovely,' said Sophie, relieved. She would be married before her baby was born.

Philip spoke to Lieutenant Pridham, who agreed to transport the wedding party to the island. Philip asked Prince Felix if he would act as witness. He was visibly delighted and suggested that his wife, Princess Irina, could support Sophie.

The wedding party was transported by small boat from the *Marlborough* and the sailors arranged a horse and trap to take them to the monastery. It took some time to locate the Russian Orthodox priest, who was initially reluctant to conduct a marriage at short notice but, once told he would be officiating in the presence of Russian royalty, he quickly changed his mind.

The party arrived at the monastery at the appointed time and went into the chapel. Two priests dressed in white vestments stood in front of the screen next to a bath full of water. As Philip was not of the Orthodox faith, he would first have to be baptised. Philip self-consciously undressed to his underclothes and felt very naked. The group giggled at his obvious embarrassment.

The priest intoned some prayers, took some holy water and touched his head, forehead and ears and read out some prayers. Philip was moved towards the bath and immersed, first for the Father, then for the Son and finally for the Holy Spirit.

Incense rose from the censer to the ceiling as towels were brought, and in a short time Philip was dressed and the marriage ceremony could begin.

The bride and groom stood inside the entrance of the church, the priest blessed them and handed them lit candles which they would hold throughout the ceremony. The deacon led the *ektenia*, or litany, with special petitions for the couple followed by two brief prayers. The betrothal over, the wedding proper could begin.

In the Eastern Orthodox Church the sign of marriage is not the exchange of rings, as it is in the West, but rather the placing of crowns on the heads of the bride and groom. The priest led Sophie and Philip into the centre of the church, where they came to stand on a piece of new, rose-coloured fabric, symbolising their entry into a new life. The bride and groom then publicly professed that they were marrying of their own free will.

The priest placed the crowns on the heads of the bride and the groom. Once this was done, the crowns were then held above their heads by Felix and Irina. There followed readings from the Epistles and the Gospel, brief prayers and the sharing of a 'common cup' of wine, and then the priest wrapped his stole around their joined hands and led them, followed by their attendants still holding the crowns aloft, three times around the *analogion* to symbolise the pilgrimage of their wedded life together. They were married.

Afterwards the entire party drank vodka toasts overlooking the sea, and Sophie felt it was the most romantic day she had ever spent.

On return to the *Marlborough* gifts were presented to the couple. Felix gave Sophie a small Fabergé egg made from lapis lazuli and tiny rubies that could be worn around the neck. One prince gave Sophie a writing box, another prince an illustrated Bible. Philip received a Cossack dagger and some cufflinks with the engraved double-headed eagle of the Romanovs. A small sponge wedding cake was delivered as a gift from the officers and crew of the *Marlborough*. That evening Sophie was particularly touched to receive a small gold brooch with pearls and diamonds, along with a note of congratulation from the Dowager Empress. No one mentioned her pregnancy.

Two days later Pridham approached Philip as he was walking with Sophie.

'I'm sorry to interrupt you,' said Pridham. 'I've been asked to invite you to dinner at seven tonight in the wardroom. The captain thought it would be nice if you could all join us. We'll be arriving in Constantinople in a few days and at that time various members of the party will be disembarking. We thought it would be a good opportunity to say goodbye.'

'We'd be delighted,' said Sophie.

In order to feed all the passengers, three sittings for each meal were required. The most important always took the third sitting; it allowed more time to relax after the meal.

The meal was very British and probably not to the usual taste of the Russian passengers but none complained and all declared the food quite delicious. Brown Windsor soup was followed by steak pie and vegetables, and finished off with fresh fruit, cheese and biscuits, all washed down with wine. The food was declared to be quite luxurious by those who, for months, had lived off a ration book supplied by the Bolsheviks.

'If you had lived almost exclusively on fruit and vegetables, and drinking coffee made from acorns, this meal would be like a banquet,' said one of the guests.

Another said, 'For weeks we had two cooked meals: fried potatoes with onions and fried potatoes without.' There was much laughter.

'The people, however, were very kind,' said Prince Orloff. 'On more than one occasion we found flour or sugar and even some meat left at the front door. Without their generosity we might have all starved to death.'

The treatment of the Dowager Empress, who was dining in her own rooms with her daughter, was a particular source of conversation. The Bolshevik jailers were seen as being barbaric and disrespectful to the Empress. On one occasion her Bible had been snatched from her hands and confiscated, as likely to poison her brain.

Another of the diners recounted how the Dowager Empress's bedroom had been ransacked by guards who ordered her to stand in her nightdress and watch as her possessions were scattered over the floor and even a photograph of her murdered sons destroyed as it was ripped from its silver frame.

One princess recounted how a guard had walked into her drawing room wearing one of her diamond brooches on his tunic.

'To avoid any nastiness, I suggested he'd look even better with the matching necklace. With that I fetched the necklace and placed it around his neck, and he left the room quite delighted – I never saw him again, much to my relief.'

After the meal and when real coffee had been served at the table, Prince Youssoupov sought to liven up the group with an impromptu concert on the same guitar that he'd played the evening he killed Rasputin.

After the ladies had departed to another cabin to play cards, a decanter of port was placed on the table and the Prince was encouraged to tell the story of that night.

'Oh, you don't want to hear about that mad monk, surely?' said Felix, his face brightening at the prospect of telling the story yet again.

'Oh yes, please, sir,' said a junior officer.

'We'd be more than thrilled,' said another enthusiastically.

Putting down his guitar, Felix sighed with feigned reluctance. 'Oh, very well, if I must.'

He looked around the table and once he had everyone's attention he took a great breath and began.

'First, you must know that Rasputin was a devil, a bad influence in the Imperial Family, and he was ruining Russia. In fact, I'm convinced he was being paid by the Germans to lose the war. He was a debauched man and a pig who would bed anyone – man, woman, nun or priest or even goat, it made no difference to him. It was said that he could hypnotise anyone just by looking at them.'

Felix looked at the junior officer with wide eyes as if mimicking Rasputin, and the young officer giggled in anticipation of the story that was to come.

'Two friends and I decided we had to save Russia from the devil and I sent Rasputin an invitation to dinner. He thought I would let him bed my beautiful wife, Irina. You see how depraved he was?

'Since the Youssoupov Palace was along the Moika Canal and near a police station, my friends and I decided that using guns would cause too much noise, so we laced pastries and wine with potassium cyanide crystals.

'When Rasputin arrived I took him to the basement dining room.

'Usually he looked like a beggar and smelled like a farmyard animal, but that night, for a change, he'd taken great care over his appearance, obviously thinking he would be meeting my wife. He wore a silk blouse embroidered in cornflowers, with a thick raspberry-coloured cord as a belt. He had even brushed his hair and carefully combed his beard, and as he came close I could smell the odour of cheap soap. I had never seen him look so clean and tidy. At least he would meet his maker having had a bath, I thought.'

Everyone laughed.

'"There will be no one at your house but us tonight?" Rasputin asked me. I reassured him that he would meet no one and that even my mother was in the Crimea.

'"I don't like your mother; I know she hates me,' he said to me. "She plots against me and spreads slander about me. The Tsarina herself has often told me that your mother is one of my worst enemies."

'I looked at Rasputin with dread, knowing he had second sight. I suspected he could see right into my head and that he knew what I intended to do. My hands shook as I offered him a poisoned pastry. He refused, saying they were too sweet for him. I couldn't persuade the devil to eat or drink and I started to panic.

'I went upstairs to talk to my friends. On my return Rasputin had, for some reason, changed his mind and had helped himself to a few pastries and a glass of wine. He ate three or four in quick succession and I waited, expecting him to drop dead.

'Rasputin began to speak in his gruff voice, caused by too much smoking and vodka. "It seems that my plain speaking annoys a lot of people," he said to me.

'"The aristocrats can't get used to the idea that a humble peasant like me should be welcome at the Imperial Palace… They are consumed with envy and fury… but I'm not afraid of them. They can't do anything to me. I'm protected against ill fortune. There have been several attempts on my life, but the Lord has always frustrated these plots. Disaster will come to anyone who lifts a finger against me."

'I was terrified. I knew he could see into my heart and I poured out a cup of poisoned wine and handed him more of the poisoned cakes.

'"I don't want any cakes, they're too sweet," he said.

'A few minutes later he reached over to the plate and took one, then another and a third... I watched him. The poison was enough to kill a horse but, to my horror, Rasputin went on talking quite calmly. I was convinced he was the devil.

'"Pour me out some more wine," he said.

'I watched him drink, expecting at any moment to see him collapse. But he continued to sip the wine like a connoisseur. Then he rose and took a few steps and staggered.

'"What was the matter?" I asked, convinced that the poison was finally working.

'"Nothing, it's just a tickle in my throat. The wine's good, give me some more," he said.

'I couldn't believe it. The monk went on walking calmly about the room, admiring this picture and that picture and this and that piece of furniture. Then suddenly Rasputin's expression changed to one of fierce anger. I'd never seen anything so terrifying. His eyes bulged.

'"Pour me a cup of tea, I'm very thirsty," he said.

'I poured the tea and he caught sight of my guitar. "Play something cheerful, I like your singing," he told me.

'I was now petrified... the nightmare had lasted two interminable hours and I made an excuse to walk upstairs to talk with my friends. The poison didn't seem to be working and I took a gun from Pavlovich and went back downstairs. As I entered the room I saw Rasputin looking at an ebony cabinet and I said to him, "Grigori Efimovich, you would do better to look at the crucifix and pray."

'I raised the pistol and shot. My friends rushed down the stairs to see Rasputin lying on the ground. We moved the body off the bear rug where he had fallen so that his blood wouldn't stain it.

'The devil was still breathing but after a few minutes, he jerked convulsively and fell still. We were all thankful that the nightmare was over and went upstairs to celebrate and to wait for the night to get darker so that we could dump the body without being witnessed.'

Felix lowered his voice to a whisper and everyone leaned forward to hear him.

'About an hour later, I felt an inexplicable need to go look at Rasputin. I walked downstairs and felt the body. It was still warm. I shook it, and there was no reaction, but as I turned to walk back upstairs Rasputin's left eye started to flutter open. He was still alive! Then, with a sudden effort—'

Felix screamed and raised his arms above his head, making all those around him jump backwards in fright. Everyone laughed at his theatrics.

'Rasputin leaped to his feet, foaming at the mouth. The devil rushed at me, trying to get at my throat. His eyes were bursting from their sockets, blood oozed from his lips and a ferocious struggle began… This devil, full of poison, with a bullet in his heart, had been raised from the dead by the powers of evil. He was the reincarnation of Satan. He held me in his clutches. I prayed to God and by a supreme effort succeeded in freeing myself from his grasp. Rasputin fell on his back, gasping horribly, and lay motionless on the floor.

'Then after a few seconds, he moved again. I rushed upstairs and called the others.

'"Quick, quick, come down," I cried. "The devil's still alive!"

'We found Rasputin running out across the courtyard yelling, "Felix, Felix, I'll tell the Tsarina everything!" I ran after him and fired the pistol but my hand shook so much that I missed. I fired again, and missed again. Then, to regain control, I bit my hand and fired a third time. This time the bullet hit Rasputin in the back. He stopped and I shot him again. Rasputin fell to the ground but still he refused to die. Instead, he began to crawl towards the door. Eventually he collapsed and was still.'

The audience clapped madly.

Felix acknowledged the applause but raised his hand and the audience went quiet.

'But that was not the end of the night…' he whispered. 'Since it was almost dawn, we were now in a hurry to get rid of the body. I stayed to clean myself up, and my friends placed the body in the car, sped off to the location we had chosen, and heaved the heavy body over the side of a bridge and into the river. But they forgot to weigh it down – and when the police pulled him out two days later they found he had managed to untie the rope that had bound his hands.

'Rasputin's body was taken to the Academy of Military Medicine for an autopsy. It revealed that he had drunk a large amount of alcohol but, do you know, no poison was found. He'd eaten enough poison to kill two horses… but, in fact, had drowned.'

Looking down at his plate, Felix seemed to suffer some melancholy.

'Rasputin had no morals. He bewitched the Tsarina – and his popularity with women came not from the size of his prick but for the three large warts that were on it.'

Philip was not the only diner to speculate about how the prince knew of such an intimate detail of Rasputin's anatomy.

Another bottle of port was ordered. The ship's officers, desperate to hear every detail, encouraged Felix to repeat the story, which he did, with further embellishments.

# Chapter Seventeen: Malta

The *Marlborough* sailed through the Dardanelles and on to the island of Prinkipo, just twelve miles from Constantinople. When the *Marlborough* anchored, a craft approached it from the shore. A Turkish official boarded and informed the captain that any passengers could come ashore but would be subject to hygiene regulations and their clothing would be fumigated.

Unperturbed, various passengers did venture ashore for picnics and to enjoy the island. The Turks kept their promise to subject their clothes to the fumigation process. Over the next two days, much to the distress of those passengers that had gone ashore, the fumigated clothes lost their shape and even shoes shrank horribly. This caused consternation among the royal passengers, who felt they didn't have enough clothes to ruin.

A week later, on the afternoon of Easter Sunday, the *Marlborough* sailed into Malta.

Over the sixteen days it had taken to travel to Malta Philip had grown a beard, and that morning decided to clip and shape it. The sailor who acted as the ship's barber sat him down in the leather chair and set to work and a little later Philip presented himself to Sophie and Sergei.

'Don't you look distinguished,' said Sophie on seeing him, and gave him a kiss. Although she found the bristles tickled her face, she was delighted with his new look.

The passengers watched as the Governor of Malta, Lord Methuen, came on board to welcome the Empress and escorted her and her daughter to the Governor's residence, the San Antonio Palace. The remaining passengers, together with their seven hundred and fifty pieces of baggage, were taken to various hotels in Sliema, a fishing town across the Grand Harbour from Valletta.

Philip, Sophie and Sergei were allocated rooms in the same hotel as the Youssoupovs. On the second day Felix sent a note to Philip asking him if he would join him for a walk in the gardens that evening before dinner. They arranged to meet on the terrace at six thirty.

Philip had four hours before his meeting with Felix and told Sophie that he was going into town. He ordered a taxi to take him to Valletta.

At the main post office he asked if he could change some money into the local currency and send a couple of telegrams. The clerk passed the forms over the counter and Philip wrote out the messages he had composed in the taxi. The first was just three sentences in length. Philip never understood why punctuation was charged extra while the four-character word 'STOP' at the end of each sentence was free. He told himself that he must ask one day, but didn't have time that day.

The second message was one sentence longer.

Philip handed the forms and payment over the counter.

'Would you like to pay for a reply?' asked the clerk.

'May I arrange for the replies to come here? I'll come back tomorrow.'

'Certainly, sir, they'll be here for you to collect.'

Leaving the post office he walked to the nearest bank and transferred one hundred pounds into a Westminster Bank account in London.

At the time they had agreed, Philip found Felix on the terrace admiring the view over the valley.

'Isn't the smell of the orange blossom magnificent?' said Felix.

'Yes, sir.'

'How are your new wife, and Sergei?'

'They are both well, thank you.'

The pleasantries over, Felix gestured for them to walk away from the hotel. Philip concluded that this was a business meeting and Felix wanted to avoid being overheard.

'I take it that now you have escaped Russia that you will be returning to the Bank of England?'

'I'm not sure, sir,' replied Philip.

Felix looked at him questioningly. 'Why so?'

'Things have changed since being in Russia. At one time my whole world was the bank. I loved the work and the life. It was comfortable, secure and it was intensely boring and unproductive. Being a banker, one persuades oneself that the work creates wealth and stability – and it does, but only for those people who don't need it. It does very little for those who have very little, and absolutely nothing for those who have nothing. Since the war and my time in Russia, my life has changed. I've seen how self-serving my work was, not just to me personally, but to the part of society that I was so firmly attached to.'

'You sound like a Bolshevik,' laughed Felix.

'No, I could never be that. The Bolshevik system of equally shared wealth is also flawed, simply because people are greedy. The Bolshevik elite, or whoever runs Russia, will always live in large houses, protected by high fences, stuffed with the nation's treasures and with servants attending to their every need.'

'With their philosophy of communal property, how will the Bolshkeviks manage that and keep the population happy?' asked Felix.

'They'll find a way. My prediction is that they'll give the people what they want. A place to live, food, education, and they'll tell them that all property belongs to the state. The population will be happy for a time and it'll be during that period that the palaces will house the Bolshevik elite who will hang fine paintings on the walls and eat off the best china. They will simply be temporary guardians and protectors of the state's assets, and it'll all be for the benefit of the people.'

Felix laughed again. 'Very perceptive, and I'm sure you'll be proved right.'

'And my life has changed in other ways. I'm now married and wonderfully happy and soon I'll be a father. My new life won't fit into the old one, nor do I intend to make it fit.'

The Prince invited Philip to sit on a bench and, once they were both settled, he spoke.

'I understand why you might not return to England and your past life, but you will need to have something to do, and I have a proposal. There are a mass of people leaving Russia. Some have never worked for a living and possess very few skills. Others are being displaced because they have supported the wrong side in a civil war; others because they follow a religion that's no longer accepted. It won't be just aristocrats that the new Russian state will destroy. In time, whole races of people will be considered counter-revolutionary. Cossacks, Armenians, Georgians, Gypsies and Jews will all be considered dangerous at some time in the future. They will be killed or forced to leave Russia and many will leave with just the shirts on their backs. It's the way things have been done in Russia for centuries, and I see no reason why that will change. I feel it's my obligation to help my countrymen where I'm able, but it needs a special person, someone with a knowledge of international banking; a desire to help people through misfortune and not just for their own benefit. I'm not that man, but I think you are. Together we could help many of my countrymen, and I'm asking you for your help.'

Philip was surprised by the Prince's proposal. 'Can I think about it and give you my answer in a few days?'

'Of course – take all the time you need, but I do hope you agree. I will be moving to Paris in a day or so and I'm most likely to stay at the Hotel Vendor. You can leave me a message there,' and the Prince rose and left Philip in the garden alone.

Philip continued to sit on the bench and look into the distance.

In the past he would have rejected the proposal out of hand. Felix was, after all, a self-confessed murderer – even though most people believed that Felix had been justified in murdering Rasputin – and the Youssoupov family had a reputation for charitable work that had only been possible due to their huge wealth. It seemed that Felix had inherited the need to help his fellow man. Philip remained on the bench for two hours, looking out to sea, and after a couple of hours he felt a plan was coming together. He would ask Sergei what he thought of the Prince's proposal.

The only person to notice Philip struggling with his thoughts was a gardener tending the roses.

'Poor man,' he said to himself. 'I'm pleased I don't have his problems.'

****

The following morning Philip returned to the post office to collect any messages that might have been sent in reply to his telegrams.

'You've had replies from both messages,' said the clerk, handing him two envelopes. Philip opened the envelopes, read the few lines contained in each reply, placed both pieces of paper back in their respective envelopes and tucked them into his jacket pocket. They were what he had anticipated!

That evening Philip recounted the conversation he'd had in the garden with Felix to Sophie and Sergei.

Once he finished Sergei spoke. 'Felix is right about so many people needing help. Since I've been at the hotel, I've read in the newspapers that Russia lost two million men in the war, and Germany, Austria, Britain and France lost a million each. That's six million families affected by the loss of a breadwinner. Then Russia's revolution has displaced countless millions more, many of them leaving to come to Western Europe. So many need help.'

Philip could only agree with Sergei. 'The task is daunting. What could be achieved?'

'With your business brain and Felix's royal name and connections and the doors he could open to the highest in society, you could do so much good.'

'I agree,' said Sophie.

'And will you two also help me in this venture?' asked Philip.

'I can't speak for your wife, but I'd be honoured. It would give me something useful to do and with what I learned from my father about business I'm sure I could make a small contribution. Like Sacha, I've known that changes need to be made, but I can't accept Sacha's belief that violence is the only pathway to achieving what he wants. This must be a better way,' said Sergei enthusiastically.

'Could any work we do be harmed by Felix murdering Rasputin?' asked Philip.

Sergei laughed. 'I predict that in the future people will be writing books, stage plays and even making films about the murder, and Felix will always be the hero. It makes a good story. A handsome prince slays a dirty, lecherous, evil devil that has hypnotised and bewitched a royal family. Public sympathy will always be on Felix's side.'

'I suspect you're right,' said Philip.

The three of them discussed their plans well into the night.

When they retired to bed Sophie wrapped her arms around Philip and kissed him gently on the lips.

'And what's that for?' he asked.

'It's my thank you.'

'For what?'

'It's been a long time since I've seen Sergei so happy, so excited and with something to live for. Inviting him to help you with your work has made him feel useful. He's so happy and I wanted to thank you for being so kind.'

Philip smiled. 'It was no kindness. Your brother has a good brain for business, I value his opinion, and he'll be a great partner, as will you.'

'Me?' she said in surprise.

'I didn't just marry you for your looks, you know. You have such compassion and a deep understanding of people – and, besides, I want to make sure you're always close to me. I don't want to leave you where someone might be tempted to steal you from me.'

'No one will ever steal me away from you,' she said.

****

Over the next few days the three of them relaxed, enjoyed picnics overlooking the sea, visited St John's Cathedral, watched an opera from a private box at the Monoel Theatre and even took Sergei for a swim in the sea. Sophie had never been happier, as Philip and she laughed and behaved like any couple in love with not a care in the world. Sergei was pleased to be included in their plans but, on more than one occasion, pretended to be asleep in the shade of a tall poplar tree so that his sister and her new husband could have some time alone.

One morning Sophie decided that they should visit the shops in Valletta. They needed a new wardrobe: it was noticeable that their fellow Russian exiles, far from being the impoverished group expected by the hotels and shops on the island, had unpacked much of their seven hundred and fifty pieces of luggage and now appeared around the town and in the local restaurants in fashionable clothes, and for dinner wore their diamond necklaces and even tiaras. The three of them took a boat across the harbour to Valletta and strolled around the shops, where Sophie spent some of her money on new dresses and hats and the two men bought a couple of suits, shirts and evening wear.

To celebrate Philip and Sophie's marriage they decided to book a table for dinner in a restaurant just a few streets away. While Philip dressed Sophie lay on the bed and watched him. He presented himself to her and she nodded her approval, got up from the bed, adjusted his tie, kissed him on the lips and said, 'And now you must go!'

She opened the door and playfully pushed him out of the room. He turned to look at her and she waved at him and the door closed, leaving him in the corridor.

Philip and Sergei dutifully waited in the lobby. Philip was reminded of his childhood, before his mother had died, when his father had joked, 'A man washes, puts on a clean dress shirt and the most complicated part is threading the studs into the starched shirt. Women, on the other hand, have a lady's maid to help. Because there are two of them, it means it takes twice as long to be ready.'

To while away the time they drank a whisky. Philip read out a report in a newspaper about the peace conference negotiations, and a whole hour passed.

Then Philip saw Sophie at the top of the stairs wearing a long evening gown of peach silk. A matching shawl came down over her bare shoulders to fall across her stomach and disguise the fact that she was pregnant. Her golden hair was swept up to show off her long neck. She wore peach-coloured elbow-length gloves and her mother's pearls, which had been restrung in Valletta.

As she descended the stairs, men stopped to let her pass and regretted that their wives didn't look as beautiful. Women were jealous that they no longer turned heads in the same way. The clerk on the front desk caught the pageboy staring and cuffed his head with the flat of his hand, sending him scurrying towards the lift. Sergei beamed with an older brother's pride.

The restaurant was on the harbour front overlooking the fortifications and across the bay to the town of Valletta. Bougainvillea covered the front of the building and waiters with long white starched aprons moved between the tables. A first course of turtle soup was followed by lobster *chevre d'or* served with a delicious hollandaise and black truffle sauce. Then they enjoyed *poulet sauté maison*. All the food had been carefully chosen so that it could be eaten with a fork or a spoon and Sergei wasn't embarrassed at only having one hand. When the dessert trolley was finally wheeled to their table, they looked at the cakes covered in strawberries, the *compote de cerises*, the *mille-feuilles fraises*, *sorbet au champagne* and sent the trolley away. They were all full from one of the best meals they had had in months, if not ever.

Throughout the meal Sophie looked at her brother and her husband with joy. She was with the two men she loved most in the world. Their smart new evening suits, starched shirts and stiff collars made them look so handsome. Sergei, in particular, looked relaxed and happy.

She caught her husband looking at her. He looked so proud, more than a couple of times they glanced at each other to say a silent 'I love you.'

The waiter brought coffee and a flower seller approached the table. Philip purchased six white roses and presented them to Sophie.

'A late wedding bouquet,' he told her.

She picked up the flowers and smelled their heavenly perfume.

After the meal they decided that it was such a magnificent evening they would stroll along the harbour to see the stars and watch the other diners promenading. Despite the harbour being busy the three of them felt as if they were quite alone. Philip wheeled Sergei and Sophie had her arm entwined in Philip's.

Philip failed to see the two men dressed like dock workers and with their cloth caps pulled low over their faces until it was too late. One knocked into Sophie, making her stumble.

'Hey there,' shouted Philip as a warning to the two drunks.

As Philip protectively held on to Sophie one of the men pulled a pistol from his coat and aimed it, very steadily, at Philip's chest.

'No!' shouted Sergei and with a mighty effort pushed himself up from the chair. There was a flash of flame and a deafening crack.

Sophie watched in disbelief as Sergei leaped upwards and then fell to the ground, the wheelchair upturned beside him. She bent down to pick him up, hoping that he wasn't too hurt – then she saw the stain that had begun to turn his white shirt crimson.

Philip heard the gunshot and watched Sergei fall to the ground.

'Oh God,' he said, and looked into the crowd for the attacker.

*Was it him? No, he's too young, he's too old, he's got a beard... if only the woman would move, he could see the man behind her. No, it wasn't him either. Is that him? No, his wife's holding on to his arm.* He wanted to rush into the crowd, search for the men, arrest them, ask them why they had done it, but Sergei was gasping for breath. He couldn't leave him.

Sergei coughed and a brown liquid covered his chin and spattered Sophie's dress with tiny specks. The crowd groaned in disgust and some took a step back while others turned away. Others were transfixed by the sight and more people joined the crowd.

Sophie held her brother more tightly in an effort to comfort him, and stroked his hair as their mother had done when they had been ill. He seemed to draw comfort from her stroking it. Sergei smiled at her.

He coughed again and a darker liquid oozed out of his mouth and Philip pressed his silk scarf into the wound to stem the flow of blood.

It was useless. Philip knew Sergei was dying.

Sergei also knew he was dying. He could feel both his arms and legs. It was strange that he felt whole again – but he wished he didn't feel so cold.

'Promise me you'll look after her,' he said to Philip, who nodded and squeezed his shoulder. Turning his head to look at Sophie he smiled.

'I love you,' he tried to say, but no sound came out of his mouth. He had said all that he needed to. He had no pain now; everything was quiet and peaceful, he could go to sleep.

Sophie looked into his eyes and watched them glaze over. She kissed his cheek and her body shook as she rocked him like a baby and whispered, 'I love you too, my Bliznets.'

A policeman rushed over and asked one of the crowd gathering around the scene, 'What happened?'

'A robbery, and a man's been shot,' someone said.

'Did anyone see who did it?' the policeman asked.

'One had bushy eyebrows,' a man in the crowd volunteered.

**\*\*\*\***

The Malta police force is one of the oldest in Europe, dating back to 1814 when Sir Thomas Maitland was Governor of Malta. At the moment, the illustrious history of the force of which he was such an outstanding member mattered not a jot to Inspector Giovanni Debarro. He had arrived at work in a profoundly bad mood. His argument with his wife had lasted longer than normal. The usual accusations still rang in his ears. It wasn't his fault he had to work such long hours; after all, he was a police inspector. And as for her shrill accusations of him being with other women... Was it any wonder that the attractions of the curvaceous Adele were preferable to those of a wife twenty years past her prime? Was it his fault he arrived home after midnight most nights?

He knew it was going to be another hot day and, as he walked into his office, he wiped the sweat off his forehead with a grubby handkerchief. Hanging his jacket on the back of his chair, he slumped behind his desk and wished for an easy day. He felt the sticky dark patches of sweat staining the same white shirt he'd worn the day before. His lazy bitch of a wife had got it into her mind that he was with another woman, and hadn't washed a clean shirt for him as revenge. He cursed the fact that the ceiling fan still hadn't been repaired.

Perhaps he would do what he did yesterday. Walk over the street to Armando's Café, sit in the shade and do some paperwork. He could have another lunch of *bigilla*, pâté made from broad beans and garlic, followed by a large portion of the flaky pastry parcel filled with ricotta that last year had won the prize for the best *pastizzi* in the town.

Suddenly there was a knock on the door, and a young policeman walked in.

'Chief Petruzza was looking for you last night.'

'What did he want?'

'There was a shooting last night down by the harbour. A Russian was killed. The chief wants you to look into it,' replied the young man, placing a paper file on Debarro's desk.

'Christ, that's all I need,' muttered Debarro.

The young policeman closed the office door and wondered how the lazy fat slob had managed to become an inspector.

\*\*\*\*

Death is not a time for quiet reflection. Death brings with it many strangers, all demanding answers to questions about coffins, flowers, orders of service, notices in newspapers and all the minutiae that are involved in making the necessary arrangements for the dearly departed.

Sophie sat in the hotel room gazing out of the window, contemplating the peace of the fishermen's boats soundlessly going in and out of the harbour. In contrast, the hotel room was in a state of constant commotion.

There was a knock on the door. Sophie groaned. Who now? she thought.

Philip opened the door to see a small pudgy man in a crumpled suit and behind him a uniformed policeman.

'I'm Inspector Giovanni Debarro of the Malta police. I would like to ask the Count and Countess Tagleva some questions about the incident last night,' said the pudgy man.

'Come in,' said Philip.

'I take it you are the count and the lady is the countess.'

The question was rhetorical and Philip chose, under the circumstances, not to correct the inspector.

Debarro walked over to Sophie and bowed slightly. 'My sincere condolences on your loss.'

'Thank you, you're very kind,' said Sophie for the hundredth time.

'However, it's my duty to ask you both some questions.'

Philip nodded.

'When did you arrive in Malta?'

Philip recounted their arrival on board HMS *Marlborough*.

'You came on the same ship as the Dowager Empress of Russia?'

'We did,' replied Philip.

Hearing how the visitors had arrived on the island and the company that they kept, Debarro told himself that it would be prudent to undertake the investigation with as much care as the heat of the day would allow. He might have to justify his actions at a later date.

There followed an hour of questions. Is this your first time on Malta? Have you any enemies on the island? Did you know the assailants? Can you describe them? What were they wearing? Could they have been Russian? Did they say anything? Why did you choose that particular restaurant? Had you eaten there before? Was anything stolen? What type of pistol was it?

After the policemen left Sophie said she was tired and retired to bed to have a cry.

There was another knock on the door. Philip opened it to find the bellboy, who handed him an envelope. It was a note from Felix Youssoupov and his wife, sending their condolences. He placed the note on the small table adjacent to the door and noticed the white roses he'd given Sophie at the restaurant the night before. The yellowing petals were spattered with small flecks of brown.

Philip picked them up and placed them gently in the waste bin under the table.

Philip thought of Sophie. In the past few months she had lost her father and now her brother, and she didn't know where her eldest brother was. She had had to leave her country and home to flee into exile. He felt her emptiness.

Philip thought back to the night before. The whole episode was etched into his mind in slow motion. The gunmen had approached as if they were about to demand money: that would have been the logical conclusion, and the one that the Maltese police would most likely come to. But the men hadn't demanded money. The attackers had said nothing. They hadn't attempted to snatch Sophie's pearl necklace. He could only see the pistol pointing at his chest. The gunman had started to squeeze the trigger and, seeing this, Sergei had thrown himself out of his chair so that he came between the pistol and Philip. Sergei had sacrificed himself to save him.

Sophie lay on the bed in a fog. She looked at the empty wheelchair in the corner of the room. She should have done more to save Sergei, and she buried her face into the pillow and screamed with anger. *How dare Sergei leave me? I have lost all my family; now I only have Philip.*

There was another knock on the door. Opening it, Philip found Felix Youssoupov.

'I'm so sorry about the news – Irina and I are very upset. If there's anything that I can do, then please just ask. How is the Countess?' he said formally.

'Shocked, but please come in. She thanks you for the note,' replied Philip.

Felix entered the room and took off his hat and coat. He whispered, 'I thought that I would tell you that tomorrow we're leaving Malta to travel to Italy and from there go to Paris. I've made reservations at the Hotel Vendor, and once you have settled things here I hope to see you in Paris.'

When Felix had gone, Philip gently opened the bedroom door and, seeing that Sophie was awake, handed her Felix's note.

'How kind of Felix to bring his condolences; such a nice man.'

Philip sat down. 'I think you've been so strong. I know how close you were to Sergei. I promise you'll never have to be on your own again.'

'You're such a wonderful man.'

'And you're such a wonderful wife.'

Philip took Sophie in his arms and held her, and Sophie eventually fell asleep, utterly exhausted and unable to cry any more.

**\*\*\*\***

Debarro returned to the police station. He'd spent a few minutes looking at the murder scene and another couple at the morgue looking at the body.

He sighed. Foreigners always caused trouble. Every summer the island was invaded by tourists from France, Italy and other places who lost their wallets, lost their children and complained of the hotel prices. He longed for the winter when most of the visitors left and the worst crime he had to deal with was a bit of sheep stealing. After reading newspaper reports of the barbarity of the revolution he wasn't surprised that the Russians were bringing their own kind of violence to his island. He gave the description of the assailants given to him by Count and Countess Tagleva to the front desk. It would be distributed to the police force and printed in the local newspapers. There was nothing more to be done for the moment. He dropped the file on top of the others in his pending file and walked to

Armando's for a cool glass of wine and lunch. He didn't expect to catch the assassins; by now they would be long gone.

Three days later, Sergei was buried in the local Orthodox church.

The coffin was open, in the traditional Russian manner, and Sergei looked peaceful. A small bouquet of white roses had been placed on his chest.

Philip and Sophie moved forward and kissed Sergei's forehead for the last time and Philip said to her, 'Before we left Yalta I filled a small pot with earth so that our baby would be born on Russian soil. I think we should use some of it so that Sergei is buried with some of his homeland's soil.'

Sophie smiled. 'So that's why you left the boat at Yalta! You're so thoughtful; thank you.'

Philip produced a small tin and poured half the contents into the side of the coffin. Sophie placed a gold Orthodox cross on top of Sergei's chest before the coffin lid was put in place and the coffin lowered into the ground.

That evening, as the sun was going down, they returned to visit the grave and to be alone with Sergei. Sophie stroked the wooden Orthodox cross that had been placed at the head of the grave, and wept a little.

# Chapter Eighteen: The House of Tagleva

## May 1919

Two weeks later Philip and Sophie arrived at the Hotel Vendor in Paris and checked in as Count and Countess Tagleva. They were shown into a suite of rooms, one floor below Prince Felix. The change of name, which had come about by chance thanks to the portly Maltese inspector, had seemed to both of them a way that Philip could hide from further unwanted attention while ensuring that the family name of Tagleva would not be lost. Philip was pleased to have left Malta. He had been worried for Sophie. At first, she had refused to believe her brother was dead and then her emotion had changed to anger: anger at Sergei for sacrificing himself, anger at herself for not saving him, anger at his murderers, and anger at the police for not finding the man who had shot him. The one person she never directed her anger towards was Philip. All she wanted to do was to be held by him. It was the only place that she felt completely safe and secure.

That evening the two of them had dinner with Felix and Irina Youssoupov. Philip was pleased that Sophie was able to spend some time with them; they would be company for her, as he had some work to do the following morning.

The next day, Philip took a taxi to the Société Générale. He handed the clerk a visiting card and the clerk politely asked him to take a seat. Philip looked around him, thinking that the lobby looked more like a cathedral than a bank. The huge glass ceiling resembled Norman arches, and a dome of golden glass bathed the reception area in a warm glow. As in a cathedral, all conversation was carried out in hushed tones and, despite the large number of people working and holding meetings, there was very little sound.

A young man approached Philip, his leather-soled shoes echoing on the elaborately decorated marble mosaic floor.

'May I introduce myself? My name is Jean-Claude and I will be your account manager. Please follow me if you would, sir.'

After arriving at a comfortable office, Jean-Claude spoke. 'I understand from the front desk that in addition to opening a bank account you also wish to purchase a safe deposit box.'

'That's correct,' said Philip.

'May I ask the name of the account holder?'

'Count and Countess Tagleva.'

'Certainly, sir,' said Jean-Claude.

The details and papers were drawn up and copy signatures taken from Philip, who said that he would bring the Countess to the bank to provide her signature in due course.

Jean-Claude then led him down three flights of stairs and into a private room, where his safety deposit box was brought to him.

'This is box A3287,' said Jean-Claude, pointing to the number on the front. 'This is your key, and this is the bank's,' and he produced from his pocket a key on a chain that allowed it to be attached to his belt. He opened the box using both keys, and pushed back the heavy lid.

'I will leave you now, sir. Please take as long as you wish and ring the bell when you are finished.'

'Thank you, Jean-Claude.'

Philip opened the case he had brought with him and filled the deposit box with the cut diamonds, gold and platinum ingots, the ruby bracelet, the diamond and sapphire necklaces and all the other treasures he'd brought out of Russia. He added a large purse full of gold coins and another containing four strings of pearls that Sophie had given him. Finally, he placed some envelopes on the top and closed the box, locking it with his key. He rang the bell.

As he prepared to leave the bank Jean-Claude asked, 'Is there anything else I can do for you?'

'Actually, there is. I would like to send a message to the Bank of England. Could I do so from here?'

'Certainly, sir.'

Philip composed the message and Jean-Claude left to telephone the bank with the message, returning some ten minutes later.

'Monsieur, I very much regret to inform you that when I telephoned the Bank of England and, as requested, asked to speak to a Mr Philip Cummings, I was told he had left the bank's employment some time ago. It seems he was dismissed for what I was told were "irregularities". I'm very sorry. As you requested, I didn't mention your name and didn't leave a message. I hope that was in order?'

'You did very well. Thank you.'

Philip left the Société Générale.

**** 

That night Philip met Felix Youssoupov. The papers to begin an investment brokerage had been lodged with the French authorities. These had specified that Philip was the managing director while Felix, his wife Irina and Sophie were directors.

The House of Tagleva had been established.

The first priority, the security of his family, had been achieved. He could now turn some of his attention towards ensuring that the people he suspected were behind his betrayal and Sergei's death were made to pay.

Working from a hotel suite was hardly the best way to encourage confidence in customers, so Philip and Sophie decided they needed a more permanent home. They looked for a townhouse that would accommodate themselves and the new baby, as well as provide offices for Tagleva.

Despite their temporary location, Felix told all his relatives about their venture and within a few days Philip received a steady stream of exiles all looking for investment advice. Many of the Russians sent to Philip had absolutely nothing to invest, having lost everything in the revolution. They had no money or jewels, and on more than one occasion their only collateral was their title. There seemed to be more penniless princes, dukes and counts in Paris than anywhere else on earth. However, he tried to see everyone and, whenever possible, helped find a job, accommodation or helped with finances to start a business.

One morning Felix arrived and handed Philip a paper, saying, 'I thought you would be interested in this, as it affects what you might do with the packages and letters you brought out of Russia. It contains details of the Tsar's murder and from the various investigations that started within a few days of his death.'

Philip took out the papers and began to read.

### The Case of Emperor Nicholas II
### Compiled from eleven volumes of evidence
### Investigators:

*Alexei Nametkin, Ivan Sergeyev, examining magistrate and investigation committee*

### Includes testimonies from four guards at the Impatiev House:

*Medvedev, Yakimov, Letemin and Proskurykov*

*All claim NOT to have been part of the execution party, but claim to have seen the Imperial Family before and after they were killed:*

*Investigations reveal that the Imperial Family, together with their few remaining servants, Anna Demidova, Alexei Trupp, the Tsar's valet, and the Tsarevich's doctor Dr Botkin, are all dead.*

*There follows the testimony of Michail Medvedev and other members of the squad of soldiers guarding the Royal Family (but who deny being part of the murder squad).*

*Medvedev states:*

*'In the evening of 16 July, between seven and eight p.m., when the time of my duty had just begun, Commandant Yurovsky [the head of the execution squad] ordered me to take all the Nagan revolvers from the guards and to bring them to him. I took twelve revolvers from the sentries as well as from some other guards, and brought them to the commandant's office.*

*'Yurovsky said to me, "We must shoot them all tonight; so notify the guards not to be alarmed if they hear shots." I understood, therefore, that Yurovsky had it in his mind to shoot the whole of the Tsar's family, as well as the doctor and the servants who lived with*

them, but I did not ask him where or by whom the decision had been made... At about ten o'clock in the evening, in accordance with Yurovsky's order, I informed the guards not to be alarmed if they should hear firing.

'About midnight, Yurovsky woke up the Tsar's family. I do not know if he told them the reason they had been woken, and where they were to be taken, but I positively affirm that it was Yurovsky who entered the room occupied by the Tsar's family. In about an hour the whole of the family – including the doctor, the maid and the valet – got up, washed and dressed themselves.

'The Empress sat by the wall by the window, near the black pillar of the arch. Behind her stood three of her daughters (I knew their faces very well, because I had seen them every day when they walked in the garden, but I didn't know their names). The heir and the Emperor sat side by side almost in the middle of the room. Doctor Botkin stood behind the heir. The maid, a very tall woman, stood at the left of the door leading to the store room; by her side stood one of the Tsar's daughters (the fourth). Two servants stood against the wall on the left from the entrance of the room.

'Yurovsky ordered me to leave, saying, "Go on to the street, see if there is anybody there, and wait to see whether the shots have been heard." I went out to the court, which was enclosed by a fence, but before I got to the street I heard firing. I returned to the house immediately (only two or three minutes having elapsed) and, upon entering the room where the execution had taken place, I saw that all the members of the Tsar's family were lying on the floor with many wounds in their bodies. The blood was running in streams. The doctor, the maid and two waiters had also been shot. When I entered, the heir was still alive and moaned a little. Yurovsky went up and fired two or three more times at him. Then the heir was still.'

Medvedev's testimony finishes here.

Other testimonies and third party descriptions of the events are as follows:

Testimony A
'One of the assassins told me this. On entering the room, the Empress said to their chief jailer, Yurovsky, "Are we forbidden

211

from sitting down?" The jailer ordered two chairs to be brought in. The Tsar placed his sick son on one and the Empress sat on the other. Nicholas took his place at the head of the group and directly in front of the Tsarevich, thus screening him from the door. The child's doctor, Dr Botkin, stood directly behind the child and placed a hand on the Tsarevich's shoulder.'

*Testimony B*
'The assassins entered the room and Yurovsky ordered the family to stand. Yurovsky looked at the Tsar and addressed him: "In view of the fact that your relatives in this country and abroad continue to plot against the revolution, the Presidium of the Ural Regional Soviet has sentenced you to death."

'Nicholas said, "Oh, my God." The Empress and two of the servants in the room muttered a prayer and crossed themselves. The soldiers pulled pistols from behind their backs and from tunic pockets.

'The first bullet smashed into the Tsar's chest, turning his green jacket scarlet, followed by a second, third and fourth as all eleven assassins fired at him, each wanting to claim that they had killed the tyrant. In all, eleven bullets entered Nicholas's chest. Two exited through his back, one hitting the Tsesarevich in the left hand and removing two fingers. The other wounded Dr Botkin in the shoulder and was deflected downward and out of his body to hit the Tsar's valet in the leg, shattering his femur. The Emperor lurched forward and fell to the floor, dead.

'Another of the assassins pointed his Mauser towards the Empress and fired. Her head exploded, spraying blood and brains all over her two daughters, who were standing behind her. She dropped her cane as her body slumped back into the chair, then to the floor. She fell to the floor and landed on her back with a black mass of blood where her face had been. The noise must have been deafening, because the guards later complained that everyone's ears rang for a long time afterwards, and a couple of the guards were reported to have been wounded by bullets ricocheting around the room, as grey smoke made it difficult for the assassins to see and to aim properly.'

*Testimony C*

'I was told that most of those in the room had survived the first volley of bullets and the guards had to open the doors to clear the air of the gun smoke so that they could see. As the smoke cleared, the assassins saw all but three of their victims still moving, and many moaning in pain.

'The jailers entered the room for the second time. It seems that The Tsar's daughter, Grand Duchess Marie, screamed and hurled herself at a cupboard door in an effort to escape, but a bullet struck her in the thigh and she collapsed to the floor, writhing in agony. The Empress's maid, Anna Demidova, clutched a pillow to her chest and a bullet hit the metal box hidden inside, splitting it wide open and tipping some of the Empress's favourite jewels onto the floor. The second bullet hit the maid in the upper leg.

'Dr Botkin, having fallen to the floor, wounded, was now propping himself up in an effort to reach and protect the Tsarevich. A bullet was fired into the doctor's temple: he fell into the boy's lap and blood ran from the doctor's shattered head and down the boy's legs, filling his boots with blood and brain.

'As the Tsarevich looked down at the doctor, one of the guards walked over to the thirteen-year-old and emptied five bullets into the boy's chest. He hoped to put the boy out of his misery, yet the boy still refused to die, protected by jewels sewn into his tunic and undergarments. Terrified but unable to move due to the weight of Botkin's body on his legs, the young heir to the Romanov throne watched as another guard approached with a bayonet and plunged it towards his chest – but the blade hit a large ruby and slipped off his tunic. The guard pulled another pistol from his tunic and fired two further bullets into the boy's chest. Trapped in his seat by the dead doctor's body, the boy's tunic turned crimson and his head slumped forward onto his chest. He was dead.

'In the far corner of the room, the Tsar's three surviving daughters huddled together. Again a hail of bullets was fired, but they too refused to die, also protected by the jewels they had hidden in their clothes. Yurovsky approached Grand Duchess Tatiana, aimed his pistol at her head and pulled the trigger. The front of her face exploded, covering her screaming sisters in more blood and brains. The final survivors were dispatched in a similar manner.

*'The guards checked each of the bodies for a pulse and one, fuelled by blood lust, took his ten-inch bayonet and plunged it deep into the Tsar's chest, splitting his chest bone in two, before doing the same to the dead Empress. From her chest spouted a fountain of blood, covering the guard's face and hair. Horrified at the sight he had witnessed, one of the guards vomited in the doorway. The execution of the family and their retainers had taken no more than fourteen minutes.'*

*Notes: Few identifiable human remains have been found, although those that have been retrieved are not enough to account for the eleven victims that have been reported to have been killed.*

Philip handed the report back to Felix.

'I'm very sorry to read this about your family; such a terrible thing.'

'Thank you,' said Felix. 'Will this alter how you use or look after the letters and property you brought out of Russia for the Tsar?'

'No – they remain the property of the heirs of the Imperial Family. This just confuses the situation, and it may be many years before it is resolved. I suggest we wait until that situation becomes clearer. The letters I was given to take to England, I will eventually give to their intended recipients, but I need to be sure the information they contain will be used properly and in accordance with the Tsar's wishes.'

'Do whatever you think fit,' said Felix and left.

****

Sophie had been feeling a little crampy the day before, but hadn't thought much of it. Nonetheless, she decided to retire to bed early. At two in the morning she awoke with the disquieting sense that her waters were beginning to break. She got out of bed and wandered about the bedroom for an hour or so, feeling some relief that the waiting might soon be over. She shook Philip awake. 'I think I'm going to have our baby.'

Philip rose from the bed in a mixture of excitement and panic and went to call the midwife they had engaged for the birth. Sophie returned to the bed and lay there, timing her contractions. In the early stages of her pregnancy, she had been told by a neighbour that contractions were like indigestion. Sophie wondered what kind of indigestion the poor woman had suffered from! This was turning into an experience she really didn't feel ready for.

The midwife arrived. By now Sophie could feel intermittent internal twists of pain and, recalling the stories she had been told of childbirth, most of them unpleasant, she felt she was facing a vast unknown.

'I want my husband,' she said to the midwife.

'All right, dear, if you're sure, but he won't be any help – they never are.' She left to call Philip, who entered the room carrying a small box.

'And what's that?' demanded the midwife, pointing to the box.

'Russia,' said Philip, and placed the box containing what remained of the Russian soil he'd saved underneath the bed. The child would be born above Russian soil.

Sophie's contractions were now between three and five minutes apart and lasting for one minute each.

'It won't be long now,' said the midwife to Sophie, in her usual effort to be comforting.

Could this be the real thing? Sophie thought. Everyone had told her that first babies tended to take twenty hours or more to arrive, but this seemed to be happening so fast. She looked up at Philip, standing next to her, and for the first time thought he looked utterly helpless. She laughed at his helplessness through the pain of another contraction.

'Now comes the easy part,' lied the midwife. 'You can push now.'

Sophie pushed.

Two long hours later, Sophie had begun to wonder whether she would ever have the baby, and her low moaning had been replaced by tears and yelling.

'I don't think I can do this!' she shouted.

The midwife replied, 'Yes, you can. You're doing it right now.'

Sophie looked at the ceiling, then at Philip. Why had he put her in this situation? As she cried in frustration, the midwife spoke sternly. 'Look at me! Stop crying and focus all your energy on pushing your baby out. Crying isn't going to help you have a baby.'

So Sophie concentrated on pushing. She knew she was close.

At long last the midwife said, 'I can see the baby's head.'

Moments later, Michael Sergei Tagleva was born.

# Chapter Nineteen: Boulogne-Sur-Seine

Two weeks later Philip and Sophie moved into a modest three-storey house in the Paris district of Boulogne-Sur-Seine, known as Boulogne by Parisians, and set up their home.

They hired a nanny for young Michael, and a chauffeur.

Philip's joy was complete when he went to collect Mr and Mrs Evans at the Paris railway station.

Philip hugged Mrs Evans for the longest time. He felt as if the best part of his past life had returned to him. Once he had put Mrs Evans down he shook her husband's hand earnestly.

'We were so surprised to get your telegram and one hundred pounds,' said Mrs Evans, thinking his beard made him look very distinguished. 'We thought you must be dead when the bank stopped your salary. We didn't know what to do. The man from the bank explained you were missing and suggested we sold your things and looked for some employment elsewhere. But we couldn't do that, not until we were sure. We had almost used up the money you had left us when your telegram arrived. Then we got your letter asking us to come to Paris.'

'As you asked, we've put our things into storage and caught the train. Your note was quite clear about telling no one we had heard from you,' added Mr Evans.

'But what's going to happen to all your lovely furniture and beautiful things, and that lovely glass collection you had?' asked Mrs Evans.

'They're only possessions – they can all be replaced, and I've arranged with a solicitor in London for the contents of the house to be sold. By next week there will be nothing left of Philip Cummings in London.'

'Oh Lord,' exclaimed Mrs Evans.

Philip hugged them both again. 'I'm so pleased you're both well and I'll tell you everything that's happened once I get you to my house. Then everything will be clear, but now I must take you to meet my wife and son.'

'A wife and a son,' exclaimed Mrs Evans. 'How wonderful!' and she gave Mr Evans an approving nod.

'I always knew he'd marry a beauty, and the child is bonnie,' Mrs Evans said to her husband that evening. Together they began to put the house into some sort of order.

Mr Evans engaged a maid to clean upstairs and an assistant cook for Mrs Evans and began to organise Philip's expanding wardrobe. He mentioned to Mrs Evans that Philip had lost a lot of weight, as his jackets and trousers were two inches smaller than when he was in London.

'That'll be because he's not been eating my steak pie,' said Mrs Evans, adding that he obviously needed feeding up.

The household settled down to a routine of family domesticity that inevitably revolved round the nursery. Four or five times a day Sophie would visit her son and often encouraged Mrs Evans to accompany her. Mrs Evans loved playing with young Michael, who would hold on to her chubby fingers and gurgle with delight as Mrs Evans cooed back at him. Philip would pop his head around the door to check on his opening batsman each morning and evening.

When not visiting his son, Philip was hard at work setting up Tagleva Investments. Felix Youssoupov, the non-executive chairman, brought in many investors who were looking for financial advice. Very soon Tagleva's reputation for sound financial advice was being talked about in salons and at dinner parties all over Paris. Their clients included wealthy French citizens, Russian emigrés and even some English people and Americans living in Paris.

Then there were those who needed finance, and Tagleva Investments was always happy to encourage a new business venture, even if the risks were higher than a bank would usually consider. It soon became obvious that Tagleva would need to employ staff to manage the amount of work being generated. The house in Boulogne-Sur-Seine couldn't cope with the number of files they needed to track client invest-ments and the four secretaries and the bookkeeper that Philip had engaged. They also needed a deputy to help manage the business.

Each time Philip visited the Société Générale he had been increasingly impressed by Jean-Claude. On one occasion he gave Philip, from memory, the closing share values of four-teen stocks. He could offer opinions on stock movements and advice on whether to buy or to sell, and Philip noticed that on nine out of ten occasions Jean-Claude's advice proved to be correct. Philip also noticed the ease which he remembered clients' names and account details.

One evening Philip ensured that he was passing the bank just as the staff were leaving at the end of the day. Jean-Claude immediately recognised Philip and stopped to talk to him, so Philip offered to buy them both a coffee and absinthe. Over the next hour and a half Philip heard about Jean-Claude's early life and war.

'I've been a trainee banker at the Société Générale for two years. My father was a businessman who exported goods to England. He often took me with him, and that's where I learned to speak English. My mother doted on my father and so home life was very warm and secure. Both my parents worked hard and were able to send me to university, where I studied eco-nomics. Once I left university I got a junior position in a bank but within a few weeks the war began and I enlisted in the army. I was a motorcycle dispatch rider based in a French general's headquarters. I wasn't happy being behind the real fighting, and asked to be transferred to the front. I eventually ended up on the western front in the closing months of the war. When the war finished I managed to return to the bank.'

'Are your parents still alive?' asked Philip.

'No, they both died before the war.'

'I'm sorry,' said Philip.

'My father was ruined by a banker and another businessman who set out to destroy him. My father killed himself and my mother was driven mad with grief.'

'How awful – that must have been dreadful.'

Jean-Claude nodded soberly and Philip moved the conversation on to other things.

Over a couple of weeks their coffees turned into long dinners. Jean-Claude enthusiastically talked at length of his love of mathematics, how he used statistics to predict changes in the stock market, the price of wheat, copper and tin and at what point to buy and sell so that he was buying almost at the bottom price and selling almost at the top.

'The trick is not to be too greedy and not to wait too long before buying or selling. Buy a share after it has fallen by fifteen per cent and hold on to the share until it has risen above the purchase price by twenty per cent. Then it's time to sell,' Jean-Claude explained. 'It works seventy-five per cent of the time across the entire Paris Exchange.'

The conversation turned from finance to politics.

'The politicians at the Paris peace conference are forcing Germany to pay France and its allies reparations for the cost of the war. It's crazy,' said Jean-Claude. 'Half of Germany's national income for the next hundred years will be owed to someone else. Germans will live in a permanent state of poverty and it's always going to be a source of discontent. There's only one thing that Germany can do, and that is to default on its loans. Public opinion in Germany will move to extremism and hatred of the French. The whole policy to punish 'the Hun' is stupid.'

After a few weeks Philip offered Jean-Claude the job of general manager at Tagleva, at double his current salary. Jean-Claude accepted.

Philip quickly learned that Jean-Claude had a photographic memory, and he could recall not just the latest stock figures but also the final balance of customer accounts days after reading the information. He worked hard, arriving early and leaving late.

Jean-Claude also had a flair for organisation, which allowed him to easily reorganise the system so that every document could be found immediately it was required. He created a system for deciding which companies to recommend to clients as being good for investment, and he visited the companies to ensure that the information they supplied was both honest and correct. Philip saw how hard he worked and wondered when he managed to sleep or have a social life. A young man in Paris should be enjoying himself – but Philip concluded that that was Jean-Claude's business.

After seven months, the town house could no longer cope with the amount of work they were generating, and Philip felt that it was time for Tagleva to move out of the family home. Together with Jean-Claude, they began to look for larger offices. They viewed and rejected a number of possible locations before Jean-Claude found an ideal office building on Rue Pierre Charron.

Located between Avenue George V and the Champs-Elysées, the office was in the heart of Paris, near the financial and government districts and with the additional benefit of being conveniently located for Philip to walk to it from home.

Large wooden polished double doors created an imposing entrance to the five-storey building, and fine wrought-iron balconies, so liked by the Parisians, were at every window. Inside the spacious rooms would make ideal offices, with enough to allow for many years of expansion. In addition, the cellars could easily be converted into a secure strong-room.

Jean-Claude set about equipping the offices in the style expected of a successful investment house. He started with Philip's. An antique dealer delivered a large leather-topped desk to act as the focal point of the room, and this was set centrally in front of a window. A large blue and white Persian carpet was laid. To the right of Philip's desk, a large dining table would act as a meeting space and seating was provided by eight gilt-wood salon chairs covered in blue silk. Other items included a secretaire, bookcases in mahogany and a huge Napoleon III gilt mirror above the marble fireplace.

Philip was delighted with the classic look, which Jean-Claude used throughout the rest of the building.

Jean-Claude's office was similarly decorated, though with a smaller meeting table for six. Even the lift contained a silk-covered salon chair that customers could use while being conveyed to the directors' floor to meet Count Tagleva.

Jean-Claude set about employing clerks, secretaries, deposit managers, an accounting department and legal advisers. In all, forty-five employees joined Tagleva over the following six weeks. To manage the staff, they decided that two new directors should be appointed. Together they would manage Tagleva when both Philip and Jean-Claude were away.

The accountant was a lucky find. Tobias Meijers was visiting Paris from his home in Amsterdam. He and Philip met in a coffee shop. Philip needed some sugar and, since there was no sugar bowl on his own table, asked Tobias if he could use the one on his table. Their conversation quickly turned away from the delights of Paris to their mutual interest in finance. Philip learned that Tobias was unhappy with his current employers.

'They can't accept that accountant-designed systems aren't always fault-free. Traditional methods are often too trammelled by rigid theory and over-elaboration. My employer insists on having a system that's arranged solely for the purposes of strict audit and to protect them from the staff pilfering the stock rather than the benefit of those using the system on an on-going basis.'

Over the next two hours Philip and Tobias talked about budgets, budgetary control, standard costs, and costing as a management tool. Philip agreed with Tobias that 'control of waste could be better achieved through setting of standards and monitoring of performance against those standards rather than through figures on a piece of paper'. They also agreed that poor management of financial control and flexibility was 'a result of the war, when amateurs who knew little or nothing about finance were put in all kinds of important positions'.

Within a few weeks Tobias had left his employers in Amsterdam and moved to an apartment in Paris near Rue Pierre Charron that Sophie had found and decorated for him.

Philip was delighted by Tobias's acute mind and his ability, shared by so many of his countrymen, to speak and write English, French and German in addition to his native Dutch.

The lawyer, Arnaud Hourcade, applied for the job of Head of Legal Services after seeing it advertised in a newspaper. A French Canadian, Arnaud had grown up in a one-church town in Quebec with a greater need for fur trappers and traders than for lawyers. His father's law firm, as a result, was neither busy nor profitable. The lack of work was probably the reason he habitually consumed half a bottle of Hiram Walker's Club Whiskey before lunch. When his father announced, a few minutes before he slid off his stool to the floor in Charley's Bar, that Arnaud was off to New York to study law, the other men in the bar knew they would never see Arnaud again.

For Arnaud, the attraction of New York University was its reputation for producing attorneys experienced in international law and tax. This gave him the passport he needed to get as far away from Quebec and his father as he could. He enjoyed studying in Washington Square and University Heights and thought the University's motto, *Perstare et Praestare* – to persevere and excel – perfectly suited his ability to grasp opportunities whenever they presented themselves.

He found his studies weren't difficult. He easily managed to submit his essays and read the books required by his tutors and to find time to pay his university fees by playing regular games of chemmy and poker.

After moving to Paris, Arnaud advertised himself as an *avocat international, attorney et solicitor intervenant en France et aux États-Unis*. The fact he could practise in both France and the United States would, he calculated, be an attraction to the banks in Paris.

He was offered a job at Rothschild's but turned it down in favour of joining Tagleva. There would be greater opportunities for him with a smaller, expanding bank than one with many layers, traditions and a career path that depended on the death of the person above than on merit. When he was offered the job, he celebrated with a bottle of champagne purchased after winning a few hundred francs at a game of *baccarat banque* at the casino in Monmartre.

Philip was delighted that Tagleva's senior staff all spoke two or more languages, were young, energetic, intelligent and flexible in their thinking.

On the entire floor above Jean-Claude and Philip's offices a card index system, similar to the one that Philip had found so useful in London, was begun by a team of librarians hired for the purpose and supervised by Katherine du Bois. Very quickly thousands of cards held the details of every company in which Tagleva invested clients' money, the names of the directors, past accounts and main shareholders, trading history and the names of prominent staff. Sections for most European countries and the United States were established and cards for individual politicians, bankers and other influential people completed.

The day Philip moved into his new office, he arranged for a sign-writer to write above the door in gold leaf in English, French and Russian:

*The mistake that all businessmen make is the error of examining surplus value, not in its purest and beneficial form, but in the specific form of only profit.*

*L'erreur que toute la part d'hommes d'affaires est l'erreur de l'excédent-valeur examinante, pas sous sa forme plus pure et salutaire, mais sous les formes spécifiques de bénéfice seulement.*

Ошибка всей долей бизнесменов будет ошибка рассматривая остатк-значения, не в своей чисто и полезной форме, но в специфически формах только профита.

Few visitors would bother to read the golden words; fewer still would know they were the words of Karl Marx; and none would know that they had once been spoken by another Count Tagleva.

Once the gold letters above the door had been completed and the sign-writer had left the building, the liveried doorman threw open the heavy wooden double doors of the Tagleva offices.

# Chapter Twenty:
## The rise of the House of Tagleva

Each morning Philip, Jean-Claude and Tobias would meet to look through the information they had received from New York and London and consider the investments they would recommend for that day. Once decided, Jean-Claude and Tobias would contact various brokers throughout Paris to buy and sell the stocks agreed. This was generally completed prior to the stock exchange opening, and stocks could often be bought and sold before the news from America was acted upon by other investment houses. As a result, Tagleva gained a reputation for informed investments and client numbers rose further.

Word of the wonderful investment advice being offered by the establishment in Rue Pierre Charron quickly spread throughout salons and dinner parties in Paris, and Felix Youssoupov introduced Russians, French politicians and his friends to Philip and Jean-Claude. Investments poured in and profits rose. Tagleva continued to use the Société Générale as its bank and within seven months the Tagleva account contained three million francs, making Tagleva one of the bank's most valuable customers.

In Paris, Sophie and Philip would rise early and, after a light breakfast, go to the nursery to see their son. They delighted in playing with the infant, who smiled and laughed as each parent took it in turns to hold and cuddle him. After half an hour they would leave the nursery and descend the three flights of stairs to the study where the night's post and telegraphs from Jean-Claude would be waiting for them to read.

While Philip looked through the correspondence, Sophie would meet Mrs Evans to discuss the arrangements for the day. Together they planned the luncheon and dinner menus, and once this had been done they would spend a few minutes talking over a cup of tea.

Mrs Evans would often find Sophie looking through a magazine at the latest Paris fashions. On occasion Sophie even asked her opinion. Most she thought elegant, except for that 'flapper fashion from America – those short skirts, what's the world coming to?' she said to Sophie. 'And as for the new fashion for make-up, it makes women look no better than they ought.'

'Oh, do you think so?' said Sophie. 'I think it has a practical purpose. Women are now forced to enter the professional world of work and have to look their best to compete with men for employment. I think it helps to make women look very sophisticated.'

On her next day off, Mrs Evans walked to the Rue du Faubourg Saint-Honoré and bought a powder compact and lipstick, and an assistant showed her how to apply it.

Half an hour after Sophie's meeting with Mrs Evans she and Philip would walk or drive to the Tagleva offices at Rue Pierre Charron. His secretary would have arranged meetings with businessmen, politicians and entrepreneurs, all wanting Philip's advice on investments, the economy, business and foreign exchange.

Sophie had established a tradition that every visitor was offered Russian tea and a slice of her mother's favourite cake. Renamed *Framboisier Tagleva*, it contained raisins, cocoa powder, walnuts and sour cream and was declared absolutely delicious by all who tasted it – so much so, that Sophie was constantly asked for the recipe, to which she always gave the same answer: 'If I give you the recipe then you'll not come to see us, and I'd be so disappointed by that.' Philip admired the way she was able to be friends with both his clients and their wives, gently flirting with the men and listening attentively to their wives' gossip.

Tagleva was gaining a reputation for sound, careful and imaginative investments that rivalled the best institutions in Paris, even the De Rothschild Frères Bank. Clients confided in Philip that the main problem with Rothschild's was that it was 'uninspired and too conservative'. After meeting with Baron Edouard De Rothschild, the senior partner, Philip concluded that he was 'one of the last of a generation of gentlemen with a high sense of honour', but that he was just that – a wealthy man who happened to run a bank. Philip thought he had no strategy, no vigorous or innovative policies, and was caught between two philosophies: those of the old Europe and those of the new.

Bankers were not the only important contacts for Philip. Ambassadors, senators, members of the French National Assembly, and cabinet ministers all walked through Tagleva's doors to consult with Philip. It was not long before Sophie and Philip were invited to a grand dinner by the President of France at the Élysée Palace. Held in the Salon d'Argent, the room where Napoleon Bonaparte formally signed his abdication after the Battle of Waterloo, the invitation signified that Count and Countess Tagleva had arrived at the pinnacle of Paris society.

After each client meeting, dinner party or social contact, a record of what was said was entered onto a card and filed in a cabinet on the fourth floor. Each card was cross-referenced against the client's company, investments, names of directors and major shareholders and other news of note. The cards, now numbering over ten thousand, gave Philip an immediate update on any individual or company in which Tagleva had some interest.

One evening, eight months after it had opened, Philip was alone in his office. Looking out of his window on the busy street below brought back to his mind the smog-filled day in London a lifetime ago. He played through the events that had trapped him in Russia: no messages from the Bank of England, meeting Sophie and Sergei, the baker, their escape from St Petersburg, their visit in Moscow from the policeman Anatoily, their escape from the soldiers on the train from Moscow, meeting Felix Youssoupov, his marriage to Sophie, Sergei's death, Michael's birth, the creation of Tagleva. It was like a game of chess. The pieces were lined up for battle but the black queen and bishops were invisible – not missing, just invisible. Some of the moves, particularly those in Russia, were difficult to understand.

The time had come to bring the game to a conclusion.

# Chapter Twenty-one: The Cheese

Tagleva opened its London office in St Mary Axe in the City, three minutes' walk from the Bank of England. It was staffed by two financial advisers and four clerks, and details of all transactions were telegraphed to the Paris office at the end of trade each day. Twice a month Jean-Claude visited the London office to inspect the books and stay a few days to manage the office.

The decision to open an office in London was a good one. London's population of over seven million, tired of the drabness of the war years, wanted to have fun. Entrepreneurs satisfied this demand by opening clubs, restaurants and dance halls to cater for the jazz and cocktail crazes flooding in from the USA. Superstores such as Harrods and Selfridge's were full of shoppers buying up the latest Paris and American fashions.

New corporations such as ICI and British Petroleum built large head offices in central London, and factories rose up along the new arterial roads into the city, including the Firestone Tyres factory, the Wrigley factory at Wembley and Lyons food processing works at Hammersmith. As a result of the growth in employment the population of London became wealthier and boys as young as twelve and thirteen sported fashionable cloth caps and knee britches while their elder brothers favoured the American fashion of boaters and sports jackets.

When Jean-Claude visited London he held meetings in the Tagleva offices but at the end of the day stayed in a rented house just off Fleet Street, near the Royal Courts of Justice. The house had been purposely chosen and comfortably furnished as a convenient location to entertain clients and be close to the financial institutions in the City. Another benefit was that it was close to the Ye Olde Cheshire Cheese public house. The well-known drinking establishment had been a meeting point for City workers since the seventeenth century and some even said that a pub had occupied the site since 1538.

Approached through a narrow alleyway, 'the Cheese' beckons its patrons into a dark warren of narrow corridors and staircases leading to numerous bars and dining rooms. It's said that there are so many corridors that, after a few jars of strong ale, even regulars often get lost. Past customers included ambassadors, prime ministers and royalty as well as writers and journalists such as Dr Johnson, Boswell, Voltaire, Thackeray and Charles Dickens.

It was still a place where the employees of institutions that fed off each other came to exchange gossip and indiscretions and conclude business deals. Any lunchtime or evening the Cheese would be full of Fleet Street hacks, clerks from the Royal Courts of Justice, barristers from the Inns of Court, bankers, litigants and even the odd pickpocket.

The main stairwell of increasingly narrow steps led up to the atmospheric upstairs dining room where Jean-Claude could often be found holding court to the many friends who sought out his company when he was in London. Jean-Claude was always ready to buy a round of drinks, share a tip on the stock market, listen to a juicy piece of gossip in the comfort of the high-backed settles that created small booths, offering the chance of a private conversation.

One of the advantages of having a photographic memory was that the information passed to Jean-Claude at the Cheese could be accurately read by Philip the following morning in Paris.

Jean-Claude entered the Cheese at the end of his working day and sat at his usual table. Within a short time he was surrounded by the usual crowd of lawyers, businessmen and bankers, all sharing jokes and chatting. It was noisy and the wine and beer flowed.

Jean-Claude noticed that William, a friend of his, had joined the group and with a stranger.

'William, how nice to see you again, come and sit down,' cried Jean-Claude across the room.

William approached with a large smile on his face. 'Jean-Claude, this is a colleague of mine, Edward Lascelles.'

'I'm delighted to meet you,' said Jean-Claude as they shook hands. 'Do sit down. I want to hear all about you. But, first, what will you have to drink and eat?'

Edward found the atmosphere intoxicating. This man with the French accent, who William had described as 'the best company in all London', was at the centre of a large group of people and was including him in his circle. Edward felt important.

After a couple of hours the group had thinned to just seven and Jean-Claude declared they should all go on to the Embassy Club in Bond Street. Edward wasn't sure; he wasn't used to late nights, it was midweek and it was a work day tomorrow.

'Nonsense,' said Jean-Claude to Edward's protestations. 'We won't be late, it'll be fun and, besides, we've only just met. I'll look after you.'

Ten minutes later they were all piling into taxis for the short trip to the Embassy Club. Edward was excited. He'd never been into such a club before and was amazed that it should be so busy, full of so many elegant people enjoying themselves.

'The Home Secretary's tried to close the Embassy more than once, but since the Prince of Wales and his brother are both members he's always failed,' shouted Jean-Claude above the noise of the dance band.

They found an empty table and ordered drinks. A man approached Jean-Claude with an outstretched hand.

'Nice to see you again, Jean-Claude. Champagne as usual?'

'This is my new friend, Edward Lascelles. Now Luigi, you must look after Edward, he's a very important man at the Bank of England and would make a good addition to the club membership.'

Edward and Luigi shook hands.

'As a friend of Jean-Claude's, you're always welcome at the Embassy and I'll make sure you're always on the guest list,' said Luigi.

Edward was delighted.

Luigi brought glasses of champagne, together with a large plate of sandwiches.

'But we've already eaten,' said Edward to Jean-Claude

'The crazy licensing act in your country only allows alcohol to be served until half past midnight so long as it's accompanied by food. Nightclubs serve sandwiches. Often the curfew on alcohol's ignored and the party goes on till four or five – always if the Prince of Wales is here. The illegality adds to the excitement and sheer naughtiness of the club, don't you think?' asked Jean-Claude.

Edward did feel daring, and wondered how Jean-Claude could afford the club's outrageous prices. He'd never experienced anything like the excitement of the Embassy. It was exotic, glamorous and outlandish.

It wasn't until three in the morning that he finally arrived home, his head buzzing with excitement and with time for only a couple of hours' sleep before he had to be up for work. All the following day Edward was intoxicated by the Embassy Club and by Jean-Claude. Like cocaine, only banned by the government in 1920, it was a high Edward wanted to experience again and again. The following evening, despite feeling tired from the night before, Edward walked to the Cheese. It was quiet. Where before there had been a noisy crowd all enjoying Jean-Claude's company, tonight there were only a few drinkers.

'Where's Jean-Claude?' he asked one of the waiters.

'He won't be in tonight,' came the reply. 'Gone back to Paris, he has. He'll be back as usual next week, though.'

Edward felt deflated. He looked around to see if there were any faces he recognised from the night before, but the five people in the room were all strangers, and none of them looked at him or invited him to have a drink. He felt very alone. Arriving back down on the street, his shoulders slumped and he looked at his shoes as they hit the pavement that took him home and early to bed.

\*\*\*\*

Three days later Sophie and Philip were invited to a small dinner party, for twenty, at the Rothschilds. The evening was memorable for a number of reasons. For Sophie it was a chance to meet friends and to enjoy the food and atmosphere of a lost age.

Philip was looking forward to meeting two men. One was an entrepreneur he found fascinating, and the other he expected to be enlightening. The first he identified because he was drinking orange juice instead of the champagne on offer. Philip walked over and introduced himself.

'Pleased to meet you,' said the man. 'I'm Philippe de Rothschild.'

The index card that had been delivered to Philip an hour before he left the Tagleva office gave him substantial background on the man and also suggestions of topics of conversation that would be of interest to him.

### Philippe de Rothschild:

*Born in Paris, Georges Philippe de Rothschild is the younger son of Baron Henri de Rothschild (b. 1872).*

*He lives the life of a wealthy playboy, often found in the company of a beautiful woman, usually actresses. He has a love of fast cars and races them competitively. To maintain anonymity when racing, he uses the pseudonym 'Georges Philippe'.*

*In sharp contrast to the majority of the Rothschild family, he doesn't seem to enjoy their staid aristocratic traditions.*

*At the outbreak of World War I (aged 12) he was sent to the safety of the family's vineyard in the village of Pauillac in the Médoc. There, he seems to have developed a love of the country and the wine business, an enterprise that has been in his family since 1853. The vineyard is currently spending vast amounts of money to upgrade the château, adding electricity, running water and a proper access road, as well as a new system of bottling wine and storing it.*

Philip was able to ask Philippe about winemaking, and there followed a long and enthusiastic explanation of the process.

'The current system is that vineyards sell their wines in bulk, leaving the maturing, bottling, labelling and marketing to be handled by the wine merchants. In my opinion that just produces mediocre wine. My idea is to bottle the wine at the château. That way, I can maintain control over the quality of the wine and market it under the name Château Mouton Rothschild.'

'How very exciting,' said Philip. 'Though you can't guarantee that every year will result in a wine of great quality. What will you do with the wine you can't bottle as château-bottled?'

'Good question, and one that I've been struggling with for a few months, but I think I've come up with the answer. The grapes that don't produce a superb quality I intend to sell under the name Mouton Cadet. What do you think?'

'I think that's an excellent solution,' and Philip made a mental note to purchase a couple of dozen bottles of Château Mouton Rothschild as soon as they became available.

The person Philip expected to find enlightening sat opposite him during dinner: a bald-headed man with a moustache that was waxed so that it looked like cat's whiskers and which caught crumbs of food that he wiped away with his napkin. The details on his index card told Philip that Joseph Noulens was France's Minister of War in 1913 and then ambassador to Russia in 1917.

Noulens spent most of the dinner talking about the incompetence of French generals.

'At the start of the war our idiot generals told everyone that a bayonet could defeat the machine gun when wielded in the hands of a charging French soldier. Our men hurled themselves across open fields towards the enemy and were simply mown down by a hail of bullets. Hundreds of thousands of men sacrificed themselves with "Pour la France" on their lips because of the antiquated mentality of French military leaders who directed events thirty miles to the rear.'

After another course and a few glasses of wine he was jabbing a fork at Philip to emphasise his point.

'And do you know the other thing that killed thousands? Those damn stupid uniforms we had. They were another relic of the previous century. They were too bright. The men wore a greatcoat of blue wool and trousers that were a striking red, intended to instil a sense of boldness in the soldier, the generals pompously said. Even the cavalry had burnished silver breast-plates and plumed helmets. Splendid targets for the German machine guns.'

He emptied his glass of wine, which was immediately refilled by the servant that stood behind his chair.

'Even before the war,' he continued, 'I tried to take measures to reduce the visibility of the men's uniform. I was even keener to change the uniform when we discovered that the red dye was produced by the damn Boche. So we turned to the British to supply the dye.' He took another large gulp of wine. 'The first cloth the British supplied was unstable. It faded into a light bluish-grey after continued exposure to the sun, and sometimes ran when it rained. Half our soldiers ended up stained blue when it rained – bloody incompetence!'

Philip was disturbed by the woman to his right, who whispered, 'After a few glasses of wine he talks of nothing else. This is the third dinner this month I've had to listen to the incompetence of our generals and the poor equipment supplied by the British. So, Count Tagleva, to change the subject, I want you to tell me what investments you recommend for a poor, impoverished widow. I have a few francs that I could spare for the right investment.'

Philip wondered what definition this widow had of 'impoverished' and how many francs were 'a few' as he looked at her opulent diamond and ruby necklace.

****

For days, all that Edward could think about was Jean-Claude. How he'd enjoyed the evening at the Embassy Club, how when Jean-Claude laughed his whole body seemed to shake, his display of confidence and the fact that so many people seemed to know him and like him. He wished he could be like Jean-Claude. He thought back to the loneliness of his schooldays, when he was never a popular boy, but always wanted to be so.

He'd tried so hard to fit in with the boys' talk, which was of nothing else: they talked about football – football – football at every turn and after every class. Everyone but him caught the football mania. His classmates talked endlessly about the offside and the charging behind rules. He pretended to be interested; he tried to learn the names of the men who played for Blackburn Rovers, Preston North End and Aston Villa, but secretly agreed with his form master that 'every young man playing football will come to ruin'. Though he dared not say so.

Leaving the bank to go home, he thought he would pop into the Cheese to see if Jean-Claude was there. He climbed the stairs to the dining room and saw Jean-Claude talking to another man. On seeing him, Jean-Claude cried, 'Edward, I'm so pleased to see you. I've just arrived and I'm buying the drinks!'

The three of them settled down at a table. They talked of nothing much, told a few jokes, people came to say hello and after an hour drifted away, then they ate and ordered more drinks. At ten Jean-Claude announced he must leave as he had an early meeting the following day.

On the pavement they bade each other farewell, and Edward hailed a cab. The cab driver glanced in the mirror at his passenger. Judging by the smile on his face, he'd had a good evening.

The following afternoon Edward was in his office when a messenger entered and handed him a letter. Picking up the long silver and ivory paper knife he'd retained when Philip's property had been sent to his home, he slit through the envelope and opened the note inside.

*Dear Edward,*
*I had such fun last night at the Cheese and your company turned an otherwise boring evening into one of great delight.*
*I would be greatly pleased if you are free to join me tonight to see the new play,* I'll Leave It To You, *which has just moved from Manchester to the New Theatre. I have two tickets for a private box. It's by a playwright called Noël Coward. Don't know if he's any good as a playwright, but reviews are good and it sounds fun. Afterwards we could dine at the Ritz.*
*Jean-Claude*

How wonderful, Edward thought, and immediately penned a quick reply to confirm his acceptance of the invitation and handed it to the messenger. For the rest of the afternoon Edward found it difficult to concentrate and he continually looked at the clock that hung above the door. At exactly three minutes past five he walked out of the bank.

After a long bath and after carefully dressing in evening wear, Edward met Jean-Claude in the lobby of the New Theatre. They were shown to the private box.

On the way Jean-Claude asked, 'Do you know the play?'

'No, it's the first time I've heard of Noël Coward.'

'The *Manchester Guardian* wrote, "Mr Coward has a sense of comedy and will probably produce a good play one of these days."'

They both laughed at the newspaper's pomposity and Jean-Claude added, 'Though *The Times* says it's a remarkable piece of work, so we'll see which is right and raise a glass of champagne to the correct newspaper at dinner. You will be coming to the Ritz afterwards, won't you?'

'I wouldn't miss it for anything,' smiled Edward.

On a side table at the rear of the box was a bottle of champagne. Jean-Claude poured them both a glass and spread a large spoonful of Beluga caviar onto a cracker.

Noël Coward had indeed written a good play and both of them laughed a great deal. Edward was enjoying himself, especially because he was alone in his new friend's company. For almost the first time in his life he felt special and liked for himself.

Afterwards, at the Ritz Jean-Claude listened attentively as Edward told his life's story. As Jean-Claude filled his wine glass, Edward recounted how his father had paid him scant attention.

'At six, I was sent away to a preparatory school, which I hated. At Harrow I was bullied by the older boys because I was no good at sport and because I had such a close relationship with my mother. My life began when I left Cambridge and my mother took me on a tour of Europe.'

'Where did you go?'

'Paris, Venice, Florence, Pisa and Rome – it was a wonderful time. In Paris we spent two whole days in the Louvre and she encouraged me to buy some items in the flea market and then some paintings in Venice and Florence. My home's stuffed full of the stuff. It's so old-fashioned.'

'Any regrets in life?' asked Jean-Claude as brandies and cigarettes were brought to the table.

'Other than my school days? Like everyone, a few, I guess. A couple of business decisions I shouldn't have made in my early days at work… there is one regret I have. During the war I could have helped a friend and didn't. I feel sorry that I didn't.'

'What happened to him?'

'I don't know.'

'Everyone has regrets from the war. Don't let it bother you,' said Jean-Claude comfortingly.

They left the Ritz and walked towards Piccadilly Circus. Two young workers passed them and after a few yards one shouted back, 'Jaspers.'

Jean-Claude ignored the street slang. Such insults, he noticed, while rare in Paris, were commonly shouted by louts to well-dressed men walking down the street. He looked at Edward, who seemed quite embarrassed at being called a homosexual.

They said no more until they had hailed two cabs.

'Thank you for a superb evening.'

'We must do it again, very soon.'

'I would like that,' said Edward as he climbed into his cab.

Jean-Claude returned home to send his report to Philip.

Two days later Edward was again at the Cheese. Surrounded by a large group of friends, Jean-Claude was holding court and Edward felt a pang of jealousy. He'd enjoyed Jean-Claude's company at the theatre and dinner at the Ritz. It was difficult to have the same kind of discussion with Jean-Claude when they were in larger company. He didn't want to share him.

'We're off to the 50/50 club,' said Jean-Claude over the noise. 'Are you coming?'

'Yes please,' replied Edward.

When Jean-Claude introduced him to the owner of the club, the matinee idol Ivor Novello, the man who had written the tune to the wartime hit 'Keep the home fires burning', Edward was beside himself with delight. Novello, like Jean-Claude, had everything: wealth, popularity, effortless glamour and a charm that intoxicated men and women in equal measure.

'Jean-Claude,' Edward said after taking his first sip of champagne, 'Because we're friends I've been reluctant to ask for your advice in investments, but the whole of the City of London beats a path to your door, so would you be offended if I asked your advice for my own benefit?'

'I'd be offended if you didn't,' replied Jean-Claude. 'If I can't help my friends, then I wouldn't be a good friend.'

'Could I ask that our discussions remain secret? I'm not sure how my superiors at the Bank of England would react if they knew.'

'Of course. I'll tell you what we'll do. I'll allocate an account in your name at Tagleva. You'll be the only one to have access to it. Would that suit?'

'Thank you,' said Edward with feverish anticipation.

'Then can I suggest that you invest in three companies,' began Jean-Claude. 'The first is the Instone Air Line. It's an airline company that runs a passenger service for people travelling between London and Paris. It'll be very popular, as it's a fast way to travel and, if I'm right, the company will be very profitable. I also know, and this is just between you and me, that a government committee is to recommend that the main British airlines should merge to create one financially strong airline. Instone might be part of that merger. If that happens, the stock will go through the roof.'

Jean-Claude continued. 'The second investment should be in the Brown Publishing Company. It's owned by US Congressman Clarence Brown. Thirdly, I'd suggest the Los Angeles Steamship Company. It provides a fast passenger service between Los Angeles and San Francisco. Business is booming. I suggest an initial investment of three thousand pounds, spread equally between the three companies.'

Edward felt embarrassed. 'I'm not sure that I can afford to invest that amount.' He blushed.

'No matter,' said Jean-Claude. 'You pay me ten per cent as a deposit and I'll arrange for Tagleva to invest the three thousand pounds on your behalf. After the shares increase in value we'll sell a few. Then you can repay the loan from the profits and the rest will be yours to keep.'

'You'd do that for me?' asked Edward.

'Of course – you're my friend. I'll set it up tomorrow.'

# Chapter Twenty-two: Across the Atlantic

## 1923

Since the war had ended, the United States dollar had become the strongest currency in the world. Philip believed that within a couple of decades the United States would eclipse Britain in both wealth and influence.

So, following the successful opening of the London office, Philip began to think through the third stage of Tagleva's development. The next and most logical place to have an office would be in the United States of America. With offices in America, he'd told Jean-Claude, Tagleva could trade for most of the day if there were electronic communication. Ten years previously, the first transmission of speech across the Atlantic Ocean by radiotelephone had proved to politicians and businessmen alike the potential benefits. There had already been attempts to lay a telephone line across the Atlantic and very soon someone would succeed. Tagleva needed to be ready.

Four possible locations were discussed – New York, Washington, Chicago and San Francisco – as providing the best hubs for twenty-four-hour trading, when it came. Philip wanted to visit the United States and investigate the possibilities for himself.

There were other reasons to visit. Philip wanted to find out more about the 'Teapot Dome' scandal, in which the Secretary of the Interior, Albert Fall, was accused of leasing navy petroleum reserves at Teapot Dome in Wyoming and two other locations in California to private oil companies at low rates without competitive bidding.

Initially no evidence of wrongdoing had been uncovered, as the leases were legal enough, but records kept disappearing mysteriously. There remained, however, unanswered questions: how had Fall become so rich, so quickly and easily? It was claimed that the money from the bribes had gone to Fall's cattle ranch and as investments in his other businesses. Philip wondered if there might be a link to Britain.

The opportunity to travel to America came when Felix Youssoupov arrived to tell Philip and Sophie that he and Irina were moving to the United States and had decided to give up their directorships of Tagleva.

'You don't need our help any more. Tagleva's grown into a successful business and it's now time that you found directors with more experience, who can move you forward,' said Felix.

'We'll be sorry to see you go,' said Sophie, genuinely upset at the thought of them moving away from Paris.

'Well, I've decided to open up Tagleva in New York and San Francisco so why don't we all travel to New York on the same boat and we can have a long good bye,' suggested Philip.

'What an excellent idea,' said Felix. 'I'll book to sail on the *Majestic* – it's the most luxurious ship afloat, and we should try to book adjacent staterooms.' He added, 'Do you know, it even has an indoor swimming pool?'

## New York

As the boat sailed into New York the four of them stood on the first-class deck with all the other passengers to watch the Statue of Liberty slide past them. Sophie looked in awe at the size of the statue. Representing the Roman goddess of freedom, a broken chain at her feet, it was a gift from the people of France and the largest and most imposing sculpture she'd ever seen. As the ship moved towards the skyscrapers of Manhattan, Sophie squeezed Philip's arm in excitement.

The romance of his first sight of New York was not lost on Philip, yet he couldn't understand a nation that proudly declared that all men are created equal, with its Statue of Liberty that proclaimed, 'give me your tired, your poor, your huddled masses yearning to be free', while the children of frightened slaves still remained so unequal and when, only a few months before, the United States Supreme Court had ruled that Bhagat Sing Thind, a Punjabi Sikh who'd settled with his family in Oregon, could not become a naturalised citizen of the United States because he was 'not white'.

They checked in to the Plaza Hotel, where they had a suite overlooking Central Park. Sophie and Philip occupied the master bedroom while young Michael and his nanny had the second room.

Sophie was captivated by New York. She'd seen nothing quite like the bustling city, where every building seemed to have a minimum of eighteen storeys and could reach thirty storeys. Cars clogged the roads, open-topped buses transported commuters up the wide avenues, brightly coloured trams rode their tracks up and down the roads, delivery vans were everywhere and everyone seemed to be in a hurry.

On the third night, Philip took her to see Rudolph Valentino in the film *Blood and Sand*. Sophie was captivated by Valentino's sultry looks, and Philip inwardly laughed as Sophie stared at the screen, feeding herself handfuls of popcorn.

The final scene arrived all too quickly – when the matador hero is killed in the bullfight but is reconciled with Carmen, his true love, moments before he dies. As the music faded, Philip could hear sniffs and sobs from the many women in the audience and as the lights went up he saw Sophie, covered in spilled popcorn, with red puffy eyes and holding a handkerchief to her nose. He roared with laughter and was given a playful slap on the legs for doing so.

On the way out Philip thought that if women flocked in their hundreds to the picture house and could fall in love with a flickering image of a man they had never met and cry at his death, then there was money to be made in cinema. Perhaps it was worth investing…

One aspect of life in the United States that fascinated Philip and which held no logic – for him, at least – was the 18th Amendment, commonly called Prohibition. The law made it illegal to produce, import or consume alcoholic beverages on US soil. It spawned a booming industry across the whole of the United States, and vast numbers of people became wealthy smuggling cases of rum from the West Indies and Caribbean, and transporting whiskey and other liquors across the border by truck from Canada and by boat from Europe.

Speakeasies made the purchase of alcohol in New York easy, since everyone knew where to find booze. Even respectable establishments got in on the action. Claudio's Restaurant, the oldest family-owned restaurant in the country and one that Philip and Sophie had visited, found its way into the illegal spirits business. The ground floor was a fine French restaurant while the upstairs served as a speakeasy. A dumb waiter to the downstairs part allowed diners to sip from 'water glasses' that were actually filled with the alcoholic beverage of their choice.

Then there was the most popular speakeasy in the state, the Island Club and Casino on Star Island, with a clientele that included Ernest Hemingway and the actor John Barrymore. In fact, Philip thought that finding booze in America was easier than it was in England, with its strict licensing laws – it could only be achieved by being able to easily bribe the police and political authorities.

After two weeks of sight-seeing, Philip decided that it was time for him to start work. An invitation for 'Tea with Count and Countess Tagleva' proved irresistible to the elite of New York society. Philip could usually expect an acceptance within the hour. Afterwards Philip and Sophie would receive an invitation to dinner so that they could be shown off and where Philip would meet influential husbands. The husbands invariably wanted to meet Philip again, to do business. Often this meant a late breakfast, or what Americans called 'brunch'.

As a result Philip's day would start early, reading the newspapers and the streams of letters from London. The early part of his day would be filled with personal meetings with potential investors or clients over brunch, which was followed by a lunch with more people. The afternoons were booked with client meetings, and the evenings were filled with visits to the theatre, parties and dinners where he would meet politicians and city elders.

Philip was meeting the most influential people in the country. People such as Charles Schwab, the steel magnate and owner of the Bethlehem Steel Company; Richard Whitney, a member of a number of the city's elite social clubs who was on the Board of Governors of the New York Stock Exchange; and Ivar Kreuger, the head of a business investment company. Together the three men controlled more money than the US Treasury.

Philip liked Schwab and Whitney but he didn't particularly like Ivar Kreuger. In Philip's opinion, Kreuger's investments delivered impossible returns and when he heard that Kreuger never allowed his financial books to be audited he suspected that very little of his clients' money was being invested. Instead he was paying a high-interest dividend from the money he received from new investors. The scheme relied on there being more money coming into the scheme than was being paid out. For that to happen, he needed increasing numbers of clients, and Philip knew that logically the money would eventually dry up. The losers would always be those who joined the fraud late – and that would be the vast majority. What interested Philip was that Kreuger claimed that he had contacts in Britain, France and even at the Bank of England.

Philip also managed to meet some of the business owners who had supplied the American army during the war, and was particularly interested to meet the inventor of the Lewis machine gun, Isaac Newton Lewis.

After each meeting, he completed an index card on each client and these were filed in the same way as those in Paris and London. The information was sent to the Paris office, in code, and contained assessments of companies, projects, business leaders and any other information he thought useful.

After five months Philip was able to open Tagleva offices in San Francisco and New York.

# Chapter Twenty-three: Edward's fortune

## March 1924

Jean-Claude arranged to meet Edward at the American Bar at the Savoy Hotel in the Strand. Edward arrived to find a bottle of 1895 Pol Roger champagne on the table.

'What's the celebration?' asked Edward.

'I've some good news for you, and once I heard that Winston Churchill ordered this exact vintage from his wine merchants Randolph Payne & Co., I thought we'd celebrate and see if Winston's made a good investment.'

'Good news? How exciting!'

'Patience,' teased Jean-Claude.

The waiter poured the champagne and they took a sip.

'I think Churchill's made an excellent choice,' said Jean-Claude.

'So what's the good news?' asked Edward eagerly.

'You know the money Tagleva invested for you?'

'Of course,' said Edward, becoming even more excited.

'With the dividends I've managed to increase your portfolio and I've bought additional shares in pharmaceuticals as well as companies in radio and automobiles. The value of your share account is now twenty-five thousand pounds. Yesterday I took the liberty of selling some of the shares to repay the initial loan Tagleva made to you, but the income from what's left will keep you in some style. Certainly you'll be able to drink champagne every day.'

'My God, twenty-five thousand pounds? That's a fortune.' Edward did a quick calculation. 'That's nearly a hundred years of my salary from the bank.' He beamed and raised his glass to Jean-Claude. 'All down to you, my best friend, thank you so much. Let's celebrate with a meal in the Grill and, this time, I'm paying.'

They finished the bottle and walked down the stairs to the Grill Room. They began with caviar and blinis, followed by lobster thermidor, and concluded with stuffed breast of partridge. The wine waiter ensured their glasses were never empty.

At the end of the meal Jean-Claude said, 'You're drunk, Edward.'

'A little,' replied Edward and giggled. 'Nothing I can't cope with.'

'Why don't you take a room at the hotel? Tomorrow's Saturday so you're not working – and you can afford it now.'

'What an excellent idea,' said Edward as his head swam.

They walked out of the Grill and to the reception desk. When he signed the register, Edward felt a little sad. Going to his suite and to bed would be the end of the night – he didn't want this evening to finish; he was celebrating. He didn't want to end the night celebrating alone – in fact, he never wanted to be alone again. And why should he be? He could afford not to be alone ever again.

He smiled. How clever he'd been to ask Jean-Claude to invest his money for him, and what a great friend Jean-Claude had turned out to be. He wanted Jean-Claude to stay and continue the celebration.

'Let's have a nightcap in my room.'

'Of course,' replied Jean-Claude.

The bell boy carried up another bottle of champagne, let them into Edward's suite and walked away with half a crown in his pocket.

Once the door had closed, Edward turned to Jean-Claude and placed an arm round his shoulder. 'Do you know something? You're my best friend, my best friend ever.'

'Thank you,' said Jean-Claude.

'No, you are,' insisted Edward. 'I love you, Jean-Claude. I've never loved anyone so much as I love you. Would you mind if I kissed you? As a friend, of course. Oh God, sorry, I shouldn't have asked that, now you'll think me disgusting. I'm sorry, Jean-Claude, please forgive me.'

Jean-Claude raised his finger and touched Edward's lips.

'Hush, be quiet,' he said.

Edward felt a hand wrap itself around his head and pull him towards Jean-Claude. Every sense in his body was awakened; he was incapable of any resistance, even had he wanted to resist, which he didn't.

## New York

Sophie and Philip were enjoying a late breakfast in their suite at the Plaza. Philip was reading the newspaper and Sophie was finishing her bowl of cornflakes. Cornflakes had arrived in Britain the year before, but had never been served for breakfast as Mrs Evans had firmly informed her that 'these flakes couldn't possibly have the same benefit as a cooked breakfast of eggs and toast'.

When Sophie read the adverts along Fifth Avenue quoting Mary Barber, the head of the Kellogg's Home Economics Department, describing Kellogg's Corn Flakes as an essential part of a balanced diet, Sophie tried a bowl. She thought them novel, colourful and she now started her breakfast with them every day. She couldn't wait to tell Mrs Evans how delicious they were when she returned to Paris.

'Anything in the papers?' enquired Sophie.

'Not much. Russia has adopted an experimental calendar with a five-day week. It's apparently causing chaos. And some man called Hitler has tried to overthrow the German government in what the newspapers describe as a "Beer Hall Putsch". He's been arrested; likely to go to prison, they say.'

'So we won't be hearing of him again,' said Sophie.

'Possibly,' replied Philip from behind the newspaper.

'As there's nothing much in the newspapers, you'll be interested in my news.'

Philip put down the newspaper to listen to his wife's news. It couldn't be too dramatic, she was smiling.

'So…' he said expectantly.

She smiled. 'You're going to be a father again.'

'Wonderful,' he said, and walked around to Sophie to kiss her. 'I'm so pleased! How long have you known?'

'I went to see the doctor yesterday and they confirmed it. Perhaps we can give Michael a little sister to play with.'

'That would be nice. I'd love to have another girl in my family,' and he bent down to kiss her again. 'Now I must get dressed and go to my appointments. Will you be all right today?'

'Of course; it'll be eight months before you need to panic.' She smiled and watched him leave the room.

Twenty minutes later, after Philip had arranged for a dozen white roses to be delivered to Sophie's room, he walked to the corner of 57th Street and Fifth Avenue to Tiffany's for 'a little something with diamonds' for his wife.

## London that same day

Edward could only think of Jean-Claude and began to live for the nights they would spend together.

'You're so good at it,' Edward said to Jean-Claude one evening after they had made love.

'Of course,' replied Jean-Claude. 'I'm French.'

Edward giggled and wished he were French.

Over the following weeks Edward was introduced to the 'bachelor' scene in London. He was taken to places he had never dared visit before. The Lyons Corner House in the Strand, Sunday mornings at the Trocadero in Piccadilly, where gentlemen mixed with transvestites and other friends, the Hotel de France in Villiers Street where a 'gentleman's friend' could be safely entertained for the evening, Marble Arch and Hyde Park Corner where 'a pound is the tariff for a Foot Guard but a Horse Guardsmen will cost you rather more'.

Edward threw himself into his secret world with enthusiasm, regretting that, in the past, he hadn't known where to go or had been too afraid of the danger. He'd lost so many opportunities. Now he understood how to tread a pathway through illegality and danger; he felt comfortable and slightly smug at his new-found knowledge.

A week later Jean-Claude announced that he was returning to France for a few weeks. Edward thought his world would collapse. He was in love with Jean-Claude. How could he go to the Trocadero on his own, or anywhere else on his own, for that matter?

'How long will you be away?' he asked in panic.

'A week or two, possibly longer,' came the reply.

It would seem like a lifetime, thought Edward. 'When do you go?'

'Tomorrow evening. Let's have dinner before I catch the boat train.'

The following evening Jean-Claude and Edward met at a small Italian restaurant off the Strand and began the evening by sipping a martini at the bar.

A young man entered the restaurant and approached them. 'Hello, Jean-Claude,' he said.

He was a vision of classic beauty. Edward was reminded of the statue of Diadoumenos which he'd seen in Greece when with his mother.

'Edward, this is James Steinburg. I've asked him to look after you while I'm away in Paris.'

Edward shook James's hand, noting the firm grip, the penetrating look from the hazel eyes, and the perfect mouth. He knew he would enjoy being looked after. James smiled back at Edward, thinking only of the fifty pounds in his jacket pocket and the promise of another fifty pounds in two weeks if he showed Edward 'the best time'. For such a fortune, Edward was going to experience an orgy of physical self-indulgence.

## New York

Philip was relaxing in his suite at the Plaza Hotel at the end of their tour of the United States. While exhausting, the trip had been most enlightening: he'd gained a good understanding of the immense wealth the USA could generate and how he thought it would transform how business would be done throughout the world. He was pleased that he had managed to establish offices in San Francisco and New York and identified the location for a third in Chicago. He'd met people who he hoped would prove to be lifelong friends and business contacts – people such as Walter Chrysler, who'd taken control of the Maxwell Motor Company and reorganised it into the Chrysler Corporation, and Edward Smith, a founder of Peoples Trust Bank of St Albans and New York City's Sherman National Bank.

Smith had been of particular interest to Philip, as he had substantial holdings in ammunition manufacturing companies. Their meetings had added more information to the game of chess that Philip was beginning to understand. They had spent long evenings talking through Britain's armament production during the war: how at the start Britain's guns could only fire four shells a day; how the shortage of acetone meant that many shells failed to explode or exploded in the breach, killing British soldiers rather than Germans; and why it wasn't until 1917 that Britain was manufacturing more guns than Germany. In Smith's opinion, had the United States not joined the European war, then Germany would have won.

While they were in America, Sophie wanted to go to Los Angeles to see where movies were made. At various parties Count and Countess Tagleva met the emperors, princes and princesses of the silent screen: Samuel Goldwyn, William Fox, Carl Laemmle, Louis B. Mayer, Buster Keaton, Ronald Coleman, Mary Pickford and Joan Crawford.

'It's all so romantic,' she told Philip.

'I don't know; I thought they were rather boring,' commented Philip.

'Wouldn't you like to be married to a film star?' enquired Sophie.

'And swap you? Absolutely not; I've already got my Mary Pickford,' and he kissed her.

'And me my Ronald Coleman.'

'Before you're swept away by some actor, I think it's about time we returned to Paris,' he told her. 'You should have your baby so that he or she can be born on Russian soil and I didn't bring the box with me. I didn't think I'd need to.'

'Have you thought of any names?' she asked.

'If it's a boy, how about Leonid or Matislav, and if it's a girl Matvei or Halinka?'

'It'll be nice to get back home. Besides, Michael is beginning to develop an American accent.'

'One day, I suspect, we'll all speak with an American accent,' said Philip.

'Oh, I do hope not. In the north they slur their vowels so strangely and in the southern states they don't open their mouths to speak in case they catch a fly,' and she mimicked the greeting they'd heard in Louisiana: 'Y'all.'

Philip roared with laughter.

# Chapter Twenty-four: Preparing for disaster

## September 1926

Philip, Sophie, Jean-Claude, Tobias and Arnaud were sitting around the boardroom table in Philip's office in Paris. The first item on the agenda was to review Tagleva's finances, which had grown hugely. They discussed the individual progress of each office, starting with Paris, then London, New York and San Francisco. All were profitable and attracting customers in ever increasing numbers.

The second part of the meeting was taken up with political, business and social events that affected clients' investments and the advice that Tagleva would be offering clients over the following week.

The final item on the agenda was to discuss a change to investment policy. Everyone looked at Philip as he started to outline his thoughts.

'The stock market has risen by twenty-five per cent over the past year and everyone expects it to rise further. When Sophie and I were in America we found it had become common practice for people in all strata of society to invest money in the stock exchange. Sometimes people invest their entire life savings, and often this is done by taking out a loan to buy the stock.'

'We've done exactly that for some of our own clients,' said Tobias.

'But, as agreed in past meetings, only up to forty per cent of the client's investment,' added Arnaud.

'Quite so,' replied Philip. 'However, while Tagleva restricts the amount of the loan, in the United States the amount people are being allowed to borrow has risen from forty per cent to nearly ninety per cent of the money invested. We've all noticed how this same practice has been adopted in London and other parts of Europe. If the stock market falls, these loans are unsustainable. I propose that we stop making loans for investment in the stock market. In addition, we should ask all existing clients with such loans to sell some stock to repay any loan they have with Tagleva.'

'But that'll make us uncompetitive with other investment houses,' said Arnaud.

'I agree,' said Philip. 'But only in the short term, and I think it's the correct position to take. My feeling is that the stock market's been rising too fast to be sustained. If the stock market were to fall by only eleven per cent, then many people would be bankrupt. I feel we have a duty to our clients not to put them in that position.'

Jean-Claude spoke. 'If we suddenly ask all those clients to repay their loans there could be panic and people might even conclude that Tagleva itself is in financial difficulties. May I suggest we make a cautious change in policy and we ask selected clients to reduce their loans over a given period of time, say six months? We could advise that they do this by selling some of their stock and repaying their loans to Tagleva and, in addition, we will take ten per cent of any dividends, to reduce the loan still further.'

'Good idea,' said Philip.

'And if some clients ask for further loans?' asked Arnaud.

'Then we politely refuse.'

'Even if that means we lose the client to another investment house?' pressed Arnaud.

'Yes, even if we lose the client,' answered Philip.

'I think that policy is wrong. It will make us uncompetitive and, in any event, all the loans are made against other assets such as property, so Tagleva wouldn't suffer,' argued Arnaud.

'I disagree,' said Philip. 'Our clients going bankrupt isn't good for business.'

'A change in policy will cause speculation both in Paris and London,' added Jean-Claude.

'I agree,' said Philip, 'and we don't want to be the catalyst for a crisis, so we need to make this change carefully and without causing any more problems than is necessary. But

I'm convinced that the rise in the stock market is not sustainable: something will break and I'm concerned about the consequences.'

They eventually agreed to adopt Philip's proposal but the vote was not unanimous; Arnaud voted against the proposal.

Once everyone had left them alone Philip asked Sophie, 'How are the twins today?'

Sophie smiled 'Feeling better and getting over their colds. Poor things – they are too young to do anything but cry. Michael was such a love and kissed them both on their foreheads every morning, just like we do to him when he's unwell.'

'It's lovely that Michael's so protective of Matislav and Halinka and it's wonderful to now be a family of five.'

'Only a man could be delighted to have two babies at the same time,' she teased, 'but I must go now, I'm meeting friends at Maxim's.'

'Enjoy Maxim's. By the way, I have something to ask you after dinner tonight.'

'Wicket keeper or fast bowler?' Sophie said, giving him a wink, and then turned away, walked towards the door and wiggled her hips in the way she'd seen Vilma Bánky do to Rudolph Valentino in *The Son of the Sheik*.

As the door closed behind her, Philip smiled and murmured to himself, 'That's my countess!'

Half an hour later Philip walked into Jean-Claude's office.

'How are things in London?' enquired Philip.

'Having discussed the office at the board meeting, I assume you mean, how's Edward?'

Philip nodded. He regretted how Edward was being used but understood that Jean-Claude had good reasons for being so manipulative. Nevertheless he'd always considered him a friend and good company but Edward, once Philip had left for Russia, hadn't been such a good friend in return. Jean-Claude looked at Philip and understood his conflicting emotions, though he couldn't share them.

'James Steinburg's doing a great job. In fact, he describes Edward as going off like a Roman candle every time they meet, so we know all the committee decisions, all the gossip and anything else that's happening in the Bank of England.'

'Yes, I've had the reports. I'd never imagined that Edward would be that indiscreet,' sighed Philip.

'I think he always was weak, but when you were at the bank he kept it under control. All I did was light the fuse and step back. If it hadn't been me, then it would have been someone else. In any event, you have nothing to reproach yourself for. Edward's being the catalyst of his own demise.'

'I didn't come here to discuss Edward. I've decided that I want to take a less active role in Tagleva for a few months. I want to have a little time to settle some outstanding business. Could you manage things for a few weeks?'

'Of course; smiled Jean-Claude encouragingly. 'If I can be of any help at any time, just ask.'

'Thank you. That's much appreciated, and I know I can rely on you,' said Philip.

Arnaud was sitting at his desk. He hadn't been happy at Philip's proposal at the board meeting. He knew Philip was wrong. It was stupidity, he thought to himself, to turn down business and ignore what everyone else was doing. He stabbed a paper knife into the blotting pad. Such a policy would only slow Tagleva's expansion: ignoring opportunities cost money, and would harm his advancement and his reputation. Perhaps he'd made a mistake by not joining Rothschild's.

****

It was after dinner and Philip and Sophie were relaxing on the sofas on either side of the roaring fire. He sipped a cognac and she a glass of Cointreau.

'This afternoon you said you wanted to ask me something,' she said, unable to contain her curiosity any further.

'I haven't forgotten.' Philip was about to ask Sophie to take on a task that would take her away from him and the children. It would be hard work, and not popular in some quarters. Michael was eleven years old and the twins nearly three. They would miss her and she them. If he asked her in the wrong way, she'd refuse. She had every right to do so, and he had no right to ask, but he had decided he must. If she said 'no', he'd find another way. He wanted to find the right words.

'I've read Sergei's words above my office door every morning I've come to work. They've screamed at me ever since they were painted. It's time they came true. I've decided to set up the Tagleva Foundation.'

Sophie smiled. She'd been waiting for this time ever since they'd discussed the possibility years ago. She decided not to interrupt him. She wanted to hear his plans.

'Thank you for agreeing to call it the Sergei Tagleva Foundation and that its purpose will be to use most of the profits you and we gain from our shares in Tagleva to help the disadvantaged – no matter their social status, colour, race or religion. I've been looking at the news from Britain and I think that it's time that a group of people desperate for such help – the miners – are helped. The unions and the government are on a collision course. Germany's being forced by France and Italy to export free coal as part of its reparations after the Great War, and Britain's mine owners are affected by the free coal and are maintaining their own profits by reducing miners' wages and increasing their working hours. It's causing awful hardship. A lot of people, particularly children, are suffering. There's going to be unrest between miners, owners and the government – I know it. I think we should help where we can.'

Philip knew, just by looking at her, that she was waiting for him to finish. He knew she'd already guessed what he was going to ask her. As their relationship deepened, each knew what the other was thinking.

'I would like you to head the Foundation. You'd bring to it your huge compassion and love, you'd be representing your brother and I think you would be wonderful at it.'

Still she sat opposite him, waiting for him to complete the outline of his plans. She had always admired how he could so easily explain a problem and give a workable solution.

'I'll set up the Foundation with a million pounds as an initial contribution and I hope that you'll go to London and begin to make the money work. However, before you give your answer there are some things you should consider. It'll be hard work and will mean being away from Michael and the twins. You'll also come in for some criticism and opposition from friends as well as mine owners and others who won't understand your motives or what the Foundation is trying to do.'

Philip sat back on the sofa and waited for her answer. The fire roared in the grate. Sophie's face and hair were coloured gold from the flames, her silk dress shone and her eyes sparkled as much as the diamond studs in her ears.

'My one regret will be missing the children, but I'm sure that we can arrange for them to visit, and I can always catch the boat train and come to stay in Paris for weekends.'

'For much of the time, I'll be in London with you, but I'll be concentrating on the unfinished business from Russia and finishing the chess game.'

'I see, so you're close to finding all the answers then?' answered Sophie.

'Yes, it won't be long now, just a few loose ends to tie up.'

'Then my answer is yes, on two conditions: Tobias joins the Foundation and works with me and that, once the chess game's over, and the Foundation is securely set up, we settle down as a family.'

'I promise,' said Philip.

# Chapter Twenty-five: The strike

## May 1926

While Sophie and Tobias threw themselves into the work of the Foundation, Sir Charles Cunningham watched with indifference the worsening living conditions of the South Wales Miners, seeing no profit in the situation for himself.

Sophie and Tobias first travelled around the poorer areas of Britain, particularly the coal-mining regions of Wales. What they saw shocked them. Philip had told Sophie that coal production was in crisis: 'too many countries are producing too much'. To maintain their profits, the mine owners had reduced wages and increased working hours. In the past seven years pay had gone down from £6.00 to £3.90. Families were starving and the cry had gone up from the collieries: 'Not a penny off the day and not a minute on the day.'

How could it be, thought Sophie, that Britain, the land of capitalist might and unexampled compromise, could be preparing for battle between the boss and the worker? It was like being back in Russia, and even the words of Winston Churchill and Prime Minister Baldwin were similar to those she had heard all those years ago in her homeland: 'The strike is a challenge to parliament and is the road to anarchy.'

One million miners were unable to feed their families. It was the wives and the children who suffered most. Children walked the cobbled streets with no shoes; mineworkers were prosecuted for taking a small bucket of coal dust off the slag heaps that towered above their rows of homes, in the hope of keeping themselves warm at night; families went to bed with empty bellies. Meanwhile, the mine owners, the richest men in the land, would tell their servants to place more coal on the fires to keep their backs warm as they ate dinner.

Sophie established committees. The committees, made up of miners' wives, would manage the soup kitchens and distribute food and clothing. Tobias arranged for the bills to be paid, drew up contracts with shop owners to supply food and clothing which was stored in central distribution points, kept the accounts of how much people had been paid and what services they were to deliver.

'The Foundation isn't a charity,' he would say to those who questioned its right to supply free food or clothing. 'It's a business delivering essential help to hard-working people today in the knowledge they won't need it tomorrow.'

It was an explanation that most people had to think about, and by the time they had come to understand its meaning Sophie and Tobias had moved on. Tobias wasn't surprised that the mine owners hoped to break the strike by making the children suffer. That they would do everything they could to prevent aid reaching the strikers, would bully, deceive and threaten anyone who helped Sophie, was something that made him angry.

Tobias saw part of his job as being Sophie's protector, but soon discovered she needed no such help. When in Risca, in Wales's Rhondda Valley, a mine manager entered the food kitchen. He was a stocky man with knee-high jackboots and carrying a horse whip.

'You don't live here and you're on private land. Unless you leave *now*, I'll whip you out of the village,' he threatened.

Mothers held their terrified children as they all waited to see what would happen. Tobias took a step forward to protect Sophie, but she knew that such an action would only result in violence and gently put her hand on his arm to stop him.

'My dear man,' said Sophie, her Russian accent broader than usual. 'You obviously don't know who I am. My name is Countess Tagleva and I'm delighted to meet you. You can whip me if you like, but I would suggest you find something better than that' – pointing to the horsewhip. 'Where I come from it would be considered a fly swatter.'

The mine manager didn't know what to do. This well-dressed woman with the strange accent was challenging his authority. He was paid to keep workers in line; he dared not raise his whip against a titled lady, even if she was a foreigner. He looked around the sea of faces. Knowing he was defeated, he turned and walked out of the soup kitchen, red with anger.

Two days later Sophie was in London and met Jean-Claude. He told her of the latest political situation.

'The last-minute negotiations have failed. A general strike will begin in a few days. Apparently the Prime Minister is terrified by the revolutionary elements within the union movement. Workers at the *Daily Mail* have refused to print an editorial with the headline "For King and Country" that said "a general strike is revolutionary and will destroy the government and subvert the rights and liberties of the people."'

Sophie was mad with rage. 'After fighting the war and saving the nation by increasing coal production, they're only asking for the right to earn a living wage for themselves and their families!'

'A state of national emergency has been declared,' said Jean-Claude.

'The Tsar did the same thing in Russia. I don't think he truly understood that it would bring the nation one step closer to revolution. I hope the Prime Minister isn't going to make the same mistake.'

'I hope it won't be as bad as that,' said Jean-Claude.

The same day, in parliament, the Speaker of the House of Commons called on the Prime Minister, Stanley Baldwin, who rose to address the House.

'We have been challenged with an alternative government... I do not think that all the strike leaders, when they assented to ordering a general strike, fully realised that they were threatening the basis of ordered government, and have moved nearer to proclaiming civil war than we have been for centuries...'

Troops were dispatched to Scotland, South Wales, London and Lancashire. Warships sailed into the docks in the Tyne, the Clyde, Swansea, Barrow, Bristol and Cardiff. Sophie worked fourteen hours a day providing hot meals, fuel and comfort to the families of those on strike. When she wasn't in a soup kitchen – or arranging for a doctor to visit a child with measles, or delivering bread – she was meeting with friends and those sympathetic to her cause. One afternoon she was having tea with Lady Salcombe, a confidante whose husband worked in the 'corridors of power'.

'The King,' confided Lady Salcombe in a whisper, in case anyone should overhear, despite the fact that there were only the two of them in the room, 'told his ministers that he's livid with the newspapers and politicians for suggesting that the strikers are revolutionaries. His Majesty told the Prime Minister, in no uncertain terms, that he should try living on their wages before he judges them.'

How different from the Tsar's opinion, thought Sophie. Perhaps Britain wouldn't go the same way as Russia.

Transporting food and essential provisions for strikers was becoming more difficult. Only fifteen out of three hundred underground trains ran. Most of London's four thousand buses were stuck in their terminals, and only nine trams operated instead of the usual two thousand. A similar picture was repeated around the country. Nothing moved without the workers' say-so. That was, except the trucks and cars carrying food, clothing and coal for the Tagleva Foundation, and Sophie was relieved when the police and the army, ordered to halt the trucks, failed to do so. She guessed that it was out of sympathy for the plight of past comrades in arms rather than support of the strike.

Sophie watched columns of people march in the streets, just as they had done in St Petersburg. They waved flags, shouted the same slogans and, as in St Petersburg, the same soldiers and mounted policemen were ordered to break up and arrest the demonstrators. There were leaflets littering the streets. *The British Worker,* the Trades Union Congress's newspaper, declared: 'We are not making war on the people. We are anxious that the public shall not be penalised for the unpatriotic conduct of the mine owners and the government.'

In response, Winston Churchill, the Chancellor of the Exchequer, produced and financed *The British Gazette* and wrote, 'I do not agree that the TUC has any right to publish their side of the case and exhort their followers to continue the strike.'

On reading what Churchill had said, Sophie threw the paper on the floor. 'It's a disgusting rag,' she said. 'What would he know of suffering? He's the nephew of a duke. I do hope he never becomes Prime Minister.'

Passing groups of workers flying flags and marching with placards, she walked to the newest soup kitchen she had set up. She hoped that Britain wasn't falling into the same anarchy she'd seen in Russia. At the door she found a special constable and wondered if the kitchen had been closed. As she approached, the constable saluted.

'Are you here to stop people entering?' asked Sophie.

'No ma'am, I'm 'ere to keep peace. That means 'alting any trouble that might 'appen, not to stop good people coming and going. As long as people behave nicely it'll be good enough for me. The sergeant at the station said summat about preventing rabble coming to the kitchen; I've not seen any rabble yet.'

'Thank you, officer,' said Sophie. 'I'll send someone out with a cup of tea for you.'

'Much appreciated, ma'am,' and he saluted again.

As Sophie walked into the room she was greeted by a crowd of men, women and children all sitting eating soup and bread on the tables. Sophie smiled.

Two volunteers approached Sophie. 'Have you heard, my lady? The Flying Scotsman's been derailed by strikers near Newcastle. Things are serious.'

Things were indeed becoming serious, thought Sophie.

'Gawd, luv a duck, that'll cause problems for the strike,' she exclaimed, delighted to be able to use the expression she'd heard earlier that week. The two volunteers looked at each other in amazement.

'And her a countess and all,' they'd say later.

Tobias always enjoyed how she could use language in a disarming manner. Many an arrogant mine manager had been surprised by the 'language' Sophie could employ to get what she wanted. He marvelled at the long hours she could work, how easily she could charm hundreds of people to help her cause, her refusal to accept that something couldn't be done. Everyone seemed to come under her spell.

Two days after the train had been derailed, the TUC General Council visited the Prime Minister at Downing Street to announce its decision to call off the strike, provided that there would be no victimisation of strikers. The government said that it had no power to compel employers to take back every man who had gone on strike. Fearing prosecution by the courts, the union leaders agreed to end the dispute without such an agreement.

Sophie, exhausted by working such long hours, feared the workers would be even worse off than before. Mine owners, employers and the government would call for revenge. It had been the same in the attempted Russian revolution of 1905.

Over the next few months her fears were realised, as there were over three thousand prosecutions, more than half of them for acts of incitement. One Lambeth tram cleaner was fined five pounds for simply shouting, 'We want the revolution.'

Sophie would often pay such fines herself. Tobias would pass the money to the Clerk of the Court even as the accused was being taken down from the dock.

'We still have so much to do,' she told him. 'The suffering of the miners' families will last months – even years. Many have been sacked and have no chance of finding other work, and those that have gone back to work have been forced to accept lower wages. It's tragic, but most of the strikers have achieved nothing for all their efforts.'

Philip admired how hard Sophie was working, but she was tired and he was concerned about her health. 'Why don't you go home to Paris and spend some time with the children? You can come back and continue your work when you're more rested.'

'Yes, you're right, I will,' she said.

Philip ordered two dozen white roses to be delivered when she arrived home, and decided to make another donation to the Foundation's funds.

## Chapter Twenty-six: The conspiracy exposed

Members of the Reform Club in Pall Mall only have to look around themselves to know that they are at the very pinnacle of British society. The interior of the club is based on the Farnese Palace in Rome, and its saloon is regarded as one of the finest rooms in all London. The library contains over seventy thousand books on politics and history – and more than a few exaggerated biographies. Members traditionally donate a copy of any book they write to the library. If one was able to look at the list of members, one would read a list of the great and the good – including judges, Members of Parliament, generals and wealthy industrialists – and so it would come as no surprise to find the name 'Sir Charles Cunningham' included.

Sir Charles used the club in the same way that Renaissance monarchs had used their own sumptuous palaces, in which a visitor is meant to be acutely aware of their place in the scheme of things. Sir Charles liked to position himself at the apex of power in the saloon, where he could easily observe the rich and the powerful arriving for meetings, exchanging confidential news, and hatching the plots that would advance themselves or result in the downfall of rivals. Not all plots were a success, and he particularly enjoyed watching the indignation that resulted from betrayal, anger over a plot that had gone wrong, and the despair and downfall of a once proud man.

Failure was not something Sir Charles had much experience of, and occasionally he wondered what catastrophic failure might feel like. He had had the occasional setback to a plan, but his superior intelligence and guile had always overcome any human obstacle that had dared to cross him.

One day, he was reading *The Times* when he saw a tall bearded man walking towards him. He wasn't expecting a visitor.

'Sir Charles Cunningham?' asked the man.

'Yes, but I'm at a disadvantage. Do we know each other?'

'My card.'

Sir Charles took the card, read it and gestured to a seat. 'Please sit down, Count Tagleva.'

Philip took the seat opposite Sir Charles and leaned back into the soft leather.

'I take it that you're the chairman of Tagleva Bank.'

'Correct,' said Philip.

'Delighted to meet you. To what do I owe the pleasure of this meeting?' Sir Charles looked at the man opposite him and wondered why this investment banker would want to meet with him. He hoped it wasn't to discuss investments. He was able to manage his vast wealth on his own.

'Sir Charles, I have some letters that are addressed to the government, and specifically to His Majesty the King.'

'How did these letters come to be in your possession?' asked Sir Charles, intrigued and a touch concerned.

'I was given them by General Alexander Mossolov, the head of the Tsar's Imperial Chancellery.'

Sir Charles brushed a piece of thread off his trousers and watched it float to the floor. He suddenly felt very uncomfortable.

'What do the letters relate to?' he asked, trying to stay calm.

'They detail events that happened during the war, and specifically to the treason of some British nationals.'

'If you give me the letters, I will ensure the King receives them.'

Sir Charles looked at the man sitting opposite him. *I must remain calm and look as if I'm in control. I have crushed better men than this in the past, and I will do so again.*

'Would you really give them to the King when you've taken so much effort to ensure the papers are never delivered?'

'What do you mean?' asked Sir Charles.

Philip pulled an envelope from his jacket.

'The letters in this envelope detail your treason during the war: how you and various fellow conspirators worked to make yourselves wealthy by ensuring that the war lasted as long as possible. In doing so, you caused the deaths of hundreds of thousands of British soldiers, not to mention those of our allies.'

Sir Charles sighed. 'This is nonsense. I worked very hard to ensure that Britain won the war. You can't prove anything.'

'On the contrary. I've spent the past ten years collecting proof in Britain, France and the United States that confirms the allegations detailed in these letters.'

'What allegations?' sneered Sir Charles.

'That you and others established companies to supply Britain and its allies with war supplies. These ranged from uniforms to munitions, and for these supplies you used inferior quality materials but charged top prices.'

Sir Charles waved away the allegation. 'Those companies were helping with the war effort and the contracts were approved. These things have been said about so many people since the war. People aren't interested any more – you're ten years too late with such allegations.'

'True,' said Philip. 'But in your case, the facts show how you worked against Britain. That you plotted to extend the war so that Germany defeated Russia and could then bring her armies to the western front, thus prolonging the war against Britain.'

'How could I have managed that on my own?' sneered Sir Charles.

'You didn't. You had fellow conspirators in France, Belgium, Russia and even Germany. You arranged for ships carrying essential supplies to Russia to dock at ports you knew were controlled by the Germans. You sent ammunition to the army that you knew was faulty and wouldn't explode; you arranged for false intelligence to be sent to the Russian army's headquarters; and you arranged finance for the Bolsheviks. In addition to your activities in Russia, your companies supplied inferior cloth to the French army so that when the dye in the cloth ran it caused a drop in morale; deliveries were late or short; and you and your French conspirators sowed the seeds of the French army's mutiny. All of these things gave Germany an advantage and resulted in a stalemate for the Allies. It was what you had worked for, because at each turn you made money from every bullet and every new uniform.'

Sir Charles's face had turned waxen and expressionless.

Philip continued.

'Once you heard that the Tsar's secret police, the *Okhrana*, had arrested your contact in Russia, you knew that he would admit everything. You increased your payments to revolutionaries and once they were successful you plotted to ensure that the Tsar and his family would not be given sanctuary in Britain. While you weren't directly responsible for the deaths of the Imperial Family, your actions meant that they were denied the chance of exile in Britain. In effect, *you* condemned them to death. Your guilt is contained in these photographs of the original letters.' Philip handed Sir Charles the bundle of envelopes.

He opened the envelope, pulled out a photograph and read the handwritten letter, which began:

*My dearest cousin George,*
*It is with regret that I'm writing to you with details of some of your countrymen who have destroyed Russia and harmed Britain and yourself. The main details are as follows…*
*Your loving cousin*
*Nicki*

As he read the papers the colour drained from Cunningham's face.

'But that wasn't your only betrayal. You sent Sidney Reilly to persuade me to travel to Finland and meet the steamer *Novordsk*. There was no steamer – it had been sunk the month before by a German U-boat. All that awaited me in Finland was a bullet in the head. You hoped that if I died, the letters would be destroyed. When you discovered I hadn't been killed in Finland, you told the Russian authorities that I was a spy. You hoped that I'd be arrested and face a firing squad in Russia, but all your plans failed.'

'What do you intend to do?' Sir Charles asked.

'Your actions were completely self-serving, and I would imagine that your life would be in great danger if these facts were to become public knowledge – if these letters were to be published in the newspapers, for example. But a court case involving some very prominent people in the country would not be good for the country. It would cause much anger and might even incite more civil unrest. So, if you follow my instructions your treachery will remain a secret, but if you don't then I will send these letters to the King and to the newspapers, who will no doubt be delighted to publish them on their front pages.'

Sir Charles's shoulders slumped, and he looked at his feet. Exhausted, he asked, 'What must I do?'

'I estimate you made over two million pounds from the companies that supplied poor-quality goods. You'll contribute that amount to the Tagleva Foundation, which will use it to relieve the suffering of those families that lost their breadwinner due to you. In addition you'll resign from your post at the civil service and retire to your estate in Norfolk and take no further part in the management of the country. Do you agree to these terms?'

'Do I have any choice?' whispered Sir Charles.

Philip stood up and looked down at Cunningham. 'You and your group are finished. I expect the money to be received by the Tagleva Foundation within thirty days.'

Philip turned and walked away.

Sir Charles ordered a large whisky. When it arrived he drank it in one draught and left the Reform Club, never to return.

The following morning Sir Charles Cunningham wrote his resignation letter and left his office in Whitehall. The same day, strangely, various other diplomats and civil servants in England, France, Belgium and Italy also resigned from their posts. A week later *The Times* reported that a number of factories had mysteriously burned down overnight; the police suspected arson for insurance claims. In London a businessman threw himself out of a third-floor window and was impaled on the railings below. A French general was found dead in his château in Provence by his maid; the French police concluded he'd accidentally taken an overdose of the pills prescribed by his doctor for a stomach ulcer. In Berlin a politician threw himself under the wheels of a tram. Two businessmen were gunned down in Chicago and another found drowned in New York's docks. Law firms in London, New York, Washington, Berlin and Paris also suffered catastrophic fires that destroyed all their files and put them out of business. Finally, Sir Charles Cunningham retired to his estate in Norfolk.

## Chapter Twenty-seven:
## Rough justice for Edward

Jean-Claude was with a dozen or more friends at Ye Olde Cheshire Cheese, among them a couple of hacks from the *Daily Herald* newspaper. Jean-Claude liked teasing the reporters from the *Herald* for their unconditional support of a socialist revolution.

'The *Herald*'s a great newspaper,' cried one of the hacks in defence of his employer, but the usual howls of protest from barristers and the reporter from the rival *Daily Express* drowned his words.

'Don't forget, we panicked the government in 1917 with that great article, "How they starve at the Ritz". It told the great British public how you toffs were living the high life when the rest of the country was fighting for its survival.'

The crowd roared its playful disapproval once more.

'Yes, eggsactly,' slurred the *Herald*'s other hack as he waved his half-full jug of ale in the air. 'Exposed the cons-… conspicu… – you know what I mean – consumption by the filthy rich, and don't forget the government was panicked into introducing food rationing as a result of the article. And a good thing too!'

'So you'll not be wanting any more conspicuous consump-tion and another jug of ale?' shouted Jean-Claude above the noise.

'Don't mind if I do,' came the reply, and the crowd roared with laughter.

Then Jean-Claude saw Edward.

'Edward, my friend, come and sit down. How are things?'

'Fine, I think.' Edward obviously wanted a private word.

'What is it?' Jean-Claude asked him. 'You look agitated.'

'I need to talk to you. There's been talk at the bank about Tagleva.'

'Let's find somewhere quiet.' They went to find a quiet corner on another floor of the Cheese.

Once they were settled Edward spoke. 'There have been questions at the bank about Tagleva. It's not so much the investment house but the Foundation run by Countess Tagleva. She's upset too many people during the strikes, helping workers and everything.'

'Who's asking the questions?' asked Jean-Claude.

'Neville Porter – he took over the Russian desk from a friend of mine when he went missing in Russia some years ago. I think Neville's about to cause trouble for Tagleva.'

'Do you know why?'

'I'm not sure, but the point is, I wanted to make sure that my shares were safe, that if Neville caused problems at the bank for Tagleva then my money would be safe.'

Jean-Claude smiled. 'Your money's safe, I guarantee it, but why don't I transfer the share certificates to our offices in Paris? They'll be safe there. Remember, the only person who knows you own them is me. So no one in the Bank of England can accuse you of profiting from your position.'

'Oh, thank you, you're a great friend,' said a relieved Edward.

'So how's James?' asked Jean-Claude, changing the subject.

Edward's eyes lit up, forgetting his troubles at work.

'He's wonderful, thank you so much for introducing us.'

'My pleasure.'

'Now, I must return to the bank,' said Edward, and left the Cheese.

That night a coded telegraph was sent to Philip in Paris that simply stated: *Cat among pigeons.*

\*\*\*\*

Neville Porter left the Bank of England and limped towards the hansom cab waiting to take him home. He was exhausted. He hadn't expected Charles Cunningham to resign from his job so suddenly – obviously something must be wrong. He'd phoned Cunningham at home but his man had said he'd left for his estate in Norfolk. Despite repeated phone calls to the Norfolk estate, his butler said he was out. Perhaps Cunningham was refusing to speak to him. Neville felt he deserved to be treated with more respect by the man he'd helped to make so rich.

Suddenly Neville became aware of someone behind him. Turning, he saw a tall man in a heavy coat and hat. Despite his beard he looked vaguely familiar, but in the evening light Neville wasn't able to make out his features properly.

'Neville,' said the man.

'Do I know you?'

'It's Philip Cummings.'

'My God, I thought you were…'

'Dead?' enquired Philip.

Neville quickly composed himself. 'You're back in London, I'm going home, so why don't you come with me and we can have a drink?' Neville wanted to get off the street, where they might be seen together.

'That would be fine.' Philip climbed into the cab and sat opposite Neville in the cab. On arrival Neville ushered Philip into the study and limped in behind him. He poured each of them a glass of Madeira wine from the long-stemmed decanter and passed a glass to Philip. He then limped to his desk, sat in the leather chair and waved Philip to a chair on the other side of the desk.

'You look very well,' said Neville as Philip made himself comfortable.

'Thank you, but I haven't come here for a social meeting.'

'So what have you come for?' asked Neville, knowing the answer.

'I've come to ask, why?'

Very slowly, Neville opened the drawer where he kept a loaded pistol.

'Why the bank dispensed with your services?' asked Neville and continued, 'Believe me, I opposed it, of course I did, but when you'd been missing for almost a year everyone assumed the worst. With the chaos going on in Russia, people thought you must be dead. Now that you're back I will, as your friend, recommend that you be given a position. It may not be your old position or status – things have changed in the years you've been missing – but I'll do everything I can to help you; you know that.'

'I'm not interested in re-joining the bank,' said Philip.

'Then what do you want?'

'I've come to ask why you betrayed me.'

'I don't know what you're talking about!'

'If I had truly been missing for ten years and turned up out of the blue, the normal question would be, "Where have you been? What happened to you over the past nine years?". The fact that you didn't ask either of those questions proves you know exactly what happened to me.'

Neville didn't know what to say, nor could he think what to say. The whole situation was beginning to horrify him. No matter how he tried to conceal his guilt, his knowledge made him afraid. He'd assumed he'd never have to face Philip again, but the demon from his nightmares had returned and was sitting in front of him.

'Why didn't you send any communications to me when I was in Russia? Why did you destroy the communications I sent to the Bank? Why did you stop funds being transferred to me? And why did you ensure that the ship that was to bring me back to England was ordered home without me?'

Neville needed time to think.

'What happened to the final box and letters you were given?' he asked.

'How did you know I was given some letters? I didn't mention anything about letters.'

He'd asked about the letters! Why had he asked about the letters? Now Cummings knew everything: with that one question he'd admitted he knew it all. All Neville could see now was Philip tormenting him, the same way his classmates had tormented him at school.

'I assumed…' He didn't finish his answer.

Philip pulled some papers from his coat and passed them over the desk. 'I've been able to get hold of your bank statements. The clerks at the Midland Bank were most obliging. You'll see regular and large amounts of money moving in and out of your account at the Midland Bank. The dates are all during the war.'

There, laid out before him, was his guilt: the web of lies, the deceit, the betrayals, but still Neville hoped he would escape from the web that was wrapping itself tightly around him.

'Moving money in and out of a bank account is normal,' replied Neville in his most sarcastic tone.

'The significance is that the amounts are more than twice your annual salary,' said Philip. 'You worked with Sir Charles Cunningham to keep him informed of what was happening in Russia, and you moved funds around the world for him.'

'You can't prove I knew what Sir Charles was up to. It was my job to move funds as instructed,' said Neville.

'You're right. But I can prove that you knew I was travelling on board HMS *Marlborough* and that I landed in Malta. You've admitted you knew I was carrying papers that would prove your complicity with Sir Charles and that you had abandoned me in Russia. You knew your guilt was in those letters – you had to stop me. But your plan failed. The bullet that was meant for me killed someone else; someone who had become very close to me.'

Neville's hand wrapped itself around the pistol, he raised it from the drawer and aimed it at Philip's chest. He was in control again.

'I won't make that mistake again. I knew that if you managed to get back to London you'd be a problem. You were always too clever for your own good, and I guessed that you'd put all the threads together. Yes, I did abandon you. You want to know why? You had an easy life – work came easy for you. Everyone told you how valuable your work was all the time. I used to hear what they said about me in private – all they could talk about was my limp. Even when I was a child, my withered foot was all that my family could see. As a child when guests came to the house I was hidden away in the nursery because they were ashamed of me. My mother told me I would probably never marry, because who would have me? She said I should resign myself to that.'

'I never commented on your limp, even in private,' said Philip as he looked down the barrel of the pistol that was pointed at his chest.

'It was always about you and your good work. You were whole, unlike me. I was withered and handicapped. I was never going to be made whole.'

'Killing me won't make it better,' said Philip.

Neville replied, 'I can of mine own self do nothing. As I hear I judge, and my judgement is just.'

'How will you explain my death to the police?' asked Philip calmly.

'I'll tell the police that a discredited past employee came to my house to rob me. That you threatened me, that I shot you in self-defence.'

Neville raised the pistol, and Philip waited for the blast.

Neville squeezed the trigger.

Blood and brains stained the wall and slid in rivers down the wallpaper and onto the carpet. Neville's torso remained seated in the chair, his hand gripping the pistol, which still pointed at Philip but now rested on the desk blotter.

Philip rose from his chair and left the room. When Neville had pulled the trigger the lead plug inserted into the barrel earlier that afternoon caused the blast to move backwards into the chamber and had removed Neville's head instead of sending a bullet into Philip's chest.

Philip truly regretted what had happened. Neville was consumed by anger and self-hatred caused by an accident of birth. Unfortunately, his family had believed that his disability was a reflection on their own health and had chosen to hide him from sight. In the end, the same hand that had paid the thirty pieces of silver to cause Sergei's death had taken its own revenge.

# Chapter Twenty-eight: The crash

## August 1929

While the bull market had fuelled public interest in shares, and huge amounts of credit had been arranged to satisfy avarice, thinking the stock market was overvalued Philip and Jean-Claude had, as they had agreed at the director's meeting, sold almost all of Tagleva's stock, and most of their clients had taken their advice to do the same. In place of shares Tagleva had invested in art and gold. The House of Tagleva was the proud owner of paintings by Manet, Picasso, Matisse, Maurice de Vlaminck, Raoul Dufy and a couple of works by a Russian painter Sophie had insisted on buying, Marc Chagall.

Philip flew into London on an Imperial Airways flight from Paris and checked in to the Ritz. He was looking forward to hearing the world-famous economist John Maynard Keynes's speech at a dinner that night.

When the meal was over and the assembled audience were enjoying their cigars and brandies Keynes rose and began: 'We will not have any more financial crashes in our time.' The audience clapped their approval.

Keynes explained his proposal by saying, 'If investment exceeds saving, there will be inflation; if saving exceeds investment there will be recession. One implication of this is that, in the midst of an economic depression, the correct course of action should be to encourage spending and discourage saving. For the engine which drives enterprise is not thrift, but profit.'

Philip couldn't agree. He felt the unsustainable rise in share values was caused by chasing a profit and having no savings to cover for bad times.

The President of the New York Stock Exchange, E.H. Simmons, supported Keynes by saying, 'I can't help but raise a dissenting voice to those who say we are living in a fool's paradise, and that the prosperity must necessarily diminish and recede in the near future.'

The audience applauded wildly when Myron Forbes, President of Pierce-Arrow Motor Car Company, shouted, 'There will be no interruption of our permanent prosperity!'

After dinner, as Philip was being driven to his apartment, he decided that such a blind optimism that stock markets would continue to rise for evermore was creating an atmosphere of overconfidence that was bound to lead to disaster. It was nothing more than a classic bubble that, like all bubbles, would burst when confidence evaporated. Why, thought Philip, were people as intelligent as Maynard Keynes so blind to the lessons from history? Financial crashes had occurred with regularity for centuries. Examples were the Dutch tulip scandal, when people paid a fortune for a single flower bulb until the value dropped and wiped out many fortunes? Or the South Sea Bubble, where people had been frantic to buy stocks on the basis of future profits, sometimes in companies that didn't even exist? Or the crisis caused by the San Francisco earthquake, which had resulted in a banking panic.

Philip knew that Maynard Keynes and the others were wrong. They were ignoring the fact that a loss in confidence *would* happen periodically.

He thought back over the past few years when the stock market had become the focus of popular interest. It was the subject of conversation at private meetings and dinner parties throughout the United States, Britain and France. For many, it seemed a perfect reflection of the new industrial age, and this feeling was fuelled by articles in the newspapers titled, 'Everybody could be rich' and 'The Dow Jones could climb to the heavens'.

The result was thousands of people, investing in the stock market for the first time, spent much of their time doing nothing but following the stock market. Ordinary people, with no training or expertise, were able to buy stock for as little as ten per cent in cash and a loan for the remainder. Whenever he was at a dinner party he would hear of stories about working-class people who had become millionaires almost overnight. Even Calvin Coolidge, the President of the USA, had told Congress, 'No congress of the United States ever assembled, on surveying the state of the Union, has met with a more pleasing prospect than that which appears at present.'

****

It had been a busy day at the bank and Edward was sitting in his newly furnished house contemplating what he might do that evening. James was away visiting his mother, a regular engagement, and Edward disliked being alone these days. James had always encouraged him to enjoy himself and had never objected to Edward picking up other men, so it had become a regular adventure for him. He bathed and dressed and took a cab to the Trocadero.

Warmly greeted by the doorman and by a few of the regulars, he ordered a drink and sat on one of the red velvet sofas that lined the back wall. Looking around him he spied a handsome youth, around twenty, he estimated, sitting alone at the end of the bar. Doubtless, he was for rent, thought Edward, but he assuaged any feelings of guilt by assuring himself that such boys enjoyed the money he was able to pay them, that it was purely a business transaction, and they appreciated the meals and expensive gifts he gave them. He indicated to the barman to offer the boy a drink. It was accepted, as he knew it would be. After taking a sip of the beer, the boy walked over to Edward and sat down.

'Thanks for the drink, mister.'

'You're welcome,' said Edward.

'They call me Rob.'

'And people call me Edward.'

'Nice to make yer acquaintance,' replied Rob, mimicking Edward's posh accent.

They shook hands. Edward was captivated by the boy.

'What's your work?' asked Edward.

'I work on the docks,' came the reply.

Edward couldn't take his eyes off his broad shoulders, firm chest and bulging biceps hardly hidden under the tight-fitting jacket.' His eyes moved to the boy's strong thighs, used to lifting heavy cargo all day. Edward placed a hand on Rob's thigh, felt the hard muscle below the corduroy and imagined stroking the rest of the boy's muscular body. Rob smiled back at him.

'So what are you doing for the rest of the evening?' asked Edward.

'Can't stay out long, cos I'm on shift tomorrow at five.'

'What a shame,' said Edward.

'What are ye looking for?'

'Perhaps some fun, but if you're working...' said Edward without finishing the sentence.

'St James's Park is near. Now it's dark it be quiet,' replied Rob.

'I don't know,' said Edward, who'd never liked his sex in the discomfort of the open air.

'Ye won't regret it, mister,' said Rob. 'I'm a big boy – I'll give ye a good time.'

Rob took Edward's hand and pressed it against his crotch. 'Course, I'd need a few quid for me trouble.'

Rob had told the truth – he was a big boy! Edward was still uncomfortable with the thought of sex in the open. He'd heard too many stories of people being attacked, arrested or robbed, but he was driven by lust and he put these thoughts to the back of his mind. What harm could there be?

'All right, just this once,' said Edward as they walked out of the bar and towards St James's Park.

Finding a secluded area down by the lake, Rob asked for his money. Edward passed him two five-pound notes, which disappeared into Rob's jacket pocket. 'Unbutton yer trousers an' pull 'em down below yer knees. It'll stop you getting grass stains on yer trousers,' said Rob helpfully.

Edward did what he was told and fell to his knees as Rob unbuttoned his trousers, exposing his huge penis. Edward licked his lips in anticipation...

The next thing he knew, Edward heard the shrill noise of a police whistle and was blinded by a bright light from a torch.

'Gotcha,' said a policeman, who dragged Edward to his feet, pulling his arms behind his back and clicking handcuffs around his wrists. Still with his trousers around his ankles, he was dragged to the police van and bundled into the back and the door slammed shut.

Inside the van a third policeman shouted, 'Another 'ead-worker for the beak on Wednesday!' and struck him on the thigh with his truncheon.

Edward cried out in pain and threw up in sheer terror. As he lay in his vomit, he wondered what had happened. Why was he alone in the police van? Where was Rob? How had he escaped? Oh God, what was he to do?

That night, as he lay on the metal bed in his police cell and pulled his knees up to his chest, he couldn't sleep. The cold kept him awake, and all he could do was to stare at the grey prison tiles on the wall. He smelled the stale vomit that covered his jacket and began to sob.

****

Over the next few weeks, Philip watched with increasing concern as the American economy faltered. Consumer spending fell, and unsold goods began to pile up, causing production to slow further. The downturn in spending led factories to slow down production and begin to fire workers. For those lucky enough to remain employed, wages fell and buying power decreased. Many Americans forced to buy food on credit fell into debt, and the number of foreclosures and repossessions climbed steadily. Even with these indicators, stock prices had continued to rise, and by the autumn of 1929 prices had reached levels that couldn't be justified by future earnings.

On the fourth of September Philip was in his office when Jean-Claude walked in and announced that stocks had begun to fall in New York, London and Paris. The following day the *New York Times* tried to calm people's nerves by quoting Irving Fisher, a leading economist: 'There may be a recession in stock process, but not anything in the nature of a crash.'

Philip thought Fisher was wrong. Twenty days later, the stock market bubble finally burst, and investors began to dump shares *en masse*. Thirteen million shares were sold that day, and the newspapers named it Black Thursday. Five days later, on Black Tuesday, another sixteen million shares were traded on the New York stock exchange, with millions of shares ending up worthless. Investors who had bought stocks 'on margin' were completely wiped out.

That same day Edward appeared before the magistrates' court charged with 'indecent behaviour likely to cause a public outrage'. Bail was opposed by the police and Edward was remanded in custody until he could appear at the crown court. His solicitor informed him that homosexuality was a crime, as if Edward wasn't aware of the fact, and told him that, if found guilty, he should prepare himself for a custodial sentence.

He was sick to the pit of his stomach, and asked himself why he had been so stupid. He sent a message via his solicitor to Jean-Claude, the only friend he could trust, asking him to visit him in prison.

A warder brought a plate of cold porridge into Edward's cell – he'd already spat into it a couple of times outside. He placed the bowl on the small table and left still with the spoon in his pocket. Edward would have to eat the gruel with his hands.

****

Philip was up late. The past few days had been long and exhausting as he and Jean-Claude had dealt with the fallout from the financial crash. There was panic in New York and London, but thankfully Paris had fared better and seemed calmer. It was evident that countries with a large manufacturing base were being hit hardest. America and the North of England had been immediately affected; hundreds of factories had closed down. France, on the other hand, was more an agricultural society and had been affected far less than more industrialised countries.

Philip finished his croissant and coffee, thinking he should walk to work before the best of the morning was lost, when Sophie suddenly let out a cry.

'What is it, my love?'

'My God, I can't believe it.'

'Can't believe what?'

'Williams,' she said to the footman, 'Could you bring me a magnifying glass from the study?'

The footman returned with a large magnifying glass. Sophie peered through the glass at a grainy picture taken of a parade in Moscow. She moved the magnifying glass this way and that to get the clearest view of a young man at the back of the group. Still not sure, she stood up and walked to the window for better light.

'Come and look!' she shouted at Philip. Philip got up and walked over to the window.

'Look, there among the Central Committee of the Communist Party photographed in Moscow.'

'What am I looking at?' asked Philip.

'The face in the back row.'

Philip took the paper and peered at the grainy photograph at a man with the same features as Sergei, though a few years older.

He put down the paper and Sophie looked at the picture once more. There, in front of her, were the people that now ruled her homeland – and her brother was among them.

'It's my brother Sacha, I know it is. Well, I never. Father always thought he'd come to nothing – how wrong he was. I wonder why he didn't try to help us when we were in Moscow?'

'Perhaps he didn't know we were in Moscow,' said Philip.

She was pleased he was alive, even if their lives were so different that they would probably never see each other again. She wished him well.

'I must go and show Michael; he'll be thrilled to hear that he has an uncle.'

Philip went to Tagleva's offices. There, Jean-Claude was studying the telegraph printer and the tickertape which revealed the tumbling value of stocks, fell to the floor in a mound. Millions had been wiped off the value of shares. Thousands in every city were now bankrupt, and reports came in of people, hearing that they was penniless, throwing themselves out of high buildings in New York.

There were some half-hearted attempts to stem the wound to the falling confidence. The chairman of Continental Illinois Bank of Chicago was quoted as saying, 'The crash is not going to have much effect on business.'

*The Times* quoted Irving Fisher, professor of economics at Yale University, as saying, 'The end of the decline of the stock market will probably not be long; only a few days at most.' He was wrong.

The economic disaster Philip had been predicting for more than a year had arrived almost overnight.

# Chapter Twenty-nine: Jean-Claude's revenge

Two days later Edward was escorted to the prison visiting room, where he smiled gratefully at Jean-Claude.

'Thank you for coming,' said Edward. 'My solicitor tells me that I can expect three years' hard labour. I'd never survive it. You've got to help me. I've been told that I can have bail if I can raise five hundred pounds. With that I could escape to France or North Africa and live on the income from my stocks. You will help me, won't you, Jean-Claude?' Edward begged.

Jean-Claude looked at him before speaking. 'I can't.'

Edward looked at him, utterly shocked. 'Why?'

'The stock market crashed two days ago and you didn't instruct Tagleva to sell your stock. I'm sorry. Your stocks are worthless.'

'But I didn't know,' cried Edward. 'How could I? I was in here, I couldn't…'

Edward looked at his friend. What was he to do? His head spun.

'My property? There's value in my house,' moaned Edward.

'Property values have also crashed, and you owe the brokers over fifty thousand pounds for the additional shares you bought. They'll repossess your property to recover what they can. It's unlikely there will be anything left.'

'Oh God, then could you lend me the money? I have to get out of here, otherwise I'm done for,' begged Edward.

Jean-Claude looked at Edward. 'Do you remember a French wine merchant begging you for a loan many years ago? You turned him down, despite the fact that he had some good wine as stock which he was offering as collateral.'

'No… yes… I think so, but what the hell's that got to do with me?' cried Edward.

'You arranged for the business to be sold off to a friend of yours, very cheaply. The wine was sold for a fraction of its value. The wine merchant went bankrupt and you shared in the subsequent sale of the wine.'

'I-I-I don't understand,' stammered Edward.

'The Frenchman hanged himself, his wife went mad and died in an asylum.'

'Yes, yes, I remember now, but it was years ago, I never expected the man to kill himself, and it wasn't my fault his wife went mad. What's it got to do with me now? I don't understand!' cried Edward.

'The wine merchant was my father, and I watched my mother go mad in the asylum.'

Edward could only stare at Jean-Claude whose eyes were cold. Edward shrank from them. His shoulders slumped. He was crushed, there was nothing more he could do.

'Oh God,' Edward said. 'I didn't know.'

'My parents were ruined because of your greed. However, that was a long time ago, and I might even have forgiven you for that, but you failed to help the person who's become like a second father to me.'

'Who?' asked Edward, now utterly confused.

'You saw telegraphs from Philip Cummings when he was trapped in Russia, and you ignored them. You could have done something – anything. If you had, then I would be helping you now.'

'How do you know Philip?' cried Edward, fearing more bad news.

'He's the chairman and founder of the House of Tagleva.'

Edward was utterly devastated. He felt as if a ton of stones were on his chest, crushing him; he was breathless.

'But you and I were friends,' Edward pleaded with Jean-Claude, hanging his head.

'You were friends with Philip and you betrayed him. We were never friends because I knew you for what you are: a greedy, small man who would be his own downfall if tempted. I feel nothing for you. I never did. And, by the way...'

Edward looked up, hoping for some words of forgiveness.

'Rob sends you his best wishes.'

Jean-Claude left the room. Edward began to sob.

A week later two policemen testified that the accused had been seen with his trousers around his ankles having sexual relations with another man, who had managed to escape. Edward saw his father and some of his colleagues from the bank in the public gallery and wanted the ground to open up and swallow him. Whatever the verdict, he knew his career was over and his family would disown him.

The jury found Edward guilty on all charges. The judge looked at him over half-moon glasses and sentenced him to two years' hard labour. Edward was taken to the cells. Edward soon discovered that the monotony of prison – the routine, the harsh discipline, the structured schedules, the ordered uniformity – distorted his sense of time and gave him the feeling of living in an extended present. All of that might have been bearable had not he found himself the victim of other prisoners. During his first week Edward was raped three times.

It was going to be a very long two years.

**** 

Three months later Philip met with Jean-Claude in Philip's office in Paris.

'I think we should review where we are,' said Philip. 'I want to close the file on the Tsar's treasure so that we can concentrate on the Tagleva Foundation.'

Jean-Claude began. 'The group led by Sir Charles Cunningham has been exposed and dealt with, and can't do any more damage. Neville Porter killed himself and Edward is in prison.'

Philip looked at Jean-Claude. 'I know Edward behaved very badly towards your family, but he was a young man at the time and I don't think he thought through the consequences of his actions. I wonder, as you get older, whether you'll gain the same comfort from your revenge that you feel now.'

Jean-Claude looked at him. 'You're right. Edward was weak and easily led, but deep down he wasn't evil like Sir Charles, nor deranged like Neville.'

'What will you do to make things better?' asked Philip.

'I did it before he was arrested. I didn't tell him, but I sold much of his stock before the crash and invested it in gold. When he comes out of prison he'll be able to live reasonably comfortably off the income.'

Though not comfortably enough to be able to afford to rent dockers for the night, thought Jean-Claude.

'What of Sir Charles?' asked Jean-Claude.

Philip sighed. 'He's retired to his house in Norfolk. He made an anonymous contribution of two million pounds to the Tagleva Foundation. That'll help many of the people he helped to destroy. He's still left with a substantial income. His greatest loss will be the loss of the power and influence he once had. I heard that he now spends his time walking in the grounds of his house, all alone, with no visitors or invitations to dinner, just brooding on his past. He'll find that more difficult to cope with than anything else.'

'And the contents of the Tsar's last box?' asked Jean-Claude.

'The jewels will stay where they are, awaiting a surviving member of the Imperial Family. If there's no claim supported by the courts in England, Denmark or the USA after a sufficient length of time, then I suggest that we sell the jewels and give the money to benefit those in need.'

'That's not the treasure I meant,' said Jean-Claude.

'I know,' replied Philip, turning to face Jean-Claude and smiling. 'You mean the Tsar's letters.' Philip turned away from the window and sat down in the leather chair in front of Jean-Claude. 'The British people would be angry to learn that so many people had been killed just for profit. They might never allow a government to go to war again if they felt their leaders would sacrifice them for nothing more than money. I've hidden the letters and hope that there will be no reason to make them public.'

'So why not destroy the papers?' asked Jean-Claude.

'One day they might be important to prevent a government taking us into another war on the basis of a lie. In any event, I've never thought it sensible to try to obliterate or change history. The new Soviet government is doing that, and it will probably cause conflict later. Let's get some dinner,' said Philip.

# Chapter Thirty: The Hunger March

## September 1932

The Great War had rendered the British government all but bankrupt, so when the stock market collapsed in 1929 the government was virtually impotent to reduce the worst effects on the poorest of the population. In fact, it made the situation worse by cutting public sector wages by ten per cent and raising income tax to twenty-five pence in the pound. As usual, the poor paid for the government's past financial incompetence, while the rich continued to make money.

While Philip and Jean-Claude became essential resources to government ministers in Paris and London, the Tagleva Foundation became a source of practical help to those who needed it most: the three million unemployed.

Sophie quickly re-established soup kitchens in the South Wales valleys, in the industrial areas of the North of England, and in London. Hostels would shelter some of the homeless, where they could sleep in a bed, have a hot bath, a change of clothing and a meal. Schools were set up so that children could get an education, and doctors were paid to hold surgeries for those unable to pay their fees. Despite all of this, Sophie felt that she was just scratching the surface of what needed to be done.

In September, the National Unemployed Workers' Movement organised a Great National Hunger March, and three thousand people from the depressed areas marched into London to meet up in Hyde Park. Sophie organised soup kitchens along the route. It wasn't easy to persuade people to help the marchers because the press, parliament and establishment figures spoke of the marches as a threat to public order. Fearing disorder, seventy thousand police turned out to control the marchers and their supporters. With no cause, mounted police would charge into the crowd, waving heavy batons and clubs. Nearly eighty people were badly injured and needed hospitalisation.

In all this confusion Sophie moved from one soup kitchen to another, organising deliveries, keeping up workers' morale, and even lending a hand peeling potatoes and parsnips for the soup. As she finished in one location she moved to another. She was working eighteen hours a day, missing Michael and the twins but grateful that Philip would arrange for them to travel to see her every weekend.

Each evening she telephoned Philip at their home to tell him of her progress and to discuss the day's events. 'There's so much to do: these poor men and women have so little and the government has no sympathy for them. Do you know they are proposing setting up work camps for the unemployed, where up to two hundred thousand unemployed will be forced to work for the government?'

'I've heard,' said Philip. 'I'm trying to use my influence to prevent the government from setting up concentration camps. It's inhuman but, if they are set up, I'm determined that they should be humanely run.'

'You're so good,' she exclaimed and, changing the subject, 'How's Michael?'

'Missing you,' replied Philip. 'He was reading a book on Great Generals in history today and he told me that in his opinion the greatest generals were those that won battles and ordered their troops not to mistreat prisoners or their families, like Alexander the Great.'

'Oh, he's such a gentle boy,' said Sophie. 'I'm so proud of him.'

'You and me both,' said Philip.

'And the twins?'

'They're fine and missing you too.'

'I must go, my darling,' said Sophie. 'I'll call you at the same time tomorrow – love you.'

'I love you too,' and he heard the click as the receiver was replaced in its cradle.

Philip returned to his study and read through the papers he'd need for tomorrow's meetings. There were times he wished for a weekend alone with Sophie and their children with nothing to do but to please themselves. He smiled contentedly at the thought that he had easily fallen into the role of a family man. He was happy. After visiting the nursery to play with his children and having a light dinner he retired to bed early and read a few pages of his book before turning out the light and pulling Sophie's pillow towards him so that he could cuddle it and breathe in her favourite perfume. He was soon sound asleep.

The following morning, promptly at six forty Philip walked down to the dining room where he found Michael and the twins at the table with their nanny. Michael was eating fresh fruit salad. Over breakfast they discussed what Michael would be doing at school that day. Michael talked about a forthcoming mathematics test, and Philip listened with interest as his son told him confidently that he expected to do well.

'I have to do well if I'm going to be a banker like you,' he told his father.

Philip was delighted his son was full of enthusiasm, energy and ambition.

Then Michael became more earnest. 'Father, I have a problem.'

Philip doubted that it could be anything serious, but Michael's furrowed brow demanded he give his son his full attention.

'A problem shared is often halved,' said Philip, knowing that the reality was often different. In any event, the problem was unlikely to be of immense importance. Michael was top of his class in most subjects, keen on sport and one of the most popular boys in the school. He shared his mother's sense of justice: he had been in only two fights, and both of these had been to challenge a bigger bully for tormenting weaker boys. On both occasions the bully had been sent packing with a bruised nose.

'As you know,' began Michael seriously, 'I've been collecting cigarette cards and have quite a collection, but I'm missing just one from my set of kings of England – King Ethelred, to be exact.' Michael paused to collect his thoughts. 'Now, another boy has the card I'm missing and is offering me a swap. I don't want to give away more than I have to. What would you do?'

'Does he know you want this one card to make a set?' asked Philip.

'Yes, I told him so. That was a mistake, don't you think?'

'Perhaps,' smiled Philip. 'What are you thinking of doing?'

'I think I'll ask what he wants first. But I don't want to offer him too many cards... difficult, isn't it, Father? You have to offer enough of what he wants but try not to give away too much of what you have. It's complicated, because if he gets upset with me he won't swap with me in the future... and he's got the biggest collection in the school. He says his father and all his family smoke like troopers.'

Michael giggled; he'd never seen a trooper smoke.

'Is business like that?' he enquired.

Philip smiled and ruffled his hair. 'Yes, my boy, just with different types of cards.'

'Thank you, Father. I've decided that I want to be in business like you. Business must be fun if it's like swapping cigarette cards all day.'

Philip watched Michael leave the room and smiled. After breakfast, Philip went to his study to begin reading the reports that had come in from London and the United States during the night and to prepare for the day's meetings. They were the usual mix of businessmen looking for finance for their companies and a government minister wanting his advice. 'Just different types of cigarette cards,' he said to himself softly.

## Chapter Thirty-one: The Phoenix plan

At eleven the phone rang and his secretary informed him Jean-Claude was on the line. Philip asked for him to be put through, knowing that a telephone call from London before midday meant that it was important.

'Philip, have you heard from Sophie today?'

'No. I spoke to her last night and we're due to speak again this evening.'

'Philip, we believe Sophie's missing. Her maid said that she wasn't in her room when she arrived with morning tea. One of the servants said she thought she heard Sophie talking to someone and leaving the house in the early hours.'

'Has she just decided to go to her appointments early?'

Jean-Claude's voice sounded strained. 'I've phoned her first appointment and they said she hadn't turned up. I've asked all those she was due to meet to phone me immediately she turns up, but so far I've heard nothing. I've sent staff to all her favourite haunts and we are phoning her friends to see if any of them have seen her. I think we have to consider the possibility of implementing the Phoenix plan.'

Philip felt himself grip the receiver more firmly. He'd known this moment might come one day but, now that it had, it didn't make the shock of its arrival any less frightening.

Wealth brought with it the risk of attack and kidnap, and Philip and Sophie had discussed how they, and particularly the children, could be protected. They had engaged a team of security experts, headed by John Lee, who devised a plan of action for any number of emergencies. John Lee was a bull of a man with broad shoulders, balding head and a round florid face. Many people who didn't know him assumed he was more criminal than a defender of the law. In fact, he was an ex-police inspector from Scotland Yard with vast experience in protecting members of the British Royal Family. It was John Lee who had identified safe houses, arranged for secret emergency financial resources that could be accessed without detection, developed instructions for dealing with the police, prearranged distress signals had been chosen, so that the family would know that any emergency was real, not a practice. Plans were rehearsed and refined so that they could be implemented without panic, confusion or mistake. It was the Phoenix plan, and its sole objective was to protect Tagleva, the directors and their families.

'Of course,' John Lee had said when briefing Philip, Sophie and the other directors, 'the logical first step in dealing with a kidnapping, for instance, is to prevent the kidnapping happening in the first place. That means not being predictable in your movements, limiting the number of people who know your itinerary in advance and, if you feel the need, arranging for my team to provide security. Above all, be paranoid and assume people want to do you harm.'

Philip couldn't think properly, but the Phoenix plan ensured that everyone else knew what to do and would do it as planned and rehearsed.

'If that's your advice, then of course I agree,' said Philip.

'I'll be at the airport to meet your plane,' replied Jean-Claude.

Philip replaced the receiver and told his secretary to implement the Phoenix plan. She cancelled his appointments, making the excuse that Philip had a bad cold. A car was dispatched to collect Michael from school and transport him and the twins, together with their nanny, to safety. The Tagleva private plane was prepared to fly to London. Two members of the security team arrived at Philip's office to accompany him everywhere until the emergency was over.

Before Philip left for the airport he walked upstairs into Sophie's private sitting room, which adjoined their bedroom. He looked around the room at her comfortable chairs, the books and photographs in their silver frames, the malachite blotter and an unfinished letter lying on the desk. He saw her small Bible on the writing desk and picked it up. He opened the cover. Inside was a pressed flower. The petals had turned yellow with age. Underneath Sophie had written: *From my darling Philip. The Hotel Europe, St Petersburg 1916.*

He carefully stroked the faded petal so as not to damage it. He was looking into the bottomless deep into which he hoped never to descend into again; into the darkness he'd known as a child when his mother had left him. It frightened him. He wanted to drive the thoughts away, and bit his lip. 'Be safe, my darling.'

He gently closed the Bible, carefully returning it to the table, and left for the airport.

As the Phoenix plan swung into action Jean-Claude cancelled his own appointments. By the time Philip was in the air Jean-Claude knew that Sophie wasn't in hospital, had not arrived for any of her appointments, and wasn't visiting her usual friends, doctor, favourite clothes shops or restaurants.

On arrival, Philip hurried down the steps of the plane and climbed into the rear of the Rolls-Royce where Jean-Claude was waiting for him with an updated report. In the front sat the driver and John Lee, Tagleva's head of security.

'What news?' asked Philip as he settled into the leather seat. He had hoped to hear that Sophie had been found but, looking into Jean-Claude's eyes, knew the news wasn't good.

John Lee spoke. 'We know Sophie left the house at around two this morning. A maid said she was woken by the front door opening and closing and that she'd heard voices in the hallway. The maid got up to check if everything was as it should be, but went back to bed when she found nothing unusual. It was only when she took tea to Sophie's room this morning that Sophie's absence was discovered and the alarm raised.'

'There is one strange thing…' said Jean-Claude, who looked at John Lee to explain.

John Lee continued. 'We've discovered that Sophie received a telephone call on her reserved line at around one o clock this morning, an hour before she left the house. Did you phone her?'

Philip looked surprised. John Lee had advised the installation of a separate telephone system to link the houses and offices of the directors and which didn't require an operator to connect them. Known as the 'reserved lines', they were used for only for important and confidential conversations.

'No, I didn't, and I assume from your question we don't know who did,' said Philip.

'Correct,' said Lee. 'But whoever it was knew her private number and Sophie must have recognised the caller and thought it urgent enough for her to get dressed and leave the house without telling anyone else.'

Lee continued, 'I think someone persuaded Sophie that the Phoenix plan had been activated. If she believed that you, Michael or the twins were in danger she would easily have agreed to be taken to you by some strangers, particularly if they used the correct passwords.'

Jean-Claude spoke. 'John Lee thinks that someone knows the details of the Phoenix plan and is using it against us.'

'Oh my God, if that's true then Michael and the twins are in danger!' said Philip. 'If someone has access to the Phoenix plan and the passwords then they'll know all of the plans and where Michael and the twins will be.' He suddenly felt sick.

The car was speeding to London and John Lee had also concluded that one of the eighteen people who needed to know the details of the Phoenix plan had betrayed the information. It was always the flaw in the plan: people needed to know what to do in an emergency and who to trust, but if that information had been passed to a third party, then it was useless.

While Philip's plane had been in the air the family's personal chauffeur, one of John Lee's team, another ex-policeman, had collected Michael from school and bundled him into the back of a small, nondescript car. In the back Michael found the twins and their nanny. Despite Sophie's concerns Michael had been told very basic details of the Phoenix plan. John Lee had insisted. 'He needs to know the passwords and basic details so that if he's in danger he can protect himself.'

As the car was driven in a circuitous route to the safe house on the edge of Paris, Michael said to the nanny, 'Isn't this exciting? Do we know who's after us?' wanting to know all the details.

The nanny was nervous enough. Wishing the driver would slow down, she said, 'Hush, dear,' and bit her lip.

Girls – they just don't know how to enjoy a good adventure, thought Michael as he looked out of the window.

On arrival at the safe house the message 'Beaujolais is best' was shouted through the window by the Housekeeper. The chauffeur knew what that meant and, without stopping, put his foot down on the accelerator and sped away.

As the car accelerated forward and skidded around a corner, the nanny gritted her teeth and cried out, 'Oh, God, what now?'

Thrilled by the turn of events Michael willed the driver to go even faster.

John Lee had always known that the weakness of the Phoenix plan was the number of people who had access to the details, and so he had devised a second plan that would keep Michael, the twins and Sophie safe. This second plan was known to only six trusted people.

The chauffeur drove the car for twenty minutes around Paris before he was sure he was not being followed, and then slowed to drive to a small village thirty miles away. Arriving at the cottage Michael saw the familiar figure of Mrs Evans standing at the gate. Behind her stood Mr Evans with his broad smile. As Michael opened the door of the car Mrs Evans threw her arms wide and bent down so that she could envelop Michael in a warm embrace.

'Lovely to see you, young Michael,' said Mr Evans.

'It's the Phoenix plan,' whispered Michael to them both, as if sharing a secret.

Mrs Evans nodded seriously.

Michael walked back to the twins and, positioning himself between them, took a tiny hand in each of his.

'Come on, you two, I'll look after you,' Michael said as he walked them into the cottage for hot chocolate and buns.

\*\*\*\*

As Mrs Evans smiled as Michael and the twins tucked into a large plate of iced buns and the Nanny was given a cup of reviving tea in Paris thousands of cards in hundreds of drawers detailing companies and people and their connections with Tagleva were being sorted. The librarians bustled from one drawer to another, creating trails of information on individuals thought to bear a grudge against Tagleva, Philip or any of the other directors.

John Lee supervised the search in the London office, and reports were sent to him from Paris and New York each hour. Pages and pages of information were received, which were sorted into useful and non-useful information. It was a process that had been rehearsed many times over the years, and whilst John Lee and Philip suspected that Sir Charles Cunningham might be behind Sophie's disappearance, nothing could be left to chance.

The chief librarian, Katherine du Bois, sorted through a special section titled 'The Tsar's papers' herself.

Jean-Claude walked into the living room where Philip was pouring himself a coffee, and poured a second cup.

'Michael and the twins are safe with Mrs Evans. The chauffeur will stay with them until things are normal.'

'Thank you,' said Philip, much relieved.

'We will find Sophie,' said Jean-Claude encouragingly.

'I know everyone is doing everything they can, but I need to think through the possibilities that may not be in the card index.'

'Then I'll leave you,' said Jean-Claude and moved towards the door. As he opened it he looked back at Philip, who was gazing out of the window with his arms folded, deep in thought. He looked strained but Jean-Claude admired how calm he was in a crisis. He'd come to love Philip as the father he'd lost. When he'd confided in Philip that he enjoyed the company of men more than women Philip had said, 'It is what you are, Jean-Claude; you aren't the first and you won't be the last. You must live your life in the way that is most rewarding for you.'

Jean-Claude closed the door, promising Philip that he'd find Sophie. Next he went to find John Lee, who was in his office, sorting through the reports that were coming in from librarians in the card index departments.

'Any conclusions?' enquired Jean-Claude.

'A few,' said John Lee. 'We know it's not an aggressive kidnap. By aggressive, I mean by a stranger: Sophie didn't put up a struggle. We know she's not visiting friends, and we can discount illness, as she would have woken some of the staff. My initial thought is that Sophie has been kidnapped to take revenge on Philip. We know someone tried to kill him in the past. The main link to the past is Sir Charles Cunningham, but he's been at his Norfolk estate and information we've had in the past hour suggests that he's still there. My biggest concern is that someone inside Tagleva is involved.'

John Lee had been a policeman for twenty-two years, the last seven, before he retired to join Tagleva, as a bodyguard for King George V. He was a jovial man with endless tales of his time at Scotland Yard. He would take any opportunity to delight and shock an audience and often left them helpless with laughter. A favourite story of his was about the time the President of Portugal was visiting King George V at Windsor Castle and asked him what he would do if he, the President, pointed a pistol at the King.

'I told the President that I'd stand between him and the King so that he shot me instead. I remember the President looking downcast and, looking at his own bodyguards, he said wistfully, "None of my bodyguards would lift a finger to save me". The King was delighted.'

Like Jean-Claude, John Lee had come to like and admire Philip and Sophie. As their protector, he'd gladly step between a speeding bullet and them if needed.

Then the phone rang, shocking in the silence, and John Lee picked up the receiver.

# Chapter Thirty-two: Sophie in peril

Sophie woke with a splitting headache: she felt as if she had been hit over the head with a sledgehammer. She sat up. Her back ached. She rubbed her arm to take away the pins and needles. A panic began to develop as she looked around the room, she assumed her prison was a storeroom of some sort – it had walls of bare red brick, large planks of unpolished wood, a small table with a carafe of water, a washing bowl and towel. High up in the ceiling, quite out of reach, was a window covered in green algae that let in very little light. Another small window was at head height, too small for an adult to climb through, and protected with a metal bar. At the other end of the room was a wooden table with some books, a couple of candles in wooden candlesticks and a potty to relieve herself. Someone expected her to be imprisoned for some time.

She felt sick. Rising from the bed she walked over to the jug of water. She poured some into the metal mug and drank it to remove the dryness in her mouth. She looked at the heavy metal door to the room, the only one in the room – there was no escape.

The training she had been given by John Lee came back to her. The first lesson had been: *Don't panic! Your adrenalin will be pumping, your heart pounding, and you'll be terrified. Calm down. The sooner you can regain your composure, the better.*

What else had John Lee told her she should she remember?

*Right from the start, try to observe and remember as much as possible to help you plan an escape. Try to figure out where you are; gather information that may be helpful if you decide to escape.*

She tried to remember everything else she had been told. *What do your captors look like, how many are there, what do they sound like, how old are they?*

It was all too difficult. It had happened so quickly: how could she remember?

The confused events of the previous night began to flood back into her mind. The telephone call, on her private line; a message telling her the Phoenix plan had been activated and to travel to Paris, confirmed by the correct code. A car would take her to Dover. It was only when she opened the door to see the two strangers that she had known something was wrong, but by then it was too late. She had tried to cry for help but one of them slammed a hand over her mouth, making it impossible. As the car drove off, a pad of strong-smelling chemicals was placed over her face.

Sophie walked to the window and peered out. Below her was cold and dirty water. In the distance a barge unloaded some cargo, but it was too far away for anyone to hear her, even if she shouted. She was in a warehouse in the docks. The proximity of the water explained why the room was so cold, and she rubbed her arms to generate some warmth. Her captives had left a couple of blankets at the bottom of the bed, so she picked one up and wrapped it around her. As she sat down on the small metal bed a noise above her made her cry out in surprise. A seagull walked over the skylight and screeched out to its friends. She wanted to be as ready as possible for what might happen next, and decided to rest. She pulled the pillow towards her and clasped it to her chest as she would one of the children when they had fallen down.

'Oh, Philip, do come soon, please come.' A tear fell from her eye to dampen the cotton pillowcase.

\*\*\*\*

The atmosphere in Philip's study was tense as Jean-Claude and John Lee reviewed the latest information from the card index.

John Lee began. 'We can discount business competitors. We've narrowed down the individuals who have been denied loans in the past six months to twenty. Despite them being disgruntled, it's hardly a reason to kidnap Sophie and we've been able to trace them all. However, there's been another development. Arnaud Hourcade's missing. He may also have been kidnapped – but I suspect that he's involved somehow.'

'But why?' asked Philip. John Lee noticed Philip clench his right fist, his knuckles white.

'We don't know that yet, but Arnaud had all the details of the Phoenix plan. If he had phoned Sophie she'd have recognised his voice and would have trusted him.'

There was a knock on the door, and a clerk brought in a letter on a silver tray. Philip opened it and took out the paper. He read the three lines twice and handed it to John Lee.

*Your wife is well. Wait for further communication from us.*

*If you value your wife's safety then we counsel against contacting the police.*

*We will communicate with you again for ransom details in early course.*

Philip held out his hand. 'May I read it again?' He took the letter and read the three lines over and over again. Eventually he looked up. 'What strikes you about the letter? The language isn't what I would expect from a ransom note. The words are those of a lawyer or someone used to diplomacy. Look here.'

He laid the letter on the table so that the other two could see what he meant. 'The words "counsel", "communication" and the final phrase, "in early course", is diplomatic and legal speak.'

'That narrows the field to two: Charles Cunningham and Arnaud. There's little we can do until the second note arrives,' said John Lee.

John Lee left the room and Jean-Claude sat next to Philip. 'We'll find her,' he said comfortingly.

Philip smiled at his friend. The adrenalin coursed through his veins and fed his brain. He wanted to scream. His thoughts were clear, and he needed them to be clear if he was to save Sophie, yet he also knew that high levels of adrenalin resulted in mistakes and bad decisions. It was why he knew he must follow John Lee's advice, even if his inclination was to rush to Charles Cunningham's estate and tear it down brick by brick until he found Sophie.

For the next two hours Philip paced the room turning over all the alternatives in his mind. Now and again he would pull a notebook from his jacket pocket and scribble some notes. The only sound was the clock on the mantelpiece that softly chimed the quarter-hours.

Suddenly the door opened and Jean-Claude and John Lee walked in with another envelope.

'The post boy delivered this.' Philip opened it carefully and took out the sheet of typed paper.

'They want two hundred thousand pounds in gold bars and the Tsar's letter.' He passed the note to the others to read. 'So now we know it's Cunningham. He's the only one who would ask for the letters.'

'Will you pay the ransom?' asked John Lee.

'For Sophie's life? Yes.'

The two men looked at Philip and remained quiet. They could see that he was thinking and now was not the time to interrupt him. Philip paced the room for a couple of minutes before asking, 'Any news on Sir Charles Cunningham?'

Jean-Claude replied, 'Yes, we had thought he was at his estate. In fact, he's not been in Norfolk nor at his house in Belgravia for three weeks. We've also found out that one of Cunningham's companies recently rented a warehouse in the docks, but no one knows which one.'

Philip breathed in deeply, then spoke. 'Feel free to tell me if you think I'm making a mistake, but I think we should prepare to pay the ransom. Ask our bankers to supply us with two hundred thousand pounds in gold coin and bars and in a number of bullion boxes. We must be able to easily transport them.'

'It's done,' said Jean-Claude and left the room.

Philip turned to John Lee. 'John, I need a person you trust who can break into a house in Wilton Crescent and discreetly find and open a safe. They mustn't leave a trace of the break-in, and no one's to be hurt.'

'No problem. I can have him ready tonight.'

\*\*\*\*

That night Philip, dressed in black trousers, dark jersey and boots, was driven to meet the man John Lee had recommended. John Lee had tried to persuade Philip to allow him to enter the property but Philip had insisted.

'I know what I'm looking for. All I need is for your man to open a safe. If things go wrong, I don't want you implicated in any way.'

Wilton Crescent was designed by a Thomas Cundy for the Grosvenor family in 1821. Like much of Belgravia, it is characterised by grand terraces with lavish white houses built in a crescent shape, and is home to many prominent British politicians, ambassadors and civil servants. The houses to the north of the crescent are stone-clad, five storeys high and with identical interiors. The top storey originally housed the servants' sleeping quarters, while the middle three storeys contain the living rooms. The kitchen, butler's pantry and wine cellar are located below pavement level. It makes breaking into the house and finding one's way around very easy. On the ground floor there is a hallway, reception room, study and dining room. Philip guessed that the safe would be in the study on the ground floor.

Philip and the man Lee had found waited until past midnight in the gardens opposite, until all the servants had retired to bed and the house lights had been turned off. Then they waited another hour before carefully approaching the ground floor and the window that would allow entry into the study.

As with all windows in the close, it was a sash window, so called because the weights are concealed in a box case on each side. Often found in Georgian and Victorian houses in London, it's a classic arrangement of three panes across by two up on each of two sashes, giving a 'six over six' panel window. This type of window provides a maximum ventilation of half of the total window area – and enough room to allow a grown man to easily climb through.

Philip's accomplice had many years of experience breaking into houses. He inserted a wire into a small gap in the middle of the window and, by twisting the metal, was able to pull aside the locking mechanism and open the window. Within two minutes they were in the room and the window was closed again. The curtains were heavy enough not to allow light in or out, so no one passing the house would see the torches that Philip and his accomplice used to locate the safe.

Philip looked at the desk but could see no safe. The professional burglar discovered it located behind a watercolour painting of the English countryside. Within twelve minutes he had the safe's door open. Philip was amazed at the ease of the operation, and made a mental note to replace all the safes in his house and at the Tagleva offices with more modern ones.

The safe contained mainly papers and some pouches of gold coins. Reading through the papers took Philip about half an hour and then he replaced the entire contents. The two men left though the same window.

One hour later, Philip was back in Tagleva's London office, meeting Jean-Claude and John Lee.

'Did it go well?' asked John Lee.

'Yes. Your man was an expert, and we should make sure he always works for us – I don't want him breaking into the Tagleva offices.'

The three laughed.

Jean-Claude handed Philip a whisky.

'What did you find?'

'Cunningham's about to leave England. There was a receipt for a first-class boat ticket to Naples and on to North Africa. He's bought a house in North Africa – and paid quite a sum for it. From the plans it's a large house with lots of land round it. I also found a receipt from a solicitor for the rental of a warehouse in the Albert Dock.'

'A long rent?' said Lee.

'Three months, in the name of Wilson & Co,' replied Philip.

'Did you find the address of the warehouse?'

'No, there was just an invoice for arranging the rental, but the solicitor was a Gordon Macintyre, and he's based in Glasgow,' replied Philip.

'Without the address, finding Sophie in the warren of buildings could take an army a whole month. The Royal Albert Dock covers three miles along the River Thames, but if you include all the finger quays that allow ships to unload their cargo, then the total's more like twelve. I could see if we can get the address from the solicitor?' said John Lee.

'Yes – good idea,' replied Philip.

'And I guess we'll be told to pay the ransom very soon,' said Philip. 'Well, there's nothing more we can do at this time of night. Let's get to bed and rest for a couple of hours. It is likely to be a long few days, and we'll need all our strength.'

The three men climbed the stairs to their rooms, but none slept well.

The following morning a brown envelope addressed to Philip Cummings lay on the doormat. A servant took it upstairs to his bedroom. Philip was already up and dressed.

'This package arrived for you. I guessed that you might wish to see it immediately.'

Philip took the envelope and opened it. Inside was one of Sophie's gloves and a sheet of paper detailing how the ransom was to be paid.

*The gold is to be made up of six gold bars, two bars each in their own wooden box. I want loose diamonds to the value of ten thousand pounds in a separate wooden box, and include all copies of the letters you hold. All four boxes should be put into a trunk and deposited at the Cunard offices in London on Monday next at exactly 11 a.m. You will get a receipt for the trunk. Place it in an envelope and pin the envelope to the parish notice board in the porch of St Mary's Church in Barnes at exactly 12.15 a.m. the same day.*

*You will be told where to find Sophie the following day at 12.00 noon*

'Would you ask Mr John Lee and Mr Jean-Claude to come and see me?'

Ten minutes later the three of them were studying the note.

'I don't think we have any alternative but to follow the instructions,' said John Lee.

'I agree,' said Philip.

\*\*\*\*

Food was delivered to Sophie three times a day. It wasn't luxurious, but it was fresh and there was always enough of it. At the same time, her kidnapper left clean towels and jugs of water on the table.

More of John Lee's instructions came to Sophie. *Every scrap of information may be helpful to your survival. Try to find out the reason for your abduction and get them to show some empathy towards you. If you can build some sort of bond with your captor they may be less likely to harm you. Tell your captors about your children, your family – anything to make you sound human and likeable. You don't want them to think of you as a sack of potatoes…*

Whenever food was brought to her or the water replenished her kidnapper wore a leather mask to hide his face, and she took comfort in remembering John Lee's words: *If you're being held for a ransom, you're worth more to them alive than dead. If they are planning to release you, the kidnappers will avoid doing anything that will identify them later…* He was about her height, spoke in a soft voice and always enquired after her health and if she needed more reading material.

*Put your captors at ease. Be calm, cooperate, don't make threats or become violent, and don't attempt to escape unless the time is right. Remember to keep your dignity. Don't grovel, beg or become hysterical. Try not to cry. It's always harder for a kidnapper to kill or harm a captive if he likes you.*

Sophie thanked him for the food and the books. At the same time, she noticed that his clothes were well made, similar to those worn by office workers all over London. His shoes were polished and the heels slightly worn on the outside, and when he spoke his Adam's apple moved up and down his neck in a most strange manner.

He listened patiently as Sophie told him about her children and how she had lost her brother, saying how much she missed them all. She asked the jailer if he had family and tried desperately to think of anything else to engage him in conversation, but he didn't say much.

The most difficult times were when she was alone. She found it impossible to read the books the jailer had left and instead would endlessly walk around the room, pacing between one wall and another, rubbing her hands over the red bricks, feeling how rough they were, unpicking flaking whitewash from some. She counted the red bricks, she counted the white bricks, and created patterns from them. She arranged the table so that the books were straight and the water mug exactly positioned, then when there was nothing else to do she peered out of the window at the dark, cold water and the barges in the distance.

More than anything, she thought of Philip; her husband, the most handsome man in the world. If she were to die in this place her greatest regret would be not having a few last minutes to tell Philip that she loved him dearly, to hold him one last time, to smell the sandalwood cologne he preferred, to touch his hair, to kiss the children and to tell them to be good for Daddy.

****

The following day, a trunk was driven to the Cunard offices in London and checked it in.

'It's 'eavy,' said the porter. 'What have you got in here, gold?' and laughed at his own joke. The clerk handed over a receipt for collection, dragged the trunk to a trolley and wheeled it to the back of the warehouse.

Jean-Claude placed the receipt in a white envelope then drove to Barnes where he walked up the church path and pinned the envelope to the church notice board. The time was exactly twelve fifteen. He returned to the car and was driven away. The only person in the graveyard was the gardener, who was tending a flower bed at the side of the church and didn't look up from his weeding. Twenty minutes passed and no one came or went. The gardener rose, picked up his tools and walked to the front of the building. As he passed the porch he glanced in at the notice board. It was empty. The envelope was gone. He rushed into the porch and tried the church door. It was locked.

Throwing down his tools on the bench in the porch, he ran down the path, across the road and to the side street where John Lee was waiting in a car.

'It's gone,' he shouted.

'Bloody hell,' said Lee. 'How?'

'Someone must've collected it from inside and shut the door and left by another entrance.'

They both ran to the church, rushed around the back and saw the vestry entrance, partly obscured by ivy and a couple of overgrown fir trees.

'Damn and blast! We still have the Cunard offices being watched so anyone collecting the trunk will be noticed,' said John Lee as they ran back to the car.

On hearing the news from Barnes, Philip was very concerned.

'The Cunard office is being watched by one of my team. Anyone who collects the trunk will be discreetly followed. At this point I guess we can only wait,' said Lee.

'I can't wait here for something to happen. I want to go to the Royal Albert Dock and see if I can find her,' said Philip, feeling completely helpless.

'There may be no need,' said Jean-Claude as he entered the room. 'We've spoken to the solicitor in Glasgow. After a little persuasion he's given us the address. It's in Alnwick Street.'

Half an hour later John Lee, Philip and a group of ex-policemen recruited by John Lee were travelling in a truck towards the Royal Albert Dock. Arriving in Alnwick Street they parked at the end of the road. Philip got out of the truck and John Lee caught his arm.

'Sir, it's best you keep hidden. We wouldn't want you recognised before we can get to Sophie now, would we?'

'I suppose not,' said Philip and watched as the group walked past the hospital and towards the building where he hoped that Sophie was being held.

After what seemed an age they broke down the front door and the group of men rushed into the building. Ten minutes later they had returned to the truck.

'It's empty,' said John Lee.

'We spoke to the workers in the next building and they said that it's been empty for a month.'

'Quick,' shouted Philip. 'We need to get to the Cunard offices.'

'Why?' cried John Lee.

'I bet the trunk's gone,' replied Philip.

'But it's being watched,' shouted Lee as they climbed into the truck.

Ten minutes later the truck screamed to a halt outside the Cunard offices.

Philip and Lee dashed into the office.

The clerk looked at them and said that he couldn't release the trunk without the receipt. After pocketing a ten-pound note, he said he would check on it and walked to the back of the building, wondering why everyone was always in such a panic.

A couple of minutes later he returned.

'It's been sent on.'

'Sent on where?' cried John Lee.

'Liverpool – went on the one o'clock train.'

'Of course,' said Philip slapping his head with the palm of his hand. 'It's not the Royal Albert Dock in London, it's the Albert Dock in Liverpool. He's going to sail from Liverpool. That's how he plans to escape. What's the time now?'

'Four forty-five,' said the clerk helpfully.

'We need to get the train and hope we're not too late,' shouted Philip.

'The next train is at five and you should make it if you hurry,' said the clerk, getting involved in the excitement.

Back at the truck, Philip was angry at himself for not seeing the obvious deception. It meant that Cunningham had a four-hour start on him. His stomach churned and every car, tram and lorry seemed to slow their progress to Euston Station, each delay making him more desperate.

Turning to John Lee, he ordered, 'Tell the men to go back to Tagleva. Inform Jean-Claude what's happened and tell him that we're travelling to Liverpool. Ask him to stay by the phone and arrange a car to pick us up at the station with a couple of men to help. Any urgent messages can be sent to us for collection at the North Western Hotel. I'll buy the train tickets and I want you to find a copy of *The Times.*'

John Lee rushed to buy the newspaper and Philip ran to the ticket counter. Thankfully, there was no queue.

'Two first-class tickets to Liverpool, please,' he said.

The clerk took the two five-pound notes he offered and passed the two tickets and some change back to Philip. 'Departs at six o'clock on Platform 4. You'll need to hurry; you've only got a couple of minutes.'

'Thank you,' said Philip, scooping up the tickets and money. As he turned around he caught sight of John Lee running towards him with a copy of *The Times* in his hand.

They rushed to Platform 4, boarded the train and found an empty compartment. Three minutes later the train pulled out of the station for the journey to Liverpool.

Back at the Tagleva offices, Jean-Claude arranged for a car to meet Philip and John Lee. One of John Lee's colleagues was talking to contacts in Liverpool and arranging for some men who could 'handle themselves' to meet them.

In another part of the building clerks were phoning the shipping lines to enquire about passenger ships sailing to North Africa or Gibraltar within the following three days. There were two. The *Demerara* would be leaving Liverpool for Gibraltar, Genoa, Leghorn, Naples, Patras, Corfu, Trieste, Venice and Fiume the day after tomorrow and a ship from the Anchor Line was due to sail to Gibraltar, Port Said, Suez, Port Sudan, Bombay and Karachi the day after that.

# Chapter Thirty-three:
## The race to rescue Sophie

On board the train, John Lee was reading aloud from *The Times* a list of the ships leaving for North America. Philip listened attentively.

'The White Star Line has a number of sailings. From Liverpool to New York, the *Adriatic* and the *Baltic*. The *Haverford* sails from Liverpool to Boston and the *Regina*, the *Doric* and the *Megantic* sailing to Montreal. Cunard has the *Aquitania* sailing to New York – but why America?' John Lee asked.

'I suspect North Africa's a false trail, the same way as the London docks were,' said Philip.

'It would be consistent,' replied John Lee.

Even though the train was an express, Philip willed it to go faster. *Surely it could go faster! Didn't the driver know this was an emergency?* The steward passed their compartment, opened the door and announced the first sitting for dinner.

'Let's pass some time by having dinner,' said John Lee.

John Lee ordered, but Philip told the steward he wasn't hungry.

'The gentleman will have some soup and bread, followed by the fish,' said John Lee to the steward. 'You'll need the energy for when we get to Liverpool.'

Philip knew he was right and when the steward brought the food he finished it, without tasting any of it. John Lee devoured the mackerel pâté followed by steak and kidney pudding.

Eventually all they could do was to look out of the window at the changing scenery.

After what seemed a lifetime the train pulled into Liverpool and they ran down the platform to the North Western Hotel across the road.

At the hotel, the porter pulled a brown telegram envelope from under his desk and handed it to Philip.

'It's a message from Jean-Claude: *Cunard confirms trunk sent to Constance Exports Office Harrington Dock Liverpool* STOP *Onward dispatch on* Aquitania STOP *No passenger Cunningham booked for passage* STOP *Tom and Will to meet you* STOP.'

Philip passed the note to John Lee as two men approached.

'Mr Lee, sir.'

'You're our drivers?'

'Aye, sir,' replied the man, who looked to John Lee like someone who could handle himself. The second man was just as big, but a little older and with a red birthmark on his left cheek.

'Your names?' asked John Lee.

'I'm Tom Barrow. Everyone knows me as Tom Furnace as I was a steel worker. My friend's Will Davey.'

Will Davey raised his right hand and tugged an invisible forelock in greeting.

'All right, Tom Furnace. You know the Harrington Dock?'

'Aye, sir.'

Five minutes later the four of them were travelling towards the docks.

'Do you know the situation, Tom?' asked John Lee.

'Oh aye sir, the office in London filled me in wi' the details. Some bastards have yer wife.'

'That's about it.'

'Whatever ye need, just ask.'

'I will,' said John Lee.

****

Charles Cunningham was sitting at a table in the first-floor office of the warehouse rented for Constance Exports. In the five months since he'd established the company it hadn't exported a single item; indeed, the company didn't trade at all. Its sole purpose was to rent a three-storey warehouse building in Liverpool Docks, the place where he would exact his revenge.

Philip had destroyed him. He'd lost his job, his position in society, and he'd been blackmailed into paying two million pounds to the Tagleva Foundation. At first he sought solace in bottles of whisky. He'd spent hours walking around his gardens with no one to comfort him other than the whisky flask he carried in his coat pocket. His only company were the roses and the greenfly.

After a few months he slowly thought of a plan. He sobered up and planned his revenge with the same meticulous detail he'd used when he was at the top of the civil service. Now his plan was coming to its climax.

He'd enjoyed watching his enemy panic as they rushed around London. He congratulated himself for predicting that Philip would break into his Belgravia home, find the papers he had carefully left in the safe, that he would first search for him in the London docks and that inevitably he would arrive in Liverpool. It had surprised him that Philip had taken so long to make the connection with Liverpool. It had proved to Sir Charles that his intellect was superior.

Sir Charles knew that Philip would be unable to resist coming to rescue Sophie himself. Doubtless he would bring some heavies, but that had been planned for, along with everything else.

By tonight Philip Cummings would be dead – and Sir Charles would be on board the *Adriatic* to New York with enough gold and diamonds to keep him happy for life. It was a shame the wife had to die. She was an attractive woman, he thought, if you liked that sort of thing. His preference was for women he could control, who were afraid of him and wouldn't complain about any bruises. He doubted she would fit the bill.

\*\*\*\*

They parked the car a hundred yards from the registered offices of Constance Exports. Philip and John Lee studied the red brick warehouse. It was like all the others. The front entrance was served by the road, where trucks could make deliveries, and the back looked out onto the dock. Built almost entirely from cast iron, stone and brick, the Albert Dock was designed to be fireproof. The ground floor had storage rooms and a warehouse, and the three upper floors large storage rooms. Double doors and a hoist on each floor allowed heavy cargo to be loaded on and off ships, while the top floor had smaller storage rooms only.

It would be difficult to approach from the road as there was one large door on the ground floor to allow for deliveries and two windows on either side with steel bars. A quick or quiet entry would be impossible, and entry from the waterside required the cargo doors to be open.

'What do you think?' asked Philip.

'I think we should watch the place for any sign of activity,' replied John Lee.

'It's difficult to see what's 'appening at the back from 'ere. I wonder if we could take a boat?' said Tom.

'An excellent idea,' said Philip. 'We'd be recognised, but Will could row past without any problem.'

Twenty minutes later Will was rowing towards the warehouse in a borrowed boat. Pretending that he was unhooking some rope that had become tied around his oar, Will was able to drift towards the warehouse. The only sign of life was the rowing boat with oars lying in it.

After a few minutes Will rowed away from the warehouse and back to the far side of the dock. As he did so, he faced the building and was able to study it carefully. One window on the second floor was covered in sacking. When he was halfway across the dock he noticed the sacking being drawn aside. A face looked out – but he couldn't tell if it was a man or a woman.

Returning to the car, he reported all he'd seen. Philip and John Lee decided that both the back and the front of the building needed to be watched. Once more Will volunteered to watch the back of the building, and walked to the other side of the dock and positioned himself so that he'd be able to signal to the car should there be any movement from inside.

Everyone waited to see what would happen.

Two hours later the door to the street opened and a small man in a winter coat emerged and turned right down the road. Tom waited until he was a hundred yards away, then got out of the car and followed him – not a difficult task, as there were now quite a few people in the street. The dockyard shift was changing.

Ten minutes later Tom rushed back to the car.

'He's gone to the café to pick up some food. He's walkin' back slowly and I guess we've two minutes if we want to rush 'im as 'e opens the door to the warehouse, but we'll have to be quick – he's right behind me.'

The three got out of the car. Philip positioned himself on the opposite side of the road. John Lee walked over the road and fifteen feet from the door of the warehouse knelt down, pretending to tie his bootlace. Tom ran to the next warehouse and lit a cigarette as if he were enjoying a break from work. The small man turned the corner carrying a large package of food and a thermos of coffee. As he approached the warehouse door Lee stood up and began walking towards him. The man, balancing the parcel of food in one arm, put his other hand into his pocket to retrieve the warehouse door key. As he did so, Lee hit him in the face. Tom caught him as he fell backwards and placed a hand over his mouth so he couldn't scream. The parcel ripped open, the thermos lid fell off and hot tea spilled all over the pavement. The man cried out in pain but he made little sound, as Tom's hand was firmly clamped over his mouth.

The man felt sick. His nose was broken; he felt warm blood stream from his nose. Another blow to his head put him out cold. Philip ran towards them and reached them just as John Lee retrieved the key from the man's overcoat. They opened the warehouse door and together they dragged the unconscious man off the street and into the warehouse before closing the door.

Once inside they could see the layout of the building. A cavernous entrance rose up three floors. Storage rooms on each floor were protected with their own metal door and a single metal staircase connected each level. Sophie could be behind any one of eighteen doors. They were exposed. They froze as a door above them opened and a shadowy figure walked out onto the landing. The man looked over the balcony, pulled a pistol from his coat and fired. A bullet slammed into the plaster just to the right of Philip's ear, covering him in fragments of brick. Another shot rang out and another cloud of brick dust filled the air. The man above rushed into one of the rooms and they heard the door being closed, locked and two bolts pushed into place.

Philip hoped that it wasn't the room that imprisoned Sophie. She could be dead before they reached the first-floor landing!

Sophie heard the pistol shot and remembered John Lee's lesson.

*There are three things to plan for: the first is an opportunity to escape, the second is an attack from a jailer and the third is an attempt to rescue you.*

Sophie had planned for an escape. She'd secreted a couple of nails prised from the wall and had hidden one in her dress pocket and the second underneath the mattress.

*If a rescue attempt is made, hooray, the cavalry's arrived! But before you get too excited, keep in mind that the rescue attempt is the most dangerous time in any hostage situation. Remember to stay out of the way. Your captors may become desperate and attempt to use you as a shield, or they may simply decide to kill any hostages. When the rescue attempt starts, try to hide from your captors. Stay low on the floor if possible, and protect your head with your hands, or try to get behind some kind of protective barrier, such as a desk or table.*

Philip, Lee and Tom ran up the staircase to the first floor. They found a heavy wooden door. It was locked. He pounded on it. 'Sophie, are you there?'

Sophie heard Philip's voice and shouted as loudly as she could, 'Philip, I'm here! Thank God!'

Sophie's voice came from above them. She was on the top floor. The three climbed the stairs again to Sophie's door.

'Are you safe?' Philip shouted.

'Yes, my darling.'

'Are you alone and in any danger?'

'No, I'm in no danger and I'm alone.'

'All right – we'll have you out as soon as we can.'

Looking at the heavy metal door, Tom shouted, 'This door's gonna be the devil to break through.'

Behind the locked and bolted door on the second floor, Cunningham smiled. His planning had been immaculate. It would take over ten minutes to break down the door that imprisoned Philip's wife, and in that time Philip and his people would be burned to a cinder.

On each floor he had dragged piles of sacking soaked in petroleum spirit, and barrels of tar. The tar would release an acrid smoke that would asphyxiate, and the sacking would set light to the building. Cunningham had positioned himself so he could ignite the material across the whole landing by walking through connecting doors from one storeroom to another without the need to access the landing. In a storeroom on the ground floor he had stored enough dynamite to blow the building sky-high. The warehouse was a death trap to anyone on the floors above.

Chuckling to himself, he lit the first pile of sacking and closed the door of the storeroom before moving to the next room and repeating the process.

As he lit the sacking and the tar burned, acrid smoke poured forth. The flames quickly moved up the walls and were soon flickering and playing round the metalwork. Soon the roof was alight, disturbing the seagulls, which flew away screaming.

Determined to take one last survey of the interior before its destruction, Sir Charles looked through a hatch in the door. He could see flames climbing the staircase. He could hear Philip and his followers struggling with the door behind which Sophie was imprisoned, as the smoke filling the air had begun to make them choke.

It was time he left.

Opening up the outer cargo doors that led to the dock – and his escape – Cunningham placed the boxes containing the gold and diamonds on the winch and slowly loaded them into the rowing boat. He lowered himself into the boat and arranged the heavy boxes so that the boat was stable, before beginning to row away from the building.

'We've got about ten minutes before the whole buildin' will be alight,' cried Tom.

The three of them tried to barge the door open with their shoulders. It didn't budge. Above them they heard a loud crack as windows shattered in the heat and flames licked the ceiling of the warehouse.

The smoke was unbearable, stinging their eyes and choking them.

'Sophie,' shouted Philip, 'is there a window in your room?'

'Yes,' came the faint reply from the other side of the door.

'Can you smash it and climb out and jump into the water?'

'No, there are bars over it – I can't crawl through.'

Skirting some flaming parts of the staircase, Tom raced downstairs and picked up the crowbar he'd seen. Back at the door he rammed one end of the metal bar into the edge of the door near the lock. John Lee lent a hand, and the two of them strained against the door. Still the door refused to move. They jammed the metal bar deeper into the edge of the door gap and pulled again. Philip looked up to see the roof of the warehouse was a sea of blue and yellow flame.

On the floor below, the man Lee had hit to gain entry to the warehouse had recovered consciousness and was crawling towards the room where he'd hidden his gold. Sparks from the ceiling fell to the floor and ignited the tar-covered tarpaulin that hid his gold. The man cried out and tried desperately to pull the burning cloth away from his money. His face hurt; he could hardly breathe; his mouth burned from the smoke and his nose was clogged with blood.

Sparks fell from the ceiling but he ignored them as he pulled the sacking away from his treasure. At the bottom of the pile, exactly as he'd left it, was his box. It was safe and sound. He stroked the lid, unable to resist the urge to check the gold. Raising the lid, hundreds of gold sovereigns sparkled up at him. He had to touch them, just to feel the beautiful metal in his hands. Once he had done that, he would close the box and pull it to the front of the warehouse and to safety.

Suddenly he heard a tremendous cracking. So appalling and deafening was the sound that he was transfixed to the spot; he couldn't leave his gold. He twisted his body so he could look upwards and cried out in horror as a huge metal girder fell from the ceiling and onto his legs. He screamed as his bones splintered and he was pinned to the floor. The agony was more than he could bear, and he clenched his fists and ground his teeth.

Then he heard a strange hissing, as if a shower of rain was descending through the roof. Helpless, he watched as molten globules of tar poured from the upper floor. This terrible cascade landed on his stomach. He tried to brush the black liquid away and the skin on his hands began to burn. He watched in horror as his hands caught fire; he could feel his flesh melting. More of the black liquid fell onto his head and within seconds his entire body was covered in the flaming black syrup. He made one last effort to sit up, to escape... Blinded by the black liquid, he held out his hands to anyone who might help, but there was no one. His body convulsed.

Philip continued to slam his shoulder against the door as Tom and John Lee pulled on the metal bar. There was a crack as the lock pulled away from the door. They pushed the bar further into the gap and all three pulled with all their strength. Finally, the lock gave way. With a last push the door flew open. Sophie was lying on the floor coughing, trying to breathe what little oxygen that still remained at floor level. They picked her up and pulled her to the landing. The stairway was covered in flaming tar. Rushing through the flames and down the stairs and into the fresh air of the street, all four collapsed on the pavement, gasping for breath. The crowd that had gathered to watch the fire rushed over to see if they were all right and helped them to the far side of the street.

On the other side of the dock a crowd of dock workers had gathered to watch as smoke billowed out of the building. They felt some relief as they watched a man load some boxes into a small boat and row safely away from the burning building. A group of men ran towards the burning building to see what they could do to help. A fire in the docks was a serious hazard and could spread to other buildings if not contained. A second later the entire second storey of the building exploded. The water around the rower was peppered with brick and metal, but he was safe. The group on the street gasped as the roof of the warehouse collapsed. Then, with a clanging of bells, the fire brigade arrived.

Cunningham continued to row until he was halfway across the dock. Philip Cummings and his people were dead; he had his revenge! A few minutes more and he'd be safe. As he looked at the collapsing building he felt water lapping at his feet. Looking down, he couldn't understand why the boat was filling with water. Within another dozen strokes, the water had risen another few inches. He was sinking! He panicked. The water rose to his waist, then his chest, and he let go of the oars and thrashed at the water in an effort to save himself. When he'd arranged the boxes of gold, one had moved and it had trapped the bottom of his long overcoat. He pulled at his coat, trying to kick the box away, but it was too heavy. The boat was sinking, dragged down by the weight of his gold. He spluttered as water entered his mouth, and clawed at the water as he sank to the murky, muddy depths of the dock.

Ambulances soon arrived for all those who had escaped from the burning warehouse. They were taken to hospital, where they spent two nights, so that doctors could treat them for smoke inhalation and burns. The police interviewed them, took statements and concluded that the file was closed – but severely warned Philip that if anything like this ever happened again he was to contact the police straight away and not try to handle it himself.

# Chapter Thirty-four: Arnaud's betrayal

By the time the four left hospital, Arnaud was halfway across the Atlantic drinking an after-dinner cognac in the grand salon of the liner and looking forward to arriving in New York. Within a couple of days he'd be on board the SS *Brazil* bound for Buenos Aires, the Paris of South America.

Betraying Philip had been easier than he had expected. His tutors at law school had told him that there was no room for sentiment in business. For a business to be as wealthy as the de Rothschild Frères Bank, it could not afford to be too caring or too philanthropic. His betrayal was made easier by the opportunity he had had to take the Romanov jewels from safe deposit box number A3287 at the Société Générale Bank.

He couldn't practise law again, but with the money the jewels would bring him he would create a new life; one that he could enjoy, where he could entertain the many friends he'd have. With the money he'd earn from selling the jewels he would be the sun around which so many planets would revolve.

He sipped the golden liquid and felt it warm the back of his throat as he thought back to the events of the past few months. When Sir Charles Cunningham had offered him a substantial sum of money to hand over details of the Phoenix plan he had at first refused and told Sir Charles he wouldn't help – but all that had changed when, quite by chance, he discovered the details of the safety deposit box.

If Philip and Sophie were dead and Jean-Claude otherwise distracted, he could persuade the Société Générale to give him access to the box. He was, after all, Tagleva's lawyer.

He'd imagined that finding the key to the safety deposit box would be difficult. Then he remembered seeing a key when

Philip had unlocked a drawer in his desk. How typical of Philip's trusting character to hide the key that held the treasure that ensured Tagleva's prosperity in his office desk! Arnaud had seized the opportunity the key presented to him.

He sold the details of the Phoenix plan to Sir Charles. He had only paid a modest amount for it – half a year's salary – but then his real prize was to come. He had phoned Sophie in the middle of the night telling her that Philip was in danger, and that the Phoenix plan had been activated. He knew she'd recognise his voice and trust him completely.

From the safety of the far end of the dock, hidden in the crowds of onlookers, he'd watched as the fire engulfed the warehouse; he'd seen Sir Charles row away from the building as the first floor exploded; and it was then he knew that Philip and Sophie were dead and he could return to Paris.

Arriving at the Tagleva offices in the early hours of the following morning, he told the caretaker he needed some papers. Once in Philip's office he prised free the drawer with a metal letter-opener and pocketed the key. All he then had to do was to wait for the Société Générale to open its doors.

He couldn't believe the riches he found in box A3287. Rubies the size of hen's eggs, diamonds, diamond and sapphire necklaces, a huge emerald on a chain with diamonds and rubies, gold and platinum ingots and other treasures.

He'd never seen such riches. He held one of the diamond and ruby bracelets over his wrist and marvelled at how the stones sparkled. He looked at the rubies that, on their own, would finance a lifetime of luxury. He decided that he would keep a couple of the larger emeralds and have them turned into cufflinks, as a reminder to take every opportunity in life. Having finished his cognac he walked to the ship's casino for another evening playing *chemin de fer*.

On his arrival in New York his luggage was transferred to his state room on the SS *Brazil* for his onward journey. Arriving in Buenos Aires, he booked into one of the luxurious hotels along the Avenida de Mayo.

'Hang the expense,' he said to himself as he paid for a week in the Presidential Suite with most of the money that remained from the sum Sir Charles had given him, and ordered champagne to be sent to his room.

A week later he located the best jeweller in town, which was prepared to buy the jewels he'd described. Arnaud laid the sparkling stones on the velvet cloths. The jeweller picked up each piece in turn and carefully studied it through his eyeglass, before replacing it gently on the velvet cloth.

'Very nice,' said the jeweller a couple of times as he peered through the eyeglass. Arnaud was becoming impatient. What amount would the jeweller offer him? His card-playing told him that impatience would only reduce the price he'd be offered.

The jeweller put his eyeglass down and pulled out some scales. He weighed the gold and platinum bars. Taking a small penknife, he scratched each ingot along the side, nodded and returned the ingot to the velvet cloth.

'You've some interesting pieces here, signor,' he said, a smile creasing his sun-browned face. Arnaud beamed.

The jeweller continued. 'It'll be easy for me to sell some, and I can make up new pieces from the larger items.'

'How much will you give me for it all?' asked Arnaud, unable to restrain himself any longer.

'Five hundred American dollars, for the lot,' said the jeweller.

'Five hundred dollars? You crook, it's worth five hundred times that amount! Do you think I'm an imbecile?' Arnaud screamed.

'I don't mean to insult you, signor. The stones are nicely mounted in gold and platinum, but they're all glass. As for the ingots, I don't want them. They're lead, covered in gold and silver – they are worthless.'

'You're a crook! You're trying to cheat me,' shouted Arnaud and scooped the items back into the box. He left the shop swearing at the man, refusing to be cheated. Within a few minutes he was sitting in front of another jeweller, who gave him the same news – as did the next jeweller, and the one after that.

At the end of the morning Arnaud found himself sitting on the pavement, his shoulders slumped, staring at the water flowing along the gutter. He was in a strange country, almost seven thousand miles from home, his only possession a box of paste jewellery worth five hundred dollars and a hotel bill for eight hundred and twenty-five dollars in his pocket.

He looked at the water flowing towards the drain. How had this happened? How had he been so foolish? All he had done was to take the opportunities that were presented to him. Looking around, he noticed the body of a dog in the gutter fifty feet away. It had probably been hit by a speeding truck as it had rushed into the road, he thought. Its fur was matted and dirty but it had no visible injury, and the animal looked strangely peaceful, even though it was in the gutter and ignored by passing pedestrians.

He raised his head and saw trucks rushing past, laden with goods. Their drivers were all in a hurry to get to their destination, their hands on the horn. He looked at the dog again and wondered if its death had been fast and painless. He looked again at the large red truck speeding towards him. He opened the box, poured the contents into the gutter and stood up. The red truck was just twenty feet away.

**\*\*\*\***

Once they were all out of hospital and fully rested, Philip, Sophie and John Lee met at the House of Tagleva in Paris and related everything that had happened to Jean-Claude.

'So why did Cunningham's boat sink?' asked Jean-Claude.

'That was Will's doing,' answered Philip. 'Will rowed over to inspect the warehouse and assumed that it was for someone to make an escape. To prevent the boat going too far, he smashed a small hole in the bottom of the boat, near the rudder, and stuffed the hole with a piece of tarpaulin to prevent the boat sinking. We assume that when Sir Charles loaded the gold into the boat the pressure on the tarpaulin bung was too much, it was pushed free and water flooded in.'

'So what about the gold?'

'Lost,' said Philip. 'The mud in the docks will soon swallow up what Cunningham had in the boat, and I would guess that the hoard his accomplice had in the warehouse will have melted in the heat. No one knows that the ransom came from me and as far as I'm concerned it's a small price to pay to have Sophie safe and well.'

Philip held out his hand and Sophie gave it a gentle squeeze.

'What of Tom and Will?' asked Jean-Claude.

'I've offered them a job working in the security team and they've both accepted,' said John Lee.

'Will you try to find Arnaud?' asked Sophie.

'Finding him in South America would be difficult and would solve nothing,' said Philip.

'It was a good idea of yours to have copies of the jewels made in case we ever needed to use them as a ransom or someone got to know of them and tried to steal them,' said Jean-Claude.

'And it was your idea to hide them in the safe under my solid oak desk,' said Philip. 'I thought you'd gone mad when you told me you had bought such a large desk, but when I watched those three burly workmen struggle to move it into position I knew you'd decorated my office in style. Even if Arnaud had known where the real jewels were, he'd have been unable to move the desk on his own and even then he would still have had to gain access to the safe, know the combination and have all three keys to open it.'

## Chapter Thirty-five: Philip's pride

Over the next few years the Sergei Tagleva Foundation continued to grow and undertake more philanthropic projects in Britain, France and the USA. It built over a hundred homeless hostels, endowed schools with books and scholarships, helped farmers in countries suffering from drought to buy food and then seed when conditions improved, financed hospitals so that they provided free medicines for children and the old. The Tagleva Bank continued to finance businesses that created jobs, and acted as a reliable source of financial advice to clients, government ministers and charities.

On the thirtieth of January 1933 Tom Barrow, now the family chauffeur and a senior member of the Tagleva family security team, drove Philip, Sophie and Michael to the head offices of the South Wales Miners' Federation. The Union President handed Sophie a silver tray inscribed with thanks 'for all the work you have done to support needy miners' families during difficult times'.

Sophie was greatly embarrassed by the speeches praising her. She blushed at the many kind things that were said, and after the speeches a four-year-old girl called Maisie, in a spotless skirt and a broad smile, presented her with a bunch of white roses and told her, 'My mam says you're a saint.' Sophie felt tears well up in her eyes as she bent down to kiss the girl on the cheek.

Michael clapped loudly, encouraging the cheers of the audience each time his mother blushed with embarrassment, and looked up at his father to encourage him to do the same. He was having a wonderful day. From the other side of the room Jean-Claude looked at Philip, standing behind Michael and the twins. Philip was going grey at the temples and his beard had flecks of white, but his eyes were bright and alert as they had always been as he smiled proudly at his wife. Jean-Claude looked at the teenage Michael, standing protectively between the twins. He'd inherited his mother's complexion, golden hair and charm, and his father's good looks and sharp mind. His command of languages was the envy of many of his school friends, as he spoke French, English and Russian and was studying German at school. His ambition, he told anyone prepared to listen, was 'to work with his father and uncle, Jean-Claude, at Tagleva'.

Far away another crowd clapped and hailed their new leader, who waved from a window to the masses below. Adolf Hitler was finally Chancellor of Germany.

# *Postscript*

At some time during the 1920s various boxes containing property that had once belonged to the Russian Imperial Family were transported down the Mall in London to Marlborough House, the residence of Queen Alexandra, the sister of the Dowager Empress of Russia. At Marlborough House the contents of the boxes were inspected by King George V, Queen Mary and Grand Duchess Xenia Alexandrovna. After an hour the boxes were repacked and returned to their place of safety.

Throughout Europe there have been persistent rumours that boxes containing the remains and property of the Romanovs have made their way into the possession of the British Royal Family. As recently as 1952, Prince Dimitri Alexandrovich, son of Grand Duchess Xenia, declared that a box with some property belonging to the Imperial Family was stored in Windsor Castle.

As recently as 2009 there were rumours that the Bank of England holds a number of boxes, each embossed with the Imperial Russian coat of arms, under lock and key in its vaults deep below the streets of London.

# References and historical information

All of the Russian members of the Imperial Family mentioned in this book, together with members of the Russian Royal Court, existed. The events surrounding the Great War and the assassination of the Russian Imperial Family happened as recorded in various testimonials.

The jewellery detailed were actual items known to have belonged to the Russian Imperial Family at the start of the Great War. Many of these items disappeared around the time of the revolution.

With the exception of conversations between Felix Youssoupov, Sophie and Philip, where historical figures are quoted the opinions expressed are as they are recorded as having been spoken. These include the quotes attributed to Karl Marx, Maynard Keynes and Lloyd George. While accurate, they may have been taken out of the actual time frame/context in which they were made.

The details of Rasputin's murder have been taken from Felix Youssoupov's book, *Lost Splendor* (1953), and other sources of the events that night have been used to create the account of the murder as recounted on HMS *Marlborough*.

Even now, ninety-five years after the murder of Russia's last Tsar, Nicholas II, we do not know precisely how many people took part in the deed. One account claims there were eight and another insists there were eleven; one for each murdered member of the Russian Royal Family. It is clear, however, that the killing squad was led by two men named Yurovsky and Medvedev.

Both men penned memoirs in which they described, in great detail, the night that Nicholas II was killed. Both wrote of their pride in the role they had played in Russian history, and both held important jobs in Soviet Russia until their deaths, and remained respected members of Soviet society.

**For further information see www.thetsarsbanker.com**

# Detail on actual historical characters mentioned

In this section, I have included some details of what happened to historical characters after the Russian revolution to satisfy readers who might be wondering what happened to them.

### Russians

*The Dowager Empress Marie Feodorovna*

Mother of the last Tsar, Nicholas II. After a brief stay in the British base in Malta, she moved to England, to stay with her sister Queen Alexandra at Marlborough House in London and at Sandringham House in Norfolk, eventually returning to her native Denmark. She died on 13th October 1928 at Hvidøre near Copenhagen, having outlived four of her six children. The Empress was interred at Roskilde Cathedral.

In 2005 Queen Margarethe II of Denmark and President Vladimir Putin of Russia agreed that the Empress's remains should be returned to St Petersburg. In accordance with her wishes, she was interred next to her husband in the Peter and Paul Cathedral on 28th September 2006.

*Grand Duchess Xenia Alexandrovna*

Sister of Tsar Nicholas II. After leaving Russia, her first cousin, King George V, allowed her to settle in Frogmore Cottage, a grace-and-favour house in Windsor Great Park. She died on 20th April 1960.

*Prince Felix Youssoupov (younger)*

Born in St Petersburg in 1886, his family was extremely rich. In 1909 he moved to Oxford where he studied at University College and was a member of the Bullingdon Club. He also established the Oxford University Russian Society.

On 22nd February 1914 Youssoupov married Irina Romanov, the niece of Nicholas II. After the revolution Felix fled Russia with jewellery, including the blue Sultan of Morocco diamond, the Polar Star diamond, a pair of diamond earrings that had once belonged to Marie Antoinette, queen of France, and two paintings by Rembrandt, the sale proceeds of which helped sustain the family in exile. The paintings were bought by Joseph E. Widener in 1921 and are now in the National Gallery in Washington, DC.

After his exile he and his wife variously lived in Paris, London and Los Angeles and became renowned in the Russian émigré community for their financial generosity. In 1932 Metro-Goldwyn-Mayer brought out a film, *Rasputin and the Empress*. The main character, Prince Paul Chegodieff, was clearly based on Youssoupov. When Chegodieff's wife was shown being seduced by Rasputin, Youssoupov sued MGM and in 1934 was awarded £25,000 damages. The disclaimer which now appears at the end of every American film, 'The preceding was a work of fiction and any similarity to actual people or events is entirely coincidental', first appeared as a result of the legal precedent set by the Youssoupov case.

Felix describes in detail how he murdered Grigori Rasputin in his memoirs, *Lost Splendor*, published in 1953.

Irina and Felix enjoyed a happy and successful marriage for more than fifty years, though it seems he never abandoned his pursuit of men. Youssoupov's private papers and a number of family artefacts and paintings were bequeathed to Victor Contreras, a Mexican sculptor who, as a young art student in the 1960s, met Youssoupov and lived with the family for five years in Paris.

Felix died, aged 81, on 27th September 1967 and is buried in Sainte-Geneviève-des-Bois Russian Cemetery in Paris.

*Prince Felix Youssoupov (the elder)*

Former Governor of Moscow and father of Felix (the murderer of Rasputin), he is buried in Rome.

### Grand Duke Nicholas

Uncle to Tsar Nicholas II and Commander in Chief of the Russian Army. He lived in a castle outside Paris until his death on 5th January 1929.

### Grand Duke Peter

Uncle to Tsar Nicholas II and brother of Grand Duke Nicholas. He died at Cap d'Antibes on 17th June 1931.

### Grand Duke Konstantin Konstantinovich

Cousin to Tsar Nicholas II. He was exiled to the Urals by the Bolsheviks in 1918 and murdered, along with his two brothers Prince John and Prince Igor. His body was eventually buried in the Russian Orthodox Church cemetery in Beijing, which was later destroyed to build a park.

### General Alexander Mossolov

Head of the Imperial Chancellery under Tsar Nicholas II.

### Grigori Rasputin

Peasant, monk and spiritual adviser to the Russian Royal Family. The theatrical details of the murder given by Felix Youssoupov have never stood up to scrutiny. Youssoupov changed his account several times: the statement he gave to the Petrograd police, the accounts he gave while in exile in the Crimea in 1917, in his 1927 book, and finally the accounts he gave under oath to libel juries in 1934 and 1965 all differ to some extent.

According to the unpublished 1916 autopsy report by Dmitry Kossorotov, as well as subsequent reviews by Vladimir Zharov in 1993 and Derrick Pounder in 2004/05, no active poison was found in Rasputin's stomach. It could not be determined with certainty that he drowned. Three bullets had passed through his body, so it was impossible to tell how many people were shooting at him or if only one kind of revolver was used. Zharov concluded that the three bullet holes were of different sizes.

## Piotr Bark

Escaped to England, changed his name to Peter Bank, and was later knighted by George V for services to banking.

## Yakov Mikhaylovich Yurovsky

He served as the superintendent of the house in Sverdlovsk (now Yekaterinburg), where the Royal Family was imprisoned. He led the firing squad and claimed he personally fired the bullet that killed the Tsar. Later, he was chairman of the Urals Regional Emergency Committee (the forerunner of the KGB). He died in 1938.

## Mikhail Medvedev

He held senior jobs after the Russian revolution and served for a time as assistant to the head of the First Directorate of the NKVD (The People's Commissariat for Internal Affairs, Народный комиссариат внутренних дел, which was a law enforcement agency of the Soviet Union). He wrote detailed memoirs about the murder of the Russian Royal Family. The manuscript, titled *Hostile Winds*, was addressed to the then Soviet leader Nikita Khrushchev. In those memoirs, Medvedev disputes the leading role of Yurovsky in the killing of the Royal Family, insisting that credit for the murder should have gone to himself. He died in 1964 and was buried with military honours at the Novodevichy Cemetery in Moscow. In his will, Medvedev left the Browning pistol with which he killed Tsar Nicholas II to Nikita Khrushchev.

## English

*King George V*

King of the United Kingdom and the British Dominions, and Emperor of India from 6th May 1910 until his death in 1936.

When Tsar Nicholas II of Russia, George's first cousin (their mothers were sisters), was overthrown in the Russian revolution of 1917, the British government offered political asylum to the Tsar and his family. However, fears that revolution might come to the British Isles led George V to think that the presence of the Russian royals might seem 'inappropriate in the circumstances'.

*Queen Alexandra*

George V's mother, and sister to the Dowager Empress Marie Feodorovna of Russia. She died on 20th November 1925 aged 80 and is buried in St George's Chapel at Windsor.

*Lloyd George*

British Prime Minister during and after the Great War.

*Rt Hon. Lord Stamfordham, Lieutenant-Colonel, GCB, GCVO, GCIE, KCSI, KCMG*

Private Secretary to King George V between 1919 and 1931.

Despite the later claims of Lord Mountbatten of Burma that Prime Minister Lloyd George was opposed to the rescue of the Russian Imperial Family, letters by Lord Stamfordham suggest that it was, in fact, George V who opposed the rescue and that he acted against the government's advice.

*First Lieutenant Francis Pridham*

Naval officer on HMS *Marlborough*, Pridham wrote a book covering the rescue of the Russian Royal Family entitled *The Close of a Dynasty* (1956). He died in 1975 and was buried at sea off Portland.

### John Maynard Keynes

*Time* magazine included Keynes in their list of the 100 most important and influential people of the twentieth century, commenting that: 'His radical idea that governments should spend money they don't have may have saved capitalism.' He has been described by the *Economist* as 'Britain's most famous twentieth-century economist'.

### Edward Robert Peacock, GCVO

Peacock (1871–1962) was a Canadian merchant banker, born in St Elmo, Ontario. He is best known as a director of the Bank of England, and as receiver general to the Duchy of Cornwall, the property management arm of the British Royal Family.

### French

### Joseph Noulens

Noulens (1864–1944) was a French politician and diplomat. He became a member of the Chamber of Deputies in 1903 and served as Minister of War from 1913 to 1914 and then as Minister of Finance from 1914 to 1915. In June 1917 he was appointed the French ambassador to Russia. Following the Russian revolution, he worked with White Guards to undermine the Bolshevik regime.

### American

### Edward Smith

President of the Central Vermont Railroad. He was also President of Welden National Bank, and a founder of the Peoples Trust Bank of St Albans and New York City's Sherman National Bank. His other holdings included an ammunition manufacturing company. A Republican, Smith served as a colonel in the Vermont Militia and was a member of the Vermont House of Representatives from 1891 to 1892.

He died on 6th April 1935, aged 81.

*Ivar Kreuger*

Thanks to aggressive investments and innovative financial instruments he built a global match business becoming known as the 'Match King'.

Kreuger's financial empire has been described by one biographer as a Ponzi scheme. However, in a Ponzi scheme early investors are paid dividends from their own money or that of subsequent investors. Although Kreuger did this to some extent, he also controlled many legitimate and often profitable businesses and owned banks, real estate and a rich mine, many of which survive today.

J.K. Galbraith wrote of Ivar that he was the 'Leonardo of larcenists'.

Kreuger's empire collapsed during the Great Depression and in March 1932 he was found dead in the bedroom of his flat in Paris. The police concluded he had committed suicide. His brother Torsten claimed that he had been murdered.

**Further information can be found at**
**www.thetsarsbanker.com**

# About the Author

Stephen Davis began his writing career aged twenty-seven with a column in the *South Wales Western Mail*. A regular contributor to business magazines, he is also the author of two business books as well as a sought-after speaker and broadcaster on business issues.

*The Tsar's Banker* is his first novel, in a series that follows the fortunes of the Tagleva family and the House of Tagleva between 1912 and 1946.